THREE OF A KIND

THREE OF A KIND

A NOVEL BY
JOHN MOORE

Ekstasis Editions

National Library of Canada Cataloguing in Publication Data

Moore, John.
  Three of a kind

  Contents: Castro's paperboy -- Saturday's Soldiers -- Code 2.
  ISBN 1-896860-87-7

  I. Title.
  PS8576.O6142T47 2001   C813'.54   C2001-910405-7
  PR9199.3.M6189T47 2001

Published in 2001 by:
Ekstasis Editions Canada Ltd.   Ekstasis Editions
Box 8474, Main Postal Outlet   Box 571
Victoria, B.C. V8W 3S1   Banff, Alberta T0L 0C0

Printed in Canada

Le Conseil des Arts | The Canada Council
     du Canada | for the Arts
  depuis 1957 | since 1957

BRITISH
COLUMBIA
ARTS COUNCIL
Supported by the Province of British Columbia

Three of a Kind has been published with the assistance of a grant from the Canada Council for the Arts and the Cultural Services Branch of British Columbia.

For Marge,
one of a kind.

Part I

Castro's Paperboy

Chapter 1

"Well, you're the man of the family now...And it's up to you to take care of your mother and the kids." In the weeks following my father's sudden death in the summer of 1962, each of my uncles found an opportunity to take me aside for a man-to-man talk. Each of these inspirational chats began with exactly that same opening line. Even then, those words caused me to seriously question adult perceptions of reality.

The man of the family?

I was thirteen. Just.

Take care of my mother and three younger kids on the fifty or sixty bucks a month I made, when I could collect it, delivering *The Vancouver Sun* after school? If they could say this with a straight face, I thought, no wonder they always seemed to be worried about money.

Uncle Bob, my mother's brother, was last on the rumpus room lecture circuit. Sniffling and sighing, he'd taken to his bed the day after my father died and it was a full week before he was able to get up and face the situation and me. Nobody, not even Aunt Edie who was married to him, paid much attention to Uncle Bob's histrionic horizontal mourning. Even I caught on that he wasn't prostrate with grief so much as paralysed with sphincter-stopping fear at the revelation that someone he knew, someone his own age, could drop dead, just like that.

After seven days of having the bedclothes changed around him and subsisting on a liquid diet of one part beef-and-barley soup to five parts Canadian Club, he finally cornered me in our knotty pine panelled rec room, but he still wasn't really up to the job.

"Well, you're the...the..."

He mumbled, choking up, so I prompted him.

"The man of the family now?"

He nodded, blearily grateful for the cue.

"And you have to...to take..."

His eyes welled, then overflowed with tears. I offered a suggestion.

"Take care of my Mom and the kids?"

He folded me in a whiskery, whiskey-wet hug. "Tha's right..."

He began to sob. Before my Dad died and Uncle Bob got the weeps for a week, I'd never seen a grown man cry. I decided there and then I never wanted to again.

"I understand, Uncle Bob. Thanks a lot." I disengaged myself awkwardly from the ambient distillery fug of his embrace, "I gotta go do my papers now."

At the paper shack and on my route I could escape from my mother's unpredictable outbursts of grief, the confused questionings of my younger brothers and sister, the claustrophobic condolences of relatives and friends. Not to mention my Grandmother's callous carping and Grandad's fatalistic fundamentalism.

My Grandmother's chief complaint about my father's demise was his timing. Her booked trip to England might have to be cancelled. She went on and on about it until my mother finally lost it and started shouting.

"For Christ sake, Mother! Bill didn't die just to spoil your goddamned trip! Go! I don't need you!"

My Grandad admonished her with reflexive smugness.

"Thou shalt not take the name of the Lord thy God in vain...Thou shalt honour thy Father and thy Mother..."

I still remembered Grandad when his pockets were always full of English toffees and candies to encourage pint-size pickpockets, when he drove his old Ford panel truck like a bootlegger making deliveries, expanding if not improving my vocabulary as he advised other drivers of breaches of road etiquette and common sense. Surgery for stomach cancer had turned him into a dour frequenter of prayer breakfasts and Bible study groups of dubious denomination. It seemed to me the doctors had cut out more than a rotten length of his digestive tract. They seemed to have cut the fun out of him as well.

Grandad and I finally only had one thing left in common. We both believed everything we read. The difference was that I read everything I could get my greedy precocious eyes on, from the newspapers I delivered every day to the adult books I conned out of the local library on my mother's library card and the ones I read standing up in the drugstore until my legs ached and I was ejected by irate pharmacists who correctly suspected me of shoplifting. Grandad read nothing but the Bible and badly printed religious tracts.

He believed in The Word, alright. Though he could quote chapter and verse from all four gospels, they weren't enough for him. He spent his evenings writing out an apocryphal fifth, his own personal account of the Life of Our Lord, on reams of cheap legal-size foolscap. If the Church ever accepted the Gospel according to Grandad, the Bible was going to look more like the Encyclopedia Britannica in its own custom bookshelf in our living room than the convenient King James version they read from at my father's funeral.

"There is no God." I spoke with the absolute cynical certainty of a thirteen year old. "And if there was, He wouldn't have let my father die."

It was that simple.

I was almost sorry I'd said that. Grandad looked like I'd just spat out one of his candies. I used to suck them down to the memory of an aftertaste, even the barley sugar and ginger ones I hated, rather than hurt his feelings. But he was wrong.

Before my father died I truly believed in the power of prayer, believed that words addressed to Somebody out there actually reached an audience, the way newspapers and books reached out and moved people the writers never met. For the whole week my father lay in a coma after his cerebral hemorrhage, I prayed daily and nightly with complete confidence my prayers would be heard and answered. Jesus had restored Lazarus to life after he was dead almost as a kind of party trick, a warm-up act to his own Resurrection. My father wasn't even dead. Getting him back on his feet should be no big strain for the Almighty.

When my father's neurologist phoned to tell my mother she should hope my father would die, because if he lived it would only be as some kind of vegetable, I made a note of his name on my List. I was only thirteeen, so my List wasn't very long, but it was thorough. It consisted of the names of every single schoolyard bully, sadistic gym and math teacher and mean bus driver who ever humiliated me. I hadn't figured out exactly what fiendish torments I was going to subject these people to when I grew up, but I had found a neat book on the Spanish Inquisition in the library and I was making extensive notes on the other side of the List.

When my father came to the same conclusion as the doctor and let go the barely perceptible grip on life he was able to signal only through a slight pressure of his fingers returned when one of us squeezed his hand and spoke to him, I felt like I did when I was five and the kid across the street told me what I already suspected—there was no Santa Claus, it was your parents. Except that this was a lot worse because parents were real and I was running out of them.

I thought about putting God on my List, but I hadn't put Santa on when he turned out to be a fraud. The kid who told me so was one of the first names on my List. If God didn't exist, there was no way I was ever going to put Him on the spot. If He did, then He was doing a lousy job or having a hell of a good laugh at my expense. Either way, listening to Grandad hypnotize himself with the magic words, "It's God's will" just rubbed it in.

"Are you going to let him talk to your father like that?"

My Grandmother had no qualms about brow-beating her distraught daughter.

"Please, Jack..."

"It doesn't matter anyway." I gave a sullen shrug. "The Americans and the Russians are gonna have a war and we're all gonna die. We're all gonna be just as dead as Dad is."

There were moments when that possibility really cheered me up. My Grandmother exploded.

"What a thing for a child to say! Where do they learn such things?"

"I gotta go do my papers."

I bolted out the back door and up the street to the paper shack.

Who did my Grandmother figure would know more about such things than me, who dropped the front page news on eighty-five doorsteps every weekday and Saturday? There was always a lot of bad news in the paper, but lately it had been getting worse. A lot worse. President Kennedy had accused the Russians of building missile bases in Cuba. Looking like a big evil bald baby, Premier Kruschev had thrown a tantrum, taking off his shoe and whacking the table with it, shouting, "We will bury you!"

I knew he didn't mean a nice neat official funeral, like my father's, and he didn't just mean war like the one my father fought in. He meant The Bomb.

Kids weren't really supposed to know about The Bomb. Like sex, it wasn't exactly a forbidden subject. It just wasn't one your parents were likely to bring up unless you asked and then they seemed kind of embarrassed as they tried to decide how much of the truth to admit. It isn't easy to explain the logic of the strategy of Mutually Assured Destruction to a child. Sex was probably easier for them to talk about, since it was an area in which they'd at least had some personal experience.

I'd eavesdropped on enough adult conversations that spring and summer to sense how worried they really were. We might be Canadians, but that wasn't going to cut much ice this side of the North Pole. The Bomb and it's fallout killed without regard to race, creed or colour as fashionable politicians liked to say.

"You can bet the Russkies have that Boeing plant in Seattle on their list..."

"They're going to loft those missiles right over the Pole and we're smack dab in the middle..."

"Doesn't matter where they drop 'em. Once the wind blows that fallout shit around we're all going to look like that steak there... And if that's mine, it's about done."

There was a lot of that kind of talk mingled with the smoke of suburban barbecues that summer, the pros and cons of nuclear war argued back and forth over well done steaks and jello-molded salads. Nobody seemed to know exactly what fallout was, but as near as I could tell it was a fast-acting version of what was eating Grandad alive from the inside. Everything that wasn't burned black as a weenie roast marshmallow in the first blast was going to turn into one of the monsters in the horror movies I'd sneaked onto the stairs to watch over my parents shoulders late at night.

Somewhere I'd read that the Emperors of China used to cut off the heads of messengers who brought bad news. I thought about that a lot as I toiled up the hills of North Vancouver with two sacks of bad news slung like evil Pony Express saddlebags over my bike. But nobody ever complained on that score, never mind tried to decapitate me. Sometimes they even tipped me a dime or a quarter when I came around in the evening, once a month, to collect for four weeks worth of it. People only complained if the paper was late or if I accidentally forgot to deliver to their house. Then I would get a pink Complaint slip on top of my bundle at the shack the next day and Rick, the sixteen year old Sub-Manager, would threaten to snip off my dink with the wire cutters he used to open the bundles and wore in a leather holster on his hip like a gunfighter.

If you got more than two Complaint slips a month, the Manager would come around to the shack one afternoon especially to give you supreme shit. Shit was what you got from Rick every day for the slightest infractions of paperboy protocol. Supreme shit was delivered from The Sun Building downtown. The Manager was a man, at least twenty years old. His name was Frank and he was already losing his thin red hair. He wore cheap loud check sports coats and drove a small white car with Vancouver Sun on the doors in black Gothic script and he made you sit in the front seat while he yelled at you.

"You got two Complaints!"

I slouched into the hot vinyl seat.

"I've got eighty-five papers. Everybody else has forty. I should be allowed to have four Complaints."

"Don't you crack wise with me, smart mouth! We're gonna split your route!" Frank bellowed like an Old Testament prophet foretelling the destuction of the Temple. "You'll make half as much as you do now!"

"So split it," I sunk into a defiant sulk. "It's all uphill. Just give me the bottom half. One of those guys who complained has a big German Shepherd who chews up the paper and tries to rip my legs off every day. The other one owes me for four months."

"Four months! Why don't you collect from him?"

"Because he never answers the door when I knock. He's got a bomb shelter in his backyard and I think he's in there all the time."

"Did you try knocking on the door of the bomb shelter?"

"No."

I wondered how a grown man in the newspaper business could ask such a question. There was a kind of post-nuclear Ant and the Grasshopper story going around, rumours that people who had bomb shelters also had guns to shoot down the neighbours when It happened and everyone who'd laughed at them for ripping up the rockery to build the thing came pounding at the door to get in. I wasn't knocking on the door of anybody's bomb shelter, not for a year's subscription.

Sometimes I dreamed I was still a paperboy after It happened, delivering wads of blank newsprint to blasted front porches, sets of cement steps which rose into space like primitive pyramids in front of heaps of radioactive rubble. Downtown there was a big pile of black concrete and warped steel where The Sun Building had been and that was where the blank paper came from. I knew there were people living under where the houses used to be because they took in the blank newspapers every day, but I couldn't collect because there were no doorbells left to ring and if I didn't collect, Rick the Sub-Manager, who had fallout cancer all over his pimply face, would cut my dink off with his atomic wire cutters.

I didn't feel like I could talk about these dreams with Frank.

"Collecting is your problem! Just make sure you pay your bill on time!"

"I always pay my bill on time." In fact, my mother had covered me for the deadbeats who ate up my profit and more on too many occasions.

"If you get any more Complaints..."

"I gotta go do my papers now." I got out of his small, hot white car.

ChAPTER 2

It was a lot cooler in the shack than the front seat of Frank's car, but the dry mineral smell of printers ink was even stronger. All the paper shacks looked alike. Shiplap-sided rectangles, painted dark glossy green outside, with a wide bench running down the centre and waist-high benches that ran from either side of the doorway all around the room. What set each shack apart was the grafitti and initials cut into the wood by paperboys, a cryptic hieroglyphic history written in acronyms and obscenities incised with stubby jack-knife blades. We made our marks alongside the recognized and respected marks of paperboys past.

The other paperboys shunned me because I was in supreme shit with Frank and therefore in shit with Rick, who snipped open my bundles as if he'd rather be cutting something softer than copper wire. I didn't blame them, even though I'd known some of them, like Rob Coombes and Dougie Trumbull, since the first grade. Kids know trouble is more contagious than plague. Finally, while Rick was fiddling with his precious transistor radio, Paul sidled up to me. His house was on my route and my house was on his. We were in the same class at school and were sort of best friends.

I ignored him, looking at a front page filled with stories about a war on the borders of India and Tibet which nobody seemed to understand or give a shit about. If the Indians and Tibetans and Chinese killed each other off it was small change. Only Cuba was important and people talked about Fidel Castro the way they talked about a man who'd had too many martinis and tried to light the barbecue with a jerrycan of gas and a Zippo lighter.

"I wonder what the Russians'll do?"

"What?" Paul gave me the calculated stupid look he usually saved for teachers, cops, Rick, Frank and parents.

"Well, if the Russians are really sending missiles to Fidel Castro in Cuba and the Americans try to stop them, the Russians might drop The Bomb. Or the Americans might think they will and drop it first."

Paul shrugged. My Grandmother was probably right. Most paperboys just delivered the paper, they didn't read it. If the banner headline said WORLD ENDS TODAY! Paul would have dropped it on every doorstep on his route without a second thought.

"I was just thinking." Paul made this unexpected announcement as I stuffed the last of my bundles into two ink-grimy sacks. I waited. "I mean..." He was obviously trying to fall in with my profound meditations. "Before they drop the Bomb I'd like to know if Irene Beaumont's boobs are for real."

"Real?" I sounded stupid, even to myself, trying to rub some of the fresh ink off my hands onto my jeans. "What d'you mean, real?"

"Well, y'know." His voice dropped to a confidential whisper, "Some girls wear falsies."

"Falsies?" I repeated dimly, trying to catch on.

"Yeah. They've got these brazeers with rubber things in them that make 'em look like they've got bigger boobs. Or some girls just stuff socks or Kleenex or bumwad in there..."

Paul claimed to know more about sex than anybody in our class, girls included, but you could never tell with girls. He advertised himself as an authority on the subject of which girls in our Grade 7 class had pubic hair and which didn't, but if he wasn't sure about Irene Beaumont's boobs I couldn't see how he could claim to know anything about more private parts of her person. Her house was on the first part of my route and I hoped I wouldn't see her now. I knew I'd stare at her chest in spite of myself.

"Little Egypt came out struttin' wearin' nothin' but a button and a bow-o-o-ow..." The Coasters doo-wop hit was blasting out of Rick's transistor as we left the shack. More than his steel rat-tail comb with the point sharpened in Shop class when the teacher wasn't watching or the Sub-Manager's wire cutters he wore on his hip, the small black plastic portable radio was the ultimate teenage status symbol and when Rick opened the padlocked Sub-Manager's cabinet inside the front door with a key on a long chain that linked his wallet to his belt, he placed the radio reverently on the empty middle shelf like the relic centrepiece of a shrine. Paul sauntered along with me for the first block. My t-shirt already felt like it was fresh out of the laundromat dryer and I wasn't looking forward to pushing the bike and its two bulging blackened sacks up the hills in the afternoon sun. Paul could afford to dawdle. The top of his route was the bottom of mine, he only had thirty-eight papers and Gordy the Goof was carrying them.

Gordy was a ree-tard. We'd never heard of the mentally-hand-icapped, much less the intellectually challenged. There were ree-tards, who were born that way, and goofs, who chose to walk around wearing football helmets and overcoats in summer and talked to themselves without making any sense. Our parents told us to stay away from both in case they tried to 'interfere' with us. With his big ears sticking out from under tufts of badly cut red hair, his clownish rubbery wet lips and childish manner, Gordy was clearly a ree-tard. Rick the Sub-Manager said he was a few papers short of a full bundle.

Gordy liked to hang around the shack and help unload the bundles from the truck when it arrived. When the hated extra bundles of advertising flyers we called "stuffs" came with the papers, Gordy became a happy cog in the improvised assembly line, inserting them into every paper with the patience of a skilled craftsman. Any lazy paperboy could con Gordy into helping on his route just by letting him carry the shoulder-bag. If you let him actually deliver a paper to a house, he did it with the selfless dedication of a secret agent on a suicide mission, in spite of the Dobermans trying to rip his legs off.

I only got him to help me once, back when I had 72 papers and my Dad was still alive. It was the easiest day I ever had on my route, but I made the mistake of telling the truth when my Dad asked why I was home well in time for dinner for a change.

"That was nice of him." My Dad's fork paused with a mouthful of pork chop in mid-air. "How much did you pay him?"

I explained that you didn't have to pay Gordy. That was the beauty of it, I told him, smirking at my own cleverness. My father put down his fork with an ominous clink against the plate.

"He likes doing it."

A hollow feeling was replacing appetite in the deepest pit of my stomach. Next thing I knew, the back of my father's big hand was quivering about a quarter inch from my face. His voice was deadly soft.

"If you ever do that, or anything like it again, I'll hit you so hard you'll smirk out the back of your head for the rest of your life."

My father never hit us, aside from regulation admonitory swats on the rear when we were young and needed to be discouraged from killing ourselves or other children. Lowering his hand, he rose from the table, left his dinner and went down to the carport to work on his boat, but not before I saw his face. He looked so angry, so bitterly disappointed, I wished he had smacked me.

I never let Gordy help me again, even after my Dad died. During those first unreal months after his death, guys from the Firemens Benevolent Association would come around to pay some of the bills, do some repair jobs around the house and just talk to my mother, making sure she was okay. One of the guys who came around worked at the same firehall as my Dad. I pretended to read a book at the kitchen table while I listened to him talking to my mother over coffee in the living room.

"Bill was a very rare guy, Marge. I know I don't have to tell you that...Everybody misses him at the hall...There was this kid who used to hang around the hall all the time. A retarded kid. His name is Bobby...Some of the guys used to tell him tall stories and tease him, but Bill always had a special way with him. He used to let him play on the old antique fire engine we keep there for parades and things. Bobby called it The Old Glass Pumper and he loved that truck. When everybody else was playing poker or shooting pool, Bill would be down in the bays with that kid, polishing that old truck until she shone like glass...When we had to tell him Bill was...gone, he ran away howling like a lost puppy. He doesn't come to the hall anymore, but we've seen him hiding behind garden walls and trees along the street, watching. He's looking for Bill's car to pull in. He'd always turn up a few minutes after Bill started his shift. We don't know what to do about him. We want to tell him he can still come and polish the Old Glass Pumper, but he runs away if we come out and try to talk to him..."

My Dad had never said anything to me about some boy named Bobby, but you always believe things you're not supposed to have heard more than anything anybody tells you. After that, when the other paperboys teased or bullyragged Gordy while they waited for the truck, I stayed well out of it. Paul got Gordy to help him every chance he could.

Paul was supposed to be my best friend, but sometimes I wasn't sure I even liked him. The girls in our class were known to think he was 'cute', a dubious distinction among the boys, but it was more than that. He had a way of getting you to do things, of putting you on the spot so you'd do stuff you knew you wouldn't do if he wasn't there, like the time he got a bunch of the girls to play strip-poker in somebody's rec room, which was how he came to be the informed source on the subject of pubic hair.

That Irene Beaumont hadn't been one of the volunteers in his experiments in introductory gynecology that particular rainy afternoon obviously bothered him, because he brought her up again as he swaggered along beside me, Gordy stumbling happily in his wake.

"She's got a crush on you, y'know."

"Who?"

I kept pushing the heavy bike, playing dumb.

"Irene Beaumont, you dinkweed...She'd do it for you."

"Do what?"

"You know...Strip for you. Take off her clothes."

"Oh." I kept my voice absolutely neutral.

Like our family, the Beaumonts had moved into the area when it was just being developed, the streets were gravel with open ditches, the new houses isolated by towering firs and cedars that blocked the view and sheltered the yards from the sun after noon. Irene and I had known each other so long we'd probably bathed naked in the same plastic wading pool full of blades of cut grass and drowned bees. For years, through elementary school I used to send her all my valentines when we stuffed them into a big tissue-wrapped box in the classroom and we'd walked home together every day until this year, when we began to be teased about it by our classmates.

Lately though, Irene Beaumont had changed. Still tomboyishly slim, her sweaters had begun to bulge distractingly in front and the changes were more than physical. She and the other Grade 7 girls had taken to running in packs, giggling, whispering and shrieking a lot, usually while looking at us boys and for no good reason I could see. They always acted like they were in on a secret or joke we didn't get and I thought they were a huge pain in the ass.

To cap it all, Irene had changed her name. Not completely. Her parents would've had something to say about that. But when I made the mistake of saying, "Hi, Irene," one rare afternoon on the way home when she wasn't surrounded by half a dozen tittering cronies, she corrected me haughtily.

"It's I-ree-nay." Her nose rose between two falls of curly auburn hair. "That's how you say it. I-ree-nay Bow-mon. That's French."

All kids want to change their names at some time, as though different sounds, different letters, would transform you like a magic spell into whatever you dreamed of being or becoming. I'd tried, at various times, to persuade my parents to address me as Cheyenne, Cisco, Doc and Flash. But that was kid stuff. Irene Beaumont seemed a little old to be pulling it.

"Sounds like it would be easier not to say it at all."

My grumpy retort caused Irene Beaumont to stalk off up the hill at a pace that made it very clear she did not want me to walk her home, carry her books or send her a valentine ever again. Worse luck, the episode was witnessed from across the street by Linda Arnold, a skinny, brainy buck-toothed freckle-faced girl who wore thick glasses and knee-socks and cardigans and funny English round toed shoes, like her mother dressed her as if she was still six years old. Linda waved to me as Irene stormed the hill and I feebly waved back, thanking God she didn't seem to have any friends, not even among the pretty girls who seemed to always take up skanky, gossipy girls as best friends, so she might not have anyone to tell. I was terrified someone would find out Linda Arnold had been sending me all her valentines since she came to our school in Grade 4.

Irene, I decided, was incredibly stuck-up and I would never speak to her again, except maybe if the Russians and the Americans did drop the Bombs and we were the only two people left on Earth. I couldn't figure out how Paul got the idea she had a crush on me and I told him so, but I was happy to play along if it kept him from finding out about Linda Arnold and the valentines I had to stuff in my brown paper lunchbag and hide in the trash before it was time to compare hauls behind the backstop after school.

"I'm telling you, she really does." Paul always conveyed this aura of mysterious certainty. "She'd do it for us, if you asked her."

"Us?" I stopped the bike at the corner.

"Well, uh...yeah," Paul started getting that look my mother called sneaky all over his face like ice cream. "I mean, unless you've got a crush on her, or something." He wasn't just insinuating I might actually like Irene Beaumont, he was reminding me that bit of news could be all over the classroom before recess the next day if he chose to let it.

Paul could usually talk me into things that got me in supreme shit with parents, neighbours, teachers and even with the Mounties when we were caught egging buses from the bush or trespassing in the half-built new houses that were rising out of the forest all over the area. My only advantage in our relationship was that I sensed, as boys do, that down deep he was chicken. Though we were about the same size, all I ever had to do was turn on him like I was ready to make a fight of it and he'd fold. But even when he did, I always felt like I'd been out-smarted.

"You better take that back."

I lowered my bike to the sidewalk and tensed up.

"Okay, okay. I take it back...Geez...Just think about it, okay?"

I picked up my laden, leaden bike. "Okay. I'll think about it." After all, he was my best friend.

"Okay!"

His grin made feel like I'd been suckered again in a way I wouldn't find out about until I was called to the Principals Office. Paul skipped off down the street, Gordy waddling behind him like a faithful dog, to do his papers.

ChAPTER 3

I thought about it, but not very hard or for very long. It wasn't that I wasn't interested in sex. I was so interested in it, thought about it so much that I was secretly worried that if I lived long enough to grow up it would be into some kind of pervert. Aside from Linda Arnold, Irene Beaumont was probably the only girl or woman, female teachers included, I hadn't tried to imagine without their clothes on and it didn't seem like a good time to start, since she wasn't speaking to me, as far as I knew.

I was glad to be rid of Paul, even though it meant I had to start pushing my bike uphill, along block after winding block of big split-level and post-and-beam houses, each with neat green patches of lawn wherever the contours of the lot would allow and rockeries around the bases of giant firs and cedars. Fractured by the branches, thick streams of buttery afternoon sunlight divided everything into dazzling, humming brilliance and slabs of cool shadow where I stopped to sit on the curb and read another paragraph or two of the news.

Dinner smells began to drift on the breezeless air, the hot fat scent of pork chops and chicken frying, the oniony aroma of baking meatloaf. The whole neighbourhood was as peaceful as a golf course or a graveyard. It was hard to read the front page stories and imagine war anywhere, let alone the end of the world everywhere. Then a car stopped unexpectedly in the middle of the street.

"Hey, kid. You're supposed to be delivering that paper, not reading it."

An early commuter, he wanted his evening paper. I had to ask his address so I'd remember not to deliver to his house. I couldn't place him. I only ever saw the men, the husbands and fathers who lived in the houses on my route on Saturdays sometimes, if they were out cutting their immaculate lawns, or in the evenings when I came around to collect. All those rainy and sunny afternoons hauling the paper, I moved through a world of women and almost all of them seemed mysterious, knowing and infinitely more desirable than any of the squirrelly giggling girls in my class at school.

I shared that feminine world with one other man. His house, a low flat-roofed rancher, was screened from the street by a tall laurel hedge and had a real cement swimming pool nobody ever seemed to use. In summer, the water was always still turquoise and perfect as a mirage. Every time I delivered his paper on one of those brain-poaching scorched earth days, I would stand and just look at at, actually feeling the cool blue fingers of water rushing along my hot sweaty body.

I often heard the piano inside the house when I dropped the paper. I even recognized the erratic unpredictable phrasings as jazz. This time, the door opened just as I flopped the paper down on the mat. I picked it up and handed it to him.

"Thanks, man."

He tossed it behind him on a hall table like he couldn't have cared less. It was four-thirty on a hot sunny afternoon and he was wearing a tuxedo that looked like he'd slept in it, except he looked like he hadn't slept in a year or so. An unravelled bow tie dangled from his unbuttoned collar. Dark curly hair tumbled over his forehead. A cigarette drooped from the corner of his mouth and it stayed there while he talked.

I don't remember what else he said to me, only that he called me "man" without making it sound like part of "the man of the family now." As I walked away, I heard the piano start up again, so I stopped at the corner to listen and read a bit more of the paper. That's how I found out who he was because I found myself looking at a picture of him. I only knew his last name was Perry from my collection book. His real name was Mac Perry and he played piano at a famous downtown cabaret where my parents used to go sometimes on special occasions to see someone like Frankie Laine or Peggy Lee perform. The article said Mac Perry was one of the finest young jazz pianists in the world today and quoted Oscar Peterson, whose name I did recognize.

What floored me was that this famous guy had called me "man" like we were friends and taken a newspaper with all these great things written about him and his picture and everything and tossed it aside like it was just another edition filled with bad news he didn't need. Everything about him, his music, the tired half-lidded eyes, the rumpled tux, spoke to me of a whole other world I'd only read about, a world of musicians and gangsters and artists and people who stayed up all night every night and didn't give a shit if the world ended tomorrow or not.

On the Ed Sullivan Show boring old comedians made fun of the Beatniks, the way they called certain things "cool", though nobody seemed to know for sure what they meant by it. I didn't know exactly what it meant either, but I knew I'd just met it in the flesh. Mac Perry was Peter Gunn and Humphrey Bogart and everything I'd read about by flashlight in books by writers like Sartre and Camus whose names I wasn't sure how to pronounce with my Grandad's old tube radio turned down so low I could barely hear The Crystals choiring 'He's A Rebel' and The Drifters crooning 'Up On The Roof.' Mac Perry was everything I wasn't going to be because I had to grow up fast and take care of my Mom and the kids, if we didn't all get fried by the Bomb first.

From that day, Mac Perry was the only competition Fidel Castro had in my private pantheon and Castro's house wasn't on my paper route. I'd read a lot about Fidel Castro in newspapers and magazines and though I didn't understand all of it, he was my hero. All my friends had heroes, but theirs were football players, baseball players or hockey players like Rocket Richard and Gordie Howe. When our homeroom teacher asked who our heroes were one day, Linda Arnold and a few of the egghead kids in class named people like Dr. Frederick Banting and Winston Churchill. When she came to me, I foolishly confessed my admiration for Fidel.

"But Jack," Miss Carey was so obviously appalled you'd've thought I'd said Adolf Hitler was my guy, "Castro is a Communist."

I knew that. I had a copy of The Communist Manifesto under my bed. It was easy to swipe from a bookstore because it was so small, but I knew the ideas weren't small and most of the governments of the world didn't think so either. People talked about being a Communist like it was the worst possible thing you could be, worse than a pervert. The fact that Communists were supposed to be atheists only made it appeal to me more.

I was too canny to debate Miss Carey in homeroom. I knew I'd stuck a Keds sneaker in my mouth and I wasn't about to chew on it with her. I'd already mastered the teenager's defense, play sullen and dumb no matter what comes. All I knew for sure was that Fidel Castro wanted a better life for his people. Apparently just because of that, the Americans thought he was the Anti-Christ. They'd tried to overthrow him the year before by landing a bunch of other Cubans he'd kicked out of Cuba at someplace called The Bay of Pigs, where Fidel and his army proceeded to kick the living shit out of them all over again.

Fidel might be a rebel, even an outlaw, but all I saw was a man who fought for something he really believed in against the odds and won. At least he was winning so far, though I realized the Americans could probably bomb the whole island of Cuba under the ocean if they really went to it. For me, there was something irresistibly honest about Castro, about his beard and his cigars and the way he wore ordinary combat fatigues when he could have ordered up any fancy uniform he wanted and awarded himself a chest full of medals.

I used to imagine what it would be like to be Castro's paperboy, delivering the Havana Sol or Tiempo or whatever to his house. I never pictured him in a Presidential Palace, but always in some palm-shaded villa open to the Caribbean breeze, like photos I'd seen in Life magazine of Ernest Hemingway sitting on his terrace with a glass of rum pretending to write. Like Mac Perry, I figured Fidel would be cool, not interested in the headlines he made, somebody who'd rather talk to real people like the kid who brought the paper.

My route ended at the tree line, at the top of Prospect Road.

There were no more houses, only mountains sheathed in thick cedar and fir forests. In one of the last houses on the street, a radio was playing Del Shannon's monster hit, 'Runaway,' and I wished I could just run off into those mountains and become a guerilla, like Fidel, or Robin Hood in Sherwood, and come out after years of fighting to take care of my Mom and the kids and everybody.

Chapter 4

"I gotta go collecting."

It wasn't easy for a thirteen year old boy to come up with a legit excuse to roam the suburbs after dark. My collection book, two long rectangles of steel with the receipts held in by two sleeved bolts, was a visa to another world of dark deserted streets from which I could watch people in illuminated windows like silent Punch and Judy shows, untouchable even by the Mounties.

"You live around here, sonny?"

A disembodied voice from the dim cockpit of a police cruiser, hidden behind the sudden blinding glare of a hand-held spotlight. Years later, I could still recognize a cop car without turning around, just from the creepy ticking hiss those big V8s made at idle.

"Just collecting for my papers." I brandished my collection book like a diplomatic passport.

"Okay. Make sure that's all you're doing."

I recognized the voice then.

"You want to pay me now?" I asked blandly.

"Uh...I guess so." He grunted reluctantly, fishing a couple of bucks awkwardly out of his uniform pants pocket. Relieved, I traded him a receipt.

"Dogs give you a hard time?" His question seethed with barely concealed malice.

"They're okay."

I didn't want to admit they scared me so bad I almost peed my pants every day. He and another RCMP Constable named Peterson shared a rented chalet style house on a thickly wooded lot near the top of my route. They kept a pair of dogs, a smallish German Shepherd bitch and some kind of Lab and Rotweiller mutt, both of whom tried to de-ball me a couple of times a week. It took all the nerve I had to deliver the paper in broad daylight, waiting for the inevitable ambush from the shadows. No way would I go down that long dark driveway at night.

"Lucky you caught me. Constable Peterson brought home a new dog tonight. We got him because he flunked out of police dog school. He tore up a couple of the trainers. His name is Champ. You watch out for him."

The dashboard lights glowed off a thin white line of teeth set in a nasty grin. I consoled myself with the thought that those teeth would be all that was left of him after they dropped the Bomb, but the sky above was blue-black and full of stars and the only thing falling was the bottom out of my stomach. With any luck, they'd start the war tonight and I wouldn't have to do my papers tomorrow.

"Champ." I repeated expressionlessly, memorizing the name.

"That's right. He's a big one."

His transmission whoosed into Low as he gunned it up the hill.

"Collecting for *The Sun.*"

A woman opened the next door I knocked on. I held out my collection book like a hymnal.

"Well, uh, my husband isn't home right now."

I stood there stubbornly, too shy to actually ask what that had to do with it, willing her to root through her change purse, a few drawers, the pockets of her husband's jackets, the cushions of the couch, a kids piggy bank.

"Can you come back another time? My husband always pays the paperboy."

Except he was hardly ever home. They owed me for three months already, but it was no time to bring that up because she hadn't meant it as a question. She was already closing the door.

"I guess so."

The door clicked shut and locked. The porch light snapped off right away and left me standing in the dark butted by confused moths. I made a mental note to add her name to my List and, when I fought my way out of the mountains and took over what was left of the country after the war, my first new law would be to make failing to pay the paperboy on time punishable by summary firing squad against your own front door.

The next doorbell I rang was answered by Irene Beaumont.

I did a double-take. "This isn't your house." Like she wouldn't know.

"Of course it isn't. I'm baby-sitting. The Morans have gone to the theatre."

She made it sound like they'd been assumed directly into Heaven. I didn't care if they'd gone to Cuba or the moon. I wasn't going to get my money here either.

"What are you doing here?"

"I...I'm collecting...you know...for the paper."

"I see." Irene held the door marginally more ajar and bit her lower lip thoughtfully. It hadn't occurred to me before that the outward signs of profound cogitation could be so attractive. "I suppose I could pay you and get the money back from the Morans when they come home."

"You could?"

"I don't see why not. Why don't you come in while I get my purse?"

My cheeks were hot as I inched into the vestibule and closed the door behind me. Irene darted up the stairs, very gracefully, I thought. I didn't know what to think, really. Irene was acting very weird, like someone saying lines from a movie or play, pretending to be so grown up, but she had invited me into a house where she was baby-sitting. Only technically, I reminded myself.

Still, getting let in to a house where a girl was baby-sitting was a very big deal. Girls our age were just old enough to start getting baby-sitting jobs on the weekend, which meant they were alone, except for the kids, in a strange house on Friday or Saturday night. By lunch recess on Friday, my friend Paul had compiled a comprehensive secret schedule of who was baby-sitting where on what nights. How he came by this information, none of us guys knew, but we suspected he had spies in the other camp.

We spent the weekend evenings biking from one strange locked house to another, greeted by multiple shrieks of dismay and delight, since the official baby-sitter always had one or two girlfriends closeted with her already. Most of the time we stood under windows on twilight lawns alive with midges, craneflies and mosquitoes while Paul tried to talk us in and the girls, like coy Juliets, hung over the sills and teased us, safe behind dead-bolted doors.

Once in a rare while we were actually let in, having sworn the deadliest adolescent oaths not to tell anybody, which meant that everybody except parents and teachers would know by morning recess on Monday. Plied with Orange Crush or cream soda, we danced to scratchy 45s like the Marvelettes 'Please Mister Postman,' jiving clumsily, boys a step behind the girls, and twisted to Chubby Checker and The Isley Brothers.

We practised kissing, using dares and games like Post Office and Spin the Bottle to get things started. Sometimes we tried to do more, but most of us were like mechanics without the shop manual. More interesting things were always rumoured to happen, like Paul getting some of the girls to play strip-poker, but they never seemed to happen when I was along. I had kissed a few girls I didn't especially like and once fondled something that might have been the beginning of a breast through the sweater and blouse and training-bra Maureen Taylor was wearing at the time, but that was about it. Jane Rogers had allowed me to put my hand on her knee while we were kissing, but when it crept a few inches higher, I was startled aback by the sudden arrival of her tongue in my mouth. As I jerked back, she looked down at the bump my hand made under her plaid skirt and shrieked, leaping up to go and tell the other girls.

I told myself Irene Beaumont wasn't really letting me into a house where she was baby-sitting. She was only doing it, paying me for the paper and all, to show off. She came back downstairs just as gracefully and handed me a deuce with a flourish.

"Thanks." I tried to keep both grudge and gratitude out of my voice as I give her the slip in return.

As I turned for the door, Irene unexpectedly called me back. "Uh...Would you like a Coke or something?"

"Uh...Well, I'm supposed to be collecting... " Then it dawned on me that she really and truly was inviting me into a house where she was virtually alone. "But, uh, yeah. That'd be cool."

It was very strange, the two of us sitting upstairs in the living room, watching tv and drinking Cokes just like a married couple with kids asleep down the hall. On tv they were showing some pictures supposed to be of Russian rocket bases in Cuba, but they were taken from so high up they could have been baseball fields. I thought it was interesting though and I was glad to have something to talk about because being there alone with Irene was making me kind of nervous and I wasn't sure why.

"How do we know that's even Cuba? It could be anywhere. That could be one of their own missile bases they've taken a picture of."

Irene was shocked. "They wouldn't lie on television, Jack."

She didn't want to talk about Castro or the Russians anyway. Instead, she abruptly asked me if I like anyone at school.

"Yeah, well, sure. I guess." I hedged cautiously. "Paul and Ron and Terry and.."

"I mean girls."

I knew perfectly well what she meant. "Yeah, well...one, I guess...Do you like somebody?"

"I asked you first."

This was the kind of game girls liked and the boys did too, except they'd rather be caught wearing a dress than admit it.

"If you tell me who you like, I'll tell you who I like."

We fenced around like that for a bit, Irene's curiousity almost but not quite getting the better of the girls "never tell" code. Then she started asking me for hints. It was an impromptu word-association game with no rules.

"Caterpillar...Zebra...Tiger..."

I teased her obliquely, just for the pleasure of observing that captivating thought process at work again in real earnest. She was wearing a striped sweater, but she didn't seem to catch on. I'm not sure what I'd've said or done if she had. By the time I finished my Coke and had to get going, she still hadn't guessed, but she seemed pleasantly flushed and not at all disappointed, so maybe she figured out more than she let on. Reverse Psychology was a trendy new concept some of our parents were trying out on us, but their attempts at it were oafish and transparent. Pubescent girls on the other hand, were like Zen masters when it came to saying one thing and meaning another so simply you couldn't fail to misunderstand it.

ChàPTER 5

For the first time, as I pumped up the hills after leaving the Morans', I didn't curse the old standard bike that was all my parents could afford and pray for a three-speed Schwinn. I felt inexplicably light and strong, my legs driving the pedals like pistons, careless of the grade.

Why did I drop hints that pointed, however vaguely, to Irene herself? It was a good joke on Miss Stuck Up, I told myself, but she hadn't acted stuck up, really, and I was genuinely grateful to her for paying me for the Morans paper. I wasn't so sure I wanted Irene Beaumont turned into an atomic fried pork-curl by the Bomb. If the two of us were the only two people left after It happened, it might not be such a terrible thing after all.

"Collecting for *The Sun*."

Grudgingly, the man fumbled in his pants pocket and came up with a couple of crumpled dollar bills.

"It's four dollars." I forced myself to speak firmly. "You owe me for two months."

"Why didn't you collect last month?"

"I tried...You kept saying to come back."

"Well, why didn't you?" He was growling now...

"I came back four times."

"George!" The woman's voice was a bark from behind the door. "Just pay him and get rid of him! You're letting in bugs!"

He tossed the bills at me and slammed the door as I bent to catch them fluttering down. The wind brushed across my forehead. As I rode away, I remembered a book I'd read about the first atomic bomb they dropped on Hiroshima. I imagined him sitting in front of his tv, screaming as the shock-wave blew his picture window into huge knives of glass that pinned him to the melting upholstery of his Laz-E-Boy recliner.

I didn't try to collect from Mac Perry's house. Though the lights were on, he was never home at night. Sometimes his wife was there. I didn't like collecting from her. She was beautiful, I guess. She looked sort of like Cleopatra was supposed to look, with long blue-black hair and dark kohl-lined cat's eyes that seemed to stare right through me into the night. She was an actress. I had seen her name in reviews of plays in the paper. She made me think of the women in vampire movies, the Brides of Dracula.

She never spoke to me. Never said "Hello" or "What do you want?" when she opened the door. She never smiled or frowned, just looked through me, walked away, came back with two dollars and shut the door before I could say "Thank you" or anything.

Instead, I turned the corner and rang the bell at the next house. As I'd hoped, Mrs. Lytle answered the door. Mr. Lytle was a tall reedy horn-rimmed guy with an absent-minded look. I didn't have anything against him except that he was married to Mrs. Lytle and I couldn't do anything about that.

If I could be said to truly have a crush on anybody, it was Mrs. Lytle. I didn't even think of it that way, my feelings about her were so confused and unprecedented. She wasn't as obviously attractive as some of the women on my route.

Not like Mrs. Canetti, who answered the door in tight leopard-spotted toreador pants, her brass-blonde hair piled in a tall beehive and her blouses cut too low to leave anything to my fevered imagination as she bent down to leisurely rifle through her huge purse for my money. She always seemed to have a cocktail glass in her hand, which she'd sometimes give me to hold, inviting me to take a sip, if I wanted. I tried once. The smell hit my nose like model airplane glue or the purple gas my Dad used in the lawnmower.

Mrs. Perry just made me nervous. Mrs. Canetti scared me spit-less with her half-lowered eyes and her dizzying perfume and double-entendre laden drawl I wasn't always sure I understood.

Mrs. Lytle wasn't much taller than my own five feet. She wore glasses with tortoiseshell frames and her rust-coloured hair curled under in a simple wave above slim shoulders. There was a freshness about her, a coolness that was nothing like Mac Perry's coolness, but like a willow tree on a hot summer day, a patch of shade beside a stream. Talking to her was like being with a friend, not some alien adult.

"Hello, Jack. Come in while I find my purse."

From the hall, I could see Mr. Lytle and the tv. He glanced at me, but seeing it was only the paperboy, he turned back to the screen where they were still showing pictures of the missile bases and President Kennedy was threatening to search Russian ships bound for Cuba by having the U.S. Navy pull them over on the high seas. Mrs. Lytle saw me watching when she came out of the kitchen with two dollars.

"Isn't it frightening?" She whispered to me, hugging herself.

"Are you scared?"

She nodded. "I try not to think about it all day, but at night, when it's dark and quiet, I can't sleep I get so afraid, thinking I might not wake up, or there might not be anything to wake up to..."

"That's when I get scared too."

I was amazed. I'd never heard any adult admit to being scared of anything, except once, when I asked my Dad if he was ever scared in the war."Every single minute for four years," he told me, but he wouldn't tell me why or anything more about it and I couldn't believe him. I'd seen him come home from the Fire Hall and cough little puffs of black smoke all day. That meant he'd been inside a burning building, getting people out and fighting a fire that could fall on him at any moment. And once, when he grabbed for the rod too soon when he was fishing and a big tyee took the herring and ripped three hundred yards of line off the reel in seconds, the knob on the reel hit him on the thumb and raised a big swollen blood blister under the nail. Hiding behind a tree, I watched as he went out into the back yard, took out a jacknife and pierced the nail to let the black blood gush out. He didn't wince, just gave a small tight smile as he shook the blood off into the grass.

As I glided down the hills homeward through the meticulously assymetrical suburban streets under the lunar glare of the streetlights past houses turned in on themselves, lit by the soft blue glow of tv sets tuned to the inescapable news, I thought about Mrs. Lytle being afraid to go to sleep and I wished I could miraculously vault the unbridgeable decade between us to hold her while she slept. Maybe she, not Irene Beaumont, would be the only woman to survive imminent end of the world.

What with Irene, Mrs. Lytle, my Mom and the kids, Mac Perry and Fidel Castro, whose chances were zip, the passenger list on my imaginary ark was getting longer. The number of people I wanted to survive still wasn't a fraction of the number of dinkweeds on my List I wanted to see burned into x-ray shadows on their own living room walls though. That category included most of my relatives, teachers, Rick the Sub-Manager, Frank the Manager, all the other people on my route along with their dogs, the doctors who failed to save my Dad, the Japanese who gave him the head wound that caused him to die twenty years later and especially all of the people in the U.S. and Russia who'd built enough of these bombs to kill everybody in the world seventeen times over, the papers said. Even at thirteen, I could see that once would be more than enough.

I wished I could do something. But what? Later in bed that night, with my light obediently out and my flashlight disobediently on, hooded by a fold of the blanket, I put aside a very odd book by Colin Wilson I'd been trying to read and got out a pad of lined foolscap and a pen instead. Maybe I wasn't Fidel Castro's paperboy, but I could write to him and tell him what I thought, couldn't I?

How to start? Dear Mr. Castro? Dear Comrade Castro? I discarded Your Excellency immediately. I chewed on the end of my pen, one of the long plastic jobs they still used to teach us the Palmer method of correct penmanship.

Finally, I settled for "Dear Mr. Castro" and started to write. I wasn't sure a letter would even get to him. The Americans might be blockading the mail too, for all I knew. But it was better than lying there in the dark, waiting for an unscheduled unimaginable dawn to break over the world.

ChaPTER 6

At last I staggered to the stop of my route. I only had half a dozen papers left and the houses were mostly on the flat, along a new road that had been pushed through to link the top of Delbrook with the top of Lonsdale, raising the tree line another quarter mile up the sides of Grouse and Fromme mountains. The view of Vancouver was enough to give you a nosebleed and no matter how whacked out I was when I made it to the end, it was almost worth it all just to sit there and look out over the city all the way to Mount Baker on a clear day.

There were several unfinished houses framed in along the new road, the contractors hurrying to get them closed up before the fall rains started in hard. No doubt they would be added to my spine-crushing list of customers. It seemed sort of silly to me to be building new houses when they stood a good chance of being turned into instant ruins by the Bomb.

I squatted on the curb to catch my wind and read the last of the paper. I was so tired my eyes were wandering. I'd been up most of the night finishing my letter to Fidel Castro, but I still hadn't figured out what to do with it. I knew it would take extra stamps to get all the way to Cuba, but I couldn't get to the Post Office during the hours it was open because I was in school or doing my papers. I thought of asking my mother to mail it, but she was still so upset after my father's death I was afraid my writing to Castro might just make things worse and she'd start thinking I was an emotionally disturbed child, as they were starting to be called.

So I kept the letter in my pocket all day, addressed to Fidel Castro, Havana, Cuba, in now slightly smeared ball-point ink.

Opening the last section of the paper, I glanced reflexively at the bra and girdle ads. Paul always held them up to the light, insisting you could really see something sometimes. I couldn't figure out why he bothered, since we'd all seen more in the Playboy magazines he sneaked out of his father's den and brought up to the shack in his paperbag to get in good with Rick the Sub-Manager.

All of a sudden I was aware of somebody or something breathing heavily on my neck. Turning my head as slowly as a sunflower, I looked up into the dripping jaws and dangling tongue of the biggest German Shepherd on earth. It began to drool, wet and warm, onto my shoulder. Weak in the knees, I managed to stand up, very slowly, whispering "Good dog" and "Nice puppy" as fervently as I'd ever prayed, hoping the idea would get across.

"Champ?" It was an all too reasonable guess.

His huge ears twitched erect. They came up to my shoulder. He must have been at least half Great Dane because he could easily have torn my throat out with all four paws comfortably on the ground. I had every reason to think he might do exactly that, but I didn't have much going in the way of choices and he seemed friendly so far. Taking a paper from my sack, I started down the cops driveway as slowly as a condemned man on the Last Mile. Champ padded along beside me while I continued to mumble "Good boy" like a litany.

Everything was fine until the other two dogs bolted out of the bush, snarling like starved hyenas. Then Champ backed away from me and started barking too. The way things were looking, they'd have to identify my remains from a shredded copy of *The Vancouver Sun.*

I kept my eyes on Champ, talking softly to him in the calmest voice I could fake. The other two had learned to be wary of me. I'd learned a trick of holding the rolled paper out in front of me up high and when they jumped for it, I'd throw a swift kick into their exposed bellies. If they'd just gone in straight for my legs, they'd have had me down for dinner, but they never wised up. They always went for the paper and caught a Keds in the gut. Now they snapped and growled, but wouldn't attack. Champ was the x-factor, like Castro, unpredictable and with a reputation for violence.

Gradually Champ calmed down and stopped barking. The house was below the level of the street and driveway, so I tossed the rolled paper like a stick grenade the last thirty yards to the doorstep. The other two dogs immediately pounced on it and tore it to bits, but I didn't care. I was already more than halfway back to the street, escorted by Champ.

"Good dog, Champ. Good boy."

That came from the bottom of my heart, as I mounted my bike. He stood in the driveway, his head cocked to one side almost sadly as I rode away, sweating relief from every pore.

When I'd dropped the last of the bad news, I coasted down the hills, sacks slung over my shoulders like twin guerilla bandoliers, empty but for my collection book. Swinging into Mac Perry's drive, I dropped the bike and pounded on the door to make myself heard over the piano that was banging out what sounded like theme music for the end of the world. Finally the music stopped and the door swung back.

"Hi, man. What's happening?"

"Uh, hi...I'm collecting, you know, for the paper?..."

"Oh yeah. Cool." He took todays paper from my hand, glanced at the front page and whistled. "Wow, man. These cats are crazy, eh? Like wild. I mean, like, I like to blow, but these cats, they're really gonna blow."

Tossing the paper behind him, he pulled a whack of bills out of his tux pocket and fanned off too many. I'd never seen so much money in one man's hand all at once, not even my Dad's on payday.

"It's only two dollars, Mr. Perry..."

"Hey, man, just take it. It's cool. It's your Christmas tip. A little early this year in case, like, Christmas might be cancelled or something. Take your chick out and spend it all in one place. You got at chick, man?"

"Well, sort of...but not really."

"Well, get one and find out what's happening before it's over, like..."He scratched his curly head, "Ah, shit, man. Maybe you're better off not knowing..." He closed the door as if he wished he hadn't brought it up.

I wanted to shout, "Wait! Tell me! I want to know before it all...Tell me what to do!" but he was gone. I picked up my bike and coasted around the corner. That was when I saw Mrs. Lytle, bending over with a trowel at the little rock garden, like island in the middle of their lawn, and I turned into the drive.

"Uh, hi, Mrs. Lytle."

"Hello Jack."

She straightened up with a smile, which was just as well since I'd been staring so hard at the curves stretching her white shorts that I almost forgot why I stopped.

"Mrs. Lytle? Could you do me a big favour?"

"Well, I don't seen why not." She wiped her hands on her shorts, which drew my attention back to them."If I can, of course."

"Could you mail this for me?" I held out my now crumpled letter. Her eyes widened when she read the address. She had deep green eyes.

I nodded, hoping she wouldn't start in asking what a kid like me would have to say to the revolutionary leader of a small country trapped between two of the most powerful nations on earth and who consequently had his hands full. I didn't want to have to argue that millions of kids wrote to Santa Claus every year and he wasn't even a real person.

"I think that's wonderful, Jack." She smiled so warmly I was relieved and unnerved all at once. "Of course I'll mail it for you. I was just going down to the store for a few things. If the Post Office is closed, I have plenty of stamps in my purse."

"Gee, thanks, Mrs. Lytle." I tried not to stare at her pale slim thighs as I fumbled in my pockets for my money and attempted to avoid encouraging the beginnings of an erection. "I'll pay you for the stamps..."

"Don't worry about that, Jack. I'll tell you how much it is and you can pay me back later."

"Okay. Uh, thanks again."

I hurriedly remounted my bike to hide the bulge in my jeans.

Free-wheeling downhill with the wind cooling my flushed face, I felt like I was flying, weightless with inexpressible joy. My words were on their way to Fidel Castro. He might even read them himself. And famous people didn't throw away their letters either. They had secretaries and people who saved them and kept them for other people to read when they were writing books about them. My letter might become a part of a history book, even if only in the last chapter.

I knew words were more than just shapes on paper or sounds in the air. When I heard Nikita Kruschev or Fidel Castro speak languages I didn't understand, I felt their meaning. I could remember what it was like to be almost able to read, seeing the big neon signs on a block of Granville Street when we were caught in a traffic jam in my Dad's brand new 1955 Ford station wagon and I sat in the back seat, recognizing some of the big bright letters while others remained just huge arbitrary shapes of colour.

Later, when I could really read, I stood in the small branch public library in the Capilano Highlands one day, distracted by a big orange and black Monarch butterfly that had strayed into the building and caught my eye on the way to the Juvenile section. I followed it, intending to open a window or something to let it out, until it lit high on a top shelf deep in the Adult stacks. I stayed there for the rest of the day, roaming the labyrinth of forbidden shelves, the Dewey Decimal System like the equation of a fission reaction in my brain as I dipped into one volume after another. Everything I'd ever wanted to know, the answer to every question every adult had ever side-stepped or promised to answer "when you're older," and the answers to questions I hadn't even thought of yet, were all there and all I had to do was turn the pages. When the librarian came around to tell me, with a disapproving look, that the library was closing, I remembered the butterfly. It had disappeared, but the endless shelves of unread books remained.

Words had risks, too. Adults always talked about the dangers of "knowing too much for your own good", so it was a good idea not to let on how much you did know, ever. Which was why I was very careful to get straight C-plus marks on my report cards, even when I knew I could get A's in some subjects if I wanted. Parents loved to say "Nobody likes a smartass kid" and they were right. Nobody does, especially other kids.

Unfortunately, I made the mistake of letting on to Paul about my letter to Castro during recess.

"Castro? Why'd you write to him? He's a Commie!"

"So?" I regretted my big mouth already.

"My Dad says, if there's a war, we're gonna kill all the Commies. Especially Castro." He looked so smug it made me vicious.

"If there's a war, those atomic bombs are going to kill everybody, including your Dad."

"You're just saying that 'cause your Dad's dead!"

"They're gonna kill you and me, too." I could see my calm certainty was scaring him. "It won't matter who's a Commie and who's not. Besides, you don't even know what a Commie is and I bet your Dad doesn't either, you dumb dinkweed."

Whatever he knew, he shot his mouth off widely enough that our homeroom teacher got wind of it and made me stand up in class just before the final bell.

"Jack? I understand you've written a letter to a famous person all of us should know more about, especially at this time."

In the first month of school, we'd all been sent home twice early in the afternoon for drills with the air-raid sirens wailing. During the summer, the tall spindly gray towers topped by enormous horns had sprouted, silent and ominous, among the firs and cedars. Walking home, we heard them, not loud exactly, but unbearably monotonous, their inhuman howl reducing all other sounds to insignificance.

"Would you like to tell the class about your letter, Jack?"

"No, Miss Carey."

I strained to keep my voice as neutral and polite as I could. Kids had been known to disappear into hideous private schools with Inquisitional forms of corporal punishment that made The Strap seem like a pat on the hand, rumour had it, just for saying "no" to a teacher. The big classroom clock said five minutes to three. The silence went on forever, worse than the air-raid siren wail, but I was determined Miss Carey wasn't going to turn me and my letter into some Grade One "Show and Tell," not when she'd acted just as dumb as Paul when I told her Fidel Castro was my hero. Everybody was staring at me, including Irene Beaumont. Miss Carey seemed to sense how angry I was, but she didn't punish me for my defiance.

"Well, class, a letter is a person's private business when that person lives in a democracy. But I think we could all benefit by Jack's example and take a greater interest in current events."

It sounded to me like Miss Carey was more frightened than she wanted to let on herself. She knew as well as I did, maybe better, that there might not be any more "current events" to study, that the tv screens and the front pages of newspapers might all soon go blank forever. I sneered at Paul as the chime of freedom finally echoed down the polished linoleum halls and the whole building trembled with the thunderous scuffle of kids stampeding to the double doors under the red EXIT sign. Outside, I saw Irene, lagging a bit behind her crowd of giggling cronies and looking over her shoulder. I ducked into the woods, ran half a mile up the trail to outdistance the others taking the short-cut and walked home alone. Later at the shack, as we stuffed our papers, Paul sidled up to me. Gordy was doing his stuffs.

"What's the matter? I didn't tell anybody anything..."

"It's okay."

I knew he was lying and he knew I knew. I just didn't want any more trouble because we were friends and worked out of the same shack and mostly because I'd also stupidly told him about Irene Beaumont letting me into a house where she was baby-sitting. If he spread that around, there'd be so much whispering, giggling and teasing that Irene Beaumont might never speak to me again even if we actually were the last two people on earth after the end of the world.

Paul drew me into the sepia shadows at the back of the shack, his voice a sibilant whisper.

"So, what'd you do with her?"

"We watched tv. She gave me a Coke."

"No, dinkweed. I mean, what did you do?"

"Well, nothing much, I guess."

"Nothing? Irene Beaumont let you into a house where she was alone baby-sitting and you didn't do anything?"

"We didn't have time. I was supposed to be collecting. She paid me for the Moran's paper so I wouldn't have to come back again."

"She did that? I told you. She must really have a crush on you to do that!" He shook his head, impressed and disappointed. "But you should have done something. Kissed her, at least...I'm telling you, she'd do it if you just asked her..."

"I gotta go do my papers." I hefted two sacks that would have crippled a longshoreman.

Chapter 7

The summer that year was swept suddenly away by a Pacific storm like a dragon that just swatted the Northwest with its tail in passing. Even so, wind-driven horizontal rain flooded every creek on the North Shore, washing out a lot of the old wooden yellow bridges like the one near the shack, whose dark understructures of heavy creosoted beams were painted with quotations from Scripture in neat block letters by some anonymous evangelist. Most of Greater Vancouver was without electric power for twenty-four hours and naturally that was the night I baby-sat my brothers and sister for the first time.

Some friends of my Mom and Dad's had decided it would do my Mom good to get out for an evening. I had to argue like a sea-lawyer to avoid the everlasting shame of having a baby-sitter when I was all of thirteen. If Irene Beaumont could baby-sit, I certainly could.

About eleven o'clock, when the power went out and some of the tall trees in the area began crashing down on the roofs of neighbouring houses, I realized my Mom wasn't going to make it home anytime soon and I was truly on my own with the kids.

Herding the frightened half-awake kids downstairs to my bedroom, where I figured they'd be safer if a tree did fall on our house, I tucked them all into my bed. I was incidentally prepared for something like this. Since I'd been getting ready for a nuclear war, this

Pacific cyclone was a kind of training exercise.

For months I'd been squirrelling things away under my bed, candles, batteries, pop bottles filled with water, cans of beans and soup and jars of peanut butter, pinched from the cupboards one at a time, assortments of cookies skimmed from baking days and packets, sealed in coffee tins my Dad used to keep nails in. I also had my Dad's .22 calibre Colt Woodsman long-barrelled revolver and two boxes of cartridges. It was my Armageddon survival kit.

After a couple of soothing fig newtons, the kids dozed off and I sat reading Joseph Conrad's "Typhoon" by candlelight. It made me feel safer somehow. From time to time I peered out into the howling darkness as nature staged a dress rehearsal of the end of the world.

When my mother finally got home the next morning, she and everybody else made a big deal out of how well I'd handled it. I was too tired to point out that I'd been prepared for something much worse. Schools were closed for the day, which was good because I needed sleep, but later that afternoon *The Sun* called to make sure I would be available to do my papers. Somehow, despite a night without power, they got the paper out.

The rain eased off a bit, but there was still enough falling to turn my paperbags into two sacks of cement. My bags had never been white and new. I inherited them with the route when it was sixty-three papers and was taking the previous paperboy so long to do that he was missing the piano lessons it was supposed to help pay for.

At first I tried to keep my papers dry, but old sacks, blackened with printers ink and threadbare at the corners from being dragged across asphalt, straining their seams from carrying twice the intended load, were about as waterproof as cheesecloth. There were times when, on the whole, I'd rather have had piano lessons myself.

Eventually I quit trying. Most people left the paper on the porch in the rain for an hour or so anyway. When the papers got really soaked, the front page and some of the inside ones would become transparent and the words, in different type sizes, would overlap and bleed into each other so it looked like a newspaper printed in some foreign language.

Sometimes late at night, the same thing would happen to the

words on the pages of the book I was reading. They would lose their meanings and become what they had been before I learned to read, arbitrary shapes on paper grouped in rows in an order that suggested meaning, but as alien as the illlustrations of cunieform writing in our Grade Seven history textbook. It was modestly titled *The Story of Civilization* and I'd already read it cover to cover, just in case I might have to write the final chapter myself. I wanted to get a feel for the form.

Standing in the relentless rain outside Mac Perry's house, listening to the music flow from his invisible fingers, I'd still almost rather have had the piano lessons and endured the social scorn. I'd never shown any special musical talent, but day after day, listening to him play as I delivered the paper made me feel things even words had never made me feel. The notes and chords vibrated with shades of meaning, yet they had no literal meaning at all. They were precise, yet indefinable, purer because on those afternoons he was playing them for himself, for their own sake or the sheer hell of it.

The music stopped suddenly and the door opened. I waved from the driveway and Mac Perry, ignoring the paper, called me in. I tried not to drip on anything.

"You look like a wet rat. Cuppa java to warm up?"

I nodded. I knew what java was. I'd only been allowed to drink coffee since my Dad died, but I was determined to like it, even though I had to add lots of cream and sugar to get it down. It was what people drank in coffee houses where jazz was played and people stood up and recited poetry they'd just written. Mac Perry put cream and sugar in without me having to ask and led me into the living room.

A grand piano stood in the centre of the room like a huge black beast, its mouth propped open with a stick. A couch, easy chair and coffee table were all jammed into an alcove that should have been the dining area. The walls displayed a couple of big abstract paintings that looked like somebody had up-chucked blood and ink on them. Above the fireplace was a very weird looking painting of a naked woman in blues and greens that was just recognizable as Mrs. Perry, but reminded me more of Mrs. Canetti across the street. I tried not to stare at it as I warmed my hands around the hot mug.

"I...I really like your music..."

48

"Cool."

Mac Perry sat on a drummer's spindly stool instead of a piano bench. Putting a glass half full of amber whiskey on the shelf of dark wood above the keys, he began to play, lightly and effortlessly, like a man relaxing by stroking a large dog behind the ears. As he played, he hummed and whispered to the piano, laughing now and then like he'd made the big black thing talk back to him.

"Dig it?" He ran his fingers softly over the keys, ending high, on a note that seemed like a question mark.

"It's like...It's like it's...alive."

He chuckled and smiled.

"It's wood. From trees, man. Like the trees outside. The hammers are padded with felt. Wool, from sheep. The keys are ivory. The bones of animals. Yeah, it's alive alright."

He began to play harder, making the piano snarl and growl, and I sensed strange animals moving in the mist outside under the watching trees. Sipping my coffee, I drifted over to the sliding glass doors that opened onto the patio. The door was open, letting the sound and smell of rain into the room through curtains that were almost transparent.

I was looking at the back of Mrs. Lytle's house. Around the corner, but still sort of next door, their backyard was just below the Perry's patio. Mrs. Lytle was standing just inside the open back door. I knew she couldn't see me. She wasn't trying to see anything. She was listening to the music Mac Perry was playing and it seemed to me that she was crying, but it was probably just all the rain running down everything that made me think so. I felt guilty, watching her when she thought nobody could see her and suddenly I wanted to be out of there, back out in the rain. Mac Perry paused to take another bite of his drink.

"Thanks for the java, Mr. Perry, but I gotta go finish my papers."

"Any time, man. And call me Mac. Mr. Perry was my old man... Stay cool."

From the look of the rain, I wasn't going to have any trouble doing that. The music shuddered behind me like the soundtrack for a storm. I was drenched and cold all over by the time I crested the last of the hills and there was no view to admire, just a grey wall of wet cloud.

Champ was waiting for me, tongue hanging out, his fur steaming in the rain. When I threw the paper to the other two dogs, it was so wet they could hardly tear it up. Wads of wet newsprint kept getting caught in their teeth, making them cough like cats full of hairballs. I hoped they'd both choke. I figured the RCMP Constables had to be the worst informed people on my route. When the world ended, they'd have to ask their dogs what happened. Stroking Champ's wet head, I almost wasn't afraid of him. If *It* really did happen, I imagined he might somehow survive too and be my dog, the only dog left in the world.

Rain stinging my eyes, I rode carefully back down the slick slippery hills. As I pedalled along the flat stretch past the first houses on my route, I noticed the paper had been taken in from the doorstep of the haunted house. The house wasn't really haunted. Until a year ago, it was just another well-kept contemporary post-and-beam. Then one day last spring machines showed up, big yellow John Deere bulldozers and Finning back-hoes. Leaving huge tank-tracks in the lawn like the footprints of dinosaurs, they clanked around to the back of the house and began excavating a large pit that took up most of what had been the backyard. They were followed by a convoy of cement trucks.

In the suburbs, that kind of activity meant only one thing. The neighbours, including Paul's parents, were thrilled. A swimming pool was the ultimate status symbol in the suburbs and everyone for blocks was talking about it, parents trying to remember if they'd met the Mordens at PTA meetings or cocktail parties or run into them at the Shop-Easy. We were quizzed about how well we knew the Morden kids, but nobody knew anything. The Mordens, it seemed, had always kept pretty much to themselves. Then the pool was roofed over and exhumed soil bermed up over the roof and walls, revealing it for what it was—a blunt ziggurat of the Atomic Age.

There were pictures of ziggurats in *The Story of Civilization*, early types of pyramids, flat-roofed and sometimes stacked so they looked like steps, in Egypt and Mesopotamia. It seemed both prophetic and appropriate to me that mankind's first form of monumental architecture was also going to be its last. The neighbours didn't see it so philosophically. Added to their disappointment over the pool was a quiet outrage that Morden, by building The Thing as it came to be called, was announcing that he intended to sit out the coming Apocalypse with his family in the bunker, presumably supplied with food and water and presumably armed and prepared to shoot any of his less prudent neighbours who survived The End and took it into their heads to drop in.

Never popular, the Mordens were ostracized. Mr. Morden was referred to as The Nut and The Thing became the butt of complaints at barbecues and dinner parties. The first time it rained, it became apparent that Mr. Morden, who was supposed to be an engineer, had neglected to put in proper drains because the bomb-shelter had to be loudly and professionally pumped out. Fingers were wagged, heads shaken, "I told you so's" exchanged, along with jokes as corrosive as radiation.

Not only had Mr. Morden made no attempt to disguise, let alone beautify The Thing, but once it was finished the Mordens abandoned any pretence of keeping up appearances. The tracks of the machines that left the lawn looking like a tank parking lot were never filled in, though by now they were hidden by grass that hadn't been mown in months.

It got worse after Mrs. Morden left with the children a few months ago. The pastel pink paint on the cedar siding was streaked with pale green mold. On the spacious sundeck, the railings were grey, white paint peeling off like irradiated skin to reveal a skeleton of splitting two-by-fours. Part of the railing had actually fallen off into the yard, but it didn't matter because nobody used the sundeck or the yard anymore.

Nobody ever saw Mr. Morden now. I was the only person who knew he was still in there because I delivered the paper and somebody took it in every day. In a way, I sort of felt like I understood Mr. Morden, though I was afraid of him and his spooky house. I hadn't collected from him in months. At night his house was always as dark as the scene of a crime. Yet I felt a kind of bond with him. We both knew the same thing nobody else seemed to want to know.

Later that night under the covers I started another letter to Fidel Castro. I told him about Mr. Morden and the air-raid drills at school and even a bit about Mrs. Lytle. I could talk to him without worrying about it being spread around school, at least. As I wrote, I imagined him reading my letter on his sunny terrace overlooking the sea, a cigar smouldering in an ashtray, a glass of rum on the table at his elbow among the maps and plans and all the other stuff he had to read. I fell asleep over my letter and dreamed I was with him, sitting there watching sunset light up the sky for the last time, but I wasn't afraid. For the first time since my Dad died, I felt safe. I knew we were only waiting for the glowing dust to settle. Then I would help Fidel make the world new again.

When I woke up, the birds were whistling outside my window and the batteries in my flashlight were dead.

Chapter 8

Coming home from school the next day, already soaked from the rain, I opened the kitchen door and there was my mother, white as a blank page, clutching the countertop for support and staring at me like she'd just seen a ghost. As it turned out, she'd been expecting one, but the expression on her face chilled me more than my wet jacket.

"It's only me."

"God...I thought it was your father." She sagged against the counter, beginning to cry quietly. "Your footsteps sound so much like his on the stairs. I keep expecting him to just walk in and ask what's for dinner."

"I...I'm sorry." I wasn't sure exactly what for.

Realizing how much she'd scared me, she put her arm around my skinny shoulders. "It's alright now...I was just getting ready to say 'Bill! How could you do that to me? How could you scare me like that? How dare you leave me with four little kids like this?'..." Her voice was getting shrill and scary.

I'd never seen her so mad. She left that to my Dad, except for the usual motherly snappishness and the odd threat of the wooden spoon when we were persistently obnoxious. I didn't know what to say or do, so I did what I always did.

"I gotta go do my papers." Grabbing my sacks I dragged them down the stairs and up to the shack through the rain.

Anger is the hard bitter centre of grief. It was like one of those hated candies mistakenly picked from Grandad's pocket. The more you sucked on it, the worse it tasted. As I trudged up the street, licking my own tears, I realized they tasted not of sorrow, but of rage. I was as mad as a thirteen year old boy can be at his dead father.

I also wanted to know why he'd disappeared just when I needed him most. It wasn't only that I was too young to be the breadwinner and the man of the family. It wasn't even the father and son talk about sex we hadn't really gotten around to. I'd hoped that would clear up a few questions raised by whisperings at school and the shack which, as far as I could tell from my reading, were the purest bullshit. But on top of everything else, the world might come to an end any day now. Was this any kind of time for a man to go and die and leave his family?

I knew it was stupid to be angry, which only made it worse. My father hadn't wanted to die. Like everybody else, he probably thought he was going to live forever. Mr. Morden in his bomb-shelter obviously thought so. Without a bomb-shelter, I still believed I would be miraculously spared to lead my chosen people out of the burning ruins into the green mountains where we would build a new society, a better world, like Fidel in the Sierra Maestra.

Officially, my father died of a cerebral hemorhage, a stroke. I wondered what it felt like. Was it a blinding white light, brighter than a thousand suns, or darkness like the softly rising dark that rises like a drowning wave when you're just falling asleep? My father owed the last twenty years of his life to the sudden great white light of the Atomic Bomb. After he died, my mother gave me the account he'd written of the time he spent as a prisoner of war in Japan, working as slave labour in a steel foundry outside Nagasaki. In it he explained how the Japanese guards held drills, herding the prisoners into caves and mine shafts that were rigged with dynamite, obviously planning to execute and bury them the moment the first American troops landed in Japan. Only the landings never happened because two whole cities, one of them only twenty miles away, had been vapourized in a demonstration, like a coming attractions trailer at the movies, of what the end of the world would look like.

54

Unofficially, my father died of a joke. Among the recollections in that diary was the story of how he got the wound that would kill him, like a bomb with a delayed action fuse, two decades later. Sweating the the foundry, he and a friend tried to improve their starvation rations by trading for salt on the black market. They got caught. After questioning by the sergeant of the guard, which included a free karate demonstration, they were lying on the floor, eyes swollen shut, mouths full of blood. His friend leaned over and said something, at which my Dad broke into uncontrollable laughter.

He woke up a week later in the dirty shed that served as an infirmary. As he put it, he needed a hat three sizes bigger. Apparently the joke hadn't translated well. A guard had slammed his rifle butt down like a piledriver on my Dad's skull. After that, he got terrible headaches, one or two a year, always in that same spot. The most frightening memories of my childhood weren't of his anger, but of him standing in a corner of the dining room with clenched fists, slamming his head into the angle where the walls met.

Nowhere in the diary did he say what the joke was, what the words were that caused him to laugh in the face of death as surely as they would one day kill him. I read it again and again, keeping the fragile notebook with its fading pages in a plastic bag in a drawer beside my bed. A lot of the things adults laugh at are mysterious when you're a kid, but as far as I was concerned the wisecrack that killed my father was the ultimate incomprehensible adult joke but one. That one was that the unthinkable weapon which saved my Dad's life in Japan was now going to incinerate his family and the world he fought and suffered to save.

If I was going to keep crying, and I thought I might, I didn't want to do it at the shack. I'd never live it down and no matter how short life might be, I wasn't going to spend it being taunted as a crybaby. Outside in the rain it wouldn't show, so I stuffed my papers into the sacks as fast as I could. Paul sidled up to me, puffing on a forbidden cigarette, pinched from his mother's pack, no doubt. He didn't particularly like to smoke, he just swiped them to give to Rick the Sub-Manager to suck up. He whispered out of the corner of his mouth not occupied by the Export A.

"So? Did you ask her yet?"

"Huh?" I tried not to look at him. Gordy the Goof was waiting at the door with Paul's paper sack proudly slung over his shoulder. Paul sighed, exasperated.

"Irene Beaumont...Did you ask her?...You know..."

"Why don't you ask her yourself?" I jerked my sacks off the bench and stormed out into the downpour. He followed me to the door whining.

"What's the matter with you?...Wha'd I say?"

"Nothings the matter with me!" I slung my sacks across my bike saddle.

"All I said was..."

"Fuck off!...Just fuck right off, okay!"

We were at an age where we told each other to fuck off all the time, but I'd overheard a man in an argument outside the fire hall where my Dad worked use the latter expression and I was impressed by the extra emphasis and freshness the word right brought to the shopworn original. So was Paul. He jerked back.

"Jeez...Wha'd I do, for Chrisake?"

Rick the Sub-Manager was impressed too. His pimply pompadour-framed face poked out the door like an evil hand-puppet. "You watch your lip, kid. Or I'll fix it for you..." Fine one to talk, since he was the one who'd done most to expand our socially unacceptable vocabularies.

Out of control, I was sobbing now, but I hoped nobody could tell because the rain was hammering my hair flat and running down my face in streams. My voice was a weird shriek.

"You're supposed to be the Sub-Manager! You're supposed to be in charge! Why don't you make him do his own fucking papers instead of getting that ree-tard to do them for him all the time!"

Rick's jaw tightened threateningly, but I could see his Brylcreem-sodden brain turning over the thought that he might well get into some unsuspected type of supreme shit with Frank the Manager over Gordy. Muttering something to Paul, he pulled his duck-tailed hair out of the rain and disappeared into the shack. Paul followed him, bewildered and still whining.

"Now wha'd I do?"

I should have felt better but I didn't. As I pushed my bike along the only flat part of my route, I turned around to see Paul taking his papers away from Gordy. Gordy just stood there in the rain, looking guilty and embarrassed, like he'd done something wrong and didn't know what.

Chapter 9

I dragged my bike up the hills in the rain, reading the headlines over and over again. BLOCKADE! U.S. MOVES AGAINST CUBA! I even delivered to Mr. Morden. I should've cut him off a long time ago for not paying me, but I knew it was as much my fault for being afraid to collect from him. I didn't feel any better until I got to Mac Perry's door and found it ajar with music coming out of it like an invitation to a party. I stood there for awhile, just out of the rain, listening, then I pushed the door open a bit further and put the paper inside so it wouldn't get any wetter. At last there was a lull in the music. I heard the rattle of ice in a glass and I stepped inside.

"Mr. Perry?...It's me. Jack the paperboy...Your door was sort of open. I put the paper inside so it wouldn't get wet..."

"C'mon in, man. Ya don't want me to think you're too dumb to come in out of the rain, do ya?"

I didn't want him to think that. I was already halfway down the hall. He hadn't turned on the lamps even though it was a dark day. An open pack of Pall Malls, a steel Zippo lighter, a glass ashtray the size of a hubcap and glass of whisky were laid out on the top of the piano like a still life painting in the luminous gray light. He greeted me with a wry grin.

"Coffee's on the stove if you want a warmer...Help yourself."

Alone in the kitchen I finally stopped feeling like a kid who fucked everything up and hurt or frightened people without meaning to or understanding why. He trusted me to look through his cupboards for a cup, through his fridge for cream, to find the sugar and pour my own damn coffee while he was busy with more important things at the piano. When I sat down in the living room, out of his line of vision so I wouldn't distract him, he was playing music that sounded like the rain, music that made me start to see things in my head, rainy afternoons in strange and beautiful cities.

When he stopped to refill his glass from a bottle of Dewar's tucked out of the way behind one leg of the piano, we were interrupted by a soft knock at the sliding glass door. With a shrug, he got up and pulled the gauze curtain aside to reveal Mrs. Lytle. Chuckling softly, he let her in out of the rain too.

"I heard you playing, Mac and I just..." She stopped suddenly, catching sight of me on the couch when she followed his quick glance. She blushed. "Oh, hello, Jack...I..."

"Draw a better crowd in the neighbourhood than I do in the clubs. Join the scene. Coffee or?..."

She agreed to coffee. Mac showed her the way to the kitchen and helped her get a cup, making me feel somehow prouder that he'd just told me to help myself. For a moment I thought I heard them whispering in there, but the rain was really loud with the patio door slid back and I wasn't sure. Mrs. Lytle joined me on the couch with her coffee, smiling shyly at me like we had a secret. Mac returned to the piano, took a big swallow from his glass and shook a long unfiltered Pall Mall from the pack to the corner of his mouth with a slight flick of a wrist. The Zippo clicked, flared, snapped shut and re-joined the pack in one smooth motion. He took a long drag on the cigarette without looking at us, smiling to himself, then he laid it in the ashtray.

"Now that I've got such a select and discerning audience, I better get with it and pull out my best licks."

He began to play again and I've never heard music like it since. I was back in that strange misty city of dripping gardens and dully glittering rooftops, the gurgling tinkle of drainpipes and wet horses clopping along slick cobblestones, only Mrs. Lytle was there too and we were walking through the streets, going nowhere, just walking and getting wet and not caring and she was holding my hand.

She actually was holding my hand. Sort of. She'd put her hand, no bigger than my own when you looked down at them like I was doing, over mine and her touch was cool and warm at the same time, soothing as the sound of rain outside the window when you're in bed a night and you don't want to go to sleep because it feels so good to be lying there warm in the dark listening to the radio on very low and the rain playing the world like a huge piano, making different sounds on the streets, the roofs, the trees. Mac talked to us as he played.

"This used to be Debussy...*Un Jardin Dans La Pluie...A Garden In The Rain*...Man, he'd flip if he could hear what I'm doing to it... Hey, who knows? Maybe old Claude would dig it, eh? He was a cool cat in his time. Sometimes he'd write little tunes like this and play them without using his thumbs, or with three fingers of each hand, just to bug the critics, play games with their minds...Maybe I should call it *Patio Furniture In The Rain*..."

He laughed at his own joke, glancing out at the dripping deck chairs and chaises on the patio anyone else would have folded up and put under cover. I didn't care that I didn't get the joke. I made a mental note to look up Debussy, Claude, in the Encyclopedia Britannica my Dad had bought us a few months before he died, but I was in no hurry. Mrs. Lytle squeezed my hand as Mac Perry played on and I wanted everything to stay exactly like that forever or end in an instant in some ultimate explosion, because I knew I would never be that happy ever again.

It didn't and finally I had to say "I gotta go finish my papers."

In bed that night I listened to Sam Cooke singing "Cupid, draw back your bow...And let your arrow go...Straight to my lover's heart for me" and thought about Mrs. Lytle while I worked on another letter to Fidel. I knew what lovers were, or were supposed to be, and it was close enough to how I felt about her. It was hard to keep my mind on Fidel and the approaching end of the world when the radio kept playing songs like The Marvelettes 'You Really Got A Hold On Me' and Gene Pitney's 'Half Heaven, Half Heartache.' I tried to explain to Fidel that I really loved this woman and it was the most important thing in my life and I had to live and get older so I could do something about it.

I knew Fidel would understand. After all, he must have left a woman somewhere, in the city of his youth or in a village of the Sierra Maestra, a woman who believed in him, loved him and waited for him to finish his revolution and come back to her, a woman he dreamed of as he smoked his cigar on the terrace and waited for another tense dawn that might be his last. I figured he must be able to pick up radio stations from Miami and I wondered if he too laid awake listening to Ray Charles sing 'I Can't Stop Loving You' or the Shirelles chant 'Soldier Boy' and thought about just running away to her, with her, into the mountains and letting the world go to Hell on its own time.

Sometimes I wished I could be like Paul and not really know anything or care about anything other than whether or not some girl had rubber things in her bra. I seemed to know just enough to make myself miserable but not enough to know what to do about it. When Mrs. Canetti bent over giving me almost as unobstructed a view of female breasts as Paul's purloined Playboys, I knew it wasn't accidental. When I threw the paper on the cops doorstep and the door was opened by a young woman in a turtleneck sweater not quite long enough to conceal her black underpants, I knew she wasn't the cleaning-lady. When I went to collect from Mrs. Lytle one time and found her wearing a black leotard and standing on her head, doing something she called 'yoga' in the middle of a living room scented with the smell of burning rope, I knew I wasn't smelling dinner burning.

I'd never seen marijuana, but I'd read about it and it was another thing I wanted the world to be around long enough for me to try, but I didn't tell Fidel that. I'd already made the mistake of telling Paul one afternoon when we were hanging around in the shell of a half-framed house after doing our papers, reluctant to go home because our mothers were cooking liver or something equally repellent for dinner. Paul was aghast, as if I'd suggested we murder our surviving parents.

"But that's...dope!"

"Not really." I'd done my research at the library. "Heroin or morphine or opium. They're dope. This is just..."

"It's dope!" Paul backed away from me through an unfinished wall like a ghost that'd seen a ghost.

"Forget it, okay?" I shouldered my mercifully empty sacks.

I thought of asking Mac Perry about it. Drugs weren't associated with rock and roll, but there were often small articles in the papers I delivered about jazz musicians being arrested at the border for possession of the illegal weed. I just didn't know how to bring it up, since he treated me like a regular guy and everything. I was afraid I might make myself look stupid and make him treat me like some smartass kid and ruin it all. I was just so afraid the world might end and I might actually not survive. I might end with it without ever having lived, without having experienced anything. I would never make love with a woman or even see any more of a real woman naked than those tantalizing glimpses of Mrs. Canetti's breasts. I would never have a chance to really love someone like Mrs. Lytle and walk with her through the deserted streets of that rained-on city I would never find on any of the coloured maps in the atlas that came with my encyclopedia.

CHAPTER 10

I had pretty much made up my mind to risk making a fool of myself and ask Mac Perry about things, about women in especially, the next time he asked me in for coffee, but things didn't work out that way. It was still raining hard so hard you'd have thought that if there was a God, he might have changed his mind about nuclear Armageddon and opted for the old tried and true Flood again. Maybe a lot of people were thinking the same thing because though the headlines screamed RUSSIANS MOBILIZE! ALLIES BACK U.S. BLOCKADE OF CUBA! and even warned WE'RE OVER THE BRINK!, there was also a front page picture story on how the most popular rubber masks for the coming Halloween were caricatures of President Kennedy, Kruschev and, of course, Fidel Castro.

With the rain rattling down I couldn't hear the piano outside Mac Perry's house. The door was closed, but the handle turned when I touched it and I followed the door into the foyer. "Mr. Perry?" There was no answer, no music, nothing but the sound of the rain behind me like static from a distant radio station as I walked down the carpeted hall. It seemed odd that it got louder as I got closer to the living room.

I guess I understood or even expected what I saw then because I didn't announce myself with anything as gauche as a stage cough. That was one of Irene Beaumont's French affectations that had mysteriously caught on among the girls in our class. Every time a boy said or did something clumsy, stupid, foolish or just plain boyish for that matter, on the school grounds he could count on at least two or three girls to drawl loudly in unison, "How go-oh-sh!" We didn't know what it meant, but we knew we when we were being mocked. It was me who hunted down a French-English dictionary in the Reference section of the library and explained to the guys it was French for "clumsy dipstick," which certainly was an accurate description of what I felt like standing in Mac Perry's hallway.

Mac Perry and Mrs. Lytle were standing behind the big black piano near the open patio door with the white gauze curtains billowing into the room. They were kissing each other, she him as avidly as he her, and they were pressed together like the pages of a wet newspaper. I backed quickly and silently down the hall and out into the rain.

It eased off a bit as I finished my route, trying not to think too much about what I'd seen. Champ had taken to following me as I delivered to the last block of houses and I was grateful for his company and protection since every other dog on the top half of my route took off like they'd been sniped with a BB gun the moment they caught sight of him. I sat on the curb for awhile in the drizzle, rubbing his huge head, looking out over the city buried in fog as thick as the aftermath of a blast. Looking like the Batmobile in the comics, a black RCMP cruiser rose out of the mist and stopped beside us. Constable Mackenzie rolled down the window.

"Getting along pretty well, you two." He sounded disappointed. I just shrugged. "Well, watch out he doesn't turn on you." He stomped the gas, spraying gravel as the car lurched down the driveway under the dripping firs.

They'd never complained about their paper being ripped to shreds by the other dogs before they could read it, but Constable Mackenzie looked like he might be in the mood to bring it up. Giving Champ a goodbye scratch behind the ears, I straddled my bike and took off as fast as I dared down the glistening hills. I didn't slow down or look around as I passed the Perry house or the Lytle house. I'd seen enough of what I wasn't supposed to see for one day. I couldn't help listening for the music, but the only sound in the street was the wet hiss of my bike tires as rippling road fell away beneath me.

I glanced at the Morden house on the home stretch, more out of morbid curiousity about the steady progress of dilapidation than anything else. Abruptly reversing my pedals, I skidded to a stop.

Not only had the paper been taken in, there was a light on in the house itself. My collection book was at the bottom of one of my bags, a jigsaw of uncollected receipts. Without knowing why exactly, since I'd already written the money off, I walked my bike under the shelter of the sagging sundeck, leaned it against the mold-flecked siding and knocked on the door. Maybe I wanted to make the day come out right somehow. Maybe I just wanted to do something to take my mind off what I'd seen in Mac Perry's living room. Maybe I figured after that nothing adults did could surprise me, so it was a good time to confront Mr. Morden.

I was right and wrong. Mr. Morden took my mind off things alright, but he surprised me too. I was shocked when the door snapped open immediately and he stood there with me almost knocking on his chest. He didn't look anything like himself as I remembered. He looked like he was wearing clothes borrowed from a bigger man. The collar of his shirt dangled around his neck like a loose noose. Green army fatigue pants flapped around his skinny legs and his dirty looking bare feet were shoved into muddy laceless Oxford brogans.

"What...do you want?" He sounded like Boris Karloff in a bad mood.

"I...I'm collecting...for the paper." I couldn't get my voice above a whisper all of a sudden.

Curtly he motioned me inside. The house smelled stale and worse than stale. From where I stood in the vestibule I could see into what used to be the rec room, filled with pieces of broken furniture and what looked like bags of garbage with stains showing through. As I stepped inside I noticed Mr. Morden didn't smell any too fresh himself and his clothes looked greasy with dirt in places. The vestibule itself was full of newspapers. Newspapers piled on newspapers, halfway up the walls in places, some obviously read, their pages roughly folded back to inside stories, others obviously added to the pile with their front pages unturned. They weren't tied up neatly in string bundles for disposal, just piled loose in tottering stacks, probably in chronological order like some demented history of the last days of mankind. I was only there to collect for four months, not for all this.

"You owe me for four months..."

"Four months?" He slammed the door behind us. "Four seconds is more like it..."

"Excuse me?" I'd been taught to say that when an adult said something I didn't understand.

"Four seconds! Four seconds is what we'll have...Four seconds to run, to hide..." He glanced toward the back of the house as though calculating how many seconds it would take him to sprint to the sunken door of his fallout shelter, bar the door behind him and cock his shotgun.

"I tried to collect, Mr. Morden..." I was careful to avoid an accusatory tone. "I really did but nobody answered and..."

"Pay? You really think I should pay? That anyone should pay? For this?" His voice rose to a shriek and he gestured dramatically to the wall of yellowing newspapers behind him. He had a point I guess. When the firestorm came all that useless bad news was going to go up in a very small puff of smoke.

I held my collection book up in front of me like an inadequate radiation shield. "I just deliver the paper, Mr. Morden..."

"For this? People have a right to real information! Not this!" He was screaming now and I was scared. "They have a right to know! An obligation to know! Even if they don't want to know! This tells them nothing! Nothing about what will really happen! There will be a shock like an earthquake! A wind like a hurricane of fire! Buildings will be blown to dust in an instant! There will be nothing left of most people but their shadows! Their skin will turn black and peel off in a second! In another second their flesh will melt! Their bones will turn to ash and be blown away before they can fall to the ground!" His eyes glowed in the dimness, the pupils like two pellets of plutonium.

It was the first time I'd ever met an adult who was really crazy. Gordy the Goof was sort of crazy but he couldn't help it and he was basically happy, smiling his idiot smile even when he was teased or conned into doing our work for us. Gordy was better off than Paul, who only knew a little bit more, enough to make him greedy and sly. Gordy knew too little and he wasn't really crazy. Mr. Morden knew too much and he definitely was.

"It doesn't matter." Mr. Morden went quiet as suddenly as he'd become agitated. I'd been edging surreptitiously toward the door, thinking of making a break for it, but he put his hand in his pocket, hauled out a fistful of crumpled dirty bills and held them out to me. I took them nervously, afraid he might grab me and start screaming again.

"This is too much money, Mr. Morden..." By my quick count he was all paid up and there was at least an extra five dollars, but he waved it away with a tired flick of his wrist. Between him and Mac Perry I was financially better off than at any time since I'd taken over the route, even if it did look like I might not have time to spend it.

"It doesn't matter." His eyes were glazed over now, sunk back into his head looking at something I couldn't see. "I know...I was there...I saw...I saw..."

My hand froze on the doorknob as I pulled the door ajar. I could only whisper again. "What did you see, Mr. Morden?"

"Nagasaki." His voice was a horrible rasping gurgle. "August eight. Nineteen forty-five. I was a prisoner of war...I worked in a ship-yard near the city...I saw...I saw..."His eyes flickered for a moment, then dulled again. "Never mind. Don't bring me any more papers. No more...No more."

"Okay, Mr. Morden." If I put in a Stop Delivery tomorrow, I'd be up the whole five bucks.

As I rode the rest of the way home, I realized Mr. Morden must be about the same age my Dad was, though he looked much older now. They'd both been prisoners in Japan, both near Nagasaki. They might even have met in some camp and not recognized each other after twenty years, except that Mr. Morden had really seen The Bomb that saved them. And now it was haunting him and hunting him down like an implacable ghost, across the years and thousands of miles to this disintegrating ordinary house on a quiet suburban street.

In bed that night I tried to start another letter to Fidel Castro, then I remembered the one I'd just written was still in the pocket of my wet jeans and why it hadn't been mailed. I'd been going to ask Mrs. Lytle to send it for me. Creeping through the dark back basement with my reading flashlight I found my damp wadded pants in the laundry and retrieved it. I put it on the beside table to dry out. I'd have to figure out some other way to get it to the post office. I wanted to write to Fidel again anyway to tell him about Mr. Morden, about what he'd seen that I was sure neither Fidel or Kruschev or Kennedy had seen except in films, how it scared him so much it made him crazy twenty years later.

Instead I kept thinking about what I'd seen in Mac Perry's living room that afternoon and I didn't think he'd be very interested in that at the moment or in the hollow feeling I had inside which was like being very hungry except that I had no appetite and had left almost my whole macaroni and cheese dinner congealing on the plate. My mother thought I was "coming down with something", probably from getting soaked to the bone and chilled delivering my papers. I fell asleep with my flashlight and my radio on again, listening to Mary Wells sing 'You Beat Me To The Punch.'

CHAPTER 11

"Do you remember the dream you had last night?"
My mother watched as I made a sandwich of my breakfast, two pieces of toast swabbed with raspberry jam with a hard-fried egg and slices of bacon between them. On a school day she'd have nagged me about sleeping in and ignoring her repeated wake-up calls until it was almost time to leave for school. I'd invented the breakfast sandwich as a way of getting around her complaint that I never had time to eat in the morning, then discovered I really liked my bacon and eggs that way, but she should have at least made her usual observation about how disgusting it was, especially since it was Saturday and I didn't have to go to school. That she didn't and her elaborately casual tone of voice warned me something was up. I'd sort of figured that out when she let me sleep in almost 'til noon without calling me once and made me breakfast after the kids had already had their lunch.

"Uh-uh."

Raspberry seeds stuck between my teeth, making them feel like they were too big for my head. My mother seemed determined to pursue the subject of my unconscious life.

"You had a bad dream. You were shouting. I came down to see if you were alright."

That explained how my radio and my flashlight had been turned off, the flashlight replaced on my night table.

"I shook you to wake you up. You looked right at me and said, 'There's gonna be a war.' Do you remember that?"

I shook my head, not just playing dumb for a change. I'd had a lot of those kinds of dreams lately, but I didn't remember this one.

"Do you stay up every night listening to the radio and reading?"

"Not every night." I equivocated through a mouthful of salty bacon, leathery egg and sweet jam. I was pleading the Teenagers Amendment—stall, split hairs until your parents tear theirs out, admit as little as possible without actually lying because lies don't hold up and just make the shit deeper, confine your answers to "Nope," "Nothing" and "I dunno."

Turning away from the sink, she wiped her hands and took an envelope down from the mare's nest of junk on top of the fridge and put it on the table in front of me. I recognized the writing, like a spy confronted with his code book. It was my letter to Fidel Castro, the one I hadn't been able to give to Mrs. Lytle to mail because of what I saw in Mac Perry's living room. At the last minute before falling asleep I'd taken it out of the drawer and put it on the night table so I wouldn't forget to take it with me in the morning.

"Do you want me to mail this for you?" Her voice was very quiet.

"Would you?" I stared down at my sandwich, oozing a yellow thread of unhardened yolk.

"First thing Monday morning...And if you must read at night, Jack, don't use a flashlight. You'll ruin your eyes and waste batteries. Use your bedside lamp. That's what it's for."

I nodded mutely, ashamed of myself for not asking her in the first place, and took my breakfast with me as I slipped out the back door. I was glad I didn't have school, but I wasn't looking forward to the afternoon. *The Saturday Sun* was the thickest, heaviest edition of the week and I had extra papers then, people who only had the week-end paper delivered.

Normally I would have called on Paul and spent the afternoon goofing around with him, but I knew he'd only start bugging me about Irene Beaumont again, so I avoided his block and rode up past Mr. Morden's house, eerily calm in the watery light. It had stopped raining for a while overnight, but clouds were rolling in from Vancouver Island over Georgia Strait again and it looked like it would rain again. Nothing harder so far than a little more Strontium-90 from H-Bomb tests into the grass and into our milk, some adults said, but I spotted the roofed over skeleton of a house under construction and dodged inside just in case.

I hadn't been there five minutes, hadn't even begun to imagine the lives of the people who would one day live there if we didn't all get fried first, when I heard someone call "Jack?" from where the planks and framing indicated the front door was going to be. Even in an undertone, I knew that voice. It was Irene Beaumont. I climbed back down from my refuge in the unsheathed rafters.

"I saw you when you went by our house. What are you doing here?"

"Nothing much." I gave her the shrug. Uninvited, she came up the roughly framed-in stairs. We wandered around the house, sort of together in the gloom, as the rain began to hammer overhead like a crew of God's own roofers. Irene made comments as we passed through only slightly more than imaginary walls, identifying the rooms.

"This will be the master bedroom."

I nodded. It was big enough to hold a chest of drawers, dressing table and a big double bed like the one my Mom now slept in alone. I wondered fleetingly where Mr. Morden slept now his wife was gone, or if he slept at all. I could see his house from the bedroom window where the wind blew in, darkening the wood of what would be the sill if the house did get finished.

Irene evidently wanted to take up our verbal "show me yours and I'll show you mine" game where we'd left off. She started asking me who I liked again as she darted in and out between the upright two-by-four studs, penetrating the walls like a playful ghost. I was a little uncomfortable in the bedrooms of a house destined to be on my route. No matter what the people who bought it were like or how they finished the house, I would always think of them confronting each other in that room as I delivered their paper. It seemed strange to think that they would sleep and make love and maybe even conceive children in that very room, a room whose hidden shape I knew more about than they did, right down to the knot-holes and the manufacturers stencils on the wallboard.

Finally while she was invisible in the hall or the small bathroom she called the "on sweet," I put an end to her irritatingly coy questions with a straight answer. I don't know why I did it. I knew I'd probably regret it even as I opened my mouth, yet saying it somehow made me feel calm and powerful inside myself.

"I like you Irene. I always have. Since we were kids."

I felt a guilty stitch under my heart when I thought of Mrs. Lytle, but I was still trying not to think too directly about her and the implications of what I'd seen in Mac Perry's living room. Irene appeared through a puzzle of struts like an ethereal spirit in the dimness.

"Do you really, Jack?" At least she wasn't laughing yet.

"Yes."

I was already doomed. If she wanted to, she could tell everybody in school I had a crush on her and they could all have a good laugh. Instead of looking triumphant, as she should have, she moved tentatively closer to me.

"Do you want to kiss me?"

"Yes."

That monosyllable hadn't let me down so far. Irene stepped up so close the points of her boobs were touching my shirt. I dismissed a passing thought of what foam rubber might feel like as irrelevant. Her head was thrown back like that of a sacrificial victim. As I bent to kiss her, her lips seemed so much softer than mine, somehow elusive, and the scent of her hair filled my head, like the smell of hidden flowering broom on the wind in spring. We stood there with our faces pressed together, holding each other carefully by the shoulders, for a very long moment, unsure of what to do next. Breaking the kiss, she stepped back.

"Is there anything else you want to do?" Her voice was a tense whisper.

The one syllable that had worked so far failed me at last. I thought I knew what she meant, but I wasn't sure and I didn't want to say "Like what?" and look like some dumb dinkweed who didn't know what came next and give her even more of a hold over me. As for telling her what I might really like to do, I just couldn't find the words.

"I guess not right now." I almost wished Paul was there. He would've known what to say. "I gotta go do my papers pretty soon."

She might have been a little disappointed, but I could tell from the way she took my hand and smiled in the aquarium shadows that she was also relieved. The air in the room smelled just like it does after a flash of lightning. She put her soft warm mouth to my ear.

"I like you better than anybody, Jack. Always. Since we were kids."

We were even.

I was nervous later as I stomped up the three two-by-six steps into the shack, but Rick the Sub-Manager didn't say anything about me mouthing him off the day before. Instead he made me wait beside my two huge bundles of weekend editions until he'd opened everybody else's bundles before he snapped the strands of copper wire with a vicious twist of his cutter.

"You got mail, smartass."

He sneered as he poked the envelope that had been trapped under the bindings of one bundle. It was addressed to my route number and hand-stamped COMPLAINT in huge red letters.

"You get any more of those, Frank's gonna take you out back and make you suck his dick one of these days."

I almost asked him how many times you had to do that to get to be Sub-Manager, but I knew he'd cream me if I did, so I kept quiet. So far I'd done alright just saying what was on my mind straight out for one day, but it seemed like a good time to quit while I was ahead. I opened the envelope, took out the pink carbon COMPLAINT slip and read it. It said, "Customers Name," then "Const. Mackenzie," followed by the familiar address of the cops who had Champ and the two worst mutts on my route. I folded it, stuffed it in my pocket and started shoving my bulky papers into the sacks. I'd made friends with a dog that was supposed to terrorize me and this was how they were getting even.

Once Rick the Sub-Manager was back at his cabinet, listening to Duke of Earl on his transistor and snapping his fingers in time, Paul came over and stood beside me as if nothing had happened. I'd noticed he did this, with kids at school, especially with girls when one of his outrageous suggestions was rebuffed, with teachers, even with Rick. He never said he was sorry or anything. He just acted like he'd forgotten all about whatever it was you'd been mad at him for. I was surprised by how often it worked. He was so persistent people just seemed to get tired of being mad at him and started doing what he wanted again.

He wanted good grades without doing too much homework and he wanted to be in the good books of teachers so he wouldn't wind up on the invisible list of "trouble-makers" whose every move was monitored while they were on school grounds. He wanted girls to like him in spite of themselves and his unceasing attempts to do things their mothers would not only have paled, but called the cops, to hear. He wanted to be Rick the Sub-Manager's toady, there to hand him the clippers if Rick was "busy" having a smoke, listening to his radio or reading confidential dispatches from the Circulation Department. He wanted Gordy the Goof to be his personal unpaid bearer on safari through the dog-infested jungles of suburbia. He wanted to be my best friend in spite of me.

Gordy had been hanging around, picking his nose and eating the boogers, by the yellow bridge over the creek fifty feet from the shack when I got there. He waved and smiled in his genuinely goofy way. Now he stuck his head in the door, looking around eagerly.

"I tol' you to stay outa here, you fuckin' geek!"

Rick snapped a kick with his black winkle-picker pointed shoe that missed Gordy's head by a foot, but it scared him. Smile crumpling, he backed off to the edge of the road and stayed there, patiently scuffing unreadable runes in the mud with the toes of his soaked laceless Hush Puppies. I knew Rick only did it to make sure I wouldn't have anything to tell on him, just as Paul had no intention of hauling the heaviest papers of the week himself. That made me feel a lot worse than the Complaint slip.

"You seen Irene?"

I felt like Paul was trying to distract me from thinking about Gordy and the trouble I'd caused on account of him, and that was okay. I wanted to be distracted.

"Yeah." I told him I'd seen her earlier that day and where.

"Well?"

"Well?"

"Did you do anything?"

"Sort of...Well, I kissed her."

I don't know why I told him, except that he was a kind of ringleader who was popular with everybody and I was a moody loner who got on the wrong side of everybody and he'd decided to be my friend for some unknown reason and include me in on stuff I never would have done on my own and I guess I wanted to impress him.

"Wow!...You kissed Irene Beaumont? She wouldn't let me kiss her and that was a dare in Lesley's basement... Did you do anything else?"

"I didn't have time." I felt a couple of inches taller. "I had to do my papers."

I left before he did. With only forty papers he could afford to goof around at the shack as long as he wanted and I figured he didn't want me to actually see him getting Gordy to do his route again.

As I pushed my bike up the hills I read the paper but the news wasn't getting any better and it looked like it was going to get worse in the worst way. RUSSIAN SHIPS CONTINUE ON COURSE, the headlines said, followed by, CUBA SHOWDOWN NEAR, BLOCKADE CLASH FEARED and CASTRO DENOUNCES BLOCKADE. I thought about how Fidel must feel. After all, the U.S. had persuaded most countries to boycott goods from Cuba and embargo shipments to him. There he was, trying to make his country into a decent place for people to raise their kids and nobody would deal with him but the Russians. So when they said, "Hey, mind if we put some missile bases in your country?" what was he supposed to do? Tell them to fuck right off?

Paper by paper, street by street, the weight of all that bad news was literally lifted off my shoulders. By the time I got to the Lytle and Perry houses, I could ride instead of pushing the bike, zig-zagging up the hills, stopping at the curb, still somehow hoping Mrs. Lytle would come out of her house and say something to me that would make it alright, but the streets were enveloped in a tense silence. At Mac Perry's house the curtains were all drawn as usual, but the door was firmly shut and there wasn't a sound from inside, no music, not a chord.

At the top of my route, Champ came out to greet me. He barked twice, then licked the side of my face harder than I washed it myself. Below, the other two dogs lurked in the bush, waiting for me to come down and get trapped against the front door. I rolled the paper into a cylinder and winged it in my best Little League style at the sundeck. Halfway there it opened and separated on the wind, turning into a flock of white birds, like the seagulls who flew up Mosquito Creek to drop oysters and crack them on the rocks, then floated down crying on extended wings.

Chapter 12

"It's all set."

I wasn't sure I'd heard Paul right as we bolted toward the school Exit and through the heavy doors along with hundreds of other kids free at last from the bondage of learning. I took a deep breath of wet autumn air to get the chalkdust and floorwax taste of school out of my mouth.

"What's all set?"

"With Irene, you dumb dink."

He looked far too pleased with himself for my own good. I'd seen that look before, often enough to have seen how quickly it could turn to terror as we desperately tried to double-talk, lie or beg our way out of a ride home in a police car, a long walk down the hall to the Principal's Office or a brisk walk home in the company of an irate neighbour with the prospect of being grounded for life.

"What's all set with Irene?"

All of a sudden the baloney and cheese sandwich I'd had for lunch was back at the top of my throat, threatening to come all the way out.

"You know...I talked to her."

"You what?"

"Well, you told me to ask her myself...Look, all I did was set it up for her to come up to the shack after we've done our papers. I told her you wanted to meet her there. The rest is up to you."

A couple of times that afternoon I'd caught Irene looking at me with mischievious curiousity. Now I knew why.

"But the shack'll be locked..."

"Naw, it won't." I was really beginning to see why parents and teachers hated that smirking crafty look of his. "I fixed it with Rick after you left Saturday. He was really sore at you, but when I told him what we're gonna do, he said okay..."

"Rick's gonna be there?"

Now at critical mass, the baloney and cheese was screaming to get out.

"Well, yeah. That's the best part. This gets you out of being in supreme shit with him."

"And you too, I guess."

"Well, yeah, but..."

"Only trouble is, smart guy, she won't do it."

"Sure she will! She let you into a house where she was baby-sitting. She let you kiss her. She'll do it for sure. Believe me."

"I mean, dinkweed, I don't think she'll do it with you and Rick there."

I was weasling furiously, trying to choke down the rotten baloney taste burning the back of my mouth. I wasn't just chicken. I actually hoped she wouldn't do it and was secretly afraid she might. I tried to tell myself she wouldn't come up to the shack, that her mother probably wouldn't let her out with dinner time so close, but I knew I was kidding myself. The shack was the ultimate male sanctum, impenetrable in a way no tree fort with its No Girls graffiti ever could be, even more forbidden in a way than the Boys washroom at school. There was just no way Irene Beaumont would miss the opportunity to be the first girl at school to enter that forbidden zone and tell about it.

"Look, Rick and I will pretend to leave. See? There's those two big knot-holes at the back of the shack. She'll never know we're watching. I'm telling you, it'll work..."

I looked around guiltily for Irene and caught sight of her already off the school grounds on her way home in the middle of a gaggle of giggling girls. She looked back at us as we down the cement steps. Paul was obviously determined to walk all the way home with me using every ounce of sneaky persuasion he possessed. There was no way I could catch up to Irene now unless I ran flat out and if I did, how would I get her away from her friends? And what would I say to her?

At the shack later, Rick the Sub-Manager was suspiciously friendly. He cut my bundles first and told me if I wanted help on my route today I could have it with a jerk of his waterfall coiffure toward door where Gordy waited hopefully, still banned from the shack itself until Rick was sure he had more on me than I had on him.

"I can manage."

In fact, I was feeling kind of weak since I finally had tossed up what was left of my lunch into the downstairs toilet the moment I got home from school.

"'Kay...But don't be late..."

He gave me a leer which flourished what appeared to be a fresh crop of pimples. His transistor was blasting The Crystals 'He's Sure The Boy I Love' as I pushed my bike away, trying not to look at Paul, who obviously intended to hang around and bask in the glory of his brilliant plan to resolve the question of the reality of Irene Beaumont's boobs among other things.

I was so nervous I missed a couple of houses and had to back-track. I kept asking myself over and over why I was going along with another one of Paul's schemes I was sure was going to land us in the deepest shit imaginable, why I had ever gone along with him on anything. I guess I did it because he was the only one my own age who treated me like a regular guy, even if I did do weird things like read The Winston School Dictionary during recess and talk about strange things and not have a father. Not having a father wasn't cool in 1962. It wasn't even normal and my reputation for weirdness hadn't improved when kids at school asked, "What's it like when your Dad dies?" and I answered, "You'd have to ask him."

I was having so much trouble getting the paper on the right doorsteps I didn't have time to read it until I was halfway through my route, slowing down as the hills got steeper. The front page was heavily blocked with harrowing headlines. RED SHIPS TURN BACK. AMERICAN ARMADA AWAITING RUSSIANS. U.S. CAPITAL DWELLERS HUDDLE UNDER SHADOW OF THE BOMB. They weren't huddling alone. RCAF PUT ON ALERT IN CUBA CRISIS.

OTTAWA TO SUPPORT U.S. 'ALL THE WAY.'

I bet that has Fidel shaking in his combat boots, I thought. I could almost hear him amusing his revolutionary comrades by quaking in mock-terror, "Madre Dios! Not the Canadians!" at the story that the University of B.C. engineers, notorious for their public pranks, had executed him in effigy with water pistols.

But the big headlines trumpeted his defiance. CUBA MANNING OWN MISSILES. DENIES RUSSIANS DOING JOB. U.S. WILL INVADE CUBA IF BASES STAY, the banners warned, U.S. REJECTS MISSILES DEAL. NO SWAP OF BASES. ALL AMERICANS READY FOR WAR. He was sitting on the centre of the bullseye and he didn't have a chance. Even if he launched the missiles he had, the Americans would be sure to get him good no matter what the Russians did. Russia was a long way off, twenty minutes as the Inter-Continental Ballistic Missile flies. Cuba they could hit in five with a strong spit and a tail-wind. I wondered if anyone would ever find my letters among his unanswered radioactive correspondence.

At the bottom of the front page, a small article caught my eye. Dwarfed by the blocks of type about Kennedy, Kruschev and Castro it said simply, Noted Musician Dies. I wouldn't have bothered to read it except that Mac Perry's name leaped out at me like an autograph. According to the paper I was about to deliver to his silent curtained house, noted jazz pianist Mac Perry had shot himself sometime late the night before. He had not left a note or any explanation for his drastic act. According to his widow and friends, he had not appeared depressed recently. The article referred me to background stories in the Entertainment section, all of which I immediately read. There were lots of pictures of Mac with jazz celebrities, Ella Fitzgerald and Oscar Peterson, but not a single word that told me why.

I sat on the curb outside his house for what seemed like a very long time. Like my mother waiting to hear my father's footsteps on the back stairs, I was waiting for the magic sound of his piano to make it all untrue. I knew most of what I read in the paper wasn't really true. Why should this be? Finally I took the paper with the news of his death and laid it like a wreath on the mat in front of the door that was now closed to me forever.

Chapter 13

The Lytle's house too was quiet and draped. The carport was empty, but Mr. Lytle would still be at work. I felt worse putting the paper on their doorstep than I had at the Perry's. I stood at the door and listened. From inside, I was sure I heard sounds. Ringing the bell provoked the muffled imitation of Big Ben that was familiar in the suburbs. It was such a long time before anybody answered I was about to run away when the door opened a crack.

"Oh, it's you, Jack..."

I hardly recognized Mrs. Lytle's voice. She wandered away from the door leaving it ajar and I followed her into the dim kitchen left of the hall. She sat down at the formica and chrome table behind a glass that looked like water but smelled like gin even from where I stood. I couldn't help noticing she didn't have the right clothes on for that time of the day or any time of the day. She was wearing only a thin beige slip and stockings, as if she'd come home and taken off her dress but hadn't finished changing.

"Are you...okay, Mrs. Lytle?"

I couldn't get my voice above a whisper for some reason. Hers remained an unfamiliar rasp.

"I...I think so...I'm...not...sure..."

Listless yet restless, she stood up and fussed aimlessly, putting a plate in the sink then taking it out and placing it back on the sideboard, moving the coffee percolator from one cold black stove element to another, picking up her glass and putting it down again with an embarrassed broken smile.

My cheeks were hot because I was upset or because of the way she was dressed or wasn't dressed. I wasn't sure. She kept standing up and sitting down and bending over, apparently not realizing or caring that I was seeing a lot of things I shouldn't have been seeing, more than Mrs. Canetti had ever shown me, down the lace front of her slip and above the tops of her stockings. Nearly naked, her girlish body seemed somehow rounder, fuller, more like a woman's.

"Is it in the paper?"

"Uh-huh."

"I don't want it." Her voice rose sharply. "I don't want it in the house! Don't you leave it here!"

"Okay...Okay, Mrs. Lytle. I won't. I'll take it away...I promise."

I wondered what her husband would think. I'd probably get another Complaint Slip and how would I explain that?

"I just...I just....don't understand!"

Rivulets of tears burst from her eyes and tracked her cheeks. Throwing her arms around my neck, she leaned against me and I felt my shirt getting even wetter and warmer than when Champ slobbered on me. I held her clumsily, trying not to touch anything I wasn't supposed to, which was just about everything as far as I could tell.

"Why?...Why?...Why?" The words came out between sobs.

I didn't understand my own grief over my father's death or my mother's larger grief. How could I understand Mrs. Lytle's grief that was not over her husband, but over the suicide of a man who was, I admitted to myself at last, her lover?

Mrs. Lytle's body was very warm through the thin slip and I felt sticky, awkward and uncomfortable. The sharp sour scent of gin got up my nose and made my eyes water. At least, that's what I told myself it was.

It didn't seem fair. There I was, holding the woman I was as hopelessly in love with as only a teenage boy can be, the woman I'd lain awake nights dreaming about rescuing from countless perils including Atomic Armageddon, the woman I'd imagined myself holding like this, being strong for, and all I wanted to do was run away like any kid frightened by adult pain, like I'd always done when my Dad got one of the headaches that made him smash his head into the walls.

"Mrs. Lytle?" I untangled myself from her damp embrace as gently as I could. "I gotta go now. I gotta go do my papers."

She nodded, her hands covering her face, weeping silently now. I ran, jumping off the front steps, picking up my bike and mounting on the fly. I was a block away before I remembered I'd forgotten to take the paper with me. I'd left it lying on the porch where her unsuspecting husband would pick it up and bring it into the house when he came home from work.

I guess it didn't really matter. Even the ancient Emperors of China couldn't make bad news go away just by killing the messenger. The news was the news, death was death and you couldn't keep it out of the house by locking the doors, hiding in a bomb shelter, wishing or praying, any more than you could keep out radioactive fallout.

I finished my route as fast as I could and it wasn't until I topped the last hill and my eyes kept filming over that I realized I was crying too. I felt guilty, sitting on the curb wiping my wet face with the sleeve of my sweatshirt. When my Dad died, I cried for a week and when I stopped I promised myself that after that nothing could be bad enough to make me cry ever again. Yet there I was only six months later, crying over a man who'd never given me anything but a couple of bucks and a cup of coffee and something I couldn't put into words.

Feeling hot doggy breath on my face, I opened my eyes to find Champ standing over me, ears curiously erect, trying to lick the tears off my cheeks. His big tongue slipped over my face like wet sponge until I had to laugh in spite of myself. He walked me down the driveway while the other two dogs put on a big show, but I wasn't worried because both Constable Mackenzie and Constable Peterson were right there with Constable Peterson's own car, a beautiful black 58 Chevy convertible with red seats. The hood was up and they were tinkering with the engine.

Neither of them looked very happy to see me so at ease with the big dog. I handed Constable Mackenzie the paper and took his grunt to mean "Thanks".

"Still haven't had any trouble with ol' Champ, eh?"

"Nope. He's a real good dog."

I gave Champ a farewell pat on the head and started back up the driveway. Then, when I was just a few yards from the street, I heard it.

"Get 'im, Champ!"

The scrabble of Champs nails on the asphalt froze me in mid-step as he lit out after me with a low growl. There was no point in running. He'd be on me in three huge bounds. All I could do was stand there, holding my breath, my heart heaving out of my chest, and wait for those huge canine teeth to rip through my flesh and hit bone. My shoulders hunched as I felt the powerful jaws clamp around my skinny right thigh. Then nothing. Releasing my leg, Champ simply stood beside me, completely docile.

Turning around slowly, I gazed at the two policemen. They looked angry and afraid and ashamed all at once, just like Paul and I must've looked when we were caught at some nasty prank. As a fireman, my Dad had always taught me to respect policemen and to go to them for help if I was in trouble. Looking at those two, I understood even better how Fidel Castro must have felt when he watched Batista's soldiers and policemen disgracing the uniform of their country and saw his true enemies.

"Good dog, Champ...Good dog."

I patted his shoulder and stumbled to the end of the drive. I had to walk my bike for a couple of blocks before I stopped shaking enough to mount up. Then I coasted the rest of the way, past the Lytle's, past the Perry's, past the Morden's and all the other houses quietly waiting for the end of the world that looked like it was due to happen any minute now. I just wanted to get home before it did.

I'd forgotten all about Irene Beaumont until I saw her standing at the corner a block from the shack. She bit her lip, supressing an eager smile as I pulled up. She was breathless with excitement at the possibility of getting to see inside the neighbourhood's most exclusive boys club, this mysterious male world girls were absolutely forbidden to enter.

"I've been waiting and waiting...Are you really going to take me to the shack?...Paul said..."

"No. We're not going to the shack. You know girls aren't allowed at the shack. Go away, Irene. Just go home...Please?"

I was too exhausted to even try to make up some clever lie and at thirteen the notion that simply telling the whole truth might actually be less painful is an unthinkable heresy. My head felt like it did when I had a fever, too big and filled with soggy cotton-batting. Irene began to pout dramatically.

"But Paul said you..."

"I don't care what Paul said!" I was shouting at her now. "Paul lies, in case you haven't noticed, Miss Know-it-all! I'm not taking you to the shack! I'm going home! Just go home, Irene!"

"I certainly will!" She was shouting right back at me and I remembered seeing some suave actor in a movie say to a woman "You're beautiful when you're angry". I wouldn't have said it about Irene even if I'd had the nerve. "I didn't really want to go to your dumb old shack anyway! I never asked you to take me there! I wouldn't go anywhere with you if you were the last man on earth!"

She'd obviously got that line from a movie, maybe the same one since she used it exactly the way she heard it, but it was the second time I'd been called a man without it meaning "the man of the family now" and I kind of liked it in spite of the circumstances. The way things were going I might just wind up being the last man on earth, but at that moment I was so relieved to see her stalking off in the direction of her own house, not the shack, that I laughed out loud. That only made her madder, of course. Spinning around, her arms tightly crossed over her still-mysterious breasts, she screeched at me like an eight year old girl whose skip-rope had been tangled by careless rough-housing boys.

"If you ever tell anyone I let you kiss me, I'll...I'll..."

She turned again and stomped away, leaving a threat too dire to be completed hanging in the cool autumn air between us.

Home at last, after dinner I sat in my room pretending to do my homework and trying to make sense out of everything, but all I got was a headache. There wasn't any point in writing another letter to Fidel Castro. By the time it got to the post office, the post office would probably be a pile of glowing bricks. I turned on my radio and caught the end of Sam Cooke singing 'What A Wonderful World This Would Be,' but that song was two years old.

Chapter 14

"Mom? I want to quit my paper route."
I guess it wasn't the best time to tell her, since she was in the middle of trying to get breakfast into the four of us, make sure we were decently dressed and combed and ready to go with the right books and the right lunches. Her shoulders slumped as she stirred the porridge I hated but was going to force myself to eat if I could just get out of having to go to the shack today. The shit I was going to be in there was so supreme I was almost disappointed to wake up and discover the world hadn't been blown up overnight.

"Why?"

I was ready, having spent most of the night marshalling and reviewing my arguments instead of sleeping.

"Well...First, they won't split my route and it's twice a long as everybody else's...and it's all uphill. They just keep adding more and more houses and people keep complaining because the paper is late or they don't get it...And when I go to collect they won't pay me and they keep telling me to come back and come back...And I hate it, that's all."

"Try to stick it out, Jack. We really do need the money now."

I knew we did. She hadn't had a job since she and my Dad got married and wasn't having any luck finding one. The Firemans Benefit Association was helping out, but there was still some doubt about whether she would ever get the pension from the Department of Veterans Affairs that would make all the difference.

"But what good is the money if I can't collect it?..." Argument wasn't working, so I tried whining and playing on maternal protectiveness. "And yesterday I got bit by a dog..."

"What?" She stopped stirring. "Where? Show me. What dog?"

"It didn't break the skin." I barely had a bruise and it suddenly occurred to me I could get Champ in serious trouble. He might even get "put down" if I got cornered into continuing that line of conversation. Since he was now the only friend I had left in the whole world, if he got killed and it was my fault I wasn't sure I'd be able to go on living myself. I gagged on a spoonful of porridge and pushed it away.

"Finish your breakfast."

"I'm not hungry."

I couldn't have eaten another bite if it had been my favourite, waffles and bacon.

I took the long way around avoiding streets on which too many kids were walking to get to school. It took Paul until recess was almost over to find me alone behind the big green baseball backstop and demand to know why I hadn't turned up with Irene Beaumont. All morning, every time I glanced at Irene in class she looked at me like I had a dead rat in my pocket before haughtily turning her head.

"I changed my mind."

"But why?"

I stayed stubbornly silent. After nearly getting Irene into a humiliating situation I sensed was actually more dangerous than I really understood, just from talking to Paul too much, and after nearly getting Champ killed with my feeble chicken-hearted attempt to talk my out of getting what was clearly coming to me, I'd decided that from now on I was going to be like Johnny Cloud, The Navajo Ace in the True War Comics who's motto was "Be Brave, Be Silent," and say as little as possible to as few people as possible. Lying awake most of the night hoping and expecting, not without reason, that Kennedy, Kruschev and Castro might solve my problems for me hadn't worked. When my mother called me for the umpteenth time to get up and get dressed for school, I knew the world was still there and so were Paul and Irene and Rick the Sub-Manager. Whatever happened, I was just going to keep my mouth shut and take it.

"Rick's really pissed off at you now."

"Fuck him. He's just a pimple-faced jerk who thinks he's tough 'cause he can push around a bunch of kids and a retard. That don't make him tough."

I said it with a lot more bravado than I felt. Paul shrugged, backing away another step or two. I noticed he hadn't stood close enough to me to whisper like he usually did. He was already distancing himself from me, from trouble. I knew I wouldn't be able to count on him later at the shack, that I'd never been able to count on him like you were supposed to with a friend and that I never would. It was just the way he was. He'd be friends with anybody as long as he thought there was something in it for him, but when there was trouble, he'd rat you out if he could and let you hang alone.

Rick the Sub-Manager was really pissed off at me. He stopped me at the door of the shack, daring me to push past him, a sneer twisting he pocked face into an even nastier expression than usual.

"What the fuck d'you want?"

"I just want my papers."

My voice was a croak, my throat as dry as fear itself. My intestines felt like they were trying to tie themselves into one of those complicated knots I'd never mastered in Cub Scouts.

"You'll get yer fuckin' papers alright." He stepped inside after gobbing straight down onto my sneakers. "Last...Then you and I'll have a little talk..." He was trying to sound like John Wayne intimidating some bad guy at the saloon. I tried to remind myself he was just a pus-faced teenager with a lot of grease in his hair, but he was three years older, a head taller and at least twenty pounds heavier than I was.

I figured I had about fifteen minutes of life left. If the Russians launched their missiles right now, they might just save me from the vengeance of Rick. Sitting on the plank bench in a dim corner at the back of the shack, waiting for my doom and listening to Gladys Knight and The Pips singing 'Every Beat Of My Heart' on Rick's transistor, I tried to think what Fidel Castro would do.

From what the papers said, it seemed like Fidel had decided that no matter how big the bully was, there came a time when you just didn't take it anymore. The difference was, he was a man and had an army and missiles and everything and I was just a kid who was scared limp. I thought about my Dad and his friend in the Japanese prisoner of war camp, laughing after getting beaten up. I tried to imagine what it would take to get me to laugh right then.

I probably would've just stayed there and took it, stayed and whimpered through whatever horrible torments Rick could devise, if Gordy the Goof hadn't snuck into the shack. Rick was snarling at all the paperboys, working himself up to a real good mad for when he got to me, but when he saw Gordy sitting in a corner by the door, swinging his legs under the bench and singing tunelessly to himself, he went completely rank. He grabbed Gordy's shirt front and slammed his head back against the wall hard enough that we heard a board crack. While Gordy was still holding his head and squealing like a blow-torched cat, Rick yanked him off the bench, kicking and punching him out the door and down the stairs until Gordy fell in the dirt and lay there, curled up and blubbering.

"I tol' you to stay outa my shack, you fuckin' ree-tard!"

Deep down in the smallest scaredest part of myself, I realized he'd only done that to Gordy to show me what I was going to get, to terrorize me so much I'd start bawling even before he hit me, almost like he was afraid I might be thinking of fighting back or something. In what felt like slow motion, I slipped off the bench and moved toward the door, swinging one of my paper sacks by the sling. The thick steel-sleeved collection book inside gave it a quietly satisfying weight. When I got near the door I let it swing smoothly back and up over my head, then I whipped it down with snap that came all the way up from my toes.

It hit Rick the Sub-Manager in the back of the head with a crack at least as loud as the one he'd made banging Gordy's head off the wall. It drove his face into the door frame with a shock that toppled his precious transistor from its shelf and silenced Roy Orbison's 'Running Scared' in a clatter of shattering plastic. Screaming, Rick kneeled on the floor holding the back of his head with one hand while the other grabbed at fragments of his ruined radio. I stepped past him and down the stairs like a man going to the gallows.

Surrounded by the shocked white faces of the other paperboys, Rick stood in the doorway, blood from his split head on one hand and bits of broken black plastic and transistors in the other. A bruised welt was already puffing up on his forehead where it had smacked the door frame. I pulled Gordy to his feet. He was still whimpering and holding his temples.

"If you touch Gordy again I'm gonna report you to the cops... And the Circulation Office at *The Sun*."

I thought the uttered threat of the Circulation Office might make him hestitate for long enough for me to take a lead-off to a running start. I should have known better. He lurched down the steps, throwing the bits of his precious radio to the ground, his expression shifting from shock and pain to sadistic glee.

"You little ass-hole!" He showed me the blood on his palm. "You made me bleed! You broke my transistor!...Now I'm gonna kick the living shit out of you!"

Scared as I was, I had to admire the way he used that phrase. Kicking the living shit out of someone did have a fine emphatic ring to it, like being in supreme shit or telling somebody to fuck right off. But Rick had seen so many movies he thought you were supposed to talk it up before you started in, like the bad guys always did when they had the drop on the good guys, which gave the good guys a chance to turn the tables on them and say something smart themselves before the theme music brought up the credits.

I did what my Dad had always told me to do if somebody started telling me what they were going to do to me. I hit him first, as hard as I could, while he was still mouthing off. My fist smacked squarely into his pimple-speckled nose. There was a collective gasp from the paperboys and satisfying eruption of bright red blood into Rick's mouth and down the front of his white t-shirt. There was an even more satisfying look of total disbelief on his face and just for an instant, a glimpse of what I knew was fear behind the rage.

Then he kicked the living shit out of me, almost literally. Aside from sapping him down with the loaded papersack, that first perfect punch was the only time I hit him. When I tried to grapple with him his weight, height and strength overwhelmed me and he rubbed my stinging face into the gravelly dirt like he was scrubbing a floor. When I squirmed away and stood up to him, he punched and kicked like an octopus with his longer reach, splitting both my lips, making my nose bleed and my head ring like Mrs. Lytle's Big Ben door chimes. I didn't just see stars, I saw galaxies and spiral nebulae. When I went down again and again, he kicked me in the head, the kidneys and the chest with his hard pointy shoes until finally I couldn't catch my breath to get up. Then he kicked me in the stomach so hard I peed my pants. Panting, he stood over me.

"Guess I showed you..."

Despite the fearsome licking he'd given me, he didn't sound as tough somehow as he had before. He didn't look it either. His tight roll-cuff blue jeans were caked with dirt from wrestling me down and grinding my face into the gravel had cost him patches of skin off his elbows. The polished points that felt like spear-tips when he was kicking me looked like he'd been square dancing in a pig pit. His t-shirt was inexplicably torn down from the neck, probably by me hanging onto it as he battered and tossed me around. It was covered in blood, more mine than his, and the Elvis hairdo he was forever combing luxuriously had exploded into greasy spikes matted with dirt and clotted blood. A couple of the paperboys snickered audibly. He whirled on them.

"What're you little pricks lookin' at? Go do your fuckin' papers or you'll get the same!"

Gulping for breath, his voice got all kind of squeaky, like he was scared instead of angry, and he stormed into the shack still screaming. "You rotten little fucks! I'll fuckin' kill the next one of you...I'll kill ya...I swear I'll..." It sounded almost like he was sobbing.

Paul was standing on the steps, his face a stylized mask of fearful submission. When I looked at him, he looked away like he didn't know me and followed Rick inside.

I fell down twice as I limped the two blocks home, leaning on my bike for support. I changed my soiled pants first, stuffing them into the trashcan instead of putting them in the dirty laundry. Even if my mother found them and cleaned them a dozen times, I would never wear them again. Then I gingerly washed most of the blood and dirt off myself while my Mom, who'd caught sight of me as I scooted out of the laundry room, pounded on the door of the little downstairs bathroom I'd locked myself in.

"Jack? What happened? Answer me! Unlock the door this instant! What happened to you?"

She sounded hysterical too. It'd been that kind of afternoon and I hoped it was going to be over soon, but I had just one more thing to do before it was. It was hard talking to her through two fat lips and a door, but I wasn't coming out until I was ready..

"Nothing, Mom. I'm just not going to do my papers anymore. That's all."

"Who did this to you? I want to talk to them! I'll call *The Sun!*...I'll call the police!..."

Just what I needed. Well, she could talk to Frank and Constable Mackenzie too if she wanted. I wasn't talking to anybody.

"Just forget it, please Mom? I'm okay now. I'm just not doing my paper route anymore... I'm sorry."

I added that, even though I wasn't. I came out and satisfied her that I wasn't bleeding to death from a major artery and none of my bones were conspicuously broken. I wasn't sure about a couple of my ribs. Pinching one of her Matinee cigarettes while she examined my destroyed clothes, I snuck around the side of the house that had no windows beside the big broom bush and tried to smoke it. It hurt when I inhaled but it hurt worse when I laughed and I did laugh, eventually. I felt close to my Dad then, for the first time since he died. Now we both knew what it felt like to laugh when you'd just had the shit beaten out of you.

I still didn't know what he'd laughed at hard enough to get him killed, but I knew what the joke was in my case and it was on Rick and maybe even Frank. I might have a few cuts and bruises, a sore mouth and ribs, but they had my sacks and my collection book and two back-busting bundles of papers and when a paperboy was sick or hurt they'd have to do them. They'd have to figure it out from the reciepts in the book. They'd be at it until long after dark.

On top of that, while he was so busy sucking up to Rick, Paul seemed to have forgotten that my house was on his route. I might not be able to beat Rick, but even after all I'd been through, maybe even because of it, I was absolutely sure I could beat Paul's weasely face right into the driveway and I intended to do exactly that just to round out my day as soon as I stopped feeling like I might throw up.

I waited behind the broom bush, feeling my lips and nose bruise and swell, until I heard the paper flop on our doorstep just around the corner. Then I ran around the bush, cutting him off from the street, fists up and ready.

"Alright, you fuckin' fink."

Gordy stood there grinning sheepishly and sorrowfully.

"Aren'cha gonna be a paperboy anymore, Jack?"

I turned to the street. Up at the corner, Paul was standing by the light pole, watching and shifting his weight nervously from foot to foot. I took a couple of steps down our driveway. He took an equal number of steps up the street. I sneered and started taunting him.

"Don't bother running, chickenshit! I'm not gonna chase you! I can get you any time I want! You better find a new way to walk home from school! Or I'll get you when you're doing your route! I'm gonna report your big pal Rick for what he did to Gordie! You tell him that! He's gonna lose his Sub-Manager key for sure, so he won't be around to protect you! And I'm gonna tell them about you getting Gordy to do your papers all the time! You'll have to do them yourself! And I'll be waiting for you every day! You think about that, 'cause I'm gonna get you, you gutless dogshit!"

I walked back and picked up the paper.

"Thanks Gordy, but you shouldn't do his papers for him any more."

"But I like doin' the papers, Jack."

"I know you do, Gordy. You just watch out for guys like Rick."

"I don' like Rick. It was mean what he did to you."

"He did it to you too, Gordy."

"I know...but ever'body does that to me."

"Yeah, well, they shouldn't. It's not right, Gordy. I'll see you around."

I stepped inside and shut the door. For a moment I thought of legging it out the back door, ducking under the Miller's fence, through a couple of yards and cutting Paul off further along the street. I knew the terrain of every back yard on the block. I could just slip through like a commando and ambush him in any of a dozen places, but I decided to let it go for now. He had Gordy with him and Gordy had seen enough fights he didn't understand for one day.

I'd have plenty of chances to catch Paul where I wanted him and besides, I kind of liked the thought of him having something to lie awake worrying about all night, something to really be afraid of since he was too dumb to be afraid of the end of the world. I liked thinking of him sticking close to the monitoring teachers on the grounds at lunch at recess, unable to have any fun or get up to his old tricks, sneaking off behind backstops, under concrete exit ramps or the far corner of the field to hatch his little schemes, always looking over his shoulder for me, never knowing when I'd land on him like a hundred-megaton bomb. I just hoped the world wouldn't end before I got my chance.

Looking down at the paper I was still holding, I realized I was going to get that chance after all. NIKITA TOSSES IN CUBAN TOWEL! WORLD HAILS JFK-NIKITA ACCORD! RUSSIA TO SCRAP CUBA BASES. ANXIOUS WORLD VOICES RELIEF WITH EASE OF WAR THREAT. Holding the paper on my lap, I sat on the stairs and read.

Nothing was going to happen. The Russians were going home and taking their missiles with them. The Americans were letting them go and they weren't going to invade Castro's Cuba, at least not right now, so Fidel was safe at least. Everything was going to be like it used to be except that my Dad was still dead and Mac Perry was still dead and I didn't have a best friend anymore or a reason to hurry right home after school either. Having fucked up with both Paul and Irene Beaumont, my social life at school and in the neighbourhood was over almost as totally as if we had all been blown to cinders. About the only kid I could think of who'd hang around with me now was Ted Brauer, who lived more than two blocks away and went to Catholic school. It was a good thing I liked him because I figured we'd be seeing a lot of each other from now on. The only girl in class who would speak to me after Irene got through with my reputation would be Linda Arnold, which was not so good a thing because not only would it give Paul and company even more opportunities for ridicule, she was also smarter than me.

Leaving the paper in the hall, I went down to my room and laid on my bed. I turned on the radio. I wasn't sure how I felt. My face and ribs still hurt and I'd taken a beating for nothing, since Gordy was still doing Paul's papers. Two of the three men I admired most were inexplicably gone. I'd probably never see Mrs. Lytle again now that I wasn't her paperboy, but that was okay. I would be seeing Irene Beaumont again, though, and that wasn't okay since I had the awful feeling that maybe I really did love her and she was never going to speak to me again as long as I lived, which looked like it was going to be longer than I'd anticipated.

Worst of all, I'd let my mother down terribly, just when she needed me most, and my Grandmother and the other relatives would have plenty to say about that, none of it good. Now that the Cuban missile crisis was over there wasn't going to be the threat of war to take their minds off me. I was listening to Elvis singing 'Return To Sender' when my mother knocked on the door softly and let herself in.

"Are you alright?"

I nodded. I didn't know what to say. I wanted to apologize for losing my paper route and hanging around with Paul and worrying her and lots of things, but I couldn't find the words. I never have.

"There's a letter for you."

She handed me a scuffed buff envelope. The writing on the stamp was in Spanish and I recognized the word Cuba immediately. She left me alone to open it. I peeled the end of the envelope back carefully and unfolded the single sheet of paper.

"Dear Comrade! Thank you for your good wishes to the Popular Revolution of The Cuban People! In their Struggle against Imperialist Oppression! The Revolutionary Government of The Cuban People wishes only Peace to All the Peoples of the World! To the Victory of the Revolution!"

It was kind of silly really, a typed form letter that was just a bunch of badly translated slogans strung together with lots of exclamation marks, but that didn't matter. All that mattered was the signature, the ink-scrawl that was no more than a single dominant initial with a squiggle, which needed no translation or exclamation point.

Fidel.

I folded the paper carefully, then unfolded it to read it again to make sure it was real. It was only a bunch of mechanical words except for that signature. That was scribbled by a man's hand, by his hand. Even if he hadn't written or dictated the letter, he had taken a moment of his time when he believed his country was about to be invaded or annihilated to sign it and have it sent thousands of miles to a boy in a country which sided with his enemies and who might well be nothing but a handful of ashes before it arrived.

When my father died I felt I hadn't been a good enough son, that I hadn't made him love me enough to give him the will to come out of his coma and live. In a way, I felt the same about Mac Perry. He'd invited me into his house, into his life in a small way, and I couldn't help wondering if there might have been something I could have done or said if I'd been more perceptive and articulate that would've stopped him from playing the one loud, single, final note that silenced his music forever. Instead, all I had done was write fan letters to a hero who might just as well be no more real than Zorro on tv or Batman in the comics, but for one thing—the letter in my hand.

Closing it against my chest, I tried to remember exactly what I had written and to imagine Fidel reading my words, alone late in the warm tropical night, wrapped in the smoke from his cigar. I was holding an actual piece of history in my hands. I couldn't save my father or Mac Perry, but in the half-doze that was slowly turning into sleep I could almost make myself believe that I had saved the rest of them, my Mom and the kids, Irene Beaumont, Mrs. Lytle, Gordy, Champ, Constable Mackenzie, Mr. Morden, even Paul and Rick the Sub-Manager and the whole unknowing and ungrateful world.

Part II

Saturday Soldiers

ChAPTER 1

Strung out in single file, ten paces apart, we followed Sergeant Wolff into the mist. Thirty feet above, the autumn fog had burned off, but at the bottom of the ravine it still swirled around the gray trunks of the cedars and hung in their drooping branches like the silent aftermath of an explosion. The fog was cold and it crept down the collars and snaked up the sleeves of our camouflage jackets, but it was comforting. If we couldn't see them, they couldn't see us either. The trail was spongy with dead pine needles and the steady liquid mutter of the creek on our right flank seemed to muffle the accidental noises of moving men, the tinkle of carelessly buckled harness, the rasp of canvas and fatigues, the thump of a combat boot against a hidden root, a whispered command.

Faces blackened under dark blue berets, we looked like a tribe of fugitive racoons, peering out from behind the stumps and boles of the biggest trees and emerging from under the cover of huge ferns as the Sergeant jerked us forward on an invisible line. Twenty paces back, I was silently cursing the tangle of wild blackberry canes that were trying to reclaim the trail. I'd got my pack briefly hooked on them, provoking a dry rattle from the brambles and a martyred look around from the Sergeant. He didn't waste time trying to kill me with a look. The one he shot me made it clear he had complete faith in my ability to manage that all by myself and he had more pressing things on his mind.

Suddenly dropping into a crouch, he signalled us to do the same and stay put. I looked over my shoulder and passed the signal on, but the rest of the squad were already playing statues. That was one order everybody always obeyed on the double. Even with the warpaint and battle dress they still looked more like a troop of Boy Scouts than soldiers.

The Sergeant motioned my buddy Ted, ten paces ahead of me, to come up to him. With his habitual distracted smile on his face, Ted was chewing a blade of grass and watching a big black beetle navigate around the unnatural obstacle presented by the toe of his boot. He missed the signal and I waved him forward impatiently. With a sigh I could almost hear, Sergeant Wolff gave me the come-along sign as well. I couldn't tell if it was regret or revenge I saw in his face.

When I drew level with him and Ted, I could see around the bend in the trail and the problem. Twenty yards or so ahead our point man Dougie Trumbull was hunched under a big forest fern, waiting for the Sergeant to give him the high-sign. Directly across from where he sat another trail branched off to the right, following the creek, while the main trail continued on slightly to the left. The trails forked at the foot of a steeply rising ridge. We weren't in one ravine but two and the heavily wooded centre ridge would be a natural place from which to patrol both ravines and lay ambushes in either direction.

Sergeant Wolff drew us in close so he could whisper.

"I want you two to take the right fork. Work your way along a hundred yards or so, staying close to the inside bank so you can use the cover. Use the terrain. See if you can find a way up to the top of that ridge."

"What do we do when we get there?"

I knew I'd made a mistake the moment I moved my lips. Sergeant Wolff favoured me with a look he reserved for his least useful and most expendable recruits.

"I trust you to figure that out if you get there. If that ridge is inhabited, like I think it is, you might want to make some very loud noises so the rest of us can join the party. Do you think you can do that?"

"Sure Sarge."

Ted always was an optimist, but Sergeant Wolff hated being called "Sarge." He gave us a pained look. We tried to look grim and intrepid. He shook his head wearily.

"Go."

Ted cheerfully led off, for which I was momentarily grateful. We worked our way up to the fork on our knees under the ferns, where Dougie winked at us from inside his cape of lacy green fronds. He gave us a "Good luck" thumb-up. Nodding silently, we slipped into the overgrown lesser trail. The fog was thicker in this narrower ravine and we cut our spacing down to two yards so we could whisper. As soon as we lost sight of Dougie, our last contact with the squad, I got nervous.

"What d'you think?"

Ted gave me a thoughtful look.

"I think I'd rather be in bed with Linda Arnold."

I gagged to stop myself laughing out loud. Linda Arnold was the plainest girl in our Grade Ten class. I'd known her since elementary school and she hadn't changed, skinny legs, no discernable super-structure, lifeless long straight hair, braces on her teeth, sensible English shoes, old-fashioned dresses with high necklines and low hems and no makeup. She had a monstrously high IQ and had been my Biology partner for the year. For someone so smart, she was awfully squeamish, so I had to do all the dissecting of pithed still-jerking frogs and foetal pigs formaldahyde, gritting my teeth and re-swallowing my tuna sandwich lunches, the price of preserving my tough-guy image. She'd followed me around through junior high school like a lost puppy and Ted and the other guys ragged me mercilessly about her obvious crush on me as though it was the mark of Cain.

"Why the fuck do you have to bring up Linda Arnold now, for Christ sake?"

Ted smiled benignly.

"I'd just rather be in bed with her than here. That's all."

He pointed up the ridge, then to the trail ahead. I saw what he meant. The overhang of earth and gorse that had allowed us to scuttle along in a crouch had played out. A few small ferns screened the trail, but if we tried to take it even on our knees we'd be totally exposed to the ridge above. There was only one way, on our bellies, along a track that was muddied by seepage, rain and the disquietingly recent imprint of boots.

Ted went first, his FN rifle laid across his arms in the manner prescribed for crawling under barbed wire and machinegun fire. With a stifled groan, I followed. It only took a few yards for a shovelful of mud to find its way under my web-belt and plaster itself against my belly like a cold compress. It was a long, tense, cold mucky crawl before we surfaced behind a comfortingly big fir.

"You know what?"

Ted's eyes were fixed on the dark line of the ridge above us.

"What?"

"I'd rather be in bed with Linda Arnold too...If you'll move over and make room for me."

Ted gave me his bemused smile.

"Let's go."

I was tempted to ask where and why and a whole lot of other questions not covered by the Manual of Military Instruction which, incidentally, does not have the answers in the back. I really would rather have been in bed with Linda Arnold or anyone, or anywhere but where I was, which was the only characteristic I shared with soldiers the world over, past, present and future. At least we had the overhang for cover again, only about three feet, but enough to make you feel totally invisible when your Sergeant expected you to hide behind a blade of grass.

Ted stopped and pointed uphill with the barrel of his FN. There was a faint narrow track, probably a game-trail, with the scrub and ferns growing over it from both sides to form what was almost a low tunnel. We'd be completely hidden from above if we crawled slowly, very quietly and didn't panic. I nodded reluctantly. I had to grit my teeth to stop them from chattering, the mist was so damn cold.

Ted led off again. It was like being kids, playing Cowboys and Indians or just plain Guns, only now the thing I was carrying wasn't the old plastic Winchester or one of the wooden rifles my Uncle Bob used to cut out of planks for us with his jig-saw. It was a NATO issue Belgian-made Fabrique Nationale semi-automatic with a box-magazine for nine rounds of 7.62 ammunition accurate up to six hundred and fifty yards, which was Jim Dandy except that I'd never been able to hit anything smaller than a barn door with it at a hundred yards on the range.

It took us forever to get to the top of that ridge. The trail switch-backed a few times, but we had no choice but to follow it. A foot or so to either side would have put us into salal, Devil's Club and brambles so noisy we might as well have set off a flare. I was sweating in spite of the chilling mist. My hands felt numb and stiff, like they were borrowed from a corpse.

Ted stopped so suddenly I almost kissed his ass. He motioned me to come alongside. Ahead of us, the trail opened into a grassy meadow. Luckily the entrance to the trail was deep in the shadow of a large fir, which was probably why nobody had noticed it. On the far side of the meadow, under cover of the trees there, khaki figures were dug in, their exposed backs to us. You didn't have to be Napoleon to figure out they had a commanding view and field of fire over the trails.

Edging forward in the shadows, we checked our flanks. Having failed to notice the game trail, they hadn't bothered to post a rear guard, figuring nobody could get past them and anybody who did would have to make more noise than the retreat from Moscow coming up that way.

"Ready?"

Ted looked amused by the situation. I took a deep breath, squeezed the pistol grip of the FN so tightly I expected the barrel to squirt out like toothpaste, and nodded.

"Whenever you say."

I was watching the backs of the figures in the foxholes, counting heads, figuring the odds and not liking the arithmetic much. Ted seemed very calm when he gave the word.

"Now."

In perfect unison, we rose and charged across the few yards of magically sunlit grass above the mist, our rifles rising to our shoulders.

The blast from Ted's whistle nearly broke my eardrums. In the excitement I'd forgotten all about mine. Trying to fish it out of my camo jacket, I shouted "Bang! Bang! You're dead!" for all I was worth and finally did blow a few belated blasts for good measure, even though you're not supposed to shoot prisoners who already have their hands up. A few collapsed dramatically in their foxholes, screaming "Medic!" in stagey falsetto as they dropped.

"Hands on your heads!"

I felt like a junior SS man confronted with his first partisans.

"You point that fucking thing at me, I'll shove it up your ass!"

Corporal Stevens slapped the barrel of my unloaded FN out of his face as he climbed out of his neat, deep regulation foxhole. He was being a bad sport, but I couldn't back-talk him on account of his being a Corproal. Ted intervened, ever the voice of reason.

"C'mon, Corporal. We got you fair and square. I'll have to ask you to surrender your weapon."

"Surrender my...?"

The Corporal clutched his precious WWII vintage Sten gun, a badge of his non-commissioned rank. Ted nodded.

"You are my prisoner, sir."

Stevens looked like he might wet himself. I don't think he'd have given up his Sten except that Ted called him "Sir" as if he was a General and his fellow defenders had already tossed their rifles out of their holes onto the grass.

"C'mon, Corp. They got us alright."

Corporal Stevens flung down his Sten in disgust. He wouldn't put his hands on his head, though. Not even when Sergeant Wolff and the rest of the squad stormed the ridge and burst into the clearing to find Ted and I presiding over our prisoners, festooned with captured arms like a pair of Vikings on vacation or heroes of the Trojan War.

A young mother shepherding a gaggle of children of assorted sizes and sexes unexpectedly entered the meadow from a trail at the far end.

"What are those men doing, Mummy?"

"They're just playing soldiers, sweetheart."

CHAPTER 2

As we climbed out of the ravine and marched incongruously past the swing sets and the empty wading pool toward the Armoury, Corporal Stevens stalked ahead on his long storky legs clutching his reclaimed Sten gun menacingly. He looked like he'd be only too happy to let go a full clip into the kids on the swings who were taunting us, asking if those were real guns and if we were real soldiers. It was just as well none of us ever saw a bullet except on the firing line at the rifle range out in the bush on the Seymour Parkway. Mind you, if we'd had live ammo the Corporal would still never have got the chance to summarily execute the local kindergarten. One of us would've accidentally shot him in the back long before that. Accidents happen and in our outfit they usually happened around us.

To the officers of the 15th Field Squadron of Royal Canadian Engineers (Militia), we were the Recruit Section. To the non-coms, the Sergeants, Corporals and Lance-Corporals whose unhappy lot it was to teach us the basics of military dress, deportment and drill, we were known by innumerable colourful epithets, most of them products of Sergeant Wolff's inexhaustible vocabulary. When he was in a good mood, he'd affectionately call us "a bunch of fuckpots." When he was angry, he called us things I'd never heard before. Fortunately, I've never heard most of them since.

At the not so tender age of seventeen, I didn't know for sure what a fuckpot was and I still don't, except that it described anyone under the rank of Sergeant most of the time and all recruits without exception. Sergeant Wolff swore with the inspired maniacal foulness of a shithouse poet in an insane asylum. Swearing in Canada tends to unimaginative and repetitive, basic Saxon sex and scatology with a dash of Catholic blasphemy on the French Canadian side. Mostly we just stick the word "fuck" into any available opening between two words and let it go at that. Not Sergeant Wolff. We recruits were still too young to supress involuntary titters at the Sergeant's epic saltiness, which only egged him on to greater outburst of virtuosity, apparently oblivious to the officers cringing away from the parade square.

"Stop giggling like a bunch of tarts in a dildo factory or I'll make you stand to attention until your assholes fall off and the shit runs down into your boots!"

A story circulated in the Enlisted Mens mess that Sergeant Wolff had once been placed in charge of drilling the girls of the Navy Wrenettes. The Wrenettes shared the cinder-block building next door to the old red brick Armoury with the Air Cadets. In their black uniforms, black stockings and stiff white hats the Wrenettes looked like a troop of dangerous nuns. Hard-faced gum-popping girls culled from the detention halls of every high school on the North Shore, they were known as the Sea Sluts, the sleaziest squad of nautical nymphomaniacs ever assembled by the Department of National Defence. What roles they could be expected to play in wartime, or peacetime, if we could somehow wangle them out from under the watchful gaze of their Petty Officer, were the subject of lurid speculation in the collective imagination of every Militiaman, Air, Army and Sea Cadet in North Vancouver.

Dougie Trumbull, one of the brighter lights of the Recruit Section, once dared to ask Sergeant Wolff exactly what the Wrenettes studied over there on their Saturday morning parades. The Sergeant replied with a wicked leer and lingering unmistakeable emphasis.

"Semenship."

The Sergeant was said to be *persona non grata* next door since the drill episode. Their Petty Officer was on the sick list and Sergeant Wolff got off on the wrong foot by suggesting her indisposition was probably the result of an unmilitary attack of monthly cramps. That crack, delivered in a stage whisper as subtle as an air-raid siren, was probably what made the Staff Sergeant give him the duty.

Apparently the girls had displayed a lack of smartness in coming to attention. A man in the armed forces of any Commonwealth country comes to attention like a Coldstream Guard. The right knee jerks up smartly so the thigh forms a ninety degree angle to the hip before the heel is driven down in a brain-rattling, vertebra-compacting slam, producing a sound as loud and crisp as a rifle shot. In deference to the old skirted uniforms, however, women in the services were allowed to bring their feet together with a kind of sideways foot-dragging shuffle like the American forces use. Sergeant Wolff was said to have expressed his disgust with this casual performance at a megaphone volume his own C.O. could hear next door.

"When I say Ten-Shun...I want to hear thirty cunts sucking air!"

At seventeen or so, we recruits were already too cynical to take Sergeant Wolff seriously as a role model, but he acted the part of Sergeant to perfection, the Sergeant of every low budget war movie we'd ever seen, every Sgt. Rock, Beetle Bailey and True War Stories comic we'd ever wasted an afternoon with, and we relished his performance even when he abused us. He must've been in his late thirties or early forties. Over six feet tall, he looked like the old movie star Ronald Coleman with the thin pencil line moustache. He was always immaculately tricked out, his brass blindingly bright, his black non-com hat set squarely on his close-cropped head, the patent peak pulled down almost level with his eyebrows like a Marine in a poster.

I never found out what he did the other six days of the week. Obviously a peacetime ex-serviceman, he was probably a quiet cog in some company, a pipe-smoker with a wife and kids and a nice house in the suburbs who'd shit himself if he ever heard a shot fired in anger. Even in the midst of his towering profane rages when he was threatening to cut off our pus-filled gonads with a rusty bayonet and feed them to the crows, the twinkle in his eye would betray how immensely he was enjoying himself. Like us, he was just playing soldiers. Only he was a lot better at it than we were.

Corporal Stevens was detested as unanimously as Sergeant

Wolff was admired. Before the Squadron recruiting drive swept us up in its unsuspecting net, Stevens had been a Lance-Corporal. As far as we could tell, that was on a par with being made blackboard monitor in elementary school. A Lance-Corporal seemed to be an enlisted man raised above his comrades by a scrap of felt on his arm to be a flunky, toady, lick-spittle and stool pigeon for the Sergeants mess. Stevens was the kind of chickenshit bully who hid behind his rank to make sure he never got his battledress dirty while seeing to it that everyone in his charge stood in shit up to the eyeballs.

He'd been a Lance-Corporal for a long time because the Squadron was under strength and there weren't bodies in the ranks for him to bully and justify his promotion to full Corporal. Thanks to the misguided generosity of someone in the Defence ministry, a modest recruiting drive had been authorized. The guilty party was probably some Parliamentary Secretary or Assistant Deputy Minister who only wanted to cease being the recipient of our Commanding Officer's interminable reports on the serious threat posed to the nation's western defences by the dearth of young men trained to respond to any emergency, civilian or military, with plastic explosives in one hand and entrenching tools in the other.

Advertisements were placed in local newspapers and posted on high school bulletin boards. Young men were offered the opportunity to learn the rudiments of practical engineering and acquire valuable experience of military life, said to be useful in a later civilian career, not to mention ninety dollars a month, in return for giving up the dubious pleasure of sleeping in on Saturday mornings.

The response was less overwhelming than the crowds of eager young volunteers who flocked to recruiting centres in 1914 and 1939 to die for Crown and Empire but times were changing and so were notions of patriotism. My friend Ted Brauer looked at me like I might be having a delayed reaction to bad acid when I pointed to the notice tacked to the board outside the school office. We'd just come from an unpleasant interview with the Vice-Principal on the subject of haircuts, specifically the infrequency thereof.

Our avoidance of barbers was making us conspicuous in a predominantly upper middle class suburban high school in 1966. Even

Irene Beaumont, my childhood friend and secret elementary school sweetheart, who hadn't spoken to me in a couple of years, made a point of coming up to me in the hall one day and telling me what she thought in a voice loud enough to be heard by most of the crowd of teachers and students milling between periods.

"You ought to be ashamed of yourself, Jack Morrison! You and your creepy weirdo friends think you're so cool but you just look like a bunch of bums! If you don't care what people think of you, you should at least care about what they think of your school!"

No applause was neccessary. If not quite prepared to lynch me on her say so, the mob murmured assent and a couple of the senior varsity boys who accompanied her everywhere like bodyguards would certainly have dragged me into the nearest washroom for a forcible scissors trim, a thing not unknown to happen in other high schools at the time, had she given the word. I didn't blame her too much. She was Head Cheerleader, Prom Queen material and a prominent member of the Student Council. It was her job to uphold standards, even if it meant sounding like she listened to The Beachboys song 'Be True To Your School' until her brain melted. I even suspected the Vice-Principal, who knew from our records we lived in the same neighbourhood and had gone through school together, might have put her up to it.

Ted and I were for sex and drugs and rock and roll. At least we wanted to be. At the time, sex was more talk and daydreams than action, drugs were highly illegal, expensive and unpredictable and rock and roll meant the Rolling Stones first couple of albums.

Ted gave be a quizzical look.

"I thought we wanted to make love, not war?"

"Yeah, but think about it...We have to get haircuts anyway, or else we get expelled, which means our parents will make us get some kind of shitty jobs. This way, we get haircuts, stay in school and get paid ninety bucks a month, a hundred and eighty between us, for doing fuck all for a few hours on Saturday..."

"That'll buy a lot of nickel bags..."

"And smokes...and mickeys of Lambs Navy and lemon gin..."

"The government'll finance our bad habits..."

"I know a guy who's in. You can drink beer underage in the

109

mess..."

"We'll be like spies. Undercover. We'll infiltrate the fuckin' army."

"They'll probably make us officers, smart guys like us..."

"We'll revolutionize the army from within!"

"We'll invade the U.S. while their army's in Vietnam, capture Blaine and drink all the beer!"

"They say girls love a man in uniform..."

The following Saturday, we presented ourselves at the Armoury with a dozen or so equally unprepossessing candidates to be inducted by the company clerk, Sergeant Laporte, to whom we afforded considerable silent amusement. Lined up on the scarred polished hardwood of the parade hall in ragged ranks, we had the distance between our hair and our shirt collars measured with a naked bayonet laid against the backs of our necks, were advised to get still more radical haircuts and were called the unlikeliest bunch of slimy self-abusing festering little fuckpots he'd ever laid eyes on by Sergeant Wolff.

"It's Wolff, with two 'f's! You all know what f stands for, don't you? It stands for 'fucked'! And from now on you're double-fucked!"

As a result of this loose-linked chain of events and motivations hardly military, we were paraded the following week to witness the promotion of Lance Corporal Stevens to the exalted rank of full Corporal. Our appearance had improved only to the extent that we were all in the same uniform, issued by Sergeant Laporte with his secret chuckle as he cheerfully ignored our helpful suggestions about size and fit.

"The Army only has one size. Size Too."

It didn't take us long to figure out that meant Too Big or Too Small. At Corporal Stevens' investiture, we learned our second lesson of military life. The new Corporal was invited to dismiss the men.

"Squadron...Dis...MISS!"

Evidently nervous, Stevens broke into falsetto trying to achieve a powerful authoritative note on the critical syllable. There was stifled laughter, even among the officers. Corporal Stevens reddened and gave the new Recruit Section, to which he'd been assigned, his steeliest glare. There were mutters as we stampeded to the Enlisted Mess and the waiting bar.

"Pricks get promoted."

"We're truly double-fucked."

Corporal Stevens proved to be every bit as big a dork as we suspected. He was about twenty-four or five and looked like the guy everybody had kicked the crap out of in his high school. Tall and angular as a character in one of Don Martin's cartoons for *Mad Magazine*, he wore horn-rim glasses and must've stayed up nights spot-welding the creases in his battle dress and spit-polishing his size twelve boots. He was the kind of clown who would.

It took Ted and I about two weekends of getting raked from boot soles to berets by Corporal Stevens and Sergeant Wolff before we figured out how the officers and non-coms always looked so sharp while the ranks, especially the Recruit Section, mostly looked like khaki sacks of shit. That week, we cut our last classes on Wednesday and sought out a dry-cleaning establishment on Lonsdale Avenue which advertised alterations at reasonable rates. A visit to the shoe repair shop run by an old Italian in the same block resulted in patent shines on our crusty issue boots it would have taken months of saliva and elbow grease to duplicate. It was all done by machines or by somebody else while we dawdled over coffee and Crazy Eights like officers and gentlemen in one of the plywood booths at The Wanda Inn, an old diner run by a pompadored queer called Blake V. Elliot who'd had one hit record a few years before. He let the incipient hipster crowd use the place as a hangout on Friday and Saturday nights, though nobody ordered anything more than coffee and maybe a side of fries and gravy split four ways. He made his money off the jukebox. The only listenable tunes in it were a couple of Beatles hits, The Rolling Stones cover of Buddy Holly's 'Not Fade Away' and Bob Dylan's 'Like A Rolling Stone' and if you didn't keep feeding quarters in to play them, the machine was rigged to play the rocking Hammond organ version of 'Goodnight Irene' that had been a the only record ever made by Blake V. Elliot and the Ferraris of Canada over and over again until somebody dug around in their jeans and came up with the coin to punch in a new selection.

It cost us a few bucks, but it was worth it the following Saturday when we stood to attention in machine-pressed custom-tailored creases and watched Corporal Stevens stare back at his own angry reflection in the mirror shine of our boots, choking on his own unexpended verbal venom. I cornered Ted later in the mess.

"Did Sergeant Wolff wink at you?"

He nodded.

"He knows we know."

"And we know he knows we know."

The other goofs in the section couldn't figure out how we pulled it off. They thought we were really gung-ho or something until we told them. A week later, there was a notable drop in the volume and vehemence of the weekly inspection tirade. Despite our vastly improved appearance, no one in the squadron, officers or men, was a patch on Staff. Our Regimental Sergeant-Major was a half-pint Hitler who, like RSMs the world over, actually ran the squadron while making it appear that the officers were doing it all. The officers had sense enough to defer to him and we all got a kick out of the way the noncoms followed him around, towering over him like the grenadiers of Napoleon's Old Guard, hanging on his slightest fart like it was the revealed word of God. Staff had a parade square voice like a tiger with a hangover. It even put Sergeant Wolff's to shame, though he seldom used it. He was like a man with a big knife on his belt. He didn't have to take it out for you to know it was there.

To preserve the Armoury's wooden floors, the squadron was forbidden to wear hobnailed boots. All except Staff. He wore them with a flourish. Listening to him cross the drill hall was like hearing a full magazine fired off and when he came to attention the old building shook to its foundations. The first week after Stevens was promoted to Corporal, he turned up with his boots hobnailed in imitation of Staff's, which he never missed an opportunity to lick. We all had to bite our tongues when Staff ticked him off in front of the whole parade, telling him he'd be on report and busted back to Lance Corporal, not to mention made to polish the drill floor with a toothbrush, if he didn't have those nails out of his boots by the next parade.

"You are supposed to be a non-commissioned officer! Are you aware that there is a Standing Order against hobnails in this squadron?"

"Yes! Staff!"

Stevens' voice was a pathetic squeak.

"I don't need to say anything more, then. Do I?!"

"No! Staff!"

It was all he could say. As in the British, in the Canadian armed forces, there are only two answers permitted in response to a query from a superior rank and he'd used up both of them. Staff spun a perfect one hundred and eighty degrees on one hobnailed heel and thundered away, leaving Corporal Stevens staring morosely at his toes.

As we sauntered the last hundred yards from the ravines where we'd conducted our manouevres to the Armoury, we were strung out across the playing fields in the sun, smokes dangling from our mouths. Corporal Stevens, far ahead of us, was doing something that looked like epileptic semaphore on the Armoury steps. His voice reached us as a thin high-pitched shriek.

"Squadron on parade! On the double!"

We looked to Sergeant Wolff, who flicked his butt into one of the empty baseball dugouts.

"You heard the Corporal...On the fucking double!"

Unslinging our empty rifles, we lowered them to the classic position for an old-fashioned bayonet charge, came together and rushed the Armoury in phalanx. Corporal Stevens dashed inside as we raised the soul-stirring battle-cry of the Recruit Section.

"Fuck yooooouuuuuuu!!!!!!"

Chapter 3

We had to turn in our weapons before we could parade, which meant lining up in two improvised ranks in the muddy motor pool yard behind the Armoury while Sergeant Wolff and Corporal Stevens called us in, disarmed us, checked the serial numbers of our weapons to make sure we returned the FN rifle we'd been issued, then locked them and their own Stens in the concrete magazine in the basement. This could be a time-consuming procedure. No matter how many times they railed at us by rote, reeling off serial numbers as they slapped the stocks into our stinging palms—"This weapon is the property of the Government of Canada! You are now responsible for this weapon! This weapon and no other! At the conclusion of this exercise you will return to the squadron magazine this weapon and no other!"—somehow it never worked out that way.

Somebody would always hold somebody else's rifle while he slipped behind a tree for a quick leak and accidentally hand back the wrong one, or you could easily pick up the wrong rifle in the general melee after a smoke break. Back at the magazine, our makeshift parade would disintegrate into a milling mob anxiously arguing over sequences of infinitesimal numbers incised on weapons that were being swapped around faster than a fire sale in a Khyber Pass bazaar, while Corporal Stevens screeched ineffectually at us and Sergeant Wolff called us Godforsaken fuckpots and cursed the lack of a convenient war in which we could all be killed.

Personally, I couldn't see the point. I couldn't imagine any soldier in actual combat conditions being terribly concerned about whether or not the rifle he was holding happened to be the specific weapon entrusted to him by the Government of Canada. Seemed to me he'd be a damn sight more worried about whether or not the fucking thing was loaded, how the hell to avoid being killed and what mental lapse had caused him to enlist in the first place.

On this occasion, we outdid ourselves. In the skirmish on the ridge, with half the squad surrendering to the other half, our weapons had gone hopelessly astray. As we bickered and traded arms, one member of the Recruit Section stood apart. Mike Darling interpreted the order to Stand At Ease with a unique flair. His perenially goofy grin was supported by his left palm, his elbow resting comfortably on the stock of his up-ended rifle which in turn bore the full weight of his pudgy form, the barrel driven about four full inches into the mud. A picture of nonchalance.

"You kernel of typhoid rat-shit! You suppurating pustule on the arsehole of humanity!"

Sergeant Wolff shouldered through the mob and seized Darling's weapon, dumping the unsuspecting Sapper on his ass in the mud. Yarding Darling to his feet by an epaulet, he shook the rifle in his face, the barrel obviously choked with a solid four-inch plug of mud, bellowing at him through a mist of hot spit.

"If I ever see you treat a weapon like this again I'll shove it so far up your ass you'll blow your brains out every time you jerk off!"

Darling had done it to us again. Of all the fuck-ups in the Recruit Section, Mike Darling was unanimously agreed by officers and men to be the one fucked furthest up. His uniform fitted him like a potato sack and always looked like a bear had slept in it. His blue beret perched on the top of his head like a sinister mushroom. Instead of sensible American style gaiters over our boots we wore puttees left over from the Boer War, long bands of narrow cloth that had to be wound around the boot-top and ankle in a spiral and tucked in just so. Darling's puttees swathed his ankles in puffy granny knots like amateur field dressings until the moment he had to march. Then they immediately came unravelled and tripped him up, not that it made any difference to his marching, since he was one of those rare individuals who are totally incapable of marching in step for more than two paces at a time.

Darling reduced the Recruit Section's attempts at close order drill to something resembling an epileptic sock-hop, a sort of St. Vitus Dance Marathon, and Corporal Stevens to frothing at the mouth. Sergeant Wolff took Darling out of the formation and tried working with him one-on-one, but even he had to admit defeat when he caught himself actually repeating expletives. He compromised by putting Darling at the very rear of every formation where he couldn't throw everyone else out of step. He'd taught us the old Army trick of getting back into step quickly if you lost the cadence. You simply took a skip, like a kid, and and came back in step. It worked for everyone but Darling, who followed as we wheeled right and wheeled left and about faced, skipping along like the Queen of the May.

Drill wasn't the only thing Darling screwed up. If we dug slit trenches in the woods behind the Armoury, it was Darling who lofted a shovelful of dirt over his shoulder that landed on the Sergeant's hat. At the firing range it was Darling who turned around on the firing line to ask a dumb question, his loaded FN sweeping the startled section, a puzzled look on his face as everyone including the Sergeant dove for cover screaming.

No one, least of all Sergeant Wolff, could figure out why Darling had joined the Militia. He didn't even like beer. He always drank Coke in the mess. I had an idea because I'd known Mike Darling years before when we were both on the same Little League baseball team, not that I was man enough to admit it. Nobody, including the coach, could figure out why he was there either. Not only was he the most totally uncoordinated kid on the team, he didn't even seem to be interested in baseball. He was a born bench-warmer, the kid who got put in to play right field for one inning when we were so far ahead or so far behind it didn't matter. He'd literally sit out there in the hay, picking dandelions or watching butterflies with his glove on the ground a few feet away, completely ignoring the game, looking up curiously as a bouncing grounder rocketed past him. A groan would go up from our bench and Darling would rouse himself to jog after the ball which he would eventually return with a floppy girlish throw that rolled to a dead stop before it reached the infield. On the rare occasions he came to bat, he'd let the opposing pitcher put two straight strikes past him without getting the wood off his shoulder. Then he'd swing wild at a high wide outside curve that was nowhere near the plate, usually a full second after it smacked into the catcher's glove.

We all hated him, of course. It was a struggle for the coach to treat him fairly. Yet he never missed a practice or a game all season. I saw him once after a game in which he'd pulled some spectacular boner, following his father to a station wagon in the parking lot. His head was down and his glove dangled from the wrong hand while his father walked ahead almost as though he didn't know him. I only knew it was his Dad because he turned back to give him a look that was a mixture of pity and contempt as he gruffly barked at him to stop dawdling and get in the car. I figured the Militia was another one of his father's attempts to get somebody else to make a man of his son.

The Engineers did their best. After our first parade the recruits were herded into the basement motor pool to be initiated in a ceremony called Creamo. The lights were turned off and in the pitch dark we were told to open our button flies and jerk off as quickly as possible. First one to squirt was supposed to shout "Creamo!" There was a lot of moaning and panting in the dark for a few minutes until someone groaned "Cream-oh!" in a choked gargle. When the lights snapped on, the rest of us, who'd been paperboys or Boy Scouts, were all standing around with our arms crossed, flies buttoned. Only Darling stood there like a blinded rat, his slimy cock shrinking in his hand, a streak of jism dangling from his battledress pants like a loose thread.

Darling wasn't the only member of the Recruit Section I'd known before. I'd gone through elementary school with Dougie Trumbull and Rob Coombes and we'd been paperboys at the same shack. They'd been a Mutt and Jeff team since kindergarten. When we were in Grade Two, our teacher kept a chart on the wall where each pupil's progress was measured. Not only were one's proficiency in arithmetic and spelling recorded, but points and demerits for grooming and deportment, having the correct number of pencils in one's pencil-box, etcetera, were also displayed for all to see.

Rob Coombes consistently ran last on the chart. His fingernails were black and bitten to the quick, big kids routinely stole his pencils, his homework was frequently consumed by dogs, he could barely spell his name and arithmetic questions which involved more than his ten grubby fingers might as well have been Einstein's Theory of Relativity. He was the only kid who ever said "No" to a teacher and was once suspended for telling the Principal to "Shut up". Kids tell their teachers a lot worse now, but then it was big stuff.

Coombes always picked fights with guys who were bigger than him, which wasn't hard because he was a shrimp. In his mid-teens, he only stood about five-two in Army boots. Dougie had been sticking up for him since they were toddlers on the same street. Dougie had grown into a big good-natured oaf who could crush full beer cans and wore size fourteen shoes and his sidekick Coombes was still the mouthy little terrier who was always getting Dougie into fights.

While Mike Darling accepted being in deep shit as part of the natural order of things, Rob Coombes wore the perpetually aggrieved look of the little guy who's always getting picked on. It was lucky for him Darling had enlisted at the same time or Sergeant Wolff and Corporal Stevens would've paid more attention to him. Trouble-makers like Coombes the Army knew how to deal with.

The only other guy in the Recruit Section I knew besides Ted Brauer was Mike McConnell. Ted and I knew him from high school. He was an odd bird, though not an obviously marked loser like Darling. He dressed like the rest of us in jeans and jean-jackets, t-shirts and Beatle boots, though his blonde hair never got quite as unruly. He hung around, but never exactly with anybody. Likeable enough, he didn't seem to have any close buddies. No obvious girlfriend presented herself, though he was good-looking and had less of a problem with his complexion than most of us, myself included. He was just one of those guys you never took much notice of if he was there and never missed if he wasn't. Ted and I met him at school and at the impromtu parties kids hold in parks and parking lots when they're too young to drink indoors. When we ran into each other at the enlistment, he sort of tagged along with us. We didn't mind. He was just there. He was easy and so were we.

After tramping up the stairs from the magazine to the drill hall where the whole squadron was formed up and glowering at us impatiently, Ted, Mike and I fell in and dressed ranks, extending our right arms to touch the next man's shoulder like we'd been taught. I was glad we were in the rear rank. I still had a mud plaster from my breastbone to my knees that I knew Staff would assume I got by tripping over the two left feet I marched with.

To our suprise, it wasn't Staff who addressed us, but the C.O. himself. The Colonel was a small portly gentleman whose small military moustache looked even blonder against the background of his brick red whiskey tan. A successful engineer in civilian life, he too gave up his Saturday mornings to Stand On Guard For Thee. We rankers seldom saw him. He was occupied with his endless communiques to Ottawa. Now and then the text of one of these missives was read aloud to us by one of the officers, tongue jammed firmly in cheek, "to keep us apprised of the situation", before we were dismissed. I pitied the recipient of those turgid voluminous dispatches.

Our officers were a colourless lot. The only time the Recruit Section saw them was when the officers were formally invited to join our mess and that was often enough to make us suspect things were a lot more fun in our smoke-filled spartan bar below stairs than in the leather and mahogany officers preserve under the eaves. On these occasions the officers, in the interest of "getting to know the men," avoided the corner where the C.O. was always holding forth with a glass of scotch in hand on the subject of his intimate friendships with the Duke of Edinburgh, the Shah of Iran, the Emperor of Japan, assorted Presidents of the United States and the entire Royal House of Saud. Before retirement he had actually run an engineering firm that built oil pipelines across the civilized and uncivilized world, so you never knew how many grains of salt to take with his stories. At this parade we were all getting ready to settle into the At-Ease stance to endure another of his unending diatribes on the maintenance of

Canadian sovereignity over the West Coast and the inadequacy of the forces allocated thereto when the C.O. began reading, but it wasn't from one of his own massive missives. It was a directive from the Ministry of Defence, Ottawa. He stood to Attention, as did we all, while he read. "...15th Field Squadron...ordered to proceed to Canadian Forces Camp Chilliwack...hundred hours...October the...in concert with Seaforth Highland Regiment...quack quack..."

The C.O. always sounded like a mallard duck with a hornet trapped in its tail feathers. I couldn't get the gist, so I whispered to Ted out of the corner of my mouth.

"What the fuck's he saying?"

Ted rolled his eyes and hissed back.

"Weekend after next."

"What about it?"

"We're fucked."

"Silence in the ranks!"

Staff's sudden roar was almost loud enough to blow our berets off. With a nod in the RSM's direction, the C.O. continued his peroration.

"...there to engage in intensified training...infantry and engineering skills...quack quack..."

The C.O. folded the order into his pocket and saluted. We saluted back. Staff dismissed us with a bark that singed our ears, glaring at Ted and I. Lucky for us it was beneath his immense dignity to address the Recruit Section directly. He shit on Sergeant Wolff, who shit on Corporal Stevens, who shit on us. That's what they call Chain of Command. The Corporal curtly waved us over before we could escape into the mess, but he barely got started citing the dire punishments prescribed for talking on parade by the Manual of Military Instruction when Sergeant Wolff took over.

"I'd put you two spunk-sucking fuckpots on report, except the C.O. might decide you aren't fit to join us on this Chilliwack excursion. Where you're going, my little fart-sniffing smart arses, they'll give you a taste of real soldiering, and may God have no mercy at all on your syphilitic souls."

I detected a distinctly ominous note in the cackle of laughter that followed. Later in the mess, I pulled Ted aside.

"What do you think he meant by that?"

"I don't know. I didn't like the sound of that bit about 'intensified training.' It sounded a bit...intense."

"What the hell. Cheer up." I was giggling under the influence of my second beer. "We're going to inflict the worst defeat on the Canadian Army since Dieppe."

If anybody could do it, I thought, looking around at the happily half-shot Recruit Section, we could.

Chapter 4

The following Saturday parade was devoted to tuning us up so we wouldn't disgrace our uniforms, the often referred to but never recounted illustrious traditions of the Squadron, the C.O., the Government of Canada or the Queen on the weekend to come. The Engineering Section, the real Sappers, spent the day in the big cold but dry classroom in the Armoury basement, brushing up on the theory of bridge building, road grading and blowing things up. We in the Recruit Section spent the day outside in the machinegun rain, crawling on our bellies through soaking bushes urged on by Corporal Stevens who was wrapped in a full-length hooded waterproof poncho.

When the Corporal wearied of that entertainment, he had us dig slit trenches which filled with watery mud faster than we could shovel it out. Our enthusiasm flagged noticeably when the water rose over our boots. Properly wound, the multi-layered puttees really did possess surprising water-resistance. You could tell who hadn't mastered the art of tying them by the expressions on their faces.

"Keep digging! You call those trenches? The Canadian Army doesn't enlist midgets! These trenches wouldn't protect the Seven Dwarves!"

I still hadn't learned that pointing out the obvious is no path to promotion in the military.

"We're not digging, Corporal. We're bailing."

Ted backed me up.

"He's right, Corporal. We're at the bottom of a drainage slope and we've hit the water table."

A vein in Corporal Stevens' temple throbbed.

"I've been in the Engineers for seven years! Are you trying to tell me you know more about the water table than I do? You couldn't find the water table with a diamond drill and a sponge! Keep digging or I'll put you both on report!"

You could tell Corporal Stevens lived for the day when he could put someone on report. Mostly all he could do was threaten because if he put a man on report it had to go before the C.O. himself. Then Stevens would have to show a damn good reason for interrupting the Colonel's dictation of his latest lengthy memo to the patient Sergeant Laporte.

You could be put on report for persistent sloppiness in uniform and Corporal Stevens had been persecuting Mike Darling along those lines, obviously singling out the luckless clown of the section for his first demonstration to the C.O. that he was worthy of his promotion. I didn't know for sure, but I suspected Sergeant Wolff told him to back off. It was apparent to everyone that Darling was trying in spite of himself to be a good soldier, if only on Saturdays.

You could be put on report for disrespect, telling a commissioned or non-commissioned officer to go fuck spiders, for instance, or for insubordination, refusing to obey a direct legal order. You could be put on report for being drunk on parade or absent without leave. You could be put on report for the murder or rape of a civilian. Sergeant Wolff had explained all this to us with forceful clarity, slapping his Sergeants baton into the palm of his hand by way of punctuation. Nobody, not even the Sergeant, said anything about the rape of a Wrenette. Among ourselves, we figured it had a lot to do with whether or not she out-ranked you.

Still, the threat of being put on report was serious enough because they docked your pay as part of your punishment and that's what all of us, with the possible exception of Mike Darling, were there for. It was enough to make us lower our voices to a mutinous mumble taken up by Dougie Trumbull and Rob Coombes, invisible in their deepening ditch.

"Maybe we'll hit China..."

"And maybe it won't be raining there..."

Corporal Stevens strode off smugly to the shelter of the old wooden Mahon Park grandstand to enjoy a dry smoke. As he deserted his command, Ted pulled out a damp Players Filter and lit up.

"If we do hit China, we could join the Peoples Liberation Army. They don't have officers, not even generals."

"They don't?" Entrenching tools were downed all over the position as soggy smokes were lit and sucked to life. "Who gives the orders?"

"They decide everything by committee. Democratically."

"That'll never work!"

The identically outraged faces of the Graham twins appeared over the crumbling lip of their mud wallow. The Grahams were the only real dorks in the Recruit Section. They'd only just moved to Vancouver from some fly-shit town on the Prairies. They'd been in the Militia there, though not in Engineers, and in Army Cadets before that, they missed no opportunity to remind anybody who would listen. We knew they really did stay up nights ironing their uniforms and polishing their boots with real spit. They slept at Attention, thumbs glued to the seams of their pyjama pants instead of fondling their dicks and dreaming about the enemy country beyond the tops of Wrenette stockings like the rest of us.

The Grahams were doubly furious when Ted and I outshone them on parade and furious squared when they found out how we did it. They told Corporal Stevens, whose ass they missed no chance to kiss, and he got at least half as mad as they were when Sergeant Wolff refused to take us to task.

"I don't care if the whole fuckpot section are dressed by their valets, as long as they don't look like walking sacks of shit on my parade. I'd be surprised if some of this lot really knew how to tie their own shoes, never mind polish them!"

The Grahams regarded the Recruit Section as a brief purgatory from which they momentarily expected to be plucked and elevated into the paradise of the Engineers. That they were military geniuses might have gone without saying if they hadn't been so determined to remind everyone, including Sergeant Wolff, of the fact. Add to that their habit of repeating what the other twin had just said in a kind of split-second echo delay and I was amazed the Sergeant didn't promote them just to save himself two pains in the ass.

There was a nasty clang in the trench next to ours as Dougie and Rob hit bedrock. With a leg up from Dougie, muddy Rob Coombes scrambled to the edge of their water-filled hole which was now almost deep enough to drown him. Squatting miserably on a heap of mud, he set fire to an Export A whose paper was almost transparent.

"Y'know, maybe the Chinks have got the right idea. Maybe we should form a committee and take a vote about digging these holes."

Graham One checked in.

"You can't do that!"

I threw my entrenching tool out of the bog Ted and I had been digging in.

"Okay. Let's take a democratic vote on something."

Graham Two echoed on cue.

"You can't do that!"

Ted had a suggestion.

"I move Corporal Stevens, with this vastly superior military experience, be detailed to complete construction of these vital positions."

There was a chorus of "Aye" from the Recruit Section followed by suggestions.

"With his mess kit spoon..."

More Ayes.

"With his lily-white hands..."

Still more Ayes. Everyone had stopped digging, even the Grahams, who were whispering to each other.

"What's going on here?"

Corporal Stevens stomped down the trail, his poncho flapping behind him. The Grahams came to Attention beside their trench, their voices a shrill counterpoint.

"Sapper Morrison and Sapper Brauer were counselling us to commit high treason, Corporal."

"They were holding a subversive meeting, telling us we should be like Communists in the army of China and vote on whether or not to obey the orders of our superiors."

"Wha?...What?"

Stevens was stunned. That we were a bunch of uniformed juvenile delinquents he already knew, but he was having some difficulty adjusting to our new roles as agents of the International Communist Conspiracy.

The Grahams were obliged to take cover in their slit trench, producing a satisfying double splash, as the rest of the section siezed their downed tools and began pelting them with shovelfulls of soggy dirt. Ted and I manned the pile of mud they'd diligently excavated, scooping it in on top of them as fast as we could. Corporal Stevens screamed, much louder than the muffled shrieks of the Graham twins who were by now in serious danger of being buried alive.

"At ease! Halt! At ease! At ease, damn you!"

When order was finally restored, the Grahams crawled up out of the mud, which is where most of us thought they'd come from in the first place and recently at that. Stammering and at the brink of tears, Corporal Stevens ordered us back to base.

"I want these holes filled and all of you back at the drill hall! On the double!"

He ran away to tell Sergeant Wolff.

"I'll get you for that."

The Graham voice in my ear made me turn around.

"Any time you want to try."

I recognized the sinking feeling in the pit of my stomach as the first symptom of a fist fight. Ted sauntered over and stood beside me.

"Bring your fucking fink brother, so I'll have something to do."

I could have kissed him.

When we finished filling in our trenches the little clearing in the forest looked like the site of half a dozen fresh graves. The Grahams finished theirs first and left, hot on the Corporal's heels, without even thanking Ted and I and the boys for doing half their work for them. Covered in mud from boots to berets, for once they looked worse than the rest of us. By the time we got back to the shelter and relative warmth of the Armoury the Corporal was just finishing his hestitant but full report of our misconduct. Sergeant Wolff's belly-laugh shook the termite-ridden rafters.

"Conspiracy? If this gang of willie-waggers conspired to hold a circle-jerk, they'd come up a hand short!

He surveyed the ranks of dripping, oozing Sappers before him with evident relish, particularly when he saw the Grahams, who obviously expected to be called as witnesses at a drum-head court martial. Sergeant Wolff smiled at them and twirled the ends of his moustache.

"You look like shit! Especially you two! Now I want you all downstairs to the classroom on the mother-fucking double or I'll rip off your sausages and have the cook fry them for my lunch! You're going to get some instruction on the equipment you'll be using next weekend. Dismiss and double it down!"

We tumbled back downstairs, curious as khaki cats about what new implements of destruction the army was about to entrust to our fumbling hands.

"Hey Sarge? Are we gonna get to blow something up?"

Though we'd only been in the squadron a couple of months, we were already jealous of the veteran engineers. Not that we gave a rogue fart about building bridges and such, but one of the subjects they studied was the fine art of blowing up things. Pacifist leanings nothwithstanding, all of us were as eager to play with plastic explosives as kids waiting for a turn at the Play-Doh bucket.

"The day the army's fool enough to let you fist-fucking fuckpots anywhere near a powder magazine, I'll put on a dress and enlist in the cock-sucking Wrenettes!"

We filed into the cold bunker classroom and deployed on hard folding chairs behind trestle tables. Nobody cracked wise about the accomodations. It was better than where we'd been. We faced an old teachers desk without a chair and a chalkboard whitened with dust. I couldn't resist shooting my mouth.

"Corporal Stevens is slacking his blackboard monitor chores."

"Silence in the ranks!" When we were settled, Sergeant Wolff's manner changed to ominous courtesy. "At ease, gentlemen. Make yourselves comfortable. You make smoke if you have 'em. The demonstration will begin shortly."

I should have sensed something was up from the smirk that skulked under his moustache as he left the room, but I was busy trying to ignite a wet Rothmans. Moments later, Corporal Stevens rushed in, pulled the metal cotter pin from the top of a black object anyone who'd ever seen a war movie would recognize immediately, dropped it on the desk and bolted back the way he'd come. Nobody but the Graham twins moved, but they made up for the rest of us, shouting "Fire in the hole!" in unison as they knocked over empty chairs diving for cover and grovelling on the cement floor in approved military style.

The rest of us sensed that much as Sergeant Wolff might want to murder us, he'd hardly be likely to resort to something as messy and unpredictable as a hand grenade to do it. How would he explain it to our parents? To the army? Besides, a single grenade would probably only maim most of us anyway. We sat and smoked, nonchalantly eyeing the grenade on the instructors table until Ted Brauer finally got up, sauntered forward and threw himself across the desk dramatically, smothering the grenade with his floppy beret. We applauded. As Sergeant Wolff entered the room Ted rolled the grenade along the floor. The Sergeant trapped it like a soccer player under his boot and picked it up, tossing it and catching it like a piece of fruit he was thinking about eating. His smile was as small and tight as the RSM's ass.

"Smartarse fuckpots."

What followed was a tedious lecture on the hand grenade, as anti-social an item of hardware as you wouldn't want to encounter anywhere. Filled with gunpowder and activated by a time-fuse inserted through the screw-off baseplate of the serrated steel near-sphere, it was surprisingly heavy for its size, which is why it had to be thrown stiff-armed, like a discus, not tossed like a baseball. I thought of my Grandad who had been a Mills Bomber in the Winnipeg Grenadiers in the Great War. I remembered him telling me about crawling across no-man's-land at night, through the barbed wire, to the edge of the German trenches where he watched them sitting around their fires roasting potatoes and telling stories in a language he couldn't understand. I never asked him why he hadn't rolled one of his grenades down among them like he was supposed to do.

The lecture over, we were paraded, reminded to bring full kit to the following Friday evening muster for our training weekend and dismissed. We ought to have gone to the mess, gulped a couple of quick beers and boarded the trucks that would drop us off in our neighbourhoods, but the Grahams, on whom most of the mud had now dried, were not in a forgiving mood. They were already taking off their web belts and berets, which theoretically meant you were no longer in uniform.

"Outside."

Ted followed me, as did the entire Recruit Section. The mess barman must've tipped off Sergeant Wolff, because he turned up just as the four of us, the Grahams, Ted and I, were squaring off to do battle in the motor-pool yard.

"I fervently hope and pray you prickless puddles of piss are planning to deliberately disgrace the uniform of the Queen."

I was relieved to see the Grahams looked even more nervous. It made me bold.

"I won't hit the uniform, Sergeant...Just his mug."

Sergeant Wolff tapped his non-coms baton against his palm with an echoing splat. The officers carried effete swagger-sticks, little leather riding crops, but all Sergeants packed these three-foot long two-inch thick varnished wooden batons which had six ounces of lead drilled into the top of the shaft, disguised by the silver regimental crest. This, Sergeant Wolff had explained during our first parade, was for "dealing with unruly or insubordinate soldiers." He thwacked his baton into his palm again and looked like he could hardly wait to demonstrate.

"Carry on. I won't put you on report...I like to handle discipline in the Recruit Section personally."

The Grahams backed down before we did, putting on their web belts and skulking off up the street while the rest of us adjourned for a beer. We invited Sergeant Wolff to join us and he responded by buying us a round.

"You fart-holes pull any of this shit next weekend, I'll have all your balls poached on toast for my breakfast."

I hoped his remark didn't reflect on the culinary standards of the Canadian Armed Forces, Camp Chilliwack.

Chapter 5

Sharply outlined against the autumn evening sky, the floodlit Armoury glowed with the crisp tidiness of a real military installation on Friday night when we mustered after dinner to leave for Camp Chilliwack. Draped in the unreal glare of half a dozen ancient arc lights tucked up under the eaves, the red brick, dark green trim and lime coloured lawns looked unnaturally precise, like a miniature painted building in someone's HO scale train layout. The impression was intensified by the joint Ted and I smoked in the privacy of the dark grandstand at the soccer field overlooking the whole park.

We weren't taking any weed with us. The penalties for mere possession were a minimum two-years-less-a-day and we suspected that for the weekend, at least, we might be subject to Military Law. For all we knew, they could shoot us and it wasn't the kind of thing we could ask the Sergeant about. Besides, privacy and free time were likely to be at a premium in a real army camp. Hidden in our kitbags, by prearrangement with the rest of the section except the Grahams, were a couple of monster Graveyards.

Graveyards were more common, if not more popular, than the mickeys of Gilbey's Lemon Gin we tucked behind our belt-buckles on Friday nights, giving us an odd square-crotched walk and the girls cause for anxious speculation about the male anatomy. Lemon gin smelled like furniture polish and possibly tasted worse, but it blended well with innocuous Seven-Ups ordered in coffee shop booths. Unfortunately it could only be obtained by hanging around liquor stores in the less reputable parts of lower North Van and trying to bribe in-bound patrons, some of whom were susceptible to the lure of a couple of bucks that would buy an extra ration of Andrés Cream Sherry. It was that or a humiliating round of begging and pleading before someone's university age brother.

Graveyards were easier to come by, especially if your parents were social drinkers. They consisted of one or two ounces, an amount hopefully too small to be noticed, skimmed from every open bottle in the family liquor cabinet into a single flask. Each Graveyard was a unique, impossible to duplicate blend of various whiskies, gin, vodka, light and dark rums, sweet and dry vermouths, usually with more generous doses of sherries and ports which could be siphoned off in greater quantities because they came in dark bottles that made the dropping levels less noticeable. Graveyards were invariably livened up by eclectic jolts of akvavit, assorted liqueurs and liberal lashings of aromatic bitters.

Sometimes these random formulae produced a potion concocted by whichever Archangel serves as God's Bartender, a nectar which could be swilled straight out of the bottle, sweeter than mothers milk ever was. More often, they tasted like something that would make a goat gag. We cut them with Coke or orange juice to get them past our tatebuds. The effects of such elixirs on a bunch of teenage boys are hard to recall, much less describe, but Robert Louis Stevenson came close in *The Strange Case of Doctor Jekyll and Mister Hyde*. I dimly remember a couple of friends being rushed to Lions Gate Hospital Emergency to be revived. They weren't called Graveyards for nothing.

Ted and I were early and still too high to want to hang around the drill hall. We dropped our duffel bags, Graveyards buried among the socks, underwear, fatigues and the tangle of ammunition pouches and musette bags none of us knew how to put on, just inside the door. Slipping back outside before the Sergeant could spot us we doubled, cheerfully for a change, across to where the unmistakeable silhouettes of Wrenettes had been observed against the light streaming from the open door of the Air Cadet hall. A single cigarette end, like a navigation beacon, guided us to a group of girls passing around a single butt.

"You guys got any smokes?" they whined in response to our enthusiastic greetings. We had smokes. The temperature of our reception rose perceptibly. We passed the pack around. By the wavering flame of my Dad's old Zippo I recognized Nasty and used the ploy of gallantly lighting her smoke as an excuse to wedge myself between her and the other girls. I was so eager I nearly set fire to her blinding bangs.

"What're you guys doin' here?"

I wasn't having gender recognition problems. It was just the form. In Nasty's case I could have picked out her distinctive hip swivel from a dozen black skirts at a thousand yards, as could any North Van boy who had a nodding acquaintance with a razor. Her voice was the grumbling moan of a bandsaw cutting across the grain.

"They're making us go over to Pat Bay, the naval base on the Island...Some kinda training shit...The whole weekend's tits up."

"In that case, I wish I was going with you."

Cary Grant had nothing on me when it came to witty double entendre, but that bit of suave repartee rated me a sardonic snap of the gum she continued to chew while she smoked one of my Rothmans. Nasty was Nancy Nistasi, permanent guest in the detention halls of Hamiliton High, North Van's toughest school, not to mention Juvie Hall and a frequent subject of my daytime fantasies and nocturnal emissions. Not even the stodgily conservative Wrenette uniform could disguise her shape, disintinctive in its way as the Bismarck's—a sleek cruiser hull fitted with battleship turrets. Around North Van, her reputation was shadier than Messalina's and she was barely out of the gate.

The first shots in the sexual revolution had been fired, but for most of us the distant echo of the salute to freedom was about all it amounted to. Women were still something to be stormed, like the Winter Palace. Girls remained divided into the two traditional catagories, those who'd let you and those who wouldn't, and there were never enough of the former around. Though I suspected Nasty's experience was vastly exaggerated in the Highlands Pool Hall where we all hung around, she was nonetheless manifestly a girl who would under the right circumstances.

I'd been laying siege to her, if nothing else, ever since the wonderful Saturday I discovered she was a Wrenette. Neither an officer nor a gentleman, I felt that at least here my professionally pressed uniform, urbane wit and superior intelligence might make an impression impossible in the civilian world where Nasty was constantly accompanied by half a dozen of the duck-tailed greaseball thugs who often beguiled an idle moment by mercilessly bullying punks like me. I was amazed Nasty put up with me in those stolen precious moments before and after our Saturday parades.

After all, I was skinny, frequently pimply smartass whose teen-idol pompador was being rapidly overgrown by a suspicious tangle of un-Brylcreemed hair around the ears and collar. Despite knowing how to talk tough to dorks like the Grahams, I was an incompetent street-fighter who'd emerged from a few unmemorable scraps with tell-tale black polish streaks on my face from having been kicked in the head by somebody's pointed winkle-picker oxfords. Most damning of all, I didn't own or even have access to a car. I was known for employing words of more than two syllables on occasion and the novelty may have amused her, even if she didn't know what the fuck I was talking about.

The language barrier didn't stop her from understanding exactly what was on my mind as I edged her deeper into the shadows. She co-operated amiably enough, handing her half-finished smoke to Big Jenny, the tall heavy-set girl who always got sentry duty while the others necked. She even took her gum out of her mouth, but for all her apparent willingness to stand in the dark and endure my fumbling hands, her own remained unhelpful, pressed into the small of my back and toying annoyingly with the hair on the back of my neck in the currently popular movie star manner. Immobile, her head thrown back, eyes closed, she could have been asleep standing up but for her tongue. The only organ of her body to evince any interest in the proceedings, it was an electric eel in a river of Wrigleys Spearmint juice.

I murmured an assortment of endearments cribbed from old war movies..."separated by duty"..."we move out at dawn"..."who knows when we'll meet again?", that kind of thing, in an attempt to inject a little of the urgency becoming obvious even through the thick serge of my battledress pants into the event at large, but without result. Nasty kissed as avidly and stirringly as ever, but female under-garments were both relatively unfamiliar and a lot more substantial in those days. To approach them, I had to brave the ramparts and bastions of the Wrenette uniform, which seemed to have been designed by a descendant of Vauban or Maginot.

My campaign of manoeuvre had achieved none of its objectives when we were interrupted by the call to arms. Big Jenny began hissing warnings into the shadows.

"Knock it off, you guys! Here comes..."

Bidding Nasty a grunted saliva-choked farewell, I bolted around the dark corner of their drill hall with Ted hot on my heels. He'd been chatting up a stringy-haired, flat-chested Wrenette called Gladys for weeks. We reached the safety of the road and turned toward the Armoury, composing ourselves.

"You get anywhere?"

My question was purely a matter of form, since there wasn't anywhere to get as far as I could see.

"I'm really getting into her mind, Jack."

"Her mind?" I groaned, hands in my pockets trying to strangle my erection." You're supposed to be getting into her pants."

"She's got a really interesting mind, Jack."

His infuriating tranquility was shattered by the bull roar of Sergeant Wolff, waiting for us at the drill hall door.

"If you two candy-ass commandos are through terrorizing the Tampon Squad, our Commanding Officer is hosting an informal little soiree for all ranks on the parade square! On the fucking double!"

The entire Squadron was waiting for us as we burst through the doors and quickly dressed ranks at the rear of the Recruit Section. My erection had subsided sufficiently for me to come to attention without discomfort. I couldn't figure out why all the officers from the C.O. down to the non-coms were either smirking or glaring or both every time they looked in my direction. I even caught some of the Sappers turning to stare during the C.O.'s brief address, exhorting us to acquit ourselves like men and bring no dishonour upon the venerable name of the Squadron. The instant we were dismissed, Sergeant Wolff took me aside.

"The Army's trying to move with the times, son, but we're not quite ready for makeup yet."

Aghast, I realized I had Nasty's distinctive hot pink lipstick smeared all over my face like a drunken clown. Sergeant Wolff rubbed it in with savage glee.

"As for the way you smell, let me remind you that poison gas was outlawed by the Geneva Convention after World War One."

I dashed to the latrine, pursued by a barrage of laughter from the entire Squadron. I managed to rid myself of the most obvious of the traces of Nasty's lipstick and eye-watering perfume in time to plunge down the stairs with my kit and receive an FN rifle from Corporal Stevens, accompanied by somewhat hurried admonitions about serial numbers and responsibilities for said weapon and no other. A spontaneous cheer went up from the Recruit Section truck as I clambered over the tailgate, the last man in.

"Shove it, you fuckpots."

The canvas-backed olive drab five ton lurched underway. We were all there but the Grahams, who were sucking up to the real Sappers and weasled into one of their trucks. Corporal Stevens was aboard, but thinking of his own comfort as usual, he was riding up front with the driver in the sealed cab where there was a heater. That was his first mistake. Letting us bring up the rear of the column, though customary, was the second. No following headlights would illuminate any mischief or debauchery we might get up to.

Graveyards of varying hues in various flasks appeared from half a dozen kit-bags in unison, but we observed the Mess formalities. Dougie Trumbull stood up, clinging to a metal strut in the swaying truck, brandishing a bottle and offered the solemn toast.

"Gentlemen! The Queen!"

Echoes of "The Queen" from a dozen throats were immediately followed by gurgling, gasping and gagging which would hardly have amused Her Majesty.

"Gawk! That's fuckin' awful!"

"Bleagh! Taste's like rat piss!"

"You've tasted rat piss?"

"Anybody bring any orange juice or Coke?"

"This one's not bad..."

"Pass it over..."

Rob Coombes dug frantically in his kit-bag.

"I can't find my Graveyard..."

"Never mind. There's lots to go around. We'll find it later..."

By the time the convoy rolled onto the Trans-Canada Highway most of us were flying high or gaining altitude rapidly. As we rumbled into the rural darkness beyond New Westminister, the advantage of being the rear-guard became apparent. When following cars pulled out to pass the slower Army trucks, we could dispose of the incriminating bottles by flinging them off to the side into the fields and dark dripping trees. It had begun to rain heavily, but we were surprisingly cosy under canvas, having abandoned the hard bench seats for a huge central chaise longue improvised on the deck out of massed kit-bags.

Lounging and smoking, passing bottle after bottle of Graveyard Cocktail, we taught each other filthy rugby songs, salty sea chanties, lewd limericks, told jokes so old they weren't so much dirty as grimy and swapped lies about girls whose pants we'd almost gotten into. At the section's insistence, I enlarged on my combat experience with Nasty, exaggerating for effect and leaving the rest to their fevered imaginations. At one point, I seem to recall Rob Coombes swinging from one of the overhead struts like a crazed chimpanzee before losing his grip and falling among the supine recruit Sappers like direct hit from a mortar, scattering spilled booze and vomit in all directions. Shortly after, the truck slowed down and turned off the highway.

"Wha's happenin'?"

"I thing we're here..."

"Where?"

"There...y'know...here..."

"Oh shit..."

"Oh shit is right..."

A blind scramble for weapons, web belts and berets ensued.

"This isn't my kit..."

"Don't sweat it...Everybody grab a bag. We'll sort it out when there's light."

Ted's voice was reasonable, but slurred beyond disguise and there was light all too soon. The trucks ground their gears to a halt and the angular profile of Corporal Stevens appeared between the canvas flaps over the tailgate.

"Everyone fall out, er, fall in and form ranks on my...Oh my God!"

He must have been downwind of us. We fell out, literally. The clatter of steel helmets and rifles hitting the asphalt was deafening. The lights of the base were terribly, painfully bright. The Corporal seemed to have lost his voice. Falling in proved much more difficult. We had a problem forming straight lines and dressing ranks, since half the section was legless and had to be supported by the other half. Somehow Rob Coombes had lost his beret, a serious breach of military etiquette.

Looking as though he might be going to swallow his moustache, Sergeant Wolff introduced us to Sergeant Plante, a very big and very formidable looking Sergeant of the Queens Own Rifles of the real Army. Sergeant Plante's nose twitched. No doubt we smelled like a bombed distillery. The rest of the Squadron was lined up in perfect ranks, trying to pretend they were in some other army. I expect they were only waiting for Sergeant Plante's order to form a firing squad and proceed with our summary execution. When he spoke, Sergeant Plante's voice was so deadly soft my heart sank to the heels of my boots.

"We'll go by the book, Sergeant Wolff. Not the Manual of Military Regulations, but The Good Book...The last shall be first...Get these...men...out of my sight and into barracks immediately. I'll inspect them in the morning, when I hope the wind will have changed. Reveille is at oh-six-hundred." He turned to Stevens. "You may dismiss your parade, Corporal."

That last crack brought tears to Stevens' cheeks. When he screamed "Dis-MISS!" it came out as a hideous croak and he stumbled away, trying to distance himself from our disgrace. Sergeant Wolff stood his ground, tapping his lead-weighted baton softly into the palm of his hand.

"That was only your first step, fuckpots, and you're already up to your noses in the shit-hole. You know where the next one puts you?"

Even in our stupours, we knew.

CHAPTER 6

My experience with the military timetable was confined to war movies where a grim faced officer would order an equally grim-faced Sergeant to "Tell the men we go in at oh-six-hundred." Go in they would, preceded by a grand barrage of artillery. Corporal Stevens was the only person I'd ever met who'd answer a simple request for the time of day with something as incomprehensibly precise as "Thirteen hundred hours, twenty-seven minutes."

The more profound implications of Sergeant Plante's warning about the time completely failed to penetrate our liquified unmilitary minds. The only barrage that preceded oh-six-hundred in our unit was the irregular cannondade of explosive farts and belches from a dozen drunkenly snoring Sappers. It seemed like I'd no sooner closed my eyes and passed out before the room lit up like a film studio and Sergeant Wolff was bellowing the traditional armed forces morning greeting.

"Drop your cocks and grab your socks! Hit the deck! On the fucking double, ladies!"

As we bounded out of bed, one of the Grahams bare feet touched down in a puddle of slimy vomit deposited by some Sapper who'd been too weak to make it to the latrine. Arms and legs flailing, he seemed to be running on the spot for an instant before landing on his backside in the mess with a wet smack and a squeal of rage.

Sergeant Wolff added insult to injury by pointing the big baton directly at him.

"Get a bucket and mop from the latrine and clean that festering mess up on the double!" The Graham started to protest, but the Sergeant was not in a reasonable mood. "This place smells like a two-dollar whorehouse over a chicken-gutting factory! You've got ten minutes to get this floor clean enough to eat off or by the living God I'll see you do eat off it!"

The threat of being made to eat anything under any circumstances was dire enough to stir most of us to action. Windows flew open to clear the air of the fug of mothballs, farts and puke. Mops and buckets cleared the floor re-fouling the atmosphere with a sinus-piercing disinfectant stench. Bedding was ineptly re-ordered. Rob Coombes was discovered still asleep on the floor, wrapped in a blanket torn from a spare bunk. Evidently he'd been unable to find his way back to the top of the two-tiered bunk he shared with Dougie Trumbull after a midnight visit to the latrine and had bivouaced on the floor.

The big latrine need a brisk scrubdown as well, having sustained superficial flak damage from the erupting guts of the Recruit Section during the night. My own fitful sleep had been punctuated with retchings and groanings during the brief interval of blessed unconsciousness. The condition of the latrine had been brought to our attention by a snotty Lance-Corporal of the Seaforths, who occupied the adjacent barracks and shared the latrine and shower, which joined the two long barracks at the centre like the middle bar of a capital letter H.

Testy remarks were exchanged, not only between us and the Seaforths, but between their Lance-Corporal and Corporal Stevens, who took the junior non-coms peremptory orders to our ranks as a challenge to his own authority. The Seaforths retreated muttering, outranked and confronted with an unpredictable band of badly hung-over Sappers armed with indescribably foul-smelling mops. By the time Sergeant Wolff returned to inspect us we'd cleaned up the worst of the mess and stood by the ends of our bunks, more or less showered and shaved and more or less dressed, except for Coombes who was clomping around with his boots on the wrong feet looking for his missing beret.

"I can't find my beret! I've lost my fucking beret!"

Mike McConnell helped him root through the gear dumped and jumbled on his bunk.

"Jesus! You can't lose that! It's got the regimental insignia on it!"

Mike was right. In the Army, headgear occupied an especially sacred niche. Without it you weren't strictly speaking in uniform. Most of us knew that because the same rule applied to the RCMP, with whom we'd had more experience. I had a momentary inspiration.

"I don't think you need it right now! I don't think you wear hats in barracks or the Mess Hall! We'll find it later."

Mercifully I was right for once. We'd no sooner jammed Coombes kit back into his duffel and taken our places when Sergeant Wolff stormed the barracks. Corporal Stevens squeaky announcement, "Section ready for inspection, Sergeant!" betrayed a distinct lack of confidence that this was so. The Sergeant toured the room, sniffing the air disdainfully and eyeing our rumpled bunks with naked contempt.

"These beds look like a troop of tarts entertained the Turkish Navy here last night! I suppose your mothers still make your beds at home! Serves them right for having you, you bunch of botched abortions! You motherless mothers' mistakes! Get these beds squared away before breakfast! Tomorrow morning I'm going to bounce a quarter off every bunk in this barracks and woe betide the fuckpot if I hear any change come down! Dismiss to the Mess Hall and parade in full equipment in forty-five minutes!"

Coombes was still whining as we set off across the grass for the mess. I did what I could to reassure him.

"Don't panic. We're on manoeuvres, right? Not formal parade. It'll be mostly fatigues and forage caps or helmets. We'll figure something out."

The mess hall was full of the enormous men of the Queens Own Rifles. I could appreciate the lead in the Sergeants batons better, now I could see what they were up against. They looked like an entire football league in olive drab. One of the reasons doubtlessly lay spread out before us as we lined up, plates in hand, at the cafeteria style kitchen that seemed to extend for the entire length of the hall. Parades of pancakes, squadrons of sausages, battalions of bacon, the scrambled eggs of a task force of chickens, rank upon rank of toast and deep cannisters of jam—suddenly we were starving.

Mike McConnell, the skinniest man in the section, ate us all under the table, going back for seconds, then thirds. Even a few of the regulars noticed his heaping plates. Three meals a day like that and we'd look like CFL linemen too. As we burped our way back to barracks through the sunny but still chilly autumn morning, it almost seemed worth defying adolescent lethargy and brutal hangovers to be alive and awake at such a marvelous unfamiliar hour. Corporal Stevens snarled at us to be on the parade square in five minutes and nipped off to toady to Sergeant Plante and the Sergeants of the Seaforths already gathering on the asphalt square. Inside, we realized he hadn't said anything about how we were to dress. Somebody said we were going to the range.

"The ground's still wet..."

"And there's a few fuckin' clouds up there..."

"It's cold, man..."

Abandoned by our Corporal and separated from the rest of the Squadron, who were housed in a different barracks, we had no one to ask and no time to reach a consensus. So we dressed to suit ourselves, some in battledress for warmth, others in easily washable fatigues, some donning olive camo bush-jackets, others in ochre coloured canvas toppers called Ranger jackets. Headgear was equally eclectic, a mix of berets, peaked forage caps and old British style soup plate steel helmets. As we clumsily dressed ranks beside the Seaforths, immaculate in battledress and pom-pommed tams the colour of old porridge, we looked like a band of cut-throat mercenaries.

I'm sure I saw Sergeant Plante turn away, biting his lip. The Seaforths were putting on a show, fancy rifle-work we called Monkey Drill, the butts and stocks of their weapons crashing and slapping in perfect unison as they spun them around like baton twirlers, over and under and through the whole manual of arms and then some. Their accompanying squad of cadets matched the older Militiamen stroke for stroke, impeccably tricked out in battledress and Glengarry caps with the Highlander ribbons streaming down their backs.

Sergeant Wolff had mysteriously re-appeared. He looked at them, looked at us, looked at Corporal Stevens and pursed his lips, giving his moustache a sardonic tilt. The Corporal seemed to be praying fervently but silently, whispering co-ordinates to some divine artillery commander who could obliterate us with a straddling salvo.

Sergeant Plante inspected the Seaforths first, probably to give himself time to regain his composure. At last he came to us. We were uncomfortably aware that the Seaforths and their cadets, ordered to Stand At Ease, were all straining their peripheral vision so as not to miss a moment of our humiliation and trying to outdo each other with snide sidelong looks. Their Sergeant was obliged to bark a terse, "Eyes Front!"

The Sergeant moved through our ragged ranks with a straight face, but he stopped in front of Rob Coombes. My breakfast dropped a few degrees. It was elementary school all over again.

"Let me see your rifle, Sapper."

"Present arms!"

Sergeant Plante reacted to Corporal Stevens superfluous shriek with a pained look. Coombes awkwardly presented his weapon, almost dropping it on the Sergeant's foot. The Sergeant caught it in his infinitely more capable hands and opened the breech. He stared into the lozenge of darkness for what seemed like a long time before hooking a finger inside to remove a remarkably large pebble.

"Do you have any idea how this stone came to be in the firing mechanism of your rifle, Sapper?"

"N-no, sir...I mean, n-no S-sergeant."

"I believe you will find there have been some improvements in ammunition in recent years."

The Sergeant's tone was mild. He closed the offended breech and handed the rifle back carefully, making sure Coombes had a firm grip before he released it. Handing the stone to Corporal Stevens, who seemed to be trying to see how long he could hold his breath, Sergeant Plante calmly escaped from our ranks and invited Sergeant

Wolff and the Seaforth Sergeant to take charge of the parade. Corporal Stevens nearly missed his cue, bewildered by the pebble in his hand, unsure whether to hold onto it as evidence to be used in a Court Martial or to dispose of it, preferably by inserting it in an orifice of Sapper Coombes. Too intimidated by his surroundings to simply drop it discreetly on a designated Canadian Armed Forces parade ground, he slipped it into his pocket with a gesture of disgust, like a man concealing a handkerchief he's lent to someone else.

We marched the mile or so to the rifle range, the Seaforths leading off in perfect step, followed by their contingent of synchronous cadets. Our Recruit Section brought up the rear, the Engineering Section having paraded separately and been trucked off in comfort to build a bridge somewhere in the woods. Our own rear was brought up by Sapper Darling, skipping madly along in a desperate attempt to get into step.

Sunlight gilded the bracken and the birds stopped singing in deference to the number of armed men passing through their woods. The occasion lacked nothing but music. Spontaneously, some smartass Recruit began to whistle the Colonel Bogey March. Our concert was taken amiss by some of the Seaforths, who cast threatening glances over their shoulders but refused to break cadence to make something out of it, especially after Sergeant Wolff joined in. In a subdued voice, he suggested some unrepeatably lewd lyrics we might sing to the tune, if we cared to, which of course we did. He almost seemed friendly as he nodded to the immaculately snotty bastards marching ahead.

"Don't let them get you down. They won't look so pretty by the end of the day."

At the range, we were issued with full clips of live ammunition and forbidden to load until we were called to the firing line. A dozen at a time, we entered the long permanent trench, stood at a sandbagged loop-hole, slapped the heavy mags into our rifles and opened fire on Sergeant Plante's command. We were to fire at will and expend every round we'd been issued. Sergeant Plante checked our empty mags and breeches personally as we exited the trench. We fired four mags each at fifty, one hundred, three hundred and six hundred yards, enough to leave our ears ringing for weeks and almost as much fun as blowing things up.

After the first round, I wasn't sure I'd survive until lunch. The FN is fitted with a metal ring on the forestock, numbered from one to eight, which adjusts the amount of gases from the firing explosion allowed to remain or escape from the chamber. This affects both the range and recoil of the weapon. A higher setting lowers the range and softens the kick. My rifle was stuck at two, as I discovered when it nearly broke my shoulder on the first shot. Nothing my numbed fingers could do would move the ring. I was cursing and sucking my aching fingers when Dougie joined me. He couldn't budge the ring on my rifle either. Finally he handed me his.

"Here. Mine's loose as a school combination lock. I've got more padding than you."

"Thanks. I owe you one. Just remember to trade back later or Stevens'll shit his khakis."

I finished the rest of my magazines feeling like I'd been kicked by a pony instead of a Percheron, too grateful to care much whether or not I was hitting the man-shaped targets. The only untoward incident occurred when I was stationed beside a Seaforth cadet who couldn't resist asking, "What costume party are you guys going to?"

I stepped on the mirror-polished toe of his boot to hold him in place and kept my voice down.

"Shut your pimply face, you little pus-boil. At least we don't wear dresses on parade."

A cheap crack at the expense of their kilts, but that and the possibility I might still have one round up the spout shut him up quick.

As it turned out, the rifle switch was lucky for Dougie too. He put half a dozen rounds into the bulls-eye at six hundred yards with my FN. After the shoot, Sergeant Plante approached us with a peculiar expression on his square hard face. I could hardly believe it was respect. There was silence in the Seaforth ranks as he read out the results. In spite of Mike Darling, who admitted he couldn't see anything beyond fifty yards even with his Coke-bottle glasses, we had clearly out-shot the Kilties and their cadets across the board.

Chapter 7

Lunch was a picnic affair, hot soup and cold sandwiches catered at the range from a mobile kitchen truck. Military picnics were no exception to the general rule, we discovered, as a large formation of dirty gray clouds moved up the valley and settled directly over the camp. The spicy scalding goulash soup was a welcome pickup, after which we sat around smoking and savouring our triumph, but I could feel the damp creeping through my bush-jacket and battledress and pitied the guys who'd worn fatigues. My only problem was going to be keeping reasonably clean. My uniform had to last at least another whole day and who knew how many parades and inspections.

Given that, I had a hunch what was coming when they marched us off after lunch to a large open field surrounded by second-growth maples and alders that had lost almost all their leaves. I nudged Ted and pointed to the ground.

"We're going down."

He nodded.

"Obviously the army's never heard that when you're down, the only way to go is up."

Sergeant Wolff had been eavesdropping from behind.

"If you fuckpots wanted to go up, you should have joined the bum-fucking Air Cadets."

We were separated from the Seaforths by a few hundred yards

and a screen of scrub, a decision by the non-coms of both groups who'd noted the deterioration of intra-service relations. The Kilties had made it plain on morning parade they resented being lumbered with a gang of undisciplined puke-sacks dressed in military motley, lowering the tone of their formations and drawing the contempt of the regulars and the wrath of the Sergeants. As an infantry regiment, they liked even less our having bested them on the firing range. They made it very clear on the march that they considered the proper duty of Sappers to be the digging of commodious latrines for the infantry. We were no happier about the arrangement. We'd rather have been with the Engineers, building a bridge or, even better, blowing something up.

With a loud display of crisp commands and ant-like energy, the Seaforths set about removing the stain on their regimental escutcheon by showing us how real infantrymen dig their own graves. After seeing us embarked reluctantly on the task of digging a lot more unnecessary holes in the ground only to have to fill them in again, Sergeants Wolff and Plante decamped to visit the rest of our Squadron at the bridge site, leaving Corporal Stevens in charge.

The weather was leaving less and less doubt about its intention to rain like a barrage. We were going to be hip-deep in mud again. Sensing the turn the weather was taking, Stevens limited himself to a brief review of the principles of foxhole construction and promptly retired to the warm dry cab of the truck parked some distance down the road, from which, he reminded us, he could maintain constant radio contact with Sergeant Wolff. I could imagine the Sergeant's delight at receiving shovel by shovel reports on the progress of a bunch of holes in the ground.

With the Corporal out of the way, our enthusiasm evaporated. Coombes stopped digging and sat on a dead log, eyeing the sky.

"It's gonna piss."

Dougie kept digging away doggedly.

"Of course it's gonna piss. It always pisses when we dig slit trenches."

Dougie was making remarkable progress in the soft soil. I dropped my shovel and lit a smoke. Ted did the same, getting a look on his face I'd learned to recognize.

"I've got an idea..."

"Uh-oh. Take cover..."

"Exactly."

He began outlining his plan as Mike McConnell and the others gathered around. The verdict was unanimous.

"It's fucking brilliant."

Only the Grahams refused to participate. Obstinately, they continued to dig their own two-man trench. The rest of us stripped off our jackets and ties and went to work on the double, one shift of the bigger guys like Dougie and Ted digging while Rob Coombes and Mike Darling filled the burlap sacks we'd been supplied with and Mike McConnell and I and some others foraged in the woods, dragging back fallen branches and dead trees, stripping them with the blades of our entrenching tools.

By the time the rain started two hours later, we'd constructed a twelve by twelve redoubt, earth-bermed, roofed over with deadwood and sandbags, complete with loopholes and slit trench entrances on both front flanks. In line with sound principles of military engineering we'd raised the interior floor a couple of inches so water would drain out instead of in. We'd even planted a few uprooted shrubs out front as a gesture to camouflage or decorative landscaping. As the rain began to slash down on the Grahams and the Seaforths in their open holes, Corporal Stevens returned to find the rest of us warm and dry, sitting on scavenged stumps, taking a smoke break in the cosy bunker. He screamed like a gutshot rabbit.

"What's this?"

Ted gave him the real estate agent tour.

"It's the Enlisted Mens Mess, Corporal...We didn't have time to build in the bar. We thought it was more important to finish your office..."

"My wha...?"

As Ted led him to the small ante-room at the back of the bunker, Stevens looked like he didn't know whether to be flattered or faint dead away from shock. Clearly visible in the dim loop-holed light, the deep central shaft in the sandbagged closet was covered by a seat constructed of pieces of old planking we'd found in the woods and neatly arranged around a central hole. The Corporal whimpered and shut his eyes.

"The Sergeants will be here any minute!"

"Incoming."

Mike McConnell came to attention on sentry duty at the door. Muddy boots were entering the redoubt. Ducking their heads, Sergeant Wolff, Sergeant Plante and the Seaforth Sergeant filed in, looking less than fresh from inspecting the flooded mud pits in which the Seaforths and the Grahams were presently wallowing. I was too cocky to keep quiet.

"Tell them to wipe their feet."

Corporal Stevens groaned for silence, giving me a look that told me he wouldn't forget or forgive. Wearing the fixed mocking smirk of a moustached Mephistopheles, Sergeant Wolff eyed the Corporal as if pondering what parts of his anatomy could be removed with a rusty bayonet for a change. Sergeant Plante, on the other hand, inspected the premises with genuine professional interest which peaked when he came to the small room Stevens was attempting to screen with his skinny body.

"What's this, Corporal?"

Stevens was evidently too overcome with modesty to answer, so Ted explained quietly.

"It's the Corporal's command post, Sergeant."

Moving Stevens aside with a twitch of his baton, Sergeant Plante peered inside. After a moment he stepped back and raised his arm in a slow formal salute to the whole section, though he addressed his remarks to Corporal Stevens, who looked like he was thinking of taking a header down the hole.

"In thirty-five years in the armed forces, I've never seen a better fortified shit-house. You may dismiss the men, Corporal."

We emerged into the rain as the Seaforths filed past in their soaked serge, caked with mud, eyes wide in grimy faces, spattered chins dangling in disbelief as they gaped at the Underground Hilton. Ted looked back at the bunker wistfully as we fell in behind the squishing infantry.

"Guess they'll make us fill it back in now..."

I grinned and nudged him, making sure the other guys heard as well.

"Nope. I heard Stevens ask Sergeant Wolff about that. He seemed kinda in a hurry to get on with it, y'know? But Wolfie said Sergeant Plante wants our C.O. and the Seaforth C.O. to see it first."

Mike McConnell and Rob Coombes stifled chuckles.

"No wonder Stevens looks like his stripes are falling off."

"I thought the Sergeant liked it..."

"If he did, you can bet that creep Stevens will find some way to take credit for the whole thing and get himself promoted to Sergeant for showing initiative."

We clambered into the trucks to be driven to the next event in the Khaki Olympics, the grenade range. After a bumpy one-cigarette ride the trucks pulled over at a T-intersection with a straight quarter mile of wide gravel path leading to a low cement block-house. As we were disembarking, Coombes realized he'd lost his tie. He'd left it hanging over the branch of a tree back at the bunker. Dougie shook him in exasperation.

"For Christ sake, Robbie! At this rate you're going to turn up for final inspection stark fucking naked! We can't go back for it now. Button your battledress all the way up and maybe nobody will notice. We'll figure something out when we get back to barracks."

We were taken in charge by Sergeant Plante and the Sergeant of the Seaforths. Corporal Stevens stayed with the truck, looking relieved to be relieved of us. Crowding into the one big room out of the drizzle, we were each issued two heavy black grenades and two fuses and ordered to rough trestle tables lining the walls to arm them. That was a fairly simple procedure we'd been taught the week before. You just unscrewed the thick threaded baseplate, inserted the fuse and threaded the plate back on. It wasn't much fun with cold fingers, but the only real difference was the knowledge that, unlike the dummies we'd practised on, these ones were filled with something a lot more volatile than sand. Once they were armed, there was nothing between us and a very final bang but the ringed metal cotter pin that held the firing lever in place. We all made sure those pins were pushed in right up to the ring.

Half a dozen at a time, we were called out to the range behind the block-house to throw these deadly things as far away from ourselves as possible. The Seaforths and their cadets went ahead of us, as usual, closely guided and monitored by range marshals from the Queens Own. They weren't taking any chances with a bunch of weekend warriors when a single mistake could result in multiple deaths and maimings. As the grenades cracked and banged beyond the heavy walls, the rest of us huddled around a small brown oil stove just inside the door of the block-house, smoking and trying to keep warm. The trestle tables displayed pair after pair of armed grenades, like fruit in a deadly bazaar.

The Seaforth Sergeant wasn't a bad guy. Around Wolfie's age, he'd been in the regular Army in '51 and gone to Korea with the UN peace-keeping forces. He was regaling us with tales of how they used to keep warm in their foxholes by smuggling girls in from nearby villages when Mike Darling finally finished arming his grenades and joined us. Reaching out as if to warm his hands, he placed his two grenades, stuffed with gunpowder and now fuses, on top of the stove and blithely spread his fingers to catch the heat.

I experienced the longest instant of my short life.

Conversation ceased in mid-syllable. Mouths opened silently. Eyebrows rose with agonizing slowness as we all stood still in a cosy circle warming our hands in front of two rapidly poaching live bombs. Darling looked bewildered by the abrupt silence, like a man suspected of farting in mixed company.

With what I'm sure was really only a split-second's hesitation, the Seaforth Sergeant scooped up the grenades and dashed outside to fling them into the shallow ditch beside the path. He may have shouted "Fire in the hole!" or something appropriate. I didn't notice. His action freed us all from paralysis and we were occupied with flattening ourselves against walls and flinging ourselves under the flimsy tables, which resulted in half a dozen more grenades rolling off and bouncing loudly and ominously on the concrete floor as we winced and cringed.

There probably wasn't any real danger. It would have taken more than the faint heat from that stove to set off the grenades. It was just the idea. The Seaforth Sergeant stared at Darling in speechless disbelief, too unnerved even to be angry. He shook his head ponderously, like a man in deep shock.

"You guys...You really are..."

"A bunch of fuckpots?"

We dissolved in hysterical laughter and insane giggles.

At that moment, another lot of us were called to throw. Around the back of the block-house there was a low cement wall divided into individual stalls, each fitted with a thick small window of perspex through which the explosion could be viewed from a sensibly prone position. The drill was to pull the pin on command with the fingers of the left hand—not the teeth, as we were reminded for the umpteenth time—toss the grenade into a trench littered with old tires about thirty feet ahead, then dive down to watch the quick yellow flash as it exploded.

It was kind of disappointing, really. The sound was more of a sharp flat crack than a satisfying destructive boom. We'd been told the base-plate was the single most dangerous part of the schrapnel casing since it tended to remain in one piece. Occasionally one would whistle threateningly overhead and strike a whining ricochet off the blank back wall of the block-house.

I stepped into my stall, leaving one grenade on the sill provided. Sergeant Plante stood directly behind me, which may have made me nervous. I got the pin out without fumbling, but when I approached the wall I forgot everything I'd been taught, squeezing the lever to the bomb like I was trying to get juice out of the thing, terrified I might drop it at my feet, and when I finally did throw it, I tossed it at the trench like a baseball. Thrown that way, the weight of the grenade causes an instantly agonizing jolt of tendonitis in the elbow and the bomb becomes a lot more dangerous to the person who threw it than the intended recipient. Grabbing my elbow I groaned and stood watching, fascinated, as the small black egg dropped and bounced dead well short of the trench which was supposed to focus the blast up and away.

Then I seemed to be hit from behind by a tank. I looked up, stunned, in time to glimpse the bright flash through the perspex and hear the block-house whipped by a lash of steel. I had trouble getting my breath, I realized, because Sergeant Plante was lying on top of me. It took me about two seconds to appreciate that if he hadn't flattened me I'd have been perforated from the waist up by a handful of hot splinters of steel. He accepted my breathless thanks with a stony silence broken only by a reminder to keep my throwing arm stiff next time.

While we were dusting ourselves off, the Seaforth Sergeant rushed around the corner of the block-house, trying not to laugh out loud.

"Who threw that one?"

Every eye turned to me.

"Nice shot. Half the schrapnel and the tail-plate went right over the block-house. Some of it hit your truck. We could see the canvas jump like somebody was beating a rug. That asshole Corporal of yours was out having a smoke. He's face down in the ditch right now, waving a white handkerchief."

Chapter 8

We were a lot more popular at dinner than we had been at breakfast. The rest of the Squadron stopped pretending we were a penal battalion and saved us a table near them in the Mess Hall. Some of them even spoke to us. Gossip gets around faster in an army camp than a high school girls washroom. They'd heard about us out-shooting the Kilties and about the miniature Maginot Line. They'd especially heard about us nearly ventilating Corporal Stevens and causing his dive into a muddy ditch. Whispered congratulations passed down the chow line.

Dougie crashed the line, slipping in between Rob Coombes and I with a sly wink. As Coombes turned, Dougie slipped a green noose over his head and slid the knot tight, closing his collar. With a flick of his wrist he stuffed the tail of the tie down the front of Rob's battle-dress tunic.

"Try not to lose it again."

Coombes looked down, gratitude spreading across his face like sunshine.

"You found my tie!"

"Shhh! It's not your tie, so shut the fuck up."

"Whose is it?"

Dougie sighed.

"It was Corporal Stevens. Now it's yours. You never lost yours. You don't know anything. Right?"

I grinned at Dougie as we shuffled past the steaming cauldrons of gloriously hot food.

"How'd you snatch it?"

"Stevens was in the shower, trying to get the mud off. He left his dirty uniform on the bed in the Corporal's room by the barracks door. I just slipped in on my way out and swiped the tie. He's over at the camp laundry now. He'll probably think he dropped on the way or something."

I heaped both our plates with fluffy mounds of mashed potato and saluted him with the sticky ladle.

"You're a born commando. A fucking military genius..."

Two minutes later, Corporal Stevens stormed into the Mess Hall, his collar conspicuously open, staring at our throats like he might be thinking of cutting one or two, but he stormed back out again without saying anything. Mike McConnell paused between shovelling spoonfulls of stew into his face.

"What's with Stevens?"

I managed not to smirk as Dougie and I exchanged winks.

"Beats me, but I think he ought to set a better example for us than to come in to dinner improperly dressed."

After dinner we were more or less confined to barracks. The rain was coming down on full automatic. The Enlisted Mens Mess on the base would only admit and serve those of us who could produce ID proving we were eighteen or over. The civilian drinking age was still twenty-one, but it was eighteen in the military on the sensible principle that if you were old enough to die in a uniform you were old enough to disgrace it. But on no account was our Squadron's customary slight bending of the rule going to be tolerated in the real Army, Corporal Stevens assured us as he left the barracks, accompanied by the Graham twins, to drink up our shares of the army's beer. He knew most of us were just under eighteen. He couldn't stop peering at our necks though.

Having failed one grade in elementary school, Mike McConnell was just past his eighteenth birthday. In the interest of recruit morale, he was going to stay with us, but we all urged him to go have a few and smuggle us out a couple of brews if he could. There was no tv in the barracks, not even a radio. Those things, along with pool and ping-pong tables, checkers, crokinole and darts, were available in the Recreation Facility. We'd looked in on the way back from dinner and found it full of Seaforth cadets sucking on Cokes. Having informed them that cartoons didn't come on tv at that time of night, we settled into our drab prison for what looked like a very quiet evening.

At least it looked like it until Rob Coombes finally discovered his missing Graveyard, which had crept into one of those useless heavy canvas musette bags none of us knew what to do with. There was a full twenty-six ounces of brownish, poisonous-looking liquid in there and our hangovers had abated sufficiently that it almost appeared fit for human consumption. Ted and I had been quietly lamenting our decision not to bring a few joints along.

"What d'you think?"

"Beats Pepsi, potato chips and ping-pong."

Dougie slipped back to the Rec hut to pick up a few Cokes to cut it with. In no time, things in the barracks were looking livelier. The official army ashtrays were big hammered steel things the size of hubcaps. Dougie discovered that one of them would slide across the polished floor like an ice cube on a sheet of hot glass. He and I started kicking it back and forth as a joke. Without commands or discussions, teams began to form as others joined in. Bunks were dragged away from the walls at either end of the long room to form goals. An improvised bar was set up on a windowsill out of the line of fire.

The game was a cross between hockey, rugby and the old schoolyard standby, British Bulldog. There were no rules. Nothing was out of bounds or out of play. There were injuries but no substitutions and no time-outs. No quarter was asked or given. Blood from split lips and noses mingled on the floor with spilled Coke and booze. We fought over and under intervening bunks, down the central alley and in and out of the big tiled latrine, recharging our drinks as play continued. Score was kept in ballpoint on the barracks wall, ranks of scratched lines that looked like a diagram of a Recruit Section parade.

We were still at it when a couple of Seaforth heads emerged from the latrine doorway.

"If you guys don't knock it off we'll call the MPs! We're trying to sleep! Reveille is at oh-six-hundred, you know!"

We had to show them we could talk military too.

"Bandits at twelve-o-clock high!"

The big ashtray, by now smashed completely out of shape, hit the latrine door like a round from a German 88. The heads withdrew, but the furious pounding on the door continued. Dougie Trumbull gave himself a battlefield commission and took command.

"Charge!!!"

We charged as one man. Pushing them back all the way through their own door to the common latrine with the initial overwhelming force of our assault, we took advantage of the time they wasted whining to their Lance-Corporal to drag a spare double bunk into the latrine and jam it solidly against their door from the inside, wedging blankets and doorstops at strategic points.

"Let 'em piss their beds."

"I wonder if Sergeant Plante'll want the C.O. to see this too..."

The pounding on the door was getting too loud in the latrine, so we returned to the barracks to pick up the game, but we were running low on fuel. There was a glassy clink from the doorway and we suspected a sneak attack from next door until Mike McConnell staggered in with almost half a dozen bottles of beer bulging various pockets like contraband artillery rounds.

"Reinforcements!"

We whacked him on the back with the enthusiasm of surrounded Legionaires greeting the relief column. He began handing stubby bottles around to be shared. I took advantage of the diversion to kick the battered ashtray the length of the room and between Coombes startled legs for a goal.

"So how's the real army?"

Mike was clearly having some trouble maintaining a military posture.

"Ish great...Great guysh...Ish so great I'm gonna join up..."

"What?"

I tried to focus on his face and keep my beer upright as Dougie plowed through us, ashtray in hand, to fling it against the far wall for the equalizer. He knocked Mike sideways onto a bunk and me on my ass on the floor. Neither of us spilled a drop. We could drink like real troopers if nothing else. Mike nodded seriously. He sounded like he was talking through a sock in his mouth.

"Yeah...I's talkin' to some guys from the Queens Own in the Mesh...Sergeant Plante's 'er too. They invited him. He's a good guy, y'know? I mean, he's laughin' about some of the stuff we been doin', but he's not really mad at ush, I don't think...Nobody likes those Seaforth fuckers. They think their shit don' stink..."

"They'll find out different later on tonight."

"Wha?"

"Never mind. What's this shit about joining up? You didn't sign anything didya?"

I had a mental picture of us pulling out at the end of the weekend and leaving Mike shackled in the custody of a burly MP because he'd signed for a twenty year hitch. Maybe these training weekends were just a front for some secret press-gang recruitment scam run by the regular army out of its Mess, plying unsuspecting Militiamen with drink and the persuasive blandishments of sauve Sergeants.

"S'true...Soon as school's over...I'm joinin' in the regs..."

I was having trouble sitting up, but I didn't think I could let this pass without an argument.

"Have you flipped, man? You want to spend years of your life in places like this?...This is like fuckin' prison, except you get paid, and the pay is shit...It's fuckin' awful here. Gettin' up at six in the morning. Digging holes all day and filling them in. Marching. Drilling. Polishing brass then blacking it over. Being called a fuckpot by morons whose only claim is some birdshit on their shoulders. It's totally uncool, man...I mean, if you want to join up that bad, go to university on the ROTP and come in as an officer. Pays better and..."

Mike looked deeply offended.

"Don' wanna be a fuckin' officer...Just wanna be inna infantry. A reg'lar enlisted guy..."

Ted lifted his legs as the ashtray zinged under the bunk we were sitting on.

"Hey, Jack. If he's figured out what he wants to do, maybe we should just let him do his own thing, y'know?"

Doing Your Own Thing was still a very new concept and I was-n't entirely clear on what it entailed. The trickiest part seemed to be figuring out what your Thing was. I shrugged reluctantly. Mike grinned and shook hands solemnly with both of us.

"Thanks, guys. I wanted to tell you guys, even before I tol' my folks, 'cause you're like, my best friends, y'know?"

He stretched out on the bunk, still in jeans and windbreaker, and dropped into a satisfied sleep. Ted and I half-heartedly rejoined the game, but after a goal-mouth scramble in which I caught a fat lip we took refuge on the top bunks in a corner of the barracks.

"D'you think he's serious?"

"About enlisting? Or about us being his best friends?"

"Both, I guess."

I was glad Ted noticed that too. Friendship meant something new and special to us, something adult, different from the neigh-bourhood alliances of childhood. Ted had lived on the outer invisible edge of my neighbourhood since we were kids, but we'd hung out together only sporadically. He attended Holy Trinity, a Catholic school over on Lonsdale, and usually hung out with kids who lived further down the hill. We palled around for a while just after my father's death when I was thirteen, but then I went into junior high and he was sent to Vancouver College, the Catholic high school downtown, and his parents moved over to the other side of Lonsdale.

In junior high my childhood friends and classmates were immediately polarized into one of two opposing camps we called Greaseballs and Hersheys. Greaseball guys wore black pointed shoes, knife-creased gray flannel slacks, expensive sweaters and spent a lot of time in the school washroom smoking and combing their Bryl-creemed hair in imitation of Elvis, to whom they listened along with Dion & The Belmonts, The Everlys, The Righteous Brothers and James Brown. I liked their music, but their idea of a good time was to drink vast quantities of beer and go out looking for fights. After a few cartilage-crushing punches in the nose and gut-churning kicks in the nuts, I decided this was a limited form of entertainment. Their girls, like Nasty, dressed as much like whores as they could without getting expelled, but unless you had a car or a rep as a tough guy, you couldn't even get a hand-job.

The Greaseballs opposite numbers were called Hersheys because they imitated everything American, specifically Californian, which was the only part of the U.S. that counted. They wore Bleeding Madras short-sleeve shirts and sleeveless pullovers, white jeans and white socks in penny loafers. They listened to surf music, Jan and Dean and The Beach Boys and they didn't dance The Dog. Their girls were cute in that well-scrubbed cheerleader way, like Irene Beaumont, but when the lights went down the furthest you were going to get with them was "Don't. I'm not that kind of girl," unless you were on the varsity team.

People I knew in both camps reacted with equal horror when I mentioned drugs or confessed to liking the new British rock bands, like The Rolling Stones, who were just breaking into the AM radio charts. Having washed the grease out of my hair and let it start to grow, not to mention walking away from a fight with a former pal who challenged me over this bizarre behaviour, I was out with the Greaseballs and the Hersheys wouldn't have me. I hated surf music anyway.

The rest of high school was stretching before me like a prison sentence served in solitary when Ted blundered back into my life and my English class on a transfer. Dressed in an eccentric ensemble of black jeans, motorcycle boots and a paisley shirt topped off with an ascot scarf of all fucking things, when the teacher asked him his name he thought the question over for half a minute before answering. I had a hunch we were going to be friends. He always maintained the faintly amused expression of an idiot saint, even when the toughest greaseballs in school tried to beat him up. He'd stand there, refusing to lose his temper, smiling distantly at the flurry of feet and fists coming at him, then he'd just grab the guy, toss him into the bushes and wait for him to get up without even trying to stomp him while he was down. Finally when they were puffed out, scuffed and dirty they'd gasp, "You had enough?" like they'd given him the whipping of his life. Ted would smile.

"Yeah. I guess so."

Only I knew why he smiled and why he never gave any of those mincing, pompadoured closet-faggot thugs the shit-kickings they deserved. He hadn't been transferred. He was expelled from Vancouver City College. One of his classmates made fun of his name and called him a Nazi on the school bus. Ted lost his temper and beat the kid half to death at the back of the bus before the driver could pull over and restrain him. Ted told me that when he realized what he'd done and that he would have kept punching and kicking the boy until he really was dead if the driver hadn't stopped him, he'd vowed never to lose his temper ever again.

After the fights, I'd hand him his jacket and we'd walk up the hills, talking about how stupid school was, about Zen, Hermann Hesse, Camus, Sartre, reincarnation, rock and roll and the meaning of life. Both of us had felt that sense of being terribly alone, of thinking thoughts nobody seemed to have thought before, that loneliness which makes adolescents such slaves to fashion and ruthless persecutors of the eccentric. We'd both reacted to not fitting in with the crowd by thumbing our noses at it in different ways.

Neither of us had ever talked about these things with Mike McConnell. He was just another one of the slowly growing crowd of outcasts, the mis-matched gang of incipient hipsters and failed hoods who hung around at The Wanda Inn Cafe on Lonsdale or in Carisbrooke Park, sharing lemon gin, joints of hard to get Mexican weed and splitting the odd expensive hit of LSD four ways. He may have overheard some of our long talks over coffee or in the park, but I couldn't recall him ever participating. Both of us were a little embarrassed about the way he'd included himself in an intimacy we'd thought was private. We both thought he was a good guy, but we didn't think of him the way we thought of each other and we were quiet for awhile, trying to see our relationship from this new third angle.

"Y'know, I think revolutionizing the Army's going to be tougher than we thought."

Ted nodded, looking over at the sleeping Mike McConnell.

"At least, we're not at war with anybody. I mean, it's weird to think that just down in Seattle guys our age are doing the same things we're doing this weekend, but when it's over, they're going to Vietnam to do it for real."

"Yeah. Maybe we should split this scene before it revolutionizes us."

We didn't have time for further reflection because Sergeant Wolff stomped in, a glassy-eyed Corporal Stevens in tow, and ordered every dirtbag fuckpot into his fart-sack and lights out in thirty seconds. He mentioned that liquor in the barracks was a serious offence on the base, ordered the immediate removal of the barricade in the latrine and promised that one drop of puke on the floor in the morning would cause us all to scrub the entire barracks with our toothbrushes.

We obeyed with only token groans, most of us too worn out by the game and the day in the fresh air anyway. After lights out, we barely had strength left to plant the empty whiskey and beer bottles under a bunk just inside the door of the snore-filled Seaforth barracks. Finally it was all we could do to stay awake long enough to slip the sleeping Corporal Stevens limp dangling hand into a mess tin full of lukewarm water in the hope he'd pee the bed.

CHAPTER 9

Our Sunday morning parade was only marginally less raggedy-ass than Saturdays. Corporal Stevens was in an especially savage mood. He hadn't peed the bed, but he had gotten up in the middle of the night badly needing the latrine and stepped in the pan of water. Coombes still had no beret, so we all wore fatigues and forage caps to camouflage the fact. We couldn't steal one of the Grahams, they'd figure that, and we couldn't cop a hat from the Seaforths because they wore those damn tams and Glengarrys.

After another immense breakfast, we were marched to the obstacle course. It was called the Assault Training Facility or something equally military, but it was just a bunch of ditches to be jumped, walls to be vaulted, netting to be climbed, ropes to be swung from and, of course, mud to be crawled through. The Seaforths were revving their engines like street-draggers. They were going to knock us into the ditches, hang us in the netting and make us lick the mud off their boots. Mike McConnell eyed them as they warmed up by doing fifty jumping-jacks in perfect unison.

"Here's where we get creamed."

I was in no mood to countenance defeatism after our unexpected triumphs of the day before. We couldn't quit now. Forget the C.O. huffing and puffing about "his boys" in the Officers Mess and actually coming out to see us parade this morning, forget the Sergeants secret joy at seeing the infantry mocked by a gang of fuckpots, forget the good wishes of the Engineers, who promised to teach us to blow things up if we could contrive to kill or seriously wound our own Corporal. We just couldn't roll over and take a shit-kicking from this bunch of toy soldiers.

"Bullshit. I saw you jump a six foot fence without touching it, crawl through a culvert and outrun a German Shepherd and two cops the night they busted the party up at the park. You telling me this is tougher than the course we ran that night? Shit, just pretend the cops are after us and we've got it beat."

Every one of us, with the possible exception of Darling, knew what it was to hurtle at flank speed through familiar neighbourhoods hearing the steady thud of those big cop boots coming on behind, jumping fences and hedges blind, praying no starved Doberman was waiting on the other side. Most of us also had the advantage of cross-country training in high school, which taught us to make the best use of available cover, deception, and unauthorized shortcuts down creekbeds and ravines which could be parlayed into a liesurely smoke break in the bush somewhere before emerging to tag on to the rear of the straggling wheezing class and finishing the run without attracting suspicion or breaking a sweat. We took the course in a breeze. The Seaforths naturally accused us of tripping, holding, elbowing, gouging and outright cheating. All perfectly true, but as they say, all's fair in love and war. I sensed the Sergeants were getting weary of their whining anyway.

The final event of the morning was a race in six-man inflatable commando canoes across the neck of a small lake a few hundred yards from where our Engineer Section was completing their bridge. Corporal Stevens divided us into two crews, while the Seaforths and cadets made up a dozen. Surreptitiously, we shuffled the teams to put Dougie, Ted, Mike McConnell and I in the same boat. The Grahams rounded out our six, not because we revised our opinion of them but because they were so totally gung-ho. Coombes didn't like being left on the clown boat with Mike Darling and the like, but he knew we were up to something so he kept his mouth shut for a change.

As we prepared to launch, eyed by glowering Kilties, I was glad we'd opted for fatigues. The boats were awkward craft with stiffened keels and rubbery sides. We were going to get very wet and cold this time, sunny morning or not. Gripping the side handles in one hand and paddles in the other, we hurled ourselves on command into the freezing lake, howling like Apaches.

The soggy near-capsize boggle we made of boarding stalled whatever momentum we'd gained by taking a run at it. Luckily, the Seaforths weren't doing any better. Several of their boats actually did turn turtle in the shallows while the rest of the fleet floundered, their flailing paddles thrashing the water to a useless froth. As soon as we got everybody paddling in the same direction, straining to keep to the cadence Dougie was calling, we began to gain on the one Seaforth boat which escaped the melee and was pulling strongly for the far shore.

At the halfway point, they started looking over their shoulders, which cost them a stroke or two. From the far bank, shouts reached us as the Engineers stopped work and gathered to cheer us on. Whether we caught up now or not, it was worth it just to hear those guys, the real Sappers who'd pretended they didn't know us two nights ago, screaming for us. As I plunged my paddle in the swirling foam again and again I knew we weren't going to win. My shoulders would pop out of their burning sockets or my lungs would collapse first, but it felt wonderful to be alive at that moment on the water in the cold autumn sunshine.

"Stroke! Stroke! Stroke!"

Dougie was getting hoarse as the two canoes almost collided fifty yards from the shore. The race forgotten, there was a flurry of paddles and punches as the rival crews grappled, each trying to push the others gunwales under water. One of the Grahams actually punched a Seaforth who'd almost dragged me overboard, causing him to let go and cup his bloody nose in both hands.

"Thanks."

"Don't mention it."

In the corner of my eye, the sun caught on something bright in Mike McConnell's hand for an instant as he reached across to grab their stern and spin their boat away from ours. The canoe was taking water, making it heavy and sluggish as we struggled to regain our stroke. It wasn't until we were within a few yards of shore and the cheers were deafening that I realized we actually were going to win. I looked over my shoulder in time to see the Seaforth canoe going down by the stern twenty yards back as most of the crew abandoned ship and swam for it, leaving two paddlers in the bows hopelessly whacking the water until it rose to their chests.

Our second crew, Coombes, Mike Darling and the other clowns, beached their boat about the time the cheering and hat-tossing stopped and the Sergeants started listening to the protests from the Seaforths. They'd dragged their boat ashore, half-deflated and waterlogged, and were pointing out the large clean rip in the stern. There was a conference of non-commissioned heads.

Glowering, Sergeant Wolff ordered the Recruit Section to form ranks. Reluctantly he requested we turn out our pockets. I noticed he didn't make it an order. As we all complied, he inspected us, tapping the cargo pockets of our fatigues with his baton. When he finished this odd inspection, having turned up nothing more than a lot of soggy smokes, he turned to Sergeant Plante and shook his head, telling us to re-stuff ourselves. A microscopic smile lurked under his moustache.

Sergeant Plante answered with a nod of resignation, cocking his head in our direction, his lips pursed in thought. Then he let rip with a real Army top-kick blast of thunder so fierce we nearly peed our pants, not that anyone would have noticed, we were so wet.

"Sergeant Wolff! Inform your men that willful damage to Canadian Armed Forces property is a subject on which I have strong opinions and no tolerance whatever! Now, DIS-MISS!"

We were invited to inspect the bridge our Engineers had built. It looked like a big green Meccano set to me, but we were duly impressed. We'd have been more impressed if they'd blown it up to celebrate our victory, but you couldn't have everything. I managed to get close enough to Mike McConnell for a confidential whisper.

"What did you do with the jack-knife?"

He gave me a look a cop would walk a mile to slap off his face and broke into a mischievious grin.

"It slipped out of my hand in the water. Cold fingers. Lucky, eh? It's on the bottom of the lake."

After we were trucked back to barracks we were ordered to

change into battledress for lunch, then parade in full equipment, helmets and packs included, which meant Sergeant Wolff had to help most of us untangle and put on our webbing. I felt sorry for him. He looked like a man trying to dress a dozen kids for school.

"You fuckpots can button your own flies, I assume?"

Ever the smartass, I couldn't resist making a crack about defective army equipment, a covert reference to the canoe incident, while he was adjusting my harness. With a quick snap of his wrists he drew the webbing so tight across my chest I couldn't inhale and lifted me an inch or two off the floor. I had a superb view of his upper sinuses.

"Listen up, you mouthy fuckpots! If I ever find out which one of you cut that boat I'll peel the skin off his arse with a hot bayonet and use it to patch the fucking hole! Do you read me loud and clear?"

"Yes, Sergeant!"

Thank God the boys answered in unison, because I didn't have enough air left to croak. He lowered me to the floor and released my diaphragm just before I passed out. The Sergeant wasn't finished.

"I want this exercise to go as smooth as a fuck with a fifty year old whore. If there's just one more screw-up, one more complaint, one more piece of lost or damaged equipment, I'll turn the fuckpot responsible over to the military authorities here on the base for disposition. If I get my ass reamed one more time on your account, I promise you none of you will shit straight for the rest of your miserable lives."

He punctuated his address with an unmistakeable gesture of his thick, heavy baton.

The afternoon entertainment was to be nothing less than full war-games. Trucked and marched to the foot of a wooded slope beyond a clearing in the forest, we were told to dig in and defend a position against an attack by infantry, the Seaforth Highlanders again. We unshipped our entrenching tools once more, moaning grumpily.

"Why can't they dig the goddamn holes and let us attack? Why do we always wind up digging fucking holes?"

Ted interrupted the muttering chorus to address Corporal Stevens directly.

"Hold it guys...Corporal? May I make a suggestion?"

Stevens hesitated. A lot of his insufferable superiority had ebbed away over the last two days. Once again, while the Sergeants umpired, he'd been left alone in command of a bunch of little bastards who'd humiliated him in front of the regular army, probably stolen his tie, tried to make him pee the bed and attempted to murder him with a grenade. I don't think he'd forgiven us for constructing that Corporal's command post in the bunker either. On the other hand, we'd come up winners all weekend and he'd been a loser all his life. You could almost see the little imp on his shoulder whispering to him to go for it, be on the winning side for once, be one of the boys, while Ted outlined his plan.

"Alright...Since we're outnumbered, the use of special tactics seems justified..."

Going to it with a will, we quickly constructed a replica of the bunker, the infamous Underground Hilton, at the foot of the hill, right down to the shrubs in front. It looked like a suburban fallout shelter, but it was actually only a solid mound of dirt, dressed up with dummy loop-holes from which sticks protruded prominently. The dirt for the fake redoubt was excavated from a number of deepish pits dug on the flanks and forward approaches. These were roofed over with branches, leaves and a light covering of soil. We brushed out our tracks, scattering dead leaves behind us, then backed into the trees, taking cover on the hill above and sending Dougie and Mike McConnell out on the two flanks as scouts.

We'd barely finished our smokes when Dougie re-appeared in the evergreen shadows, pointing to the far side of the clearing. A moment later we saw the Seaforth point men in camo jackets, daubs of war-paint on their cheeks, sneaking around in the scrub. From where we hid, they looked eerily like the real thing and I wondered briefly if this was how it looked before a fight in the jungles across the Pacific. I had to remind myself their guns weren't loaded either. The scouts faded back into the woods to report our position.

A few minutes later, they made their approach just the way Ted predicted, one small squad spread out across the clearing to draw our fire while the rest moved through the flanking woods like herds of bulls in a china factory. Corporal Stevens clutched his Sten in anticipation. He looked like he might actually be enjoying himself.

Why the Seaforths didn't twig when there was no challenge from the redoubt raises serious questions about the calibre of those who stand on guard for thee. They must've thought we actually were such dumb shits that we'd build the same fortification we'd built the day before then all retire for our afternoon naps or something. At a whistled signal, they charged, their main forces bursting from the flanks in a pincer movement converging on the bunker to go down in one single stupid wave as they plunged into the man-traps protecting the phoney fort. Their war cries turned to screams and yowls of pain as they tumbled into the hidden ditches on top of each other, twisting ankles and banging heads.

Led by Corporal Stevens, we broke cover and counter-charged, shouting "Bang! Bang!" for all we were worth, the Corporal going "Ratatatatat!" like something off the cover of a *True War Stories* comic. The Kilties took it badly, of course, scrambling out of the holes with blood in their eyes, some quite literally. We squared off, pushing and shoving, calling each other things our mothers would have paled to hear.

"I told you we should've put sharp stakes in the pits..."

A couple of punches and a rifle butt stroke or two were exchanged. We looked to be in trouble, since we were outnumbered, when the Kilties Lance-Corporal tripped Stevens down and was about to put the boots to him. That was when Mike Darling pulled his bayonet with a steely rasp that stopped everyone dead in their tracks. He stuck the point of eight inches or so of sharp steel under the chin of the astonished Lance-Corporal and did a very credible impersonation of Sergeant Wolff.

"You're under arrest! I charge you with assaulting a superior non-commissioned officer and insulting the Queens uniform! If you touch him again I'll cut your gizzard out and feed it to the fucking crows!"

We were as dumbfounded as the Kilties. Mike Darling? The fuckpot Stevens had personally tried to persecute into quitting the Squadron? Threatening a Highland company with a naked blade? Darling, who'd probably stab himself in the ass with the damn thing if somebody didn't take it away from him right smartly?

Still, for a second there he'd sounded just enough like the real thing for it to stick until Sergeant Plante's whistle ripped across our eardrums. Stepping into our midst over the supine Stevens, he took Darling's bayonet from his unresisting hand and inserted it back into the scabbard with a sharp snap. He gave the Seaforth Lance-Corporal a look that would make a King Cobra curl up and bite itself.

"I'll remind you all just once more that while you are on this base you are subject to Military Law...My law...This exercise is now complete, with a tactical victory for the 15th Field Squadron of Royal Canadian Engineers...Recruit section! Now, dismiss!"

As the Seaforths gathered their gear and slunk away, claimed by their head-shaking Sergeant, we filled in the pits and dismantled the fake bunker. Sergeant Plante waited until the Kilties were out of earshot to address us privately. His granite face looked like it might actually be capable of a smile under the right circumstances.

"Gentlemen, I wish to thank you for a most interesting two days. However, there is one small favour I would ask. If you are considering a career in the Canadian Armed Forces, please give serious consideration to the many excellent opportunities offered by the Air Force and the Navy. Above all, do not enlist in the Army. I will sleep better at nights."

I looked around to catch Mike McConnell's eye, but I couldn't see him anywhere. In fact, I suddenly couldn't recall seeing him since he went out to scout the right flank before the Seaforth attack. I nudged Ted.

"You seen McConnell?"

He shook his head and we both looked around. Mike McConnell was absolutely not there. We looked up at the wooded ridge, shining gold and green in the late afternoon sun.

"Shit. Now what do we do?"

Ted stepped out of the olive drab crowd.

"Sergeant Plante?...I believe we may have a man missing in action."

Chapter 10

The autumn afternoon was fading fast and there was a deepening chill in the air and in our uniforms as the clearing filled up with men. The Seaforths had been marched back and a detachment of the Queens Own called in from the firing range to lead us over ground they knew and we didn't. The Sergeant let us go to the foot of the hill and call Mike, but we were ordered to stay out of the trees. He didn't want any more of us getting lost, I guess.

Divided into squads led by non-coms and ranks from the regulars, we were warned the ground was difficult and told to keep short spacing, never to lose sight of the men to either side. The light was going and we would probably only have time for one sweep before it got too dark. We indicated Mike's probable direction to Sergeant Plante and he pursed his lips in that way he had. I quickly saw why. The country we found ourselves thrashing through was like the woods behind the Armoury, a maze of intersecting small ravines choked with second growth and brambles. There were a lot of hidden unexpected drops where the banks of ravines had eroded.

It was fitting, I suppose, that it was our group, led by Sergeant Wolff and a Corporal of the Queens Own, who found Mike at last. He was lying on some loose rock twenty or thirty feet below one of those scrub-screened cliffs and we didn't have to be professional soldiers to know he was dead. It was nothing like war movies where the dead always lie in dramatic poses of heroic sacrifice. Mike lay in the impossibly awkward attitude of the real dead, like a collapsed puppet or a doll wrenched by a child in a tantrum.

I didn't see his face. It was already turned toward the earth, as though death was one of those secrets of life he had learned and decided to keep to himself. Sergeant Wolff took off his own bush jacket and laid it over Mike's head and upper body as tenderly as a father drawing the covers up around a delinquent sleeping son. Then he stood up and blew three sharp blasts on his whistle, shattering the shocked silence under the trees.

We were ordered to fan out and police the area, to immediately find Mike's FN rifle, then to form a cordon around the site. At the time I thought Sergeant Wolff was brusque, even callous about the way he snapped us out of it and put us to work, though I noticed he didn't call us fuckpots for once. He simply treated us like men, like real soldiers, for the first time and we acted accordingly. In doing so we learned something, not just that life goes on, but that actually dying, like being born, is only an occasion of cosmic importance for the person doing it. For the rest of us, it's just another event, full of motions to be gone through, responsibilities to be accepted, duties to be performed.

Dougie found Mike's rifle in some bracken and turned it over to the Sergeant. Our cordon formed, we were permitted to Stand At Ease and smoke. As I lit up, a glint of silver on dark blue winked up out of the shadows at my feet. It was Mike's beret. I bent over and picked it up. Instead of turning it in to the Sergeant, I stuffed it quickly into my battledress jacket without saying anything. Nobody saw me. As soon as the rest of the search parties were out of the woods, we were replaced by the professionals of the Queens Own. Nobody said anything as we rode back to the barracks in the drafty trucks. Ted and I sat across from each other in silence, but I knew we were both thinking about what Mike had said the night before, how he'd confided in us and called us his best friends.

Dinner was a dismal affair without Mike's hollow leg to joke about. The regulars and the Seaforths were respectfully subdued. For a guy who was nobody special, Mike seemed to have left a bigger hole in our lives than he'd occupied while he was alive. The dead often do.

My father had died when I was thirteen, but a parent looms so large in your life, perspective is impossible. Mike's death was the first time I realized that the memory of a person really could be larger than the individual.

We had to parade in full dress kit after dinner to be dismissed from the base. Rob Coombes kept pacing nervously near the bunk where I was arranging my kit.

"What the fuck's the matter now?"

"My beret! I still can't find it and we have to parade in five minutes!."

I remembered Mike's beret, stuffed into my kitbag, and dug it out. He whipped it on with wide-eyed gratitude. It fit him as sloppily as his own.

"You found it!"

"Yeah...I found it under a bench in one of the trucks. I meant to give it to you before, but I guess I was thinking about something else..."

"Yeah. I know."

He touched the beret again, just to make sure it was really there on his head.

We looked better on our way out than we had coming in, not that it would have taken much improvement to achieve that effect, but I thought so and Sergeant Plante seemed to feel the same. His final address to our last full parade was short and to the point. He congratulated the Recruit Section in particular on its performance during the training exercises and expressed, on behalf of the Queens Own Rifles, the regiments condolences on the loss of one of our comrades.

"We think of casualties as only occurring in time of war...But any time any person dies in this uniform we are proud to wear, they have died for you and I and for every other citizen of this nation. In doing so, they have died for something not only greater than themselves, but greater than all of us."

Then he stepped back a pace, came to attention and saluted us. A couple of the Seaforth cadets looked like they needed their noses wiped. Mine could have done with a good hard blow, for that matter.

It's confusing to be moved by feelings you think are fundamentally a load of shit. It's like crying over sentimental songs, being aroused by pornography or stirred by the speeches of Hitler. Mike had told us he'd talked to Sergeant Plante in the Mess the night before. I wondered if the Sergeant even realized he was talking about the same boy, if he'd remembered this was the boy who wanted to enlist in the regular Army. It didn't matter. Mike had gotten his wish. He'd lived his last moments and died in the uniform he wanted to wear. The Army had him now and forever.

The long quiet ride back was as close as most of us would ever come to returning from a war. It was like coming home to a world we'd forgotten, a world that had forgotten us. It didn't seem possible that we were going to get up and go to high school in the morning. Our dismissal at the Armoury was brief. The C.O., who we'd barely glimpsed all weekend, advised us we would be notified concerning funeral arrangements for Sapper McConnell. The Wrenette hall was dark and Ted and I rode the truck up the hill, getting off early to walk part of the way home together, both of us wanting to say something about Mike but neither of us having known him well enough to have anything much to say.

There was no parade the following week. Instead the entire Squadron attended Mike McConnell's funeral at the North Vancouver Cemetary Chapel on Lillooet Road. It was officially a civilian funeral, at his parents request. You could hardly blame them for wanting to take back their son from the army that had killed him, at least for this final saddest act of parenthood. They had agreed to allow the Squadron to attend in uniform and to have the coffin draped with the flag, but that caused a bit of a screw-up because the country had a new flag as of the year before. The red maple leaf thing the government had spent an entire year arguing about now dangled from the Armoury flagstaff, looking like an airline company logo. Most people, especially old soldiers, hated it and there weren't enough of the new flags around yet for the Squadron to have a spare for funerals. So Mike's coffin was draped with the old Red Ensign, which made everybody happier and he may well have been the last Canadian soldier ever buried under that flag.

The minister was a nice young guy, but he'd obviously never seen Mike with his eyes open. The eulogy consisted of the kind of platitudes about troubled youth and the need for direction and understanding that were coming into fashion among adult do-gooders. It was an odd speech to a bunch of boys in uniform, but I guess he hadn't had much practise reading a crowd.

I didn't see anybody from school who wasn't in the Squadron, though word had got around among the outcasts Mike hung out with. Even in that small group, most people reacted by saying "Mike who?..." and frowning, remembering with a vague "Oh yeah" that was slow in coming. It was starting to look to me like Sergeant Plante might have hit the right note after all. At least he'd claimed Mike as one of his own, whether he recalled him or not, on the strength of the uniform he wore.

I was floored when the C.O. was invited to speak. Clearly coached by Sergeant Laporte, he was remarkably restrained, confining himself to a stentorian expression of the Squadron's collective grief and a reminder that next Friday was Remembrance Day, the day men all over the world pause and gather to honour the memory of the Fallen in two World Wars. He slipped in a reference to the nation's western defences against the world-wide Communist menace having been dangerously reduced by the loss of one more brave lad, just in case anyone from the Department of Defence was listening. I rolled my eyes.

"Here we go again..."

Sergeant Wolff glared down the pew at me, but he could hardly call me a fuckpot in chapel. The Skipper finished on the right note anyway, with a quotation from Donne we recognized as having provided the title of a famous novel and a major motion picture.

"Every man's death diminishes me, for I am involved in mankind...Send not to ask for whom the bell tolls; it tolls for Thee."

I glanced over at Coombes, standing stiff in Mike's beret. His cheeks looked as damp as my own. Once Mike's parents and a handful of relatives left the chapel, the Squadron filed out in good order and formed neat ranks for the short slow march to the grave site. Across the green grass squirrels hurried to gather the last of their winter stores. There was a brief prayer by the grave, then suddenly we were dismissed. No salute was fired. Ted and I were drifting along the gravel path to the road, trying not to be obvious about making a quick exit, when Wolfie collared us, his face clouded by a Sergeants deep suspicion.

"Sapper McConnell's parents have asked to be introduced to you two."

I noticed the somewhat bewildered Colonel standing with Mike's parents on the grass beside the path.

"What for?"

Sergeant Wolff's moustache twitched angrily.

"How the fuck should I know?"

Ted straightened his beret and gave me a dig with his elbow.

"Okay, Sergeant. We'd be honoured to meet them."

The Sergeant squared his own hat and chewed his lip.

"For Christ sake, don't forget to salute the Old Man. You're still in uniform."

Crisply saluting the surprised Colonel, we came to attention and introduced ourselves."

"Sapper Brauer, Sir!"

"Sapper Morrison, Sir!"

"Um...er...At ease, boys..."

The Colonel awkwardly returned our salute. In the Militia we were usually more casual than the regular forces. Once dismissed, nobody expected us to go around saluting everything in a peaked hat. Since we'd introduced ourselves, there was nothing for the C.O. to do but murmur his final condolences and rejoin his officers, leaving us with these two strangers, the parents of a stranger who, they obviously thought, had been our friend. Mike's mother was pathetically glad to meet us.

"We wanted so much to see you because Michael spoke of you two so often...We were so glad he'd made some real friends at last. After we moved from Winnipeg, when my husband was transferred, Michael never seemed to..."

Mr. McConnell, who was much taller than his wife, squeezed her upper arm gently, as if warning her not to rattle on nervously in her grief. They were probably only in their forties, but they both seemed much older to me then, prematurely aged by the death of their son.

"I asked him to invite you over to the house so many times, so we could meet you, but he never...Well, I know you boys like to be by yourselves at your age...You grow up so fast..."

I didn't know what to say. Ted saved the day.

"Mike was a really good guy, Mrs. McConnell. He was a good friend and Jack and I will really miss him. All the kids at school feel the same."

That seemed to satisfy her. Dabbing her eyes with a handkerchief, she leaned against her husband while he shook hands with us both and thanked us very much in a hollow voice. There was something in his face that gave me chill. I didn't feel like he was thanking us for being his son's best friends, but for saying the right thing to his wife in spite of the truth he and we knew—that Mike had been a moody loner nobody had really known or wanted to know.

Ted and I declined a lift home in the Squadron truck, opting to walk through the chilly but peaceful suburban streets, conspicuous in battledress, like prophetic ghosts of war. The scent of smoke was heavy in the air and big brown maple leaves flapped along gutters in the wind. We walked quickly to keep warm. I just wanted to get home, get out of uniform and into my jeans, smoke a joint out my bedroom window and flake out, listen to the new Bob Dylan album I'd picked up and forget all about the Militia, the Canadian Armed Forces and Mike McConnell.

"Y'know, man? I've been thinking...This whole Militia thing may not have been one of my better ideas..."

Ted gave me a sad knowing grin. We were friends. We did things together and neither of us would quit without the other, but Mike's death had made us see that what we'd done as a joke had a very serious punchline. We'd joined an organization whose every aribitrary order and stupid drill had only one ultimate purpose; the killing of other human beings at the risk of our own lives.

"To tell the truth, Jack, I think you might be right this time."

Chapter 11

The Remembrance Day assembly held at our high school during last period the following Thursday afternoon was typical. As many of the hip kids and greaseballs as could beat the hall monitors skipped out completely. The rest of us were herded sullenly into the gym to listen to the Principal's short boring speech about tomorrow being not just another day off school but a time to remember those who gave their lives so we might live in a great democracy and enjoy all its moral and material benefits, not the least of which was the high standard of public education represented by the the school we attended. I was a little surprised when the Principal mentioned Mike McConnell in passing and provoked a confused murmur from most of the kids who had no idea who he was talking about.

They were all restless, unable to think about anything but the long weekend, three whole days of beer and the Beach Boys and battling bra-straps, a taste of heaven before the paradise of Christmas vacation. Ted and I skulked at the back of the bleachers, trying to hide the locks curling over our collars from the Vice-Principal who was on another one of his haircut pogroms to maintain standards of school dress and deportment. His idea of how high school students ought to look in a morally and materially superior democratic society seemed to be derived from reading Archie comics, while his discipline enforcement tactics had been lifted from *Mein Kampf.*

We were becoming more disenchanted daily with democracy

and disposable income as we saw it and a new addition to the outcast crowd at school was Bud Fisher, a guy whose father actually ran for aldermanic seats in city government on the official Communist Party ticket. Bud was a big noise in The Young Communist League and he'd invited us to come to a meeting. We'd both read the Communist Manifesto and liked it, though we couldn't see how something that sounded so simple and fair in print wound up leading to what happened to a couple of our friends parents in Hungary, or the Korean War, the Cuban Missile Crisis and now the fighting that was going on in Southeast Asia. Still, we did like the idea of being subversives, having our names on lists of anti-government rebels and being shadowed by the RCMP for something more enobling than suspicion of teen vandalism.

The only sign of the times in the school assembly was that Heather Wilson, a skinny bespectacled girl who affected black leotards and was known to hang out in Robson Street cafes with the art school crowd, was allowed to read Wilfred Owen's scathing poem "*Dulce Et Decorum Est.*" Her histrionic reading fell flat on Ted and I. Though we'd never fired a shot in anger, we knew there was nothing sweet or particularly fitting about a dead boy in uniform on an autumn afternoon.

After she finished the poem Heather tried to get in a few digs about what the Americans were doing in Vietnam, but the English teacher, Mr. Johns, trotted out of the wings and hustled her off. On that Remembrance Day most of the kids at Delbrook High School couldn't have found Vietnam on a world map for a six-pack and couldn't have cared less. It was a minor problem of American foreign policy, a five minute clip on the six o'clock news before it was time for dinner and The Flintstones.

Three months later Heather would become famous, the first student in North Vancouver expelled for being caught selling a joint of what later proved to be mostly oregano and catnip to another girl in the washroom, resulting in headlines in *The Sun* and *Province* and a Principal endorsed purge of the 'anti-social elements' from the school. By the end of term, almost all the outcasts and oddballs would have either quit school or transferred out.

Ted and I didn't want out of school just then any more than any
teenager does, but we did want out of the Militia. We attended the
Remembrance Day Parade because we didn't want to let the section
down on such an important occasion, but our decision was made. We
wanted to expand our minds, not drill them, even if it meant never
getting to blow things up. The Summer of Love was still a long cold
winter away and it would be another couple of years before some of
the wilted Flower Children would make blowing things up fashionable again.

We mustered at the Armoury on Friday, Ted and I sharing the
secret knowledge that it was our last parade. We were closely inspected by Sergeant Wolff who ordered us both to find a barber shop offer-
ing a two-for-the-price-of-one special on haircuts and get two each,
an order we were to disobey for some years to come. Then we were
marched up to 15th and Lonsdale where we fell in behind a local pipe
band, which made the marching easier except for Sapper Darling who
skipped along under the solictious coaching of none other than Corporal Stevens. A strange bond was forming between those two total
losers. Stevens couldn't quite forgive Darling for having come to his
rescue in such dramatic fashion, but he couldn't forget either. Now
he seemed to need Darling to succeed in becoming a real soldier
whose brother-in-arms gesture he could accept with respect.

It was a day as cold and bright as the day Mike McConnell died
and our breath clouded the air as we swung our arms and legs in unison to the primitive piercing skirl of the pipes. I remembered my
father telling me once that brass bands were no good for real marching. After a few miles, you'd get tired of the racket and fall out of step,
but men, even those who were exhausted, shell-shocked and battle-
drained, would march all the way and into the mouth of Hell itself
behind a piper. I also recalled him telling me he'd kick my ass around
the block if he ever caught me in uniform. He'd joined up at seventeen, a year underage, and been sent to fight for seventeen days for an
indefensible outpost of British imperial prestige, a malarial scab of
rock called Hong Kong. When he died at forty as a result of a brain
hemorrhage caused by being beaten with a rifle butt in a Japanese
prisoner of war camp twenty years before, he still had grenade

schrapnel in his spine and the Canadian government still owed him back pay for four years of starvation and torture.

At the cenotaph in Victoria Park a guard from each of the services, plus a token Wrenette, manned the corners of the squat obelisk, the barrels of their white-slinged obsolete Lee Enfield rifles pointed down. Wreaths were laid, speeches made and The Last Post played by an Air Cadet bugler who only faltered on one or two notes of that desperately sad dirge.

As we marched back up Lonsdale past the faces of the curious few who happened to be out and about when all the stores were closed, someone waved to me out of the thin crowd on a corner. It took me a couple of long syncopated strides to recognize my former Biology partner, Linda Arnold. It wasn't entirely my fault. She wasn't in any of my classes that year, for which I'd been grateful, and I hadn't noticed her at school, not that I was looking.

On top of everything, she didn't look like Linda Arnold anymore. Her lank brown hair had lengthened and lightened. It was feathered back from her face in a way that, with a bit of makeup, brought out what proved to be the cool aristocratic bone structure of her slim face. The thick glasses were gone, replaced by contact lenses, I guessed. The tight blouse and longish Dr. Zhivago Russian style skirt she wore with high boots under a loose open Afghan coat accented a figure that was willowy but by no means androgynous. She looked like Audrey Hepburn's younger sister. With a haunting wistful smile, she disappeared on the arm of a guy who looked fairly straight but by no means embarrassed to be seen with her.

"Son of a bitch!"

Sergeant Wolff drew level with my elbow.

"That's no way to talk about your mother, you little fuckpot, after all she's meant to me...Now, left! Right! Left! Right!..."

I skipped back into step, straining to turn my head to catch another glimpse of Linda, just to make sure I hadn't imagined her. All the way back to the Armoury I slammed my heels into the pavement, furious with myself without being able to admit why, though I knew well enough.

They'd invited a few surviving vets of The Great War to join our

Mess. They were pretty frail in their blue berets and blazers weighted by layers of campaign ribbons and medals. Tots of whiskey laid on by the C.O. took the chill off and put some colour into their papery cheeks while we consoled ourselves with beer. One of them started hammering out old songs on the upright piano nobody in the Squadron knew how to play. In reedy old mens voices they sang 'It's A Long Way To Tipperary,' 'Pack Up Your Troubles In Your Old Kit Bag' and 'There's A Long Long Trail A-winding.' My Grandads' songs.

I thought about how strange it was that my father and mother would never have met if he hadn't transferred to my Grandad's old regiment, The Winnipeg Grenadiers, if he hadn't come back to a strange city after four years in captivity to be met on the dock by an older man in a blue beret wearing the medals of another war, who offered him a hot meal and a bed on the couch, the only bond between them a piece of cheap stamped metal, the regimental insignia.

My Grandad hardly ever talked about his war. He'd been at Ypres, the Somme, Vimy Ridge and Passchendale, where he took a bullet through the shoulder going over the top. When I was a small boy I used to stick my curious finger into the deep socket of the hole on hot days when he lounged around in baggy shorts and a singlet. The songs the old vets sang were the songs he sang at Christmas instead of carols while my aunt played the piano. He'd keep her at the keyboard all Christmas Eve, the only night of the year he'd take more than one glass of whiskey.

I didn't understand then why Christmas, not Armistice Day, was the day both he and my father would throw the cap of the whiskey bottle out the window, but I never forgot the one story my Grandad told me about it. In the early years of World War One, there were real truces at Christmas. He told me about how the Canadians and the Germans facing them had climbed out of their trenches, leaving their weapons behind, and carried all their rations into the no-mans-land between the rows of barbed wire. There they built a bonfire and sat around it sharing their grub and tobacco and pictures of their families. They sang carols. 'O Christmas Tree' and 'O Tannebaum' was the favourite because they could sing it as a round in both languages. The next day, they went back to murdering each other with barrages, bullets and bayonets as they were ordered to, but the officers on both sides put a stop to fraternizing during the Christmas truce after those first years.

More than a little tipsy, the Mess barman having been generous on the occasion, Ted and I and Dougie Trumbull and Rob Coombes left the Armoury in a car filled with equally tiddly Wrenettes. We were bound for Big Jenny's house where there were bottles of rum and no parents. I was feeling peculiar, between the beer, memories of my father and grandfather and seeing Linda Arnold looking nothing like herself. On top of everything, Nasty had absconded in a new flame-red Mustang I'd've needed to stick up a bank to buy a wheel for, swivelling right past me without even saying "Hi," like I was just some guy who hadn't had her gum in his mouth.

A good deal of military decorum went by the board when we reached our objective and got into the rum and Coke. I was glad Coombes mislaid his beret almost immediately after entering the house. Every time I saw him in it I thought of Mike McConnell and I didn't want to think about Mike. After a drink or two I realized the Wrenettes were on a humanitarian mission, consoling us over the loss of our comrade, even if they didn't recall him very clearly either, and it seemed smart to play along. The others got the idea and we were properly and sedately bereaved for a drink or two. Then the music got turned up and the venetian blinds turned down and we allowed them to cheer us up. We managed to dissuade Coombes from swinging from the chandelier, a challenge the obstacle course hadn't presented. Dougie tackled him to the floor.

"It won't hold you. You'll only fall down and lose your beret again."

"My beret! Sergeant Wolff, you're a fuckpot! Here's my fucking beret!"

Brandishing Mike's beret, which he'd found stuffed in a pocket, he fell into the arms of a Wrenette strategically placed on the couch. Ted was in the kitchen, getting into the rum and the interesting mind of Gladys. Somehow I found myself down in the rec room with Big Jenny, looking for more Cokes. I discovered she could kiss even better than Nasty. With the cruelty of youth, I wondered how she'd learned that.

I had more things on my mind than the tactical problems presented by the Wrenette uniform, so I was slow to act until it became apparent that Big Jenny knew a lot more about Combined Services Operations than I did. There was suddenly also a lot more of her to contend with than a well-worn stack of Playboy magazines had led me to expect. The more bits and pieces she took off, the less she was the 'fat chick' nobody wanted to get stuck with and the more beautiful she became. A year or so later I would encounter the word 'Junoesque' in my reading and get such a hard-on in English class at the vivid memory of Jenny that I had to cross my legs for most of the period. At the time, all I felt was that my hands were too small to seize and touch so much of everything I had ever desired. Her voice was gentle and tender as she sucked the lobe of my ear.

"Have you got one of those things?"

As luck would have it, I had one of those things, a surreptitious gift from an older cousin a year before. I'd carried the circle of foil wrap around in my wallet for so long it was making a discernable dent in the leather. As I hurried to follow Jenny's lead, I realized I had more experience with rifles and grenades than with the equipment I was about to employ. I'd seen plenty of used ones lying in the grass on the trails on the way home from school like the sloughed skins of mysterious snakes. We used to find them in very unlikely places sometimes, like the parking lot at the supermarket, which really made you think about what might be going on in any car you saw parked anywhere after dark.

With a good deal of patience and guidance from Jenny, I managed not to disgrace my uniform one last time. I suppose you could say the Army made a man out of me after all, with a little help from the Navy, of course. What surprised me wasn't the act itself, which for all the anticipation is always ephemeral, but that I'd never noticed how really lovely Jenny was before. It was like that glimpse of Linda Arnold, almost frightening in the sudden intense revelation of my utter failure to see people and things as they really were. I was so stupefied by the whole business, wondering if everything else I took for granted was about to be transformed, that I stumbled halfway home with Ted, listening to him rattle on about Gladys fascinating mind, and wandered off without even telling him about it.

My head and knees seemed to be interpreting gravity in slightly different ways. My mind wasn't doing much better. I'd like to have gone back and talked to Jenny some more, I wasn't sure about what, and maybe do that last bit again just to make sure I'd got it right. But the girls had all gone home chewing Juicyfruit gum and those awful little packets of Sen-Sen mints to get the smell of rum and cigarettes off their breath before sitting down to dinner with their parents. The smells of pork chops, chicken and roasts were drifting out of the houses I passed and I discovered I was ready to devour even my mother's shoe-leather fried liver and onions and ask for seconds. Then I wanted to go to bed and sleep until Monday morning.

Ted and I stuck to our guns, or refused to stick to them, depending on how you looked at it. The following Saturday, we turned up at the Armoury and turned in our kit to Sergeant Laporte who received it with his customary patient smile, a thick draft of one of the C.O.s memos to Ottawa wedged under his arm. He'd seen a lot of young men come and go and he struck us off the roll with the professional calm of a platoon leader doing a casualty count.

Sergeant Wolff came into the office while we were still there, the one thing we'd been afraid of. He looked us up and down, took in the paisley shirts, bell-bottom jeans and uncut hair, the stuffed kitbags at our feet, and didn't say a word. He didn't say goodbye, much less good luck. He didn't even call us fuckpots. We were less than fuckpots to him. We were civilians.

Later we sat in the grandstand and shared a thin joint, looking out over the Armoury and the hall where the Wrenettes were drilling. Occasionally Sergeant Wolff's voice would cut across the wintry air as he berated whatever pair of useless three-toed mush-brained syphillitic fuckpots had replaced us in his affections. The red Mustang sat out front softly burbling exhaust, waiting for Nasty. The tinny reverb sound of The Ventures playing 'Telstar' on the car radio drifted up to us. Then it was drowned out when someone opened one of the apartment windows facing the park and a stereo began blasting out The Rolling Stones.

"This could be the last time...This could be the last time...I don't knaaooooow...."

Ted passed me the joint.

"Hey Jack? Let's not join anything for awhile, okay?"

The scent of hot burned rope filled my nose, driving out the cinders and resin smell of Christmas already in the air.

"Not even the Young Communist League?"

He shook his head, exhaling slowly.

"How about the Now Generation?"

I was just fucking with his mind, referring to the dumb Time Magazine article we'd both just read explaining today's troubled youth to yesterday's bewildered subscribers. Ted thought about it for a moment.

"Everybody's the now generation. Most of them just don't know it."

I thought it over as I passed back the glowing roach.

"How about the human race? Think maybe we could join that?"

Ted took a last hit and flicked the tiny patch of burned paper over the grandstand rail. He grinned okay. We shook on it, the old fashioned way, the Brother Handshake not having made it out of the ghetto yet. Looking over the empty playing fields and boarded up concession stands, I imagined the human race out there somewhere, waiting for us to enlist.

Part III

Code Two

Chapter 1

It was coming up for midnight and I still had more than six of twelve hours to spin my wheels on the graveyard shift. I was away to South Burnaby in cab Fifty-One with an amiable drunk from the Avalon lounge who gave me vague directions and passed out the minute his ass hit the seat. I enjoyed the long quiet ride with the cab radio turned down to a whispering mutter punctuated by occasional liquid snores from my passenger. Autumn fog was thickening in the hollows and tidal flats along the Vancouver waterfront below as we cruised across the Second Narrows Bridge into Burnaby and I relaxed, driving the posted speed and making the most of the break while the meter ticked on like a terrorist bomb.

I'd been making money in spite of myself, whipping the cab through the hot Friday night streets from bars to parties and back to bars, the meter flag snapping up and down like a one-armed bandit on a pensioners weekend in Reno. I was glad the cab's owner was too cheap to switch to a new digital meter. The ticking of the old one was comforting as it remorselessly resolved the equation of speed and distance into time and money. Usually I goofed off on Friday and Saturday nights, wasting the first half of my shift parked on some quiet suburban street or the deserted parking lot of a darkened supermarket in an unlikely zone, pretending to read the paper and drinking gut-wrenching takeout coffee while the rookies scrambled for the weekend money.

Rookies were a bigger pain in the ass than the sprung bench seat in Fifty-One. Hotshot cowboys, they were all students or moon-lighters driving the two busiest nights of the week to pick up some fast extra cash. They ignored radio protocol, cut off each other's trans-missions and when they were on the air you could hear the rubber peeling off their tires in the background. Dispatchers hated their guts because when they cut each other off on the radio it produced an ultrasonic squeal in the radio room that could just about make your ears bleed. The cab owners hated their guts because they hated any-body who wasn't locked into paying leases, licence and dispatch fees, a mortgage on company shares, extortionate insurance rates, padded repair bills, gas, oil, tires, alimony to an ex-wife or two and the lawyer who handled the bankruptcy of their last bright idea.

Owners hated all night drivers on principle, but they hated rookies especially because they ran the shit out of the cars, pocketed every flag they could by charging flat rates and leaving the meter off, creamed a dime or quarter off every trip on the sheet knowing the owners were too greedy to take a car off the road long enough to have the meter checked, took their forty-five percent at the end of the night and left the cab parked Christ knows where with an empty gas tank and a full ashtray. The regular night drivers hated the rookies because they didn't have to spend most of a ten or twelve hour shift on a slow night sitting on a cab stand with nothing but soft static on the radio and thirty-five bucks on the sheet, getting piles, ulcers and eyestrain from reading by the dome light and worrying about where the rent was going to come from after they deducted the two packs of smokes, a dozen cups of corrosive coffee and the Rolaids to battle the greasy all night steakhouse lasagna that had settled into a ball of fire just under their collapsed ribs.

I drove graveyard shift, six at night to six in the morning, five nights a week, sometimes six, because I liked it. Around the office they'd taken to calling me Captain Midnite. The only guy in the fleet who put in more hours behind the wheel was Bradley Benson and he was a total radio junkie, cruising the streets at all hours in his own cab, picking up the odd flag to cover expenses, bringing coffee and donuts for the dispatchers, answering emergency calls from drivers, talking to the cops, flushed red from popping speed and not sleeping, wired up and wearing dark glasses in the middle of the night to hide pupils the size of poker chips. The other drivers were running an informal pool, taking bets on when Benson would crack up or crash.

I shook the drunk a few times when I got to the general area, trying to wake him up to see if he recognized the neighbourhood. All I got was "Sommerz aroun' here" each time before he passed out again. I wove through a few blocks with him slumped against the door, hoping he'd come around, but he didn't and after a while I started to feel like a murderer looking for a place to dump the body. Finally I pulled over to the curb on a side street of small darkened houses that faced an open fog-shrouded field of some kind and frisked the drunk for his wallet. I figured I might find some ID with an address and besides, the meter was racking up, I was wasting time and if I was going to get stiffed for the fare I figured I might as well find out sooner rather than later.

The address on his expired drivers licence was for Hope. A few other cards had addresses in Vancouver, none of them anywhere near South Burnaby. Or North Burnaby, for all that mattered. There was a wet five dollar bill in the fold. It smelled like beer and the meter said twelve-fifty. I turned out his pockets. A squashed pack of Export A, lint, dirty damp Kleenex and thirty cents in change. Wearily I grabbed the drunks shoulder and shook him roughly awake.

"You don't have enough money."

"Huzzat?"

"I said, you don't have enough money."

The drunk grunted and slumped back in his seat.

"Wuzza damage?"

Taking a deep breath, I leaned over and bellowed into his slack face.

"Brain damage!"

His eyes snapped open for a second, then he snuffled, shook his head and drooped, emitting a rank beery snore. I shook him hard again until he started blinking.

"Look. Try to see it from my seat. I spend ten or twelve hours a day in this upholstered meat wagon, eating food out of boxes, pizza, burgers and chow mien...I drive poor drunk slobs home who've slurped the grocery money and their wives are gonna kill them and they promise me the cheque is good and they even add a big tip 'cause they know every cabbie carries enough bad paper to poster the Great Wall of China, and I haul them in and out of the cab and heave them up the stairs and get screamed at by their wives, as if I'd taken them out and got them pissed, and I don't even call them up or go around to their houses when the cheque bounces over the bank..."

The drunk gurgled sympathetically.

"...I pick up losers in parking lots covered in their own blood and run them up to Emergency with them bleeding all over the back seat and trying to start a scrap with me to get even for the whipping they took...I give free rides home to hookers whose pimps have beaten them black and blue and taken all their money, but they won't let me take them to the hospital. I pick up fourteen year old girls hitching in the middle of nowhere because some asshole drove them somewhere and fed them six beers and fucked them and threw them out of the car with half their clothes and I crack jokes to stop them crying and drive them home to the one house on the block with the porch light still on at three in the morning and pat them on the head and send them in to face Mom and Dad...What I'm trying to say here is, I've paid my dues and, man, I've had it. Y'understand?"

The drunk hiccupped, leaned forward and threw up into his lap. I sighed. At least it was his own lap.

"Right. I just wanted you to know all that, so you wouldn't take this personally."

Careful not to get puke on my sleeve, I reached across, pushed open the passenger door and punched him on the side of the head as hard as I could. He fell out into the gutter. I laid the soggy five-spot on the seat to dry, pocketed the change, fired one of his Exports with my Zippo and tossed the pack on the dash. Yanking the wheel stick into Drive, I stomped the gas and the door slammed shut as the cab lurched away from the curb.

At the end of the block I pulled a u-turn, swirling the tattered yellow fog under a streetlight. Halfway down the street the mist had thinned across from the houses. At first I'd thought it was a schoolyard or park. Now I could make out clusters of dark tombstones rising out of the earth like the ragged skyline of an abandoned metropolis. The drunk was crawling around in the middle of the road. Like a drowning man, he raised his arm in the glare of the headlights. I swerved and put my foot down. As I shot past, a chrome bullet aimed at a distant neon artery, I thought I heard a voice cry "Taxi!"

Chapter 2

I booked myself clear on the bridge coming back. Traffic was light. It would be an hour yet before the pubs started closing and the last rush began. I listened to the zone count. Most of the night shift cabs were stacked up on stands, having coffee and a smoke before it was time to deliver the dogmeat. I caught PJ in Twenty-Seven booking away on a long trip to the better side of downtown.

"Twenty-Seven, I'm away Van West. My radio's down."

Drivers usually turned their radios down on long rides to give passengers and themselves a break from the steady gibberish of numbers and static.

"Two-Seven right."

"I'm away to the races. My pants are down."

That was Chris Newman in Sixty-Three, screwing around on the radio. PJ retorted by holding his mike up to the AM radio or tape deck and sending a blast of heavy metal music through every cab in the fleet and the dispatch office.

"Tventy-Seven, Zixty-Sree, zat vill be enuff or you are Code Two."

The evening dispatcher was Klaus Fischer, a philosophy graduate student whose thick sausage accent and total lack of a sense of humour had earned him the nickname Doktor Goebbels. The night drivers hated his guts and referred to the dispatch office on Friday and Saturday nights as Radio Berlin. Herr Doktor barked into the mike and was always threatening to put drivers Code Two, off shift, for the slightest unauthorized disturbance of the company airwaves.

"Do you read, Tventy-Seven? Zixty-Sree?"

"Gotcha."

"Zen make proper acknowledgement, please."

"Twenty-Seven right."

"Sieg Heil!"

"You are Code Two, Zixty-Sree! See Bob Sunstrom in ze morning!"

The radio was quiet.

"Do you read, Zixty-Sree?"

A long piercing contralto fart broke radio silence in every car.

"Zixty-Sree! You are Code Two! Turn off your radio! I repeat! You are Code Two!"

There was a chorus of clicks, an invisible hedge filled with electronic crickets, as drivers pounded their mike buttons, the equivalent of applause. A sitting ovation. I tapped my button appreciatively and smiled. Klaus had only another twenty minutes to go on his shift. Then everyone could relax. Gary the Gimp would take over the dispatch mike for the Late Late Show.

A couple of cars booked away or cleared and were answered only by a single loud click, the dispatchers signal that he copied but couldn't answer because he was on the phone or taking a vital shit or something. Like everyone else, I knew it was just the Doktor having a Teutonic sulk. When he finally spoke it was to me.

"Fifty-Vun, ze Lynnvood for Terry."

"Five-One right."

Terrific. Another pub trip. If this prick was going any further than around the block he was going to have to show the dough up front. I didn't mind losing a few bucks by avoiding the closing time stampede, but I'd be double-fucked if I was going to haul trash and lose money doing it. The car still smelled faintly of puke, though I'd stopped at a gas bar on Hastings to wipe off the seat and driven back with both front windows down. Then again, it could have been old puke I was smelling, something soaked into the carpet under the seats along with all the traces of beer, piss, shit and come the girls who cleaned interiors at the car wash could never completely get out of a cab. Most of them were whores on medical leave, only working a straight job until the antibiotics cleared up their latest infection and made them certified street meat again, so would they even notice?

Terry would probably be a Code Thirteeen anyway, a no load. The other company, North Shore Cabs, covered the Lynnwood stand like flies on a campground toilet. A lot of good trips went out of there to Van East, sailors mostly, coming out of the country and western cabaret with the fat girls from the East End who worked the specialty trade off the Greek ships at the North Van grain elevators and asbestos docks at Pier Ninety-Four.

As it turned out, I was wrong. I swung around the long clover-leaf sweeping exit off the bridge and pulled into the Lynnwood Hotel parking lot just in time to catch two dudes in Surrey sports-jackets, long plaid mackinaw overshirts that hung down to the backs of their knees, as they were about to get into a North Shore cab that had run a yellow at the intersection to beat me into the hole. I yelled as loud as I could as I clamped on the anchors.

"You Terry?"

The taller of the two nodded.

"Then this is the cab you called."

The guys shrugged and sauntered over, leaving the back door of the North Shore hanging open. The driver leaned over to pull it shut, glaring at me. I smiled and spit out the window.

"Better luck next trip."

He gave me the finger. I gave him three. Terry and his friend snickered as they slumped into my back seat. I reversed and gunned it out of the lot, whipping the flag down with an automatic ratchet twist of the wrist.

"Where to, gentlemen?"

"Just up to the O, man."

That was alright. I'd taken in the long greasy hair, black t-shirts, the rundown Confederate boots. I wouldn't have liked them both sitting behind me on a long trip into the boonies, but they couldn't get into much trouble between here and the Olympic Hotel. I took them the short fast way, along the Low Level Road past the wheat pools and rail lines. It was an old cement slab road, straight and fast and dark but well-patrolled by the Harbours Board Police, the RCMP and private security companies who covered the docks. The only danger was a head-on with a drunk longshoreman coming off one of the wharves after a long hard evening of boozing it up in the checkers shack at time-and-a-half.

Terry and his friend whispered in the back seat. The hair on the back of my neck stirred faintly. I'd been driving graveyard too long not to know trouble when I was hauling it and with trouble the choice was simple. Make friends with it or fight it. I reached down the side of the drivers seat until my fingers found the old glass Coke bottle filled with sand, plugged with wax and wrapped with adhesive tape, right where it should be. My mike was handy, lying on my thigh where I only had to casually touch the button to host my own radio show, not clipped to the dash a long visible yard away.

"Ask him, man...What the fuck...He might know...These guys know lots of shit..."

"Okay...okay."

Dope, I figured. Not the type for hookers.

"Hey, man?"

"What can I do you for?"

"You must know a lot of people, eh?"

"Yeah. I get to meet a lot of people in this job. I'm thinking of going into public relations."

"Like people who can get things, eh?'

I nodded. I was too tired to fuck around with these shit-for-brains hoods.

"Okay. I know all the bootleggers, hookers and dealers on this side of the water and a lot on the other side. What are you looking for?"

More whispers in the back seat. I touched the Coke bottle again, just for luck.

"We want to get a chunk, man. Y'know? A gun."

I slowed down and looked over the back of the seat.

"A what?"

"A fuckin' gun, man. Y'know? Bang, bang?"

"Yeah. I hear you. What d'you want a gun for?"
Terry looked back at me with a tight thin sneer.
"Okay. There are a lot of rattlesnakes in North Van. Right?"
"Y'got that right, man."
I turned back to the road. They were whispering again.
"I toldja we shouldna..."
The cab launched out of Low Level Road onto Esplanade where there was more light, though the body shops and high performance engine boutiques were closed up behind iron bars and rolling steel shutters for the night. Down the block, Burrard Shipyards sprouted cranes and arc lights like a rocket launching pad.
"I might know somebody."
"Yeah?"
"Depends what you have to spend. Hardware's expensive if you don't have an FAA certificate."
"We got a hunderd."
I snorted loudly. The bright lights of Lonsdale were coming up fast.
"That'll get you get a squirt gun in this town."
"Pretty funny."
I shrugged.
"At least the ammunition's cheap."
I booted it up Lonsdale and cranked it right, pulling up in front of the Olympic Hotel.
"We could maybe go two hunderd..."
"That's more like it...Tell you what. I know a guy, but he might not have anything right now. Especially for that kind of scratch. But I'll see what I can do...If I have any luck, I'll look for you here tomorrow night. In the pub. No special time. If you don't see me, don't look for me because it means no-can-do. Right?"
"Sure...Right, man. Whatever..."
"That'll be four seventy-five."
"Sure, man...Thanks a lot, eh? Keep the change, man."
They gave me five bucks.
"Terrific."
"Hey. You want a joint, man? Sort of a tip, eh?"

I shook my head, then changed my mind and took it, tucking it in my shirt pocket.

"What the fuck, thanks. You guys need any speed?"

"Naw, we're cool, but I know where you can get some acid that's..."

"I know. Clinical. Right? No thanks."

"'Kay, man. Later, eh?"

"Yeah, later." I pulled the door shut after them. "Much fucking later."

ChAPTER 3

I cleared as I turned back onto Lonsdale, North Van's great white way, and tossed a mocking salute as I passed the half dozen cars sitting on the cab stand at Second Street, waiting for the pubs at the Olympic and St. Alice hotels to excrete their carloads of human waste. Let them hump the blind drunk and the socially lame. I was heading for West Van without booking a zone until I got to the donut shop on the far side of the Capilano River where I could get a fresh coffee, a cruller and a long look at the intriguing polyester-sheathed thighs of Maggie, the eighteen year old waitress every night shift driver dreamed of laying down and fucking on the back seat of his cab while booking himself Code Seventeen between gasps of ecstasy.

There was no Code Seventeen in the drivers handbook. It had become the unofficial drivers code for "otherwise engaged with a female fare" and the driver who booked one on the air could count on an extended mobile ovation of mike-button clicks. A driver who got a personal call to pick up Maggie at the end of her shift could always count on an electronic rustle of envy and appreciation on the airwaves. None of us ever charged her, of course, but none of us ever got more than conversation either.

Doktor Goebbels didn't answer my call. It was Gary, the graveyard dispatcher, smooth and mellow and in the groove as always.

"Good evening drivers and welcome to Gary's Graveyard Revue. This morning we'll be bringing you news and views, tips and trips to keep you rollin' through the wee wee hours of this Labour Day weekend..."

There was a snatch of ragtime folk guitar music Gary always used as his theme music, played on a portable cassette deck he brought to work.

"As of this broadcast, drivers, it is twelve-oh-two on Saturday morning. The temperature is still a balmy sixty-eight degrees Fahrenheit out there, so roll down your windows and roll up your sleeves for the full Twilight Zone Count, coming up in half a sec...Cars Fifty-One, Forty-Nine, Twenty-Six and Thirty-Two are reminded that they are this morning's special guests on the Late Late Show, scheduled to hang in there 'til six in the ayem...And now, The Count..."

Ignoring Gary's impersonation of the Sesame Street counting vampire, I booted it along Marine Drive without booking my zone changes. Rookies were stacked up on all the North Van pubs, the Avalon, the Lynnwood, the Coach House, the Alice and the O, waiting for the drunk lemming rush back to a thousand rented apartments with cases of barely cool off-sales beer lugged by giggling booze-stunned fares groping each other in the back seats, fingering the cops and puking out the windows of the cab if they were lucky.

I picked up my mike.

"Zis is Radio Stalingrad signing off. Going kaput. Testing. Achtung! Eins, zwei, drei...Ist das nicht ein Mikrophon?"

"Ja, das ist ein Mikrophon!" an anonymous driver answered.

"I heard zat, Five-Vun! Do you vish to be Code Two alzo?"

The Doktor again. The fucker was still in the office. I pressed the mike button.

"Uh..Five-One. I seem to be getting some other station cutting in on my radio. I can't make it out. There's a lot of static..."

Gary came back on the air.

"Right, Five-One. I think it's just local interference. It'll probably clear up if you don't use your radio for a few minutes."

"Five-One right. I'm Code Three for five minutes."

I gave the Doktor the absent finger and lit an Export from the crumpled pack on the dash. As I crossed the Capilano Bridge into West Van I decided to drop in at the office. It was upstairs, above a real estate company next to the White Spot restaurant at the Park Royal shopping mall. Night drivers called it The Orifice and you knew which one they meant. I skidded into the restaurant parking lot, sweet-talked the waitress behind the closed take out window into giving me a coffee to go and stomped up the back stairs. There was nobody in the office but Gary at the mike and Lorraine answering the phones. She shot me a nasty look but Gary grinned. I set the coffee down at Lorraine's elbow.

"Here, darling. You may have to add sugar...Not that you're not just as sweet as candy already..."

"Fuck you, Morrison."

She mouthed it silently. She was on the phone with a client after all.

"Tsk, tsk. All those years in Swiss finishing schools. Money down the drain." I turned to Gary. "Where's the war criminal? Did he remember he left a few million things in the oven at home?"

Gary laughed.

"You really should get off his back, Jack. He's under some stress. The guy's fried from writing his thesis all day and riding the mike all night. He's shell-shocked, man."

I shrugged.

"Sure. He jumped into his Volkspanzer and schnelled it out of here, didn't he?"

"I think he heard you coming."

The radio room was a dingy hole a rat wouldn't give as a mailing address. One wall was papered with a huge map of North and West Vancouver, divided into zones with coloured felt pens. Another wall displayed a street map of Greater Vancouver. The phone girl sat behind a plywood and plexiglass partition with a wicket opening through which she passed trips to the dispatcher on memo pages she punched into a big gray time-clock before handing them on. Behind the phone girl was long rack of numbered hooks for car keys, a squat floor safe with a slot in the top for drivers shift envelopes containing the trip sheet and the owners fifty-five percent of the total. On a cheap stand in the corner there was a stainless steel drip coffee machine whose blackened flask always contained three fingers of what looked like used motor oil. Everyone, dispatchers, phone girls, drivers and owners, had a different opinion about what it tasted like.

"Battery acid."

"Diesel fuel."

"Stewed cigarette butts."

"Boiled tampax."

"I bet the night drivers piss in this stuff."

"I bet the day drivers jerk off in this stuff."

I wanted a coffee but I couldn't face scraping that tar into one of the dirty mugs lying around and dosing it with powdered Coffee Mate. Better the Donut Shop and Maggie and a lonely hard on all night. One shot of that office ratpiss and you might never get it up again.

"I'm gone. Code Four at the Donut Shop. You want a coffee on the way back?"

Gary shook his head and reached under the dispatch desk beside his stainless steel crutches and pulled out the end of a case of Lucky Lager. Crippled by polio when he was ten, he was in his early twenties and almost elegant on crutches. He had a dark maroon Econoline panel van rigged with hand controls and there always seemed to be a very quiet, very pretty girl around to carry his beer.

He was a great dispatcher, never lost a car on the board, where each car was represented by a cylindrical magnetized peg with its number painted on top. The board itself was a rectangular grid of zones and numbers, a coded map that looked a lot like a crap table. As drivers booked away trips on the radio the dispatcher moved their pegs to their destined zones, turning them so the numbers read upside down until they cleared. The dispatcher could tell at a glance which cars were away and where he could expect them to clear, as well as the locations of available cars and their order of precedence in the zone.

It was a simple system. Most of the time it was like playing chess with an invisible opponent who phoned in his moves. But when things got hot, like on a payday Friday night or Welfare Wednesday, it was more like trying to run a real Vegas crap table single handed on New Years Eve. The dispatcher was supposed to have absolute authority on the air and drivers could actually be fired for talking back, but if he let a hint of panic creep into his voice or started stammering during the pre-dinner grocery rush the drivers would eat him alive. Gary never lost his cool no matter how backed up the trips got and never got snotty with the drivers whose I.Q.s dropped as the night wore on.

Lorraine dispatched a few day shifts during the week and answered phones at night on the weekends. She wanted to be a cop but decided to settle for being an ambulance driver. She always had her First Aid book by the mike or phone, studying the elements of trauma. In the meantime she lived with a weasel-faced pill head named Rudy who dealt weed and speed through the drivers and was not the father of her kid. On the air she played favourites among the drivers and owners. To rookies and night drivers she was mercilessly sarcastic. Sometimes drivers foolishly made the mistake of asking her for a location on an unfamiliar address.

"Do you have a map book, driver?"

Every driver is supposed to carry a map book.

"Uh...I think so."

"Do you know how to use a map book, driver?"

"Uh...I guess so."

She'd dispatch several more trips until the driver's anguished voice came back on the air again.

"Uh, I don't have my map book."

"Where is your map book, driver."

"Uh, I guess I left it at home..."

"I'll put you Code Three while you go home and get it, driver. Call when you're clear."

"Uh, I mean I guess I think I lost it."

"A new map book will cost you three ninety-five at a stationary store or about five bucks at a gas station. You're Code Three. Call when you clear."

"Uh, yeah. Thanks a lot."

"Don't thank me, driver. It wastes air time."

Then she'd dispatch his trip to someone else.

Lorraine had long dusty blonde hair and wore cowboy boots,

Levis and jean jackets all the time. She used to hang around the office and go drinking with the drivers and owners. Finally the company Manager, Doug Davidson, gave her a job answering phones part time. Like everybody else, he wanted to fuck her, but more than that he wanted her to pose for his large collection of pornographic polaroids. Somehow she got to be a prime-time day dispatcher and Davidson never even got a hand-job. He still couldn't figure it out.

With the possible exception of me and Chris Newman, most of the drivers had tried to fuck Lorraine at one time or another. Even Doktor Goebbels tried his Prussian charm on her for a while with no joy. Drivers got a lot of mileage out of that for a week or two, answering, "Jawhol, mein liebchen" every time she spoke on the radio until Bob Sunstrom, the company President, made them knock it off.

Rookies always got crushes on Lorraine and some of the regular night drivers still got hung up on her on and off like a recurring tropical fever. They made dips of themselves for a few weeks, bringing her good coffee from the White Spot all day and jelly donuts from real bakeries instead of the Donut Shop where everything tasted like baked styrofoam. They hung around the office shooting the breeze with her, helping her study her first aid, then they'd start running errands for her in their cabs, taking her kid to school or picking him up, getting her groceries or laundry or picking up packages from the post office, at no charge of course. They usually got a wake up when the owner climbed up their backs for forty dollar sheets and a lot of unpaid miles when everybody else was breaking a hundred. Or when they came up short for the rent.

She was supposed to have an interesting tattoo, but nobody I knew could claim to have seen it.

"Hey, Lorraine. I'll bring you a jelly doughnut if you show me your tattoo."

"Fuck you, Morrison." It snapped out before she realized she was still on the phone. "I'm sorry, ma'am. No, ma'am, I wasn't speaking to you..."

Chapter 4

Ted Brauer was already at the Donut Shop. He drove steady nights in Thirty-Two, taking graveyards on the weekend for the long quiet hours so he could catch up on his reading. He read mostly Oriental philosophy, though he wasn't working on a Phd. Ted drove Klaus Fischer nuts because they were both German originally, but Ted's parents came from the relaxed Catholic Bavarian tradition and Klaus was pure northern Protestant Prussian. Ted hadn't spent a day in class since the year of our high school's great purge of undesirables, after which he rode the rails across Canada in late winter and met the last of the old time railroad hoboes, lived in condemned hippy houses in the slums of Montreal, then joined the new generation of hitch-hiking hoboes and planted cannibus sativa seeds along the Trans-Canada Highway all the way back to Vancouver. He typically took months to read a single book, but when he was finished he could quote most of it from memory and knew every turn, twist and flaw in the argument.

Fischer's problem was that he continually assumed their joint heritage automatically made them share certain attitudes, specifically a sort of reflex contempt for any way of doing things from wiping your ass to governing a country that didn't conform to some undefined but dinstinctively German way of doing it. When Ted was in the office he'd mutter something in German, followed by a sharp barking chuckle so you knew he was making some kind of nasty joke, only to

206

find himself drawn into a philosophical debate, which an academic isn't supposed to get into with a high-school drop out, never mind one that could split hairs with Occam's razor into the bargain. Ted was the only driver who liked him and I figured the Doktor hated him for that most of all.

Ted drove me nuts sometimes too, especially when he was having a recurring bout of Lorraine Fever, like he was now, talking about her before I could settle my ass on the stool and interfering with my moment of contemplative meditation on Maggie's spectacular thighs.

"She's really a nice kid under that tough act she puts on...and a great dispatcher. When the rush is on she can answer phones with both hands, hit the mike button with her elbow and move the pegs with her feet..."

I shrugged non-committally, stirred sugar into my coffee and tried to change the subject.

"I don't care how good she is, I wouldn't go back to driving days if God Himself was dispatching. Sunstrom's been asking around, trying to get some of us to start earlier in the afternoon and he even asked me if I'd like a few day shifts, in one of his own cars yet. I told him no way. I tried it for a week or two when I started...Getting up at five in the morning, scraping ice off the windshield. Carrying little old ladies to doctors offices and listening to their gruesome medical histories...Humping six bags of groceries up four flights of stairs for a quarter tip. Bucking traffic all day in the heat or the rain. Piss on it."

It didn't work. Ted had it bad again.

"Remember the time the guy with the gun came into the office?"

"Yeah, I heard..."

"The guy stuck up the Park Royal Hotel, right? Only he wasn't too bright and he ran out of gas a block away as he was taking off with the bread. So he ditched the car and hoofed over to the office. Guess he figured he could afford a cab..."

"Yeah, I..."

"So it's graveyard shift and there's nobody in the office but Lorraine because its a slow weeknight and the old dispatcher, Bob Neilson, has decided to close down the Avalon before he comes to work.

This guy comes in comes in looking for a cab and she notices right away he looks kind of nervous and by this time the West Van cops and the RCMP from North Van are coming along Marine Drive from both directions with lights and sirens..."

I nodded grimly. I knew I was going to get the whole story again. Cabdrivers are like cops and vets at the Legion. They never get tired of telling the same old war stories over and over again.

"Well, there are no cabs around the office and the guy suddenly panics and pulls out the gun, right?"

"Right."

"Lorraine doesn't blow her cool. She talks to the guy and makes him see there's no way out if he hangs onto a bag of stolen money and a gun. She gets him to give her the gun and the money in exchange for calling him a cab to take him through the roadblocks at the bridge...The whole time, she's still taking calls and dispatching trips like nothing's happening while the cops are burning rubber up and down the streets outside. So she calls the shop here and gets one of the drivers to cancel his Code Three and come by the office to take this guy over to the West End and promise to tell the cops he picked him up in Horseshoe Bay if they ask...When he was clear, she called the cops and told them the guy held her hostage, but got scared and changed his mind about a life of crime and left the gun and the money with her and ran off into the woods behind the mall...Quite a lady, eh?"

I put down my coffee and the cigarette I'd been thinking about lighting and pushed them carefully out of the way.

"Y'know, Ted? The first time I heard that story I thought it was so full of holes you could drive a fleet of cabs through it...And personally, I think Lorraine is a power-tripping, badge-licking, gun-sucking cunt with a capital C who probably bends over every time a guy wearing any kind of uniform walks up behind her."

I waited for my old friend to deck me. Ted sat quiet, thinking about that for a long full minute. Then he smiled.

"You couldn't get into her pants either, eh?"

I grinned like I had broken glass in my teeth. Maggie refilled our cups. Maybe it was just the way that cheap polyester uniform clung to them, but her thighs really were the kind of thing you could lose sleep over so it was just as well we were going to be up all night.

The door swung open and PJ came in with Rick Chang. Chang was FOB, fresh off the boat Hong Kong Chinese, a rookie and a bit bewildered on the air with his uncertain English and dislocated sense of direction, but he was trying hard and learning fast and I liked him. During the day he went to UBC where, he told me, he was studying "fuzzicks." He had me going for a minute there until I spotted the Physics textbook under his arm. He drove nights, five a week, with his books in the car, studying on the stand, until two in the morning. Weekends he drove graveyard back to back, like me. I kidded him about all the money he must be making once, asking him if he was planning to buy back Hong Kong from the Reds in nineteen ninety-nine, but he explained he had "many famry obrigations". Most of what he made was going back to his mother, father, brothers, sisters, his future bride, her mother, father and on and on. The night drivers immediately changed his last name to Shaw in honour of Run Run Shaw, the godfather of all the cheesy great kung-fu films, and called him Rick Shaw.

"Hi Rick. Hey PJ, what happened with your Code Twelve?"

PJ laughed.

"Oh that...Just a guy getting cute. Y'know, arguing that I took him the long way. Like I'd bother for a lousy five buck jerk trip, but there were two of them so I figured I'd better get some reinforcements when they wouldn't pay..."

Code Twelve was the drivers call for other drivers to assist, a sort of yellow alert that meant come and help me out if you're in the vicinity. If a driver called Code Fourteen on the air it meant get everybody, every driver, the cops, the ambulance, the fire department, the army, navy, air force and the fucking Boy Scouts because some whacko is really trying to kill me. PJ didn't look any the worse for whatever had happened. He seemed to think it was all a big joke.

"So I call Code Twelve and who do I get?...Bradley freaking Benson. Man, the guy must never sleep. He worked day shift today. He's not even on the board tonight, but he's out there in the dark, cruising and seeking out evil-doers lurking around the cab stands of Gotham City..."

"So? Give."

"So everything probably would've been okay until he started calling these dudes pricks and assholes and telling them the cops are on their way and they better pony up the fare right now or they'll answer to him..."

"I can see this...And what did they say to that?"

"Not much with their mouths. They let their fingers do the talking." He made a fist. "Pushed me out of the way and beat the piss out of him. Then they paid me before they took off. Who'd figure that? Man, that Benson's got some loose lugs. His mind's in neutral and his mouth is in overdrive."

The four of us moved to a booth along the wall opposite the counter. Maggie brought us more coffee and a tea for Rick.

"So where's Newman? Off to the Russian Front?"

PJ nodded.

"Yeah. You heard the Doktor axe him, eh? He wanted to Code Two early anyway. He wasn't making a dime. Fuckin' electricals in that beater are screwed up big time. He spent half the shift in gas stations trying to get his headlights to work...Big backgammon game at the Casino in the Clouds later on. He figures to get his money back out of the guys who actually worked for it. He said to come on up if it's slow. Gary has his number."

"I might..What're you doing here anyway? You're almost Code Two already."

PJ tried to look cool. Hard to do when you're smirking.

"I'm just here to pick up Maggie."

I spat coffee back into my cup, noticing Ted did the same.

"Say again?"

"Could I get a repeat on that, please, dispatcher?"

PJ was on the short side, inclined to be chubby, a goofy part dividing his blonde hair down the middle. Great sense of humour and a hell of a nice guy, thus a total loser with chicks. I thought of him as a born side-kick, the guy who always hangs around with some good-looking guy, playing straight-man and feeding him lines that make him seem wittier than Wilde and who always falls desperately in love with the women they treat like shit on their shoes. As a reward for staying up all night while they weep on his shoulder or bandaging their slashed wrists and waiting for hours in Emergency to drive them home, the girls treat him like a faithful beagle and go right back to shagging his handsome shit of a friend the minute the scars heal. Now PJ looked proud of himself. In fact, he looked quite smug.

"This Maggie?"

PJ leaned back in the booth and blew a smoke-ring.

"She's the only one here."

"Well, I'll be flat-tired on a dark road. You dog, you. Who died and made you Prom King?"

"I just asked her if she wanted to go to a little party after work. I'm taking her up to the Casino in the Clouds for a drink or two. She wants to learn how to play gammon...Nothing heavy. I might bring her to the office party tomorrow night, though."

"Not to make sure every driver in the whole company sees you with her so you can gloat your ass off or anything like that?"

PJ managed to look innocent in spite of himself.

"Never crossed my mind, but now that you mention it..."

"Wipe the canary feathers off your face. It's indecent. My hat's off to you, man. I salute you. We all salute you...And you're buying the coffee and donuts for being such a slick little fart."

"It's on me, boys."

I was happy for PJ. Lately he'd been hanging out with Chris Newman, a tall blond David Bowie clone who told everyone he was a photographer but spent most of his nights at the wheel of cab Sixty-Three. Newman dressed like he was going to a party every night while most of the other drivers barely bothered to shave. He was far too cool to ask out a waitress in a donut shop, but I suspected he'd bullet-proofed his sheets a few times dreaming of Maggie. Her turning up at a party with PJ, his current side-kick, would put a hell of a crimp in his high-waist bell bottom slacks. Serve him right, I thought, even if he is one of my best friends.

"Maggie, love? We'll all have refills and jelly donuts. Charge it to your friend here."

She smiled sweetly at PJ and winked. He lit up like an emergency flare.

Chapter 5

Two more regular night drivers drifted into the donut shop, Phil Bender and Paul Dodson, Forty-Nine and Twenty-Six respectively. Bender grinned and shook his head as he slipped into the booth behind us. Everyone called him 'Fender' because he drove like he had a death wish, but so far he hadn't knocked so much as a flake of paint off Forty-Nine, one of Bob Sunstrom's own cars. The owners did a breakdown of his sheets one week and figured he had to be averaging sixty miles an hour on every trip to make that kind of money.

Bender had driven for Black Top and Yellow Cab downtown and let us know he was only driving for a suburban company until a downtown car came available. He'd been offered a ride by MacLures, but he turned it down. They were the west side company, the taxi of choice for every hippy hophead in Kits and the West End. Their drivers would let you smoke dope in their cars, as long as you let them toke. People not in the know would walk up to a MacLures cab parked on a stand, open the back door and start to slide in, then reel back as a thick spicy cloud of ropy smoke enveloped them. Bender looked the outfit over but came back to King Cabs to regale us with tales of the dope-crazed goings on at MacLures.

"I used to wonder about those guys when I started with Yellow. I'd see these blue cabs that looked like the insurance company should have written them off two accidents ago, cruising around downtown with their top-lights off, so you knew they were hired, but they'd be doing like twenty-five, just barely rolling, with the car full of smoke and everybody inside laughing their hair off, even the driver. I got talking to one of them at a stand one night. We were sitting in his cab and it was just a total shit-pit. I mentioned it was a little funky and he might want to stop at a gas station and get one of those little tree-shaped air fresheners, but he just gave me this loopy look, then he lights a fucking cone of incense and puts in on the dash. Jesus...When I dropped into their office to check out how they ran on the night shift, man, the dispatcher and the phone girl were passing a big fat one around and they offered me a hit...Shit, you need speed, not weed, to make money in the hack business."

Bender got his from Lorraine's boyfriend Rudy, like most of the other King drivers who sometimes needed a little help staying awake and alert on long night shifts when it got too quiet. The slack times were what drove Bender crazy about working the suburbs. Wired up, he'd get all jumpy if he didn't hear the meter ticking and sometimes just book himself Code Four for lunch and boot it over the bridge to cruise for flagged trips downtown, even though it was illegal and Taxi Inspectors from the DMV were known to patrol downtown and the airport in ghost cars to enforce company agreements and report unlisenced pickups. Bender didn't care. He told me once how to beat the synchronized lights on Georgia Street. Not to be shown up, I told him I already knew.

"Sure. You can catch all the green if you do exactly twenty-nine miles an hour all the way, but the last one down at Cardero always gets you. It's out of sync."

Bender just smiled.

"If you punch the gas and do seventy-five all the way from the last light to the Cardero intersection, you can beat it on the orange."

Bob Sunstrom knew Bender was a speed freak with a heavy foot, but he also had great cop-sense and got surprisingly few tickets and he turned in such good sheets even on slow nights that Sunstrom continued to let him drive Forty-Nine.

Maggie brought Bender coffee and a cruller.

"It's a zoo out there tonight. A real animal show. You'd think they only had one night to do all their shit-disturbing instead of a long weekend."

He was right. So far there'd been two Code Twelve driver assistance calls and the pubs hadn't closed yet, plus a Code Fourteen scramble when some underage punks at a party ordered a carload of liquor, then tried to roll the driver for the load and his float when he wouldn't hand over the booze without seeing some ID. The cops had been called in on that one and we were still getting prank and crank calls from pay phones in the area as they broke up the party and the kids drifted off to parks and all night gas bars, anywhere but home, to hang out.

I shrugged it off.

"It's always an animal show. Anybody who's got the price of the tariff can use your cab as a rolling shithouse, sick-bag or motel room...After a few of them have tried to punch you out, made it with their wives or girlfriends in the back seat, wept on you, bled on you and puked on you, you just have to put yourself on Channel Thirteen and pretend you're hauling frozen meat or something..."

Ted gave me one of his looks.

"You saying it doesn't get to you at all anymore, Jack?"

I didn't want to get into yet another discussion of existential alienation with him. The night was still young, unfortunately, and it was easier to tell war stories.

"Remember Newman's first night? Man, Ted and I told him horror stories for a week when he said he was going to join this Legion of The Damned. We had him believing he'd be picking up axe-murderers on every streetcorner. So he goes out on his rookie night and for about half the shift everything's cool. Then he picks up this dude at the Av with a ratty little beard and the Charlie Manson eyes, that thousand kilowatt glow in the windows of the soul, y'know?...This guy gets Chris to take him on a magical mystery tour through the woods under Lions Gate Bridge, supposedly to the trailer court, but they wind up off on some gravel track near the old Routledge Gravel pit. It's the middle of the night and its real dark down there and Chris is starting to get a bit damp in his strides, when the guy tells him to pull over. It's pitch dark and this guy is sitting in the back seat, right behind him...Chris asks him why here and the guy says, 'Cause this is where I'm going to kill you'...Chris said he thought the last thing he was ever going to see was the lights on the bridge overhead. All those cars passing over and they might as well have been on Mars..."

Bender was interested. His own eyes had quite a glow, come to think of it, when he looked right at you instead of flicking around like he was following a pinball.

"So what happened?"

"Chris talked him out of it. The guy was just pissed and snaky and felt like scaring somebody to make himself feel sexy, I guess."

Bender whistled quietly.

"The fuckers lucky he didn't get killed. Try that shit sometime on a downtown cabbie, especially down East Hastings some night. You'd be lucky to wake up in jail or St. Pauls Emergency getting steel picked out of your guts by some intern with needlenose pliers. Wasn't Newman packing a shank or a tire iron or anything?"

"He does now."

Ted frowned.

"That's not the way to handle that kind of situation."

PJ kicked in with an ironic chuckle.

"Easy for you to say, Ted. You're big enough to make a carload of Indians dump out their beer."

Bender turned to him, nibbling his cruller.

"Say what?"

"Yep. Ted picked up a bunch of the boys from the Reserve at the Alice one night and they had a few cases of off-sales. As he's driving along Marine Drive to Mathias Road by the Capilano intersection, they start opening beers in the car. So Ted pulls over and tells them to empty the open ones into the storm sewer or they've walking the rest of the way."

"No shit? And they did it?"

Ted looked embarrassed. He nodded.

"They were okay guys. It was no big thing. It's all in how you talk to people. The dumped the open ones. It was only two beer. I took them the rest of the way and they paid me. No problem."

Bender looked at Ted with new respect.

"Jesus, you got paid? Man, those guys scare me shitless. It's the only thing I don't like about driving over here. I'd rather deal with your basic Burnaby or Surrey scumbags any time."

"They're no better or worse than anybody else. Some of them have a chip on their shoulders and maybe they have a right to. You just have to get down and be people with them. Treat them as people and make them treat you as a person."

I laughed, trying not to make it sound nasty.

"Yeah, well maybe, man, but one night I was coming out of Van Wharves late with a longshoreman going back to the hall. Good trip, but I had to fuck around on the docks at the foot of Cap looking for him for half an hour. Then on the way out, we're coming up that long lightless straight stretch through the scrub alders on the Reserve and the high-beams pick up this shit on the road ahead. It's some kind of barricade. Nothing fancy, just an old bench and some deadwood, but I had to stop the car and move it. I wasn't that happy getting out and I was damn grateful he got out to give me a hand moving the shit. Then we heard them moving around in the bushes and whooping..."

Bender went white.

"Whooping?"

"Woo-woo, woo-woo...Just like in the movies. Man, I figured the flaming arrows were next. Pull the wagons into a circle, Maw!...Anyway, we yarded just enough stuff out of the way, jumped back in the rig and I threw up some gravel getting out of there. As we took off something whacked the back of the car and took out one of my tail-lights. Try reporting that on an insurance form. Reason For Claim: Indian Attack...We never saw them. I figure it was just a bunch of Reserve kids having some fun, but that stevedore admitted he was shitting himself too for a minute there."

"See? That's what I mean. I don't get those guys at all and that kind of stuff scares me a lot worse than just getting held up."

"You got held up?"

"Oh yeah."

"Like with a gun?"

Bender cackled.

"Well, it wasn't a very big gun. I'm working the downtown and this guy gets into my cab outside the Niagara. I ask him where he wants to go and he tells me Seattle. My cab was licenced to cross the border and that's your sheet for the night right there, but you always have to call those trips in and see big money up front before the company will let you take one, so I tell the guy this and he pulls this little tiny piece out, sticks it in my ribs hard and tells me we're going to Seattle right now. It was such a dinky little thing I wasn't sure it was real. I thought it might be a starter pistol or something, but I didn't want to find out the hard way."

"What'd you do?"

"Lucky I was damn near out of gas. I showed him the gauge and talked him into letting me stop to fill up. 'Course I stopped at a self-serve up on Davie so I'd have to get out and pump it myself. He gives me this shit that he's keeping me covered, but I'm out there pumping and he's in the cab trying to be cool, but he can't really keep the gun on me from there and I'm making high signs to the kid at the cash window like a Chinese fire-drill...No offense, Rick."

"Did you run for it?"

"Nope, he did. Got so freaked out he slid behind the wheel, started her up and took off like Batman. The nozzle popped out of the tank, I got covered in gas, but he ran her straight out onto Davie, side-swiped a fucking cop car of all things, then wrapped the cab around a lamp post on the other corner. He got maybe fifty yards. Not exactly Steve McQueen in The Getaway, this dude. The cops seemed to know him...I wasn't even that scared through all the shit until the cops told me later that it was a real gun alright. A Colt twenty-five automatic and it was loaded. Not a big gun, but big enough to kill you at close range if you got hit in the wrong place. Then I got scared."

While we were talking two more drivers had taken over the booth on the other side of us. Cecil Wragg and The Count. The two biggest assholes in the company. Wragg was a towering spider-monkey, an emaciated six-five at least, who drove slouched down so low in the seat you could just see his haunted poached-egg eyes over the dash. He owned and drove Twenty-Eight, a rolling safety hazard the cops periodically threatened to take off the road. Wragg was the kind of guy you felt sorry for when you first met and hated about five minutes later. I'd come to think of him as the perfect combination of looks and personality. At least he was consistent. There was nothing about him to like.

Despite being an owner, he'd been suspended countless times for violations of company rules. One of his favourite tricks when business was slow was to scoop North Shore Cabs trips by using a portable short-wave unit he kept under his front seat to monitor their radio frequency and beat them to trips they called out in whatever area he was stalking. Everyone at King Cabs thought that one was pretty funny at first. There was a certain off-the-wall genius about a stunt like that you had to admire. It might almost have made Wragg one of the boys except that he also pulled the same kind of shit on his own company, cruising around booking zones he wasn't in and scooping trips dispatched to other cars if he was close enough to beat them to it. If he could sneak into the office and get a peek at the log of pre-dated trips and their destinations, usually long rides to the airport, he'd hog that zone an hour before or slip into it without booking it on the radio and pick off the trip fifteen minutes early. Putting a fake address on the trip sheet, he'd book on away a sudden flag to Richmond instead of saying the airport, so when the pre-date was dispatched the driver would find the fare already gone. Nobody found anything funny or admirable about that kind of shit.

The Count was a different breed of creep. He owned and drove Forty-Two. He and Wragg were almost the only owners who drove nights. They did it because the money was usually better, at least on the weekends. The Count's name was Bela Something-Unpronouncable. He was Rumanian and looked like a half-pint vampire with his short widows-peak haircut. His accent was thick as goulash so the drivers nicknamed him after the Sesame Street counting vampire. He cut in constantly on other cars radio transmissions because he was an owner and we were mere relief drivers and he always shouted into his mike no matter how many times the dispatchers reminded him not to. Whenever he was coming back from a downtown trip and had to book the bridge, he'd screech, "Forty-Two! Breedge!" and every hair on my head would stand up.

Sharing a radio frequency with a dozen other people for hours can make you as testy as sharing a motel room with them would. It's actually worse because they're all in your head. You become very sensitive to the sound of each voice and any quirky little mannerisms quickly get irritating with constant repetition. But it wasn't just The Count's accent that pissed me off. It was his unveiled sneering contempt for the night drivers, for anybody who wasn't an owner, while he sucked ass furiously around owner-managers like Sunstrom that made me want to puke. Like all the night drivers, I'd complained about his rude shit on the air to the dispatchers and managers and even told him to go fuck spiders a few times. I'd probably have left it at that, but when he took to picking on Rick Chang my intense dislike for the little fuck festered into an ass-boil of hatred that had half of every twenty-four hours to swell under pressure between my butt and the cheap vinyl of Fifty-One's drivers seat.

During a lull in the war stories, Rick shyly attempted to join in.

"I do not like...to have...trouble...with customers."

The Count couldn't let it pass. He had to lean over the booth and glare at Rick.

"Eef you dunt vant to haff trupple vith zem, you must learn to spik petter Eengleesh before you drife taxee."

Rick shrugged and looked embarrassed. I put my coffee cup down with a bang.

"Look who's talking. Dracula's dwarf cousin. What're you doing in here anyway? This joint doesn't serve Type O. Why don't you flap down to the blood bank and make a withdrawal? And take Frankenstein's fucking nephew there with you."

The Count sneered at me, at all of us, his voice a Lugosi hiss.

"Vat do you know?...Bums, all uff you. Chust bums vith ze keys to odder pipples cars."

I slid out of the booth and stood up. I showed him the fist I'd popped the drunk with.

"I know this and you better know it too, Batman. I know if you don't stay off Rick's back I'm going to drive a toothpick through your heart, fold you four ways and stick you up your own tail-pipe. You get my dreeft? That good enough Eengleesh for you?"

Fortunately the phone rang. Maggie answered it.

"Hey, Gary wants all you guys back on the road. He says like five minutes ago."

Wragg and The Count threw change on their table and split, money hunger in their eyes. It was Last Call and the pubs were spewing out our customers, the nightly crop of fermenting human vegetables headed for the compost heap of drunken sleep. Bender hit the skids fast too. He could put another thirty or forty bucks on his sheet while the rest of us pulled ten or fifteen. Rick smiled at me and followed them out. He needed the extra ten or so. Ted and I left PJ with the bill and the prospect of Maggie's company for the rest of the evening. He seemed okay with it. Out on the sidewalk I flipped my butt into the street, trying for the centreline. It dropped short and I spat through my teeth.

"Fuck. That miserable little prick picks my ass."

Ted gave his patient smile.

"Try to understand where he's coming from, Jack. I know he's a jerk, but it's the immigrant syndrome. When people are new to a country, they feel like they're on the bottom of the shit pile..."

"And the way to feel higher is to step on somebody elses face?"

"Thats right, even if it's only the guy who got off the boat five minutes after you did. Everybody needs to feel bigger than somebody, even stunted warped midgets like The Count."

I smiled and shook my head.

"Cut the sermon, Reverend Brauer. Your seeds are falling on stony ground tonight..."

"Maybe the job is getting to you, Jack. You're sure down on everybody since you quit university and started doing this.."

"I was down on everybody before that and I know exactly when it happened. It was that party a couple of years ago. Remember? That big shit-face just off Cap Road?"

"You mean the one where you went up on the sundeck and pissed down on everybody dancing in the back yard? Yeah, I think I remember that. I especially remember having to fight our way out of the place through a lynch mob of people wearing t-shirts covered with peace signs and Make Love Not War slogans."

"Exactly. I was standing up on the sundeck looking down on all those people dancing around in the backyard to The Chambers Brothers 'Time Has Come Today' and suddenly I realized they were all the assholes we went to high school with, Ted. The fuckheads who used to throw beer bottles at us from their jacked up Chevvies and threaten to cut our hair in the can. There they all were with their little fringes of hair over their ears and their tie-dyed shirts, the cheerleaders with no hairspray and no bras, giving me the brother handshake and trying to buy dope from me. That was when I realized all the shit we talked wasn't about social justice or changing the world or anything really. It was just about...fashion..."

Ted shrugged.

"Well, if it becomes fashionable not to kill people because you don't agree with them, or not to hate people just because they have a different skin colour or accent, isn't that changing the world? Or are you just pissed because the people you were rebelling against have come over to your side and you don't look like such a rebel any more?"

I laughed bitterly.

"Maybe...You always could see the worst in me and appreciate my hidden shallows..."

"I don't really think you're that shallow, Jack..."

"Hey, don't blow it. Thats why I hang out with you...It was just that I could just see them all in a few years, the guys getting their hair cut and becoming stock brokers and real estate agents, the girls buying new bras and panty-girdles after having a kid or two, all with nice little houses in suburbia, boring their kids with tales of how wild they were when they were young...Besides, I really had to take a hell of a leak and a bunch of those dumb fucks were locked in the can snorting baby powder....C'mon. Let's do the *Closing Time Tango*."

Chapter 6

"Five-One. I'm back. You need me?"

"Five-One right. The O lobby for Baker."

I did a double take.

"Ah, Five-One. The O lobby? From West Van?"

"Right Five-One...Just when you thought it was safe to go into the streets again..."

"Five-One. That's very funny. You should be on radio."

"Funny you should notice, Five-One. Everyone else is away, so I'd be very grateful if you'd get the lead out of your lingerie and pick up the Bakers at the O."

"My commotion is in motion. Five-One over and out."

"Ten-Four, Five-One. Doncha just love this big time professional radio chatter?"

I honked at Gary as I hurtled past the office. If I was lucky, this would be the one and only pub trip I'd get before the rush died. Maybe it would be Code Thirteen and I could stay off the air for twenty minutes, pretending to be looking for the Bakers in the closing time free-for-all of the Olympic pub. A guy could lose a decade in there, never mind a weekend. I could park the cab in a dark corner of the lot, meet an undiscriminating girl in the pub, check into a room upstairs and call in when the money ran out after a few days. I might not even get fired. And if I did, would that be a problem?

I didn't have long to think about it. The Bakers were waiting in the lobby. All six of them. They each had a case of beer. I didn't bother explaining that it was only legal for me to carry five. Unlike Ted, I wouldn't argue with six big Indians who'd been waiting too long already. They were going to Zeke's place. I knew it. It was on the No Service List of both King Cab and North Shore Taxi. Geographically, it was at the foot of Mathias Road, beyond a water-filled pot-hole that could swallow a cab without a trace. Zeke was the kind of guy you met once, never forgot and never wanted to meet again. At least he wasn't in the cab.

We were rolling past the car dealerships on Marine Drive when they started talking it up.

"Whad'you guys wanna do t'night?"

The reply was loud, directly behind my ear.

"I dunno. Let's kill a white man."

I stared straight ahead. All the fucking lights as far as I could see were green and there wasn't a cop in sight or I'd've crammed it, rammed a red and got myself pulled over and into protective custody. Why me? Why not Wragg or The Count or anybody else? Shit.

"Tell you what, guys. You hang tough and I'll cruise around and see if I can find you one."

They all laughed and suddenly I knew I was cool. One of the guys in the front gave me a nudge.

"Hey, man. You know Fred Nahanni?"

Know him? The only Native driver in the fleet? I not only knew him, I loved him, all two hundred and seventy pounds of him. We were like brothers. Blood brothers.

"Yeah. I drive Fred home usually when he's off shift."

"Hey, man! This guy knows Fat Freddie!"

I smiled.

"Well, I usually call him Mister Nahanni or Sir. It's healthier."

"Yeah, man! This guy really knows Freddie!"

I knew Fat Fred was a big noise in the secret men's dancing lodge on the Reserve. It made him a good man to know. He told me once about how he and his brothers and uncles used to go over to the Blackstone Hotel or the Nelson Place downtown and drink all night. Then at closing time they'd pick a fight with the waiter and brawl their way to the door through the entire pub, the other waiters, the barmen, the bouncers and finally the cops. Which also made him a good man to know.

"Here, man. Have a beer, eh?"

A bottle opened with a soft kiss. I accepted it with thanks. Not exactly a peace pipe, but what the hell. I took a long sip at the red light at Cap and Marine. When I dropped them off at Zeke's place we were all the best of friends.

"Take it easy, man."

"Yeah man. We always take your cabs. We don't like that other company. They don't hire Indians."

"Say hi to Fat Fred, man."

"Tell him the party's at Zeke's."

One of them gave me the brother handshake and another beer for the road.

"Power to the fuckin' people, man!"

"Power, man."

I guessed Ted was right after all. You just had to get down with people and be real and make them treat you as a person, especially when the odds were they could kill you as quick as look at you. I was glad to see the streetlights again when I hit Marine Drive. A few minutes later I pulled into the stand in front of the Avalon behind Thirty-Two. Ted always parked there after the pub closed because the bright light from the marquee entrance was better for reading than the interior dome. But he wasn't reading when I dropped my butt into Thirty-Two's passenger seat and lit a smoke. His face was blank and his eyes were looking at something even further away than usual.

"What's up?"

"My last trip out of the pub here...You know who it was?"

"How would I?"

"It was Rob Coombes."

"You mean Robbie Coombes we were in the Militia with? The little clown I went to elementary school with? What's he doing these days? Still fucking up and blaming the world? Was Dougie Trumbull with him? Shit, I haven't seen either of them in years. Wish I'd got that trip instead of the Bakers at the O. The Moccasin Taxi is your special gig...”

Ted shook his head.

“You wouldn't have wanted this trip.”

“Why not? Didn't he remember you?”

“Yeah, he did, but he didn't say anything for five minutes as we're driving up the hill. I was sure it was him, but he really looks different. He's not little anymore for one thing. He's still not tall but he's got a lot more muscle and his hair is shaved down to his skull. It was the tattoo on his arm that threw me off...”

“Coombes with a tattoo? Dougie must've held his hand through that...”

“Maybe he did Jack. See, the tattoo was of the globe of the world with crossed anchors behind it and a scroll underneath with the words Semper Fidelis.”

“Sounds familiar, but...”

“It's the insignia of the U.S. Marines, Jack.”

I snapped my fingers.

“That's it. Why would Rob Coombes...Oh shit. Don't tell me. Rob Coombes can't be a fucking Marine?”

I started to laugh uncontrollably. Coombes who'd been racking up demerits for grooming and deportment since first grade, the consummate unmilitary fuckup who always looked like he slept in his Militia uniform, the guy who either mislaid his rifle or managed to get rocks stuck in the breech, in the Marines? It was just too funny, but Ted didn't seem to think so.

“He's not anymore. He just got out. He'd only been back for a couple of days. He went down to the Av to see if he could find anybody he knew. I guess he did, because he asked me if everyone in this town had turned into hippy faggots.”

I eyed Ted's longish straight hair.

“Like you'd know?”

“That was his tone. I looked at him out of the corner of my eye for awhile, then I said 'Hi Rob' and he said 'Hi Ted,' but he had this sort of tough little sneer that tried to pass for a smile. That was when he asked me if we were all hippy faggots. So I asked about the tattoo, if it meant what I thought it meant and he told me he wasn't in 'Nam on a fucking sight-seeing tour..."

"The Marines sent Rob Coombes to Vietnam? What were they thinking? That the Viet Cong would laugh themselves to death when they saw him?"

"I don't think so Jack. He told me he and Dougie went down to Seattle the day after graduation and enlisted in the Marines. They volunteered for Vietnam. Join the Navy, see the world, meet new people and kill them..."

"Jesus Christ, man...Who the fuck would think?...Where's Dougie now?"

"Dougie's dead, Jack. He got killed in some hamlet. Coombes told me the name but I can't remember it. There was some kind of ambush and Coombes got hit in the legs. I noticed he limped when he came out of the pub..."

"...And big Dougie got clipped trying to save his little buddy again?"

Ted nodded.

"That's what Rob said and the way he said it you could tell he's going to be saying it for the rest of his life. You'd hardly recognize him. He's got deep lines in his face already and he just looks, well, haunted I guess you'd say..."

I didn't know what to say, so it was just as well the radio crackled as Gary called us both right then.

"Thirty-Two? Fifty-One? A couple of deliveries."

Ted picked up the mike off the seat.

"Thirty-Two go ahead."

"Get your pen, Ted. It's quite a list. Here's the address first..."

He gave Ted the address of a house in the lower part of the British Properties every driver knew was rented to three very beautiful and very expensive call girls. There was a rustle of clicks from the radio. Gary called for order.

"Please, gentlemen. Hold your applause until the performance has ended. Here's the order, Thirty-Two...Two cans of Cool Whip, one jar of maraschino cherries, two packs of Players Filter cigarettes, one head of lettuce, one length of rubber tubing..."

The clatter of mike buttons was deafening. Gary chuckled into the dispatch mike.

"I know, Ted. Believe me I'm not making this up. Honest..."

"I believe you. I just don't think I can get all this at the Seven-Eleven."

"Just get what you can, man. I told them there was a limit..."

An anonymous driver interrupted.

"Sounds like no limit to me..."

"Keep it down. Okay, Five-One? Your order is a pack of Camel cigarettes and a quart of orange juice to this address and it's the basement entrance around the side, Five-One."

I made a note of the address he gave me and took the mike from Ted.

"Got it, Five-One...Trade you trips, Ted?"

"Uh, no thanks, Jack. I think I've got it covered."

I couldn't blame him. It was every driver's fantasy that he'd take a delivery to that upscale bunny ranch one night and be invited in to make up a fourth for bridge or something. Ted waved as he pulled out of the lot, leaving me standing by my cab thinking about Rob Coombes being alive all bitter and twisted and big Dougie Trumbull being dead in Vietnam. Night shift was more interesting than days with their endless round of groceries and doctor's offices, the small talk of politics and hockey, but sometimes it was a little too interesting. The graveyard cars were the ghost cars, phantom stage-coaches who fetched the spirits of the dead on their dark nameless errands to the banshee wail of distant sirens. Our patron saint was Charon the Ferryman and sometimes the ghosts wore the faces of people we had known in the light.

The traffic had thinned out to a trickle after the rush from the bars and I was glad I'd missed the worst of it, though after talking to Ted, I wasn't so sure on the last point. The streets were getting that quiet empty look I liked, so quiet you could hear the buzz from the streetlights and the big neon signs, so quiet you could hear the traffic signals kicking over at deserted intersections and the soft sucking ripple of your own tires on hot asphalt.

I picked up the Camels and ojay and found the address among the darkened houses on Tenth, east of Lonsdale a couple of blocks. I only cracked my shins once on something in the dark before I found the hidden door to the basement suite. The guy who answered my knock looked familiar, but after a few weeks in a cab everyone does. He was about my age, tall and stringy-looking with thick glasses. He seemed preoccupied and asked me in while he looked for his wallet. As he paid for the goods and the fare, he gave me the look.

"Hey, man. Don't I know you? You went to Delbrook High, right?"

"Right."

I introduced myself. He grinned.

"Right. Right...Jack Morrison. Len Sutherland. French Eleven? Remember?"

"For sure."

We shook hands. He twisted it into the fucking brother hand-shake like most assholes did.

"Long time, man. Want a Camel?"

I didn't have to walk a mile so I took one from the pack he'd torn open and lit up, taking a deep drag. The weight almost crushed my lungs.

"These'll get it over with quick."

"No shit, man. But you get such a taste for them you can't smoke anything else. They're expensive but I needed a hit and some vitamins to keep writing and I didn't feel like walking sixteen blocks..."

I'd noticed the typewriter and a stack of paper, the overflowing ashtray and a coffee cup on the coffee table.

"What're you writing?"

Len shrugged.

"It's a play...I mean, I hope it is. I started it and a guy from the CBC liked the idea, but I've gotta get it finished by Tuesday so he can take a first draft back to Toronto..."

"What's it about?'

"Well, it's about a guy in a basement suite, y'know?"

"A basement suite?"

Len got a bit defensive. I was still trying to remember how big a dork he'd been in high school.

"Yeah. Well, why not? You have to write about what you know. Right?"

"I'm with you...but how much can you write about a basement suite?"

He looked around. The usual second hand mis-matched furniture, inherited from parents or former room-mates. A couple of gallery posters, unframed, tacked to the walls. Books, shelved on breeze blocks and boards, the souvenirs of higher education.

"Quite a lot, if you think about it....I mean, how many basement suites there are in North Van, Burnaby, Vancouver...It's like two different worlds..."

I thought about it.

"Y'now, you may be onto something there. When I'm driving around late at night I notice all these houses that're dark upstairs but there'll be a light on down in the basement. Two or three in a block sometimes..."

Len was getting excited, obviously wired on his idea.

"That's it, man. That's it exactly...The night people, all living in these damp basements with wolf spiders in the bathtub and little windows high up in the walls where your plants die and you learn to recognize visitors by their shoes passing by at eye level and, well,...where do you live, Jack?"

I had to laugh.

"Let's just say all this looks kind of familiar."

"Right on, man. So what are you doing, besides pushing a hack? You still at UBC? I used to see you out there sometimes. You doing grad work or something?"

I shook my head.

"Nope. One minute I was working on my Honours essay on Alfred Lord Fucking Tennisball and the next thing I knew all sixty pages of it were in the fireplace and I was behind the wheel of a cab."

Len nodded sympathetically.

"Say, whatever happened to that chick I used to see you with in the Student Union cafeteria? She went to high school with us. She was in our French class and in Biology...She was your lab partner, wasn't she? Lynn? Linda something?..."

"Linda Arnold."

"Yeah, Linda Arnold. Man, she was a real skank in high school. Dressed like something out of *Little Women*. Then, pow, like she just transformed overnight, like a caterpillar into this totally cool butterfly...You still see her?"

"No. I don't."

"Yeah, I guess she's married with three kids and living in Richmond by now..."

I shook my head.

"No. She isn't. She's dead."

"What?"

"You heard me."

Len whistled softly.

"Wow, man...How...?"

"She killed herself."

Len's Camel was burning down unnoticed, tying his nicotined fingers together with knots of smoke.

"Holy shit...Why would a beautiful girl like that want to off herself?"

"Because she thought the guy she was in love with was still in love with an old girlfriend of his, one of those girls who'd been foxy since the obstetrician checked Female on her birth certificate. She didn't mean to kill herself. She just wanted to scare him into realizing how much she loved him. So when her parents went out to play bridge one night, she took a lot of sleeping pills and wrote him a note and passed out on the couch. Her parents were supposed to be home before midnight. Plenty of time to find her and have her stomach pumped...Only they were having a really good time, the cards were hot and they decided to shoot the moon and have another pink gin or two and play a couple more rubbers. They didn't get home until well after two..."

"Fuck. What a drag...Who was her boyfriend?"

I opened the door. Len suddenly felt the heat of the coal between his fingers and dropped the butt, stamping it out on the cheap linoleum floor.

"Owww! Fuck!"

"Catch you later, man. My mother's calling."

Len shook his fingers to cool them.

"Hey, man...Who was the guy?"

"Good luck with the play."

I pulled the door shut behind me and stepped into a darkness filled with ghosts, all trying to flag a cab.

Chapter 7

"Five-One clear. You looking for me?"

"Not me, Five-One, but I've got a personal for you. Another delivery."

"If I wanted to be a delivery boy I'd've signed on with Pizza Pieman."

"But then you'd be making minimum wage, Five-One."

"Yeah. My standard of living would improve."

"But you'd be a pimply dork driving a crapped out Beetle instead of a professional driver at the wheel of a luxurious Detroit automobile with power steering, power brakes and air-conditioning, Five-One."

"Okay. I give up. What's the order?"

"A pack of Export A and a colostomy bag to the Casino in The Clouds."

I laughed.

"You got that Five-One?"

"I got it. You know where to page me."

"Right, Five-One. I'll put you On Call."

I picked up the smokes at the Macs on Twelfth and hit the intercom button at the Casino in the Clouds a few minutes later. The speaker crackled back at me.

"Ah, hello?"

"Taxi, sir. Need your bag checked?"

"Ah, yes. My current one's quite full. I thought you might be a Jehovas Witness. I was going to ask you to step back five feet so I could empty it on your head."

The buzzer came on like a swarm of bees in a bass amplifier. The Casino in the Clouds was a two-bedroom apartment twenty-four floors up in a twenty-five storey tower on West Fourteenth, a block off Lonsdale. Chris Newman shared it with Al Monroe, a guitar player who was currently driving cab between bands. It was expensive, but neither of them would live in a basement suite and the only thing above them here was the penthouse. The place was starkly furnished, mostly with audio and photo equipment and a few directors chairs and a kit-couch from Ikea.

The spindly photo lights and reflectors were Newman's. He usually carried a Pentax or Minolta with him in the cab, taking night pictures, mug shots of interesting fares, or experimenting with infared film. He was actually a pretty good photographer, but he spent as much time in front of the camera as behind it, using friends or a timer to shoot endless rolls of his favourite subject to experiment with later in bathroom darkroom, tinting and solarizing. He opened the door and grabbed his chest.

"Quick! Do an emergency tracheotomy with your dick and stick a smoke in the hole before my lungs collapse!"

I flipped him the smokes.

"Pay up, deadbeat, and next time get somebody else to do your fucking grocery shopping."

"Sorry to bug you, Jack, but I had to call. I'm three games down and the fucking dice are finally going my way. C'mon in. Pull up a face and sit down."

The backgammon board was on the coffee table. Al waved from the balcony, where he was showing the view to a girl I vaguely recalled seeing at a couple of his gigs before the last band broke up in a welter of adulteries and artistic differences. A couple of the other drivers were hanging out, watching the game and sucking back the brown units. I helped myself to a beer from the fridge and scoped the game.

PJ sat in a directors chair that hunched him into a butterball across the table from the couch where Newman sprawled elegantly as a Georgian rake. Maggie was perched on the arm of the couch, wearing jeans so tight my appreciation of her thighs went from immense to immeasurable. She smiled and made a little wavy motion with her fingers, mouthing her beer bottle like a popsicle. Newman rolled and PJ burst out laughing.

"Double sixes again? What'd you bring him, Jack? A pair of trick dice from the Krac-A-Joke Shop?"

"Yeah. If that doesn't work, he's going to put the plastic dogshit on your chair next time you go to the can."

Newman gestured languidly toward the boxcar cubes.

"It's all in the wrist, boys.."

I made a quick jerk gesture toward my crotch.

"And your wrist has had plently of practise..."

Newman accepted the barb with smiling condescension.

"And since I feel lucky tonight, let's double it."

PJ smiled happily.

"It's your money."

Newman was all cheery nonchalance.

"Not any more it isn't, but if I don't get some of it back it's grass-clipping soup all next week again..."

Paul Dodson was standing in the corner, admiring Al's Gibson Firebird and Fender Strat in their stands. The night drivers picked on Dodson because of his whispery lisp on the radio. Every time he said "Twenty-thix" you could count on at least two or three ad lib imitations of his voice placing him at opposite ends of the board. Nobody really disliked him though. He didn't have enough personality to dislike. Not like The Count or Cece Wragg. Dodson leased a cab and drove it himself around the clock trying to make it pay. The other night drivers told him he was nuts, but he would patiently explain his reasoning to you with an innocence so serious it was almost lovable.

"But you thee...after I pay the leath and the lithenth and the inthurance and the meter feeth and dispatch feeth and the gath and oil and repairth, everything elth is pure profit..."

No one knew where Dodson lived. The other night drivers thought he slept in the cab parked on the street somewhere. He looked like it, thin and pasty with blue half-moons permanent as tat-

toos under both eyes. I talked guitars with him for a bit while Newman lost another game. Al's nuclear-capable stereo was pumping out
David Bowie's "Alladin Sane". It had been a bad year for rock and roll
with Jimi, Janis and Jim Morrison all dying of too much living and we
were down to cross-dressers in alien makeup. I stepped out onto the
balcony where it was cooler. The panorama of Vancouver spread out
before me from Point Grey to Burnaby Mountain, stretching away
like a carpet of light to Richmond and the horizon, the downtown
neon reflected as multicoloured streaks on the black waters of Burrard Inlet. I gave it the finger. Al waved me back from the rail.

"Don't lean against it, Jack. We couldn't get all the black shit
off. The curtains are still pretty fucked up too."

The girl immediately backed up and brushed the front of her
knit dress though she was nowhere near the rail.

"What happened? Did you guys have a fire or something?"

Al shook his head laughing.

"Not exactly...One of the boys brought up this thing the other
night. Some kind of big heavy duty distress flare he picked up at a sur-
plus store. It looked like a bazooka. Anyway, we had a few cocktails
and the usual backgammon happening when somebody decided it
would be a laugh to see if this thing worked. So we took it out here,
pointed it out at the Sears Tower across the water there and pulled the
trigger..."

Al and I were both laughing now, though it wasn't funny at the
time.

"Anyway it turned out to be some kind of rocket launcher. It let
go with a boom like ten sticks of dynamite. It would have blown in
the glass if we hadn't left the sliding doors open, but the living room
was full of black smoke and the curtains were on fire and we were all
flat on our asses and this huge bright magnesium flare was hanging
over Victoria Park from a freaking parachute lighting up half of
North Van. They must've been able to see it in White Rock. It was like
the Great White Light of everybody's acid trips...The cops totally
freaked, squealing around trying to figure out where it came from. It
was like a light-show down there...Meanwhile we're all inside with the
lights out and the windows open, trying to fan out the smoke with

towels and jackets and stomp out the flames in the carpet and curtains..."

The girl giggled.

"You guys are crazy."

I stepped back inside. Al was set for the evening. Girls always went for him, even over Newman. He was short and cute and had the face of a ruined choirboy. Between them he and Newman got more Code Seventeens than anybody in the fleet. "I'll be Code Seventeen for a while" meant "Don't call me, I'm having my fluid levels adjusted" and the driver who booked one could count on jamming the radio with mike-button clicks for a full minute at least.

"Double it again."

I looked at the board. PJ was obviously going to mop up Newman in short order again, obliviously happy at the prospect, yet Newman was calmly doubling the bet as if the fix was in. Usually he was bitchy on a losing streak. Then I looked at Maggie. She was staring at Chris with a fixed glazed expression I knew all too well. I sighed and headed for the door.

"A little exit music, Maestro...Hit the road, Jack and doncha come back no more no more no more no more..."

Newman glanced up, caught my eye and look down at the board again quickly and guiltily.

"Catch you later."

I pulled the door shut behind me without answering. There was a slight chill in the cab when I started it and the radio was just a soft static hum. I drove through the silent cooling streets for a while without calling in.

"Five-One?"

I didn't acknowledge.

"Five-One? Are you out there, Captain Midnite? This is Tranquility Base calling Captain Midnite..."

"Five-One, here."

"Working or sightseeing?"

"Give me whatever you've got. Give me your tired, your huddled messes..."

I didn't mind the late night trips. They were girls mostly, seen off on front porches or in apartment vestibules by boyfriends who'd just pulled their jeans on and couldn't be bothered with shirts or shoes since they were going right back to bed. The little things would toddle gingerly out to the cab on post-orgasmic jelly legs and I'd usher them smoothly and gently into the passenger seat. They'd whisper home addresses in soft breathy voices through puffy, slightly bruised lips and sit quietly with crumpled bills in their hands, their raw thighs glued together and moony fucked-out looks on their faces as I drove them home.

It was a good way to end a night. I felt protective toward those girls and always treated them with deference and care, opening doors and giving them my arm up the sidewalk if they needed it. More than once they nodded out on my shoulder, snuggling their heads against my leather jacket on the long late ride, the clean sweet scent of shampoo tickling my nose as I took them safely home. Once when I pulled up in front of her house, the girl looked up with sleepy wine-fuddled eyes and said "Thanks. I really had a wonderful time." Then she kissed me, long and passionately, before she got out of the cab. She made it all the way to the front door before she woke up and spun around. I just waved, cleared the unpaid fare off the meter, pulled the door shut and drove away into the night.

Chapter 8

The sky was turning from black to blue like an old bruise and I was ready to call Code Two for the night. Unexpected ghosts had flagged me down in the dark. It was the risk you took driving with a For Hire sign on your roof. Any restless night-crawling spirit or zombie from the past could get into your car for the price of the tariff. I didn't feel like hanging around on the off chance of a trip to the airport. It was a good way to round off the sheet, but a drive through Hell after twelve hours on the wheel. Gary broke the pre-dawn silence.

"Five-One?"

"Five-One, over."

"Another personal for you, Captain Midnite."

"See? You don't have to be a slut to be popular. Who is it this time?"

Gary gave me an address on East Eighteenth.

"Five-One. Are you sure that's for me? I don't think I know anybody at those numbers."

"By special request, Five-One. It's the basement suite."

"That figures."

"Five-One, come again?"

"Not important. I'm on my way."

I found the address easily, but I still didn't know who lived there. At least enough light had crept into the world that I could find the door without crippling myself. I wondered who would answer my soft knock.

It was Lorraine.

"You want to go CWR to Deep Cove, Morrison?"

CWR meant Car Waiting Return, a paid two-way trip, no dead-heading back empty. The Cove was a good longish trip too, but Lorraine was Company and I wouldn't give her the satisfaction of charging her.

"Sure. Whatever."

Rudy appeared at her shoulder wearing a speedy grin.

"Hi, man."

"Hey, Rudy."

We all stumbled out to the cab, me, Rudy, Lorraine and her five year old, Jake. We'd gone a block when Lorraine snapped my meter flag down.

"Forget it, I was about to Code Two anyway."

Drivers usually charged other drivers and Company staff a flat two or five bucks for a ride to anywhere and put it straight into their pockets. I reached over to flip up the flag, but Lorraine put her hand over mine.

"Fuck you, Morrison."

At least that was normal.

It was a nice ride to the Cove, long and quiet in the breaking dawn. Jake chattered away softly to me about the meter, the radio, the cab, telling me I was lucky to be driving a Dodge Coronet instead of one of those Plymouth Fury pigs. I let him book the trip, holding the big old fashioned Motorola mike in both grubby hands. Gary acknowledged without missing a beat.

"Right, Five-One. I'll put you CWR to Deep Cove on the board."

The Cove was pretty and silent as a postcard. Only anchored sailboats broke the flat acetylene sheen of the water. It was going to be another hot sunny day, but you could feel the ancient autumn damp creeping down Indian Arm from the mountains where winter lived.

"We're going out to the marina at the end of Panorama Drive. C'mon down and have a look at the boat if you want."

I parked the cab, notched the flag back so it wouldn't run up any waiting time and followed them down the creaking floats to the half-cabined sixteen foot runabout. The name Speedboat was freshly painted on the transom. Lorraine and Rudy had acquired the boat just outside Horseshoe Bay when it burst into flames and its owners abandoned it, sure it was going to explode. Lorraine and Rudy were out fishing and drinking with some friends in a rental and Lorraine bullied them into putting her aboard the burning boat. She put out the fire, seared her hands badly enough to have them both bandaged for a week, and towed it in to claim the right of salvage. I'd heard that story too.

Rudy pulled a bottle of Canadian Club out of the forward locker. "Jolt to take the chill off?"

We passed the bottle around as Rudy turned the engine over and got ready to cast off. The rye was cool and oily in my mouth, but it burned me alive again.

"Where you off to?"

Rudy smiled and handed me a folded envelope whose corner was stuffed with pills.

"Got some business at a commune up at Brighton Beach. Thought I'd take the kid along for the day. Those'll keep you rolling through the weekend."

"The only place I'm rolling now is into the sack, but I'll bless you later tonight."

"Right on."

"Say, Rudy?"

"Yeah, man?"

"I know this guy who wants to buy a piece. You know anybody in the hardware business?'

"How big a piece are we talking about?"

"One fifty. Maybe two."

"You don't get much bang for that kind of buck."

"That's what I told him."

"Tell you what. I'll see what I can do when I get back tonight. Call me later."

"Will do."

The engine burbled fitfully, then they were away, Rudy and little Jake waving from the stern, cutting a wide white wake across the sleeping Cove. I followed Lorraine back to the cab, watching her denimed backside with studied disinterest. We didn't talk much on the way back. Once she broke the stiff silence to thank me for letting Jake use my radio.

"No sweat. He's a good kid."

When we pulled up in front of her place again she asked me in for coffee. Another surprise.

"Sure. I might as well make it an even three quarts for my twelve."

Lorraine filled out and signed the charge slip before I could argue. Then I was sitting in her small kitchen while she made me coffee and wiped the sticky traces of Jake's toast and Cheerios off the counter. She produced a bottle of Tia Maria from a cupboard and poured a generous dose into the coffee. She leaned against the counter, holding her mug of coffee in both hands.

"How come you're always such a prick, Morrison?"

I shrugged and smiled.

"I apply myself. I work at it."

She nodded, looking at her coffee like she was thinking about something else.

"You a speed freak, too, Morrison?"

"Not me. I just get high on life, y'know?"

Lorraine looked up.

"Fuck you, Morrison."

I shrugged. She looked away again.

"Rudy's a speed freak. That's all he does...Y'know? That's all."

I sighed.

"Yeah. I know."

I stood up and went over to her, took the coffee mug from her hands and set it on the formica counter. Her hands fell to her sides. She wouldn't look up at me. Her lips were stiff when I kissed her, her jaw set, her teeth locked against my tongue. I kept kissing her, her eyes, her cheeks, her neck. Suddenly her mouth opened and she went for me like a starved piranha, biting the corner of my lower lip and

241

drawing blood. I put my hands on her shoulders, pushed her back a little.

"Slow down...Gently."

She opened her eyes. The pure mean I saw there was diluted by tears, one at the corner of each eye. Her voice was a shaky whisper.

"Fuck you, Morrison."

"I usually let people I fuck call me by my first name. It's Jack."

She turned away and went into the bedroom. I took a long pull on my coffee and hung my leather jacket over the back of a kitchen chair. Then I followed her. I pulled my t-shirt over my head and stood by the bed looking at her. The skin on her belly was a bit loose and crepey, stretched by Jake. Her breasts were heavier, softer than I expected. Lying beside her, holding her for a long time, my fingers memorized her skin, muscles, bones. Who would have thought all that silky, rosy flesh could exist under the leather and denim bullshit? I'd been awake so long I wasn't sure I wasn't dreaming.

She did have an interesting tattoo. When I knelt between her knees, stroking the long soft insides of her thighs, she caught me looking at it. A tiny red and yellow butterfly fluttering out of the thicket between her legs. Modestly she put her hand over it, grinning like a cheeky schoolgirl.

"Hey, Morrison. Where's my jelly doughnut?"

I plunged into her, laughing.

Cʜᴀᴘᴛᴇʀ 9

Saturday night started at two in the afternoon. Lorraine woke me up, shaking me for the third or fourth time. I seemed to remember doing it in my sleep once, maybe twice. Before I got my eyes open she was pulling on my chain again.

"Can you do it like this all the time?"

"Only with someone who really hates my guts."

"Fuck you, Morrison."

She rolled away from me angrily. I grabbed her waist and held her, trying it from behind this time. Her elbow snapped around and caught me a real stinger on the ear. Undaunted, I grabbed a handful of her long hair and pulled her head back, biting her shoulder and thinking of lions mating in a wildlife documentary. This was more like it, better than the look of hurt and wonder, the soft whimpering and the little tears squeezed out of the corners of her eyes when we'd done it the first time. That scared me. Too much of that and we'd never be able to tell each other to fuck off again. I thought I'd established a compelling rhythm when she raised her hips slightly, but it was only so she could reach underneath herself and give my nuts a savage twist. I rolled off her and into an agonized ball.

"Oww! Fuck you, Lorraine!"

Sitting up, she burst out laughing. After a minute or so, I did too. She still couldn't kiss worth spit. Not even when she kissed me goodbye after bluntly telling me to haul ass because she had to be on the phones at four and while Rudy's business trip should mean a whole day spent lounging on the porches and beaches of the quiet communes up the Arm, you never knew when he'd take it into his speedball brain to come back early.

I was wrung out, drier than a bug six weeks in a spiderweb. The car was mine for the weekend, I didn't have to book on 'til six, so I drove down to the Tomahawk Restaurant off Marine Drive, wolfed down a huge Yukon Style bacon and egg breakfast and washed down a couple of Rudy's pills with a gallon of coffee. I stopped in at my basement suite on West Twenty-Third, showered, shaved, watered my dying plants, decided a nap would make me feel worse and besides, the speed was good and starting to work, so I fucked around, read the *Tibetan Book of The Dead* and *The Maltese Falcon* for an hour and booked on the air fifteen minutes early.

Doktor Goebbels was waiting for me.

"Gutnen abend, Five-Vun. Sinze you are not on ze air until zix o clock precizely, you haff zirteen minutes to practise goot manners and proper radio procedures in ze prifacy of your vehicle. I succhest you make goot use of ze time."

"In ordnung, Five-One."

It looked like it was going to be one of those nights.

And it was.

There was a company party at Bob Sunstrom's house in West Van, which meant the drivers who were on the air spent a lot of time on dead-head trips, carrying other drivers and staff up there for two bucks a pop and having a drink or two for the road while they were there. By eight-thirty, most of the drivers in the fleet were half-shot. Fortunately, most of their customers were too pissed to notice.

Even I got sucked into it, driving Doug Davidson's current girl-friend, Samantha, up to the party. Davidson was still at the office, try-ing to keep the tenuous organisation from disintegrating too early in the evening. Sam was on the short side for my taste, built like a cus-tom Caddy, all curves and flares. I couldn't figure out what she saw in Davidson. She actually seemed to have something between her ears besides dead air. Maybe she was kinky. She'd certainly be a stellar addition to the polaroid collection.

It was Gary who'd told me about Doug's photo-fetish. Davidson had shown a bunch of the pictures to him as a prelude to quizzing him about the sex lives of cripples.

"What'd you tell him?"

Gary winked and waited. I laughed confessionally.

"Okay. I give up...How do you do it?"

Gary smiled.

"Simple. They get on top, of course."

I nodded.

"Simple..."

"Yeah, they do all the work, I just lay back and enjoy...And they love it. They take it so seriously, so reverently, actually sacrificially, like schoolgirl saints going to martyrdom. I mean, they're making this great humanitarian gesture, fucking a crip..."

"Wow."

"Yeah...So, you want to borrow my crutches tonight?"

I actually thought about it for a moment before I cracked up.

"You asshole."

I wished Gary was on the mike instead of the Mad Doktor. Klaus sounded wired for more than sound and ready to blow tonight. I tried to avoid going anywhere near the office. I didn't want to see the Doktor and I wasn't sure how I felt about seeing Lorraine.

"Five-Vun. Code Fifteen."

The Doktor was calling me in. Code Fifteen meant Come To The Office On Company Business. Well, if the Nazi still had a hair up it from the night before, there was no time like now to pull it out. I wheeled into the hot White Spot parking lot and stomped up the stairs.

Doug Davidson was waiting for me. He was pouring rye and seven for Lorraine and himself in paper cups and he offered me a short one in his private office, "Where the Gestapo won't notice." Davidson was forty-five years old and a bachelor who lived with his senile mother. Drivers routinely did her shopping and carried her to doctors offices and sympathized with her concerns about when young Douglas was going to find a nice girl, settle down and get married.

He owned three cabs that made just enough money to keep

them on the road and was paid a salary for managing the company and handling the drivers. The job gave him the pull to pick good drivers for his fragile cars.

"The best of the worst. The rest of these clowns drive like they're trying to raise the entry fee for a demoliton derby."

I drove one of his cars.

Even with the door shut we could hear the radio squawking and the Doktor snapping and snarling at drivers through the heavy air traffic. The office was stifling, despite the open windows and three cheap fans moving the cigarette smoke around. I snapped my head toward the radio room.

"You should take him down. He's cracking up, man."

Davidson nodded.

"I'm going to spell him for a while in a few minutes. He's really on the hot seat these days and I'd appreciate it if you guys would lighten up on him."

"You got it...So what's so important you can spare your fifty-five percent of the next five minutes?"

"I just wanted to ask you about that old guy last week, Mister Edwards. The cops might want to talk to you about him."

"What's to talk about? He was ninety-four. I could see his skull right through his scalp. Two blocks from the nursing home, while he's telling me what buildings used to be here and there when he was a boy in North Van, he gave a little wheeze and died. That's all she wrote."

"What did you do when you realized he was dead?"

"I booked away to the morgue."

Davidson looked at me thoughtfully and took a sip of his rye.

"That's what I heard, Jack. Why did you do that?"

I sighed.

"Because I'm not licensed for The Great Beyond, Dave. That was as far as I could take him. Shit, I got stiffed on the trip, you could say. I didn't take a penny off him and it's customary to pay the ferry-man, y'know?"

"Okay, okay. No big deal...I just wanted to know because it happened in one of my cabs."

I drained my cup in one swallow.

"Now you know."

"Ah, you don't, uh, feel weird or anything about driving Fifty-One after that? I mean, I'd understand if you wanted a change of cars..."

"Why should I?"

Giving up, Davidson killed his own drink.

"No reason. You can roll when you're ready."

"I'm ready."

I almost resisted the temptation to see Lorraine. I was pissed off that I even wanted to see her, but I stuck my head into the radio room anyway.

"Hey, kid? Still want that jelly doughnut?"

She was on the phone, flushed and frowned and waved me off curtly. The Mad Doktor spun around in his swivel chair, eyes glowing like the torches of Nuremburg.

"Five-Vun! Drifers are not permitted in ze radio room!"

I snapped my heels together, shot my right arm out in the Fascist salute, whirled and goose-stepped down the hall. I heard the door slam behind me and Lorraine telling Klaus to go fuck spiders. In the hall I passed Doug with a fresh drink in his hand.

"Sorry, man."

He nodded. I stomped down the stairs into the warm night. There were no ghosts in the parking lot, only the invisible pervasive aromas of fried onions, potatoes and vinegar, the comforting smells of summer that never changed.

Chapter 10

In the parking lot, I ran into Chris Newman, booking on and picking up his car an hour late, as usual.

"Where've you been? Steam-ironing a crease in your jock?"

Newman looked nervous and embarrassed.

"You seen PJ?"

"He's not on the board tonight. He's going to Sunstrom's party."

"I'm such an asshole."

I heaved a sigh toward the Marine Drive gutter.

"What d'you mean?"

"You're going to think I'm an asshole..."

"I know you're an asshole. Just tell me what happened and why you're an asshole this time."

Newman said one word.

"Maggie."

"Oh, fuck, no...You didn't...What am I saying? Of course you did."

Newman shrugged helplessly.

"She wanted to stay, man...Y'know?"

"So what? You showed PJ the door and told him to make himself scarce so you could put a glaze on the chick he's hung up on? That must've been some scene. I hope she was worth it."

Newman shook his head bitterly.

"No way, man. These young girls, they all think giving a blow-job means letting a guy put his cock in their mouths. They think fucking means lying on their backs with their legs open. They might as well be inflatable girlfriends..."

I put my arm over his shoulder sympathetically.

"I'm really sorry to hear that, Chris. I think you should write a stern letter to the local school board complaining about the inadequate standard of sex education young girls are receiving these days..."

"You think I'm an asshole."

He waited for me to disagree, to admit I'd have done the same thing for a quarter hour between Maggie's apparently deceptive thighs.

"You're right. I think you're an asshole...A totally unmitigated asshole."

Newman looked away.

"Are we still friends?"

I shrugged, opening the drivers door of Fifty-One.

"Us assholes have to stick together...Later. If I get a chance I'll drop in to the party and try to find PJ."

I turned the key and booted it out of the parking lot, but I never got to the party. At least, not to that one, though I dropped in to a dozen others, bouncing back and forth across the North Shore like a pinball in an earthquake. I was hoping for a break, a trip downtown, anything, even a carload of the fat East End hookers working the Greek ships, but the closest I got to it was another personal from Len Sutherland, a delivery of course.

I handed him the Camels as he opened the door. Flushed and punchy from lack of sleep, he tore open the pack, lit one and shooked one up for me. I lit it and took a deep calming drag and almost coughed up a lung.

"Shit, man. Your lungs will pack it up by Tuesday. How's the play coming, anyway?"

"Better than I thought. I'm just working on the part where this guy in the basement suite has an affair with the wife from upstairs, y'know? Only they don't really have anything to talk about afterwards... Different worlds. Get it?"

"I get it."

"He hears her playing this same record over and over again all day, see? The song is 'It's Only Make Believe' by Conway Twitty, and it's kind of like a soundtrack played on this old phonograph..."

"Sounds terrific, man...Say, can I use your phone?"

"Right on, man...See the record symbolizes..."

Len droned on about his play while I dialed the private office line. I was cool to Lorraine, but she gave me her home number when I told her I had business with Rudy.

"Hey, Rudy? Jack Morrison...You find anything for that friend of mine?"

"Oh, yeah, man. Can do...I'll be home for an hour or so, then I gotta meet Lorraine and go on to that company party thing and do a little business there...Can you wing by?"

"You need a ride?"

"No, it's cool. She's borrowing one of the off-shift cars and picking me up. Hey maybe I'll drive it around later and pick up some extra bread. See what it's like."

"Don't waste your time. Welfare pays better. I'll see you in twenty minutes or so, I hope. It's Nightmare Alley out there tonight and the Nazi will shit kittens if I put myself Code Three right now."

Sometimes when you were hustling and hot, everything just seemed to go your way. Before I could even clear from Len's, the Doktor was calling me on the radio with a trip out of the Olympic. I was already halfway there, maintaining radio silence, but I pretended I'd just got back into the cab. Klaus sounded slightly more in control after the break Doug had given him, but he was still as edgy as a cat in a roomfull of mousetraps. I found Terry in a corner of the pub, shooting pool on the ragged stained short table with his friend from the night before. They looked like they'd slept in their clothes in the same ditch.

"You still interested in the hardware business?'

"Right on, man!"

"Keep it down...Got the money on you?"

Terry tapped the breast pocket of his mackinaw.

"Okay. It's gonna be two-fifty. Best I could do. Hope you can come up with the extra scratch."

He gave his friend pissed-off look. The friend shrugged what the hell.

"Okay, man, but you better be..."

"Hey, you don't tell me anything better be anything, man. I'm just making a delivery, that's all. I'm doing you a favour that's nothing but trouble to me, so don't fuck me around. Just give me the money and finish your game. I'll be back soon. All you have to do is sit tight and stay cool."

As it worked out, I was back sooner than I thought. My fare out of the Olympic was Dennis O'Connor, a regular, an old time dealer and rounder who was in and out of Oakalla like it had a revolving door. We got as far as the sidewalk out front where two idiots were getting an early start by punching each other out in front of a small crowd. When I looked over my shoulder, I'd lost my fare. Pushing a couple of shoulders out of the way, I found O'Connor rolling around on the cement with one of the spectators, trying to pound the guy's head into the curb. I got in the empty cab, booked away to Lynn Valley and drove up to Rudy and Lorraine's place. I gave Rudy two hundred and and gave me an unloaded .22 calibre Colt revolver. I hefted the little pistol.

"No bullets?"

"You want to give him bullets?"

"I get your point."

Terry and his pal were still at the table when I got back to the Olympic. Terry followed me out to the parking lot and got in the cab, alone. I insisted. I took the pistol out of the back of my waistband where it was digging into my kidneys and handed it to him. He tried the action.

"Kinda small, man."

"So's the bread. You don't get a .45 for small change."

"Hey, man? No bullets?"

"Our deal was for the piece. Not for ammunition...Take it or leave it, 'cause I gotta roll like five minutes ago, man."

He took it, as I knew he would, and I was up fifty bucks. When

I cleared, I even got my break trip downtown out of an apartment a
block off Lonsdale. Two hookers, one black, one white, both beautiful and a black dude who dressed like a jockey on vacation. He and
the white chick sat in back. He motioned the black girl to sit up front
with me. Before I could pull away from the curb, he shoved enough
coke up my nose to keep a bull elephant dancing the tango for a week
and asked me if I knew where a man could get something good to
smoke. I wheeled out feeling the top of my head lift off and cruised
down to a 24 hour gas bar on Marine Drive. My tank was more than
half-full. A sleepy young guy with long blonde hair came out to the
pump.

"Hey, Bobby. I got a man here who needs a pack of smokes.
He's a real heavy smoker."

Bobby grinned the slow wide grin of the terminally stoned.

"Hawaiian or Colombian, man?"

The black guy in the back chuckled.

"Hawaiian, if you please. I have been promising these ladies I
would take them to Hawaii."

The girls giggled. Bobby came back with a rolled plastic baggie
up his sleeve and money changed hands with me making change and
picking up ten in the shuffle. We pulled out onto Marine Drive and
headed for Lions Gate Bridge as pungent smoke filled the cab.

"This man is the Man, ladies. Should we take him to Hawaii
with us?"

The girls giggled again.

"I'd love to, man, but I can't handle the radio from there. The
fucking thing starts picking up alien folk music from Mars and shit
and I can't function. Strictly Buck Rogers, y'know?"

"I read you, baby. How'd you like a little action instead?'

"Right now a little action would probably put me out of
action."

He laughed and leaned forward to stroke the black girl's shoulder.

"Do something nice for the man, honey..."

The girl shrugged and unzipped my fly. I was soaring. I almost
booked a Code Seventeen on the bridge, but I remembered Lorraine
might still be in the office and she knew the code. Why rub it in? I had

it made. Money left right and centre. A head full of clear exploding light. A beautiful woman I'd met ten minutes ago was sucking my cock. Her neck twisted sinuously, resting on my thigh. When we hit the middle of the bridge in the centre suicide-lane, the car was moving so fast it rose up out of its shocks and I screamed out the window with joy at the traffic, the lights and the city.

The man in the back seat laughed softly.

Chapter 11

I couldn't lose. At the Penthouse Cabaret on Seymour, I picked off a flag going right back to Fourth and Lonsdale, so I made money both ways and pulled up on the Second Street stand down the block from the Olympic just in time for the pre-midnight slump and a tar-pit coffee from the Seven-Eleven. Chris Newman, Dodson, and Rick Shaw were all on the stand ahead of me, waiting for Last Call. We all sat in the lead car, Newman's. Rick read his physics textbook while the rest of us swapped lies and listened to the closing half-hour of Radio Berlin.

The Doktor dispatched Ted Brauer to Bob Sunstrom's place. Then he sent Fender Bender to the same address. The party would be fucking up Ted's reading no end. West Van was usually quiet after ten or so. I'd noticed on the radio that Newman was hanging around North Van all night. He usually hated pub trips and hung out in the high rent district. His favourite customers were rich old divorcees from the British Properties, who accounted for many of his Code Seventeens. You couldn't rag him about it because he bragged that he'd fuck a snake if somebody would hold its head and proudly claimed to have dry-humped several unconscious traffic accident victims when he arrived first on the scene, before calling 911.

"If they're not wearing a toe-tag, they're in play."

I guessed he was avoiding both the Donut Shop and the possibility of a trip to or from Sunstrom's party.

Then the radio came alive. Ted booked away to the West End of downtown. I turned up the volume a notch.

"That's where Samantha lives."

A few minutes later, Bender booked away Van West, but hesitantly, putting himself On Call. Klaus was in no mood to have his Volkspanzers wandering off all over the board as the mood took them.

"Vas ist your exact destination, Forty-Nine? Vhere vill you clear?"

There was no answer. In Newman's car we turned up the radio.

"I wonder what the fuck's going on?"

"Forty-Nine? Do you read?"

"I read you, Forty-Nine. I...Whoa!"

We could hear serious rubber peeling off the Goodyears in the background that time. Bender came back on.

"Ah, Forty-Nine? I'm having, ah...Shit!"

His radio went dead and the Doktor went berserk.

"Forty-Nine! Forty-Nine! You vill pull ofer and report your precize destination immediately! Do you read? Immediately!"

Then Doug Davidson came on the air. He sounded like his eyeballs were floating.

"Uh, Fordy-Nine, here...Our deshtinashun is car Thirdy-Two, over...This is Fordy-Nine calling Thirdy-Two..."

"Mister Davidson! You haff no authorization to be on ze air! I must insist you surrender zat radio to ze authorized driver of Forty-Nine! Immediately!"

Over on the other side of town in Newmans car, we nudged each other in the ribs. Even Rick Chang looked up wide-eyed from his text book.

"This is better than fucking tv, man."

"You can't beat an old time radio show."

Ignoring the Doktor, Davidson came back on the air.

"Thirdy-Two? Ted?...Thish is Doug. I don't want to pull rank on you...I know yer onny doin' yer job, but..."

The Doktor cut him off. He sounded like he was biting the dispatch mike.

" Forty-Nine! Are you in control of your vehicle?"

Bender responded after a moment or two. From the engine sounds in the background he was trying to break the land speed record for a fully loaded taxi.

"Forty-Nine, well...Sure, I mean, sort of...That is, I...Jesus Christ!"

The transmission was cut off, then Davidson came on the air again, maudlin instead of threatening.

"Look, Ted...I like you, man. You're a good guy. One of the best of the worst. I hate to do this but that cab yer drivin' belongs to me and if ya don' pull over ri' now, I'm gonna haveta put ya Code Two, buddy..."

The Doktor bounced off the roof.

"Code Two! You are Code Two, Mister Davidson! Forty-Nine! You are nicht in control of your radio! You are nicht in control of your vehicle! You are Code Two immediately! I repeat, Code Two immediately! ...Thirty-Two! You are not responding to your radio! You are also Code Two! Immediately! You are all Code Two!"

I picked up Newman's mike from the dash clip.

"C'mon. Let's do it. All together now..."

I pressed down the button and all four of us, even Rick, began to chant in unison.

"Sieg Heil! Sieg Heil! Sieg Heil!"

At eleven fifty-five, with five minutes left to go on his shift, Doktor Goebbels signed off forever. Several sharp cracks of static burst out of the radio, as if someone was smashing the dispatch mike repeatedly against a wall, then there was silence. Klaus Fischer was Code Two.

Doug Davidson, however, was not.

"Ted?...Teddy? I hate to do this man, but yer fired, buddy. Pull that cab over right now...D'ya read me, Ted? Pull her over and gimme the keys. Yer not drivin' for me anymore. Yer canned. Finished. Unemployed. Code Two forever."

There was no answer from Thirty-Two.

"Sam?...Aw, Sam, honey. If you can hear me, tell him to pull over, hon'. I jush wanna talk to ya...He's onny makin' it worse for himself, babe. I'm gonna haveta charge him with car theft..."

Silence descended for a full minute, then Ted finally came on the air, sounding quite relaxed under the circumstances.

"Thirty-Two. I'm clear Van West."

Bender radioed in moments later.

"Forty-Nine. I'm also clear Van West."

I tapped Newman's mike button once, softly.

"The sound of one hand clapping."

Gary answered, calm as a fine day in the Bermuda Triangle.

"Thirty-Two, right. Forty-Nine, right....Good evening, drivers and welcome to Gary's Graveyard Revue, bringing you thrills and spills and big bills into the wee hours...Get your pens and pencils ready 'cause we're going to play Cab Keno, a little Bingo On The Boulevards...The wheels go 'round and 'round and where they stop, nobody knows...We'll have our first lucky number of the night right after the full zone count."

An unidentified driver chimed in.

"Did somebody say 'count'? Vun, Too, Tree..."

I looked over my shoulder.

"Here comes trouble on a forklift."

Zeke himself was staggering along the sidewalk from the Olympic carrying a full load by the look of him. I nudged Chris Newman.

"You're first on the stand."

He shook his head.

"Rick? Paul?"

Even they weren't that desperate for a buck.

"That makes it unanimous."

Zeke was the biggest and meanest Indian on the Cap Reserve. Three hundred pounds of pure rage looking for a place to touch down. Even Fat Fred wouldn't fuck with him under a full moon. He paused at the last cab, mine, and tried to open the door. It was locked. He kicked a deep dent in the door panel and punched the side window so hard we heard it crack. He stumbled to the next cab, Dodson's. Also locked. We could hear him growling and and grumbling as he went to the front of the cab and kicked in a headlight and part of the grille. Dodson winced, knowing it would be his deductible it came out of. Zeke moved along to Rick's cab. Finding it locked, he tore the AM aerial out of the front fender and whipped paint off the hood with it until he got tired of that. Finally he approached Newmans car.

We all double-checked our door locks. Zeke pulled on all four handles, lumbering ponderously around the car. Then he stepped up onto the trunk and jumped on it once, buckling it. From there he stepped up onto the roof and jumped again, buckling it too, and kicked the top-light to pieces for good measure. Finally he crashed down on the hood, caving it in and popping the hinges. Stepping down onto the sidewalk, he sauntered off along Second Street toward the St. Alice Hotel without a backward glance. Newman sighed thoughtfully.

"I think I'm Code Two."

As it turned out, we were all Code Two. The pub rush petered out fast, everyone having shot their wad the night before. The graveyard drivers, what was left of us, limped down to the office to have a beer with Gary and get the inside story on the impromptu theatre-of-the-airwaves. Me, Ted Brauer, Bender, Rick Chang and Paul Dodson were just settling in listening to Gary's account of how the Mad Doktor had blown a fuse, trashed the office and had to be restrained by a West Van cop, when Bob Sunstrom himself staggered up the stairs from the party, blitzed as a European capital, and fired us all on the spot for drinking on the job.

We all trooped down the stairs and piled into Fifty-One, Gary having thoughtfully handed me the rest of his case of beer, and I fired her up and drove around the back of Park Royal Mall, a hundred yards or so from the office, parked in the dark and we all opened fresh ones and waited. It took Sunstrom about five minutes to realize he'd fired the entire graveyard shift, including the dispatcher, and that every other member of his staff was back at his house, drunk as a pack of fiddler's bitches and passed out or puking all over his furniture, in no shape to answer the phone, much less dispatch or drive.

Tentatively, he came on the air.

"Ah, this is, ah, dispatch to...anybody?"

I handed my mike to Gary.

"Let him sweat for a couple of minutes."

"Ah...This is base, er, dispatch...Aw, c'mon, guys. Can't you take a joke?"

I nodded to Gary. He squeezed the mike.

"We're having a study-session, Bob. We'll let you know when we're prepared to negotiate."

"Negoshiate? Aw, guys...We got trips up an'..."

The soft twitter of unanswered phones filled the background. In sixty seconds or less, those people would be calling the other company. We had him. We knew it and he knew it. We let him simmer for another five minutes, then settled for no reprisals or suspensions against any of us, especially against Bender or Ted Brauer for their part in the high speed car chase that had apparently resulted in some nasty phone calls from the West Van cops, the Bridge Patrol and Vancouver Metro Police to Bob's personal number.

We even made him throw in a case of beer, to be provided for the graveyard shift, as the retroactive price of having to work the night of the company party and not being available to pass out or puke on his furniture. He balked at that, knowing it would cost him a pint of blood at Jack the bootlegger's on a long weekend, but we stuck to our guns and he folded. I fired up Fifty-One and idled back to the office.

"Solidarity forever."

Gary gave me the brother handshake.

"Power to the fucking people, man."

Chapter 12

If he'd had another half hour, Sunstrom could have let us stay Code Two forever, answered the phones, dispatched and done the driving himself. The phones stopped ringing and the airwaves went stone dead, as if the whole city had fucked itself out, rolled over and gone to sleep. I was too restless from the speed and coke to sit on a stand working on the curvature of my spine, so I cruised the silent empty streets, keeping an eye out for flags, putting endless unpaid miles on the car, not even bothering to book the zone changes.

Sometime after three I was rolling along East Esplanade when I caught sight of a King Cab that wasn't showing any lights, parked in the shadows near where the body shops and engine rebuilders on Esplanade petered out into a pot-holed alley flanked by wild brambles. I drove by, but a cold chill climbed up my aching shoulders. A block further on, I hung a u-turn and doubled back.

I pulled in close enough behind the other cab to see the thin trail of exhaust bubbling out of the pipe. I read the number off the trunk lid. Twenty-Six. Paul Dodson. Nobody had heard from him for an hour or so. I hit the high beams. Dodson was slumped over the wheel. I felt like a cat with a fur-ball caught in its throat. I got out and walked up the drivers side of Twenty-Six, taking short careful steps, my fists tightly balled. The car was idling, emitting that soft ticking big-V8 hiss, like a cop car. Gingerly I reached out and opened the drivers door.

Dodson was draped over the wheel, his head resting on his right forearm. His left hand was in his lap, still clutching a slice of the medium size Pizza Pieman Full House Special that lay half-eaten in its open box on the seat beside him. I could smell anchovies. Dodson snored roughly. There were greasy traces of tomato sauce around his slack mouth.

My breath whistled out between my clenched teeth. Reaching carefully under Dodson's chest, I turned the key in the ignition, cutting the engine. Dodson stirred, but didn't wake up. I checked his doors, making sure they were all locked, then ripped a big slice of pizza out of the box. I shut the drivers door gently, locked, leaving the window down an inch. I cut my own lights and backed away as quietly as I could.

The slice was still faintly warm. It tasted wonderful. As I was rolling back onto Marine Drive, wiping my mouth with my sleeve, Gary called.

"Five-One? You still with us?"

"Five-One, yeah. I'm on tour. What's up?"

"Well, I've got a personal for you. It's a pickup at The Black Anguish on Davie, downtown. You up for it?"

I didn't answer.

"Five-One?"

"I'm here."

"It sounded personal and urgent, Five-One. I think I can spare you for a while. I'll put you On Call."

There was no traffic on the bridge. I was at the Black Angus, a twenty-four hour steak house frequented by whores, transvestites, bumboys, junkies, drunks and other low-lifes who had no reason to go home or no homes to go to, in ten minutes flat. The hostess, who looked like she was working there while she waited for the antibiotics to kick in, directed me to a corner booth. The lone occupant was holding a wet napkin containing ice cubes, obviously provided by the management, over her left eye. At least her lip and nose had stopped bleeding.

"We have to stop meeting like this, Irene...Oh, sorry. I'm not supposed to call you that. I'm supposed to call you Tiffany or Alexis or some other bullshit alias. What is it this week?"

She reached for my hand and squeezed it.

"Thanks for coming, Jack..."

"You know, when we were kids I used to wonder what it would be like to see something really beautiful, something like the Parthenon or the Taj Mahal, bombed flat and bulldozed. I guess this is as close as I'll get."

"Please, Jack. Don't start. Just take me home...Please?"

"I wish I could, Irene. But nobody we know lives in the old neighbourhood now. I get calls up there sometimes, but I never recognize anybody."

"Just get me out of here?"

She'd been crying, but she didn't now. I put my arm around her waist and hoisted her out to the cab. I was going to settle the tab, but the manager waved me off, grateful to me for making one of his problems disappear. The hostess gave me a cold frightened look and turned away. Irene moved carefully, as though she hurt inside.

"I should take you to St. Pauls Emergency..."

She shook her head, almost doubled over in the seat.

"I'll be alright..."

"Sure you will...Still at the same place?"

She nodded. I snaked the car through the impromptu pedestrian mall that was Denman St., giving a few jay-walkers intimations of mortality. I nearly clipped a couple of guys holding hands in a crosswalk. They hugged each other in terror. One of them flipped me the finger and I shoved my head out the open window.

"You wish!...Fuck him, I did!"

Irene tried to laugh. It seemed to hurt her.

"I'm not the only one who's changed, Jack."

I crashed the orange light and Georgia and headed for the Stanley Park causeway.

"I don't think you've changed all that much, Irene. You always did want to be the girl who hung out with the cool guys. Whenever the boys built a secret tree fort, you teased and flirted with us until one of us broke the oath and snuck you up there when nobody was around. Remember how bad you wanted to be the only girl who got into the paper-shack? You didn't speak to me for years after I fucked that up for you...You'd already bragged to your girlfriends. Guess I made you look dumb for once...In high school you shook your pert pom-poms and got on the cheerleading squad in Grade Ten so you could hang out with the Grade Twelve varsity football stars...Now you think this guy Rodney and his pals are players. You know what they are? They're a bunch of janitors from Seattle who come up here on weekends and fool dumb little white chicks into believing they're big time pimps and gamblers. And you're so dumb you're out fucking a bunch of junior management trainees and giving him the money...You ever bump into any of those high school varsity all-stars in their cheap car-salesman suits theses days? In your professional capacity, I mean? I do. Most of them are already going bald and running to fat and you know they've got a knocked-up sorority sister wife at home whose ass looks like the back of a crosstown bus, but they're out on the town, asking me, the guy they used to threaten to beat up, where the action is, where they can get some blow, man. They're doing business, entertaining clients, and the entertainment turns out to be..."

Irene hit me just above the right temple. A pretty good lick for someone in her condition. I swerved into the centre suicide lane. The blinking orange lights warned it was about to change direction in favour of oncoming traffic.

"Shut up! Just shut the fuck up, Jack, or I'm getting out of this fucking car right here!"

"Go ahead. They'll find you dead in the park ahead of schedule, that's all."

Her punches faded to frustrated shoulder swats. I pulled back into the right lane just as a set of headlights flashed by from the other direction. The big cement lions looked like sphinxes as we hit the bridge. It was the second time I'd crossed the bridge with a whore in my cab that night. Whatever riddle the sphinxes were silently asking, I didn't have an answer.

"Is there anybody at your place to take care of you?"

"No. My room-mate moved to Calgary."

Her breathing was shallow but regular. I drove to the apartment

tower on Bellevue in West Van, a pink confection of curves and arch-
es the drivers called The Buck Rogers Building. I parked the cab in a
visitors slot.

"You didn't turn on your meter."

"You think I'd take money from you, Irene?"

"Fuck you, Jack."

"I've been hearing that a lot lately."

"I'm not surprised."

It seemed a long ride up in the elevator. Irene disappeared into
the bathroom immediately. The place was all brass and glass, some
fag decorators idea of an apartment. The view of Point Grey, English
Bay, the Park and the city was panoramic and expensive. I gave it the
finger again, then the whole fist. I heard the bathroom door open at
last. She ducked straight into the bedroom. I lit a smoke and stood in
the door of the darkened room.

"Are you alright?"

I sensed rather than saw her try to smile.

"It's only a flesh wound, Captain Midnite...Come and be with
me?"

I sat stiffly on the edge of the big bed. She found my hand. Her
face looked softer, younger in the dimness.

"I hate you for this, Irene....Imagine that. I actually love you so
much I hate you..."

Her voice was a whisper in the dark.

"Please, Jack. Don't...Love me or hate me in the morning. Just
stay with me now..."

"I still love you and I hate still loving you..."

"Jack? Please?..."

"I love you and I hate myself for loving you..."

She sat up suddenly.

"Turn on the light!"

Startled, I hesitated.

"Turn it on!"

I pressed the switch on the small bedside lamp. Her lips and
nose looked better. Her eye was going to shine for a few days, though.
Without makeup, she looked like the Irene I remembered, even her

angry eyes. Propped on her right elbow, she undid her camisole top and pulled it away from her left breast. Across the curved swell there was a line of small angry blisters, like the tracks of a stupid beast lost in a desert, unable to see the liquid life just beneath the surface. They looked like they'd been put there with the end of a lit cigarette.

A strangled cry stuck in my throat. I groaned as if I'd been body-punched. I put out my hand, uncertain if I meant to touch her or ward her off. It wouldn't stop shaking. She grabbed my shoulder and looked directly into my eyes.

"Jack? The man who did this tells me he loves me."

Closing the camisole carefully, she lay back.

"Please turn out the light now."

I turned it out. She held my hand under her cheek and shut her eyes.

"Stay with me?"

I slipped my fingers free. She really wouldn't want me there in the morning. Closing the apartment door quietly behind me, I realized I still had a cigarette smouldering between my fingers. I took a deep drag, remembering those burns, and gagged. Then I made myself smoke it right down to the filter.

I slouched behind the wheel of Fifty-One after I cleared. It was gray dawn, not quite light, and I was ready to Code Two when Gary gave me an airporter out of the British Properties. I'd had a good first half, with the extras, but after midnight my sheet looked pretty thin. I took it.

I found the house easily enough in the maze of winding steep streets, flanked by psuedo-mansions and architects samples. I'd been in a lot of these big houses. They might have twenty rooms, but only three of them had furniture. A short pudgy middle-aged man emerged from the dark barnlike house and dropped his two cases beside the cab before he huffed himself in. I loaded them into the trunk.

"Which way do you want to go?"

He got far too indignant for that hour of the morning.

"Don't you know?"

"It's company policy to give the customer the option. Everyone thinks he knows the fastest way out of his own neighbourhood."

"Just get me to the airport...Fast. I have to catch a plane for a very important business meeting."

That was enough for me. I drove at exactly thirty miles per hour, not a mile over. I dodged or crashed not a single orange light, never mind a red. I did not roll through stop signs like they were conditional at that hour of the morning. I stopped for the regulation two seconds at each one. I said not a word. By the time we turned onto south Granville St. the guy was starting to fidget.

"Er, say, driver? Do you think we could step on it? I'm in a bit of a hurry..."

"Are you asking me to break the law, sir? To risk my licence as a public carrier and my career as a professional driver?"

I remained calm. He didn't.

"Look, you fucking punk! I'm paying for this ride! Don't you smart-mouth me or I'll..."

I pulled over to the curb and turned off the ignition.

"You'll what, sir?"

"Hey!...I mean...Hey, you can't just..."

"Please get out of the cab, sir."

I could see the sweat on his forehead in my rear-view mirror.

"Look, driver...You don't understand...If I don't make that plane, this meeting in Montreal, I'll lose...well, a lot. Maybe everything."

His eyes clicked desperately up and down the wide empty street looking for salvation, another cab, a cop, an early bus. There wasn't a vehicle in sight, not even a garbage truck.

"Look. I'll give you anything you want...Fifty bucks. A hundred! Just get me there, please?"

"Wipe your ass with it, fatso."

The man did a double-take so violent Fifty-One rocked on its shocks. He bent over and buried his face in h is hands.

"My God! You're insane! This can't be happening to me!"

"You'd be amazed what can happen...And you'd get where you're going a lot faster if you didn't step on peoples faces on the way."

I whipped the car into Drive as I turned the ignition and got rubber out of the automatic. I cracked two orange lights and crashed a red, did a flat eighty-five all the way down Granville to the Art Laing Bridge and over. It looked like clear sailing all the way to Departures until we were peeling down the curve off ramp of the bridge and the man in the back seat screamed. Out of the corner of my eye, I saw the cop car under the abutment, the Mountie frozen in classic shooting range position and the big black gun pointed right at us. I crammed on the grabbers and locked the wheel, throwing the cab into a three-sixty spin, ducking under the dash and waiting for the windshield to explode as Fifty-One came to a stalled halt broadside across two lanes.

No shots rang out.

I peeked over the dash into the face of a very young, very embarrasssed RCMP Constable who'd been playing Dirty Harry with the radar gun to while away the boredom of his graveyard shift. The man in the back seat was weeping uncontrollably. I patted his shoulder. My sphincter felt cramped.

"Take it easy, man. Just playing cops and robbers..."

He was hicupping with fear and rage.

"The bastard...The fucking bastard...How could he?..."

"You'll miss your plane."

I fired up Fifty-One and gave the cop a look of withering contempt as I drove smoothly away. He never said a word about me doing seventy in a thirty mile an hour zone. I swept into Departures, flicked on my four-ways and had the man's bags on the sidewalk and the door open in one motion.

"C'mon, man. You can still make your plane."

"I can't...Not like this."

His thinning hair was standing up static, his tie was trying to strangle him and his suit trousers were darkened by a large wet stain spreading down both thighs.

"So you're going to be ruined because you pissed your pants? Bankrupted by your bladder? Some fucking epitaph, man."

He looked up at me hopelessly. I sneered.

"What's it going to be, man? Dignity or survival?"

He climbed out of the cab and stood up. Taking a deep breath of cold morning air, he found his wallet and handed me fifty bucks for a fifteen dollar fare. He waved off my attempt to make change and offered me his hand.

"Thank you very much. I apologize for my rudeness earlier. I wish we could have met under different circumstances, but I appreciate your work."

"You're welcome. Good luck at the meeting. Change your pants on the plane and knock 'em out of their shorts in Montreal."

"I will. I'm not afraid anymore. I'm not afraid of them. I'm not afraid of anything."

"Hold that thought, man."

He picked up his bags and marched into the terminal with his head high and his pants clinging to the backs of his stubby legs. I went into the coffee shop to get a mug of black with a pinch and phone in Code Two on the land line. Let them tow the fucking cab away. I didn't feel like driving for a while anyway.

Chapter 13

Sunday was one of those nights I wondered how anybody could call this a job. Lorraine was dispatching the evening shift and her voice got on my nerves, but I didn't have to listen to it much because the airwaves weren't even ripples. A few drivers were riding around four to a car blowing joints with the windows rolled up like they worked for MacLures, so all a flag on the street would see were demented faces hovering in a cloud of smoke.

Most of us were stacked up and sacked out on taxi stands snoozing or re-reading the Saturday papers for the twentieth time. The Americans were winning at the Olympics in Munich, but getting the shit kicked out of them in Vietnam. They'd killed about a million Vietnamese while losing fifty thousand of their own guys and now they were looking for 'peace with honour,' according to Nixon. I thought about Dougie Trumbull, about his big bones out there somewhere in the jungle the Americans were about to give back to the people who owned it.

Somebody put real fresh dog shit, not the plastic stuff from Krac-A-Joke, on the drivers seat of Sixty-Three while Chris Newman was in the office and he sat down hard on it when he got back in. He booked off early, faking the flu and talking about quitting. The last time he got the flu and quit a job he'd spent two months on his bed wearing an oversize sweater and playing John Lee Hooker's boogie riff on someone's borrowed Framus acoustic. The Casino in The

Clouds was closed until further notice.

Bender finally bent a fender trying to shave thirty seconds off a five dollar jerk trip by passing on the right on an orange light in an intersection. All three cars involved got banged up expensively and there wasn't another car on the road for half a dozen blocks. Fat Fred got so bored he played ass-tag with a bus going down Keith Road hill and lost when the bus driver tapped his air brakes. The cab was totalled to the firewall. Fat Fred called a personal for me to take him home with a short stop at Jack the Bootlegger's on First.

All the cars had gremlins from the sudden damp and the light rain that put a sheen on the streets, floating up all the spots of spilled gas and oil, turning intersections into skating rinks. I had a flat tire, replaced a headlight, a fuse and a wiper blade. I wasn't making any money. Neither was anyone else. It felt like summer was over.

I got another personal from Len Sutherland. No delivery this time. I picked up a pack of Camels just in case. When I got there, Len was in a panic and it sounded like what the cops call a domestic dispute was in progress upstairs.

"You gotta help me! You're the only one I could think of to call!"

"What's happening?"

He pointed up.

"Listen! Can't you hear?"

I listened. I caught a few phrases.

"...fuckin' bastard!"

"...lousy slut!..."

"...Goddamn bully!..."

"...fuckin' whore!..."

"I don't think they're watching re-runs of *Leave It To Beaver*."

Len looked like he was trying to jump out of his skin.

"We've gotta do something! He's been hitting her!...Look, you know that play I've been writing? The one about the guy in the basement suite and the woman from upstairs?..."

I shrugged.

"Don't sweat it. Along young writers stuff is autobiographical at first."

"You don't understand! I think he knows! He might do something to her..."

"Do something to you, more likely. Like cut your nuts off with a rusty razor and feed them to his dog...But it sounds about fifty-fifty to me, right now. Did you call the cops?"

He nodded jerkily like a windup toy.

"They came already. It quieted down for a while, then it started up again! What can we do?"

"How's the play coming?"

"Fuck the godamned play!"

I shrugged.

"Life imitates art, man. Never read Oscar Wilde?"

"How can you stand there quoting some fat dead faggot when she might be getting killed up there? We have to do something!"

I shook my head.

"No, man. Nobody has to do anything. Except die, of course. She doesn't have to screw the guy downstairs. Her old man doesn't have to beat her. She doesn't have to stay and take it. The cops don't have to stop it. We don't have to do anything. You don't have to write a play. I don't have to drive a hack...We do it because we want to."

As I left, what sounded like a plate hit a wall upstairs. In five minutes I was back on the Second Street stand, helping Rick Chang translate his physics notes, a bit strange, since I wasn't fluent in Cantonese or physics, when Cece Wragg hi-jacked the company.

It started when the train came in, the B.C. Rail from Prince George, at nine-thirty. Lorraine had called ahead for the passenger count. Twelve. It was a faint hope and Wragg was the only one who pried his ass off the stand to go meet it. A while later, he booked away on a long trip to Caulfield in deep West Vancouver. Lucky. We all silently envied him. It was quiet for a long time, then we heard him clear and book a closer zone he probably wasn't in yet. About five minutes after he cleared, Lorraine suddenly called him.

"Twenty-Eight? You're Code Two. Right now. Turn off your radio and park your cab. See Bob Sunstrom first thing in the morning."

Wragg began a sputtered protest on the air, but she cut him off.

"Don't argue with dispatch on the air, Twenty-Eight, or you'll be Code Two forever. Turn off your radio and see Bob in the morning."

A few minutes later, the whole company was off the air. The radio hummed, the way it did when a driver left his mike on the seat and accidentally sat on it, depressing the button. Nobody could call in and Lorraine couldn't call out. We were jammed. Usually these incidents lasted no more than a moment, until the driver realized what he'd done, but this went on and on.

After five minutes or so, I sauntered over to the phone booth on the corner and dialled the office number. No answer. I went back to the cab and continued to interpret physics into Cantonese. It was fifteen minutes before Lorraine came on the air again. Ted Brauer rolled in from West Van and joined us, Suzuki's *Studies in Zen* under his arm.

"What the fuck was that about?"

Ted chuckled.

"Rags finally blew it. When he went down to the train the only person who wanted a cab was this little old lady. Only there was a North Shore parked behind him on the stand and she made the mistake of getting into it..."

"Can't imagine why...unless she got a good look at Wragg."

"I think that's what happened...Anyway, Rags got all twisted out of shape because the first cab on the stand is supposed to take the fare. He puts his rig in gear, blocks off the North Shore cab like a cop making a bust, storms over to it, rips open the door, grabs the old girl and screams, 'You're mine!' He hauls her out of the North Shore, drags her over to Twenty-Eight and stuffs her in the back..."

"Jesus! Why didn't the North Shore guy pound the piss out of him?"

Ted shrugged.

"Maybe he was too shocked...Or maybe he was scared. I mean, Rags looks like a psycho on a day-pass and he's famous for being crazy. The North Shore guys know all the stories about him. He tried to buy in there once because he knows they make more money and the other owners unanimously voted against him at the meeting...

Anyway, apparently he drove this old girl all the way out to her place at about eighty, screaming at her the whole time about how first cab on a stand has priority and anyone but a senile old cunt would know that. She was too scared not to pay him, but he took her money and wouldn't give her change because he said drivers deserved tips for carrying miserable bitches like her. Lorraine said she was in tears when she called and was going to call the cops. That's why she put Rags Code Two."

"So what happened to the radio?"

Ted smiled.

"Well, all of a sudden the radio went dead, right? I'd just gone over to the Donut Shop and brought Lorraine a coffee and a jelly doughnut and we were sitting there when the radio died. A few minutes later Rags comes in and tells Lorraine he's parked his cab in a secret location known only to him with the mike button taped down and if she doesn't put him back on the board, he won't tell anybody where it is."

"So what happened, for fuck sake?"

"I think I could have got him to tell me where he'd parked it, but..."

"What'd Lorraine do?"

"She punched him in the mouth."

I cracked up laughing.

"What? Lorraine punched out Cece Wragg?"

Ted nodded.

"She's got a wicked right cross, man. Laid him out flat on the floor with one shot. Broke his nose and split both lips. Lots of blood."

"And he told you where the cab was parked."

"After threatening to charge her with assault and some other stuff I talked him out of. I took him out of the office and told her to lock the doors, then I walked over and found his cab behind Park Royal and took the tape off the button. I took the fuse out of his radio, just to make sure...She's quite a lady..."

He was getting moony again.

"This time I'll go along with you on that."

Ten seconds later she sent me to the Seven-Eleven to pick up a madman.

I knew the guy wearing nothing but his jockeys and a blanket must be my fare. There was nobody else in the store except the kid behind the counter. He shrugged and rolled his eyes. I smiled faintly. It figured.

The guy had long wild hair and strange hooded eyes, but he had a big wad of money balled up in his left fist. Half a dozen rubber bands were wound so tightly around the fist it was turning blue. He got into the back seat and asked me to take him to the laundromat around the corner. I waited while he went in to get his clothes. He brought back a black plastic garbage bag full of soaking wet garments and asked me to take him downtown and keep a sharp lookout for anyone trying to tail us.

All the way over the bridge he talked in a soft non-stop whisper, a rambling paranoid monologue I wasn't even sure was addressed to me. I just drove and smoked and pretended I was hauling frozen meat or something. After cruising around Gastown for twenty minutes, he asked me to pull into an alley. I did, tapping the taped up Coke bottle under the seat for luck.

The madman carefully undid the elastic bands around his fist, paid me the exact fare in bills and change and asked me if he could get into the trunk to change into his clothes. I put him and his bag into the trunk and closed it without letting it lock and stood by the drivers door, lighting a smoke off the butt of the last. That was when Lorraine called me again.

"When do you clear, Five-One?"

"Five-One. Pretty soon, I think..."

"What's your location, Five-One?"

"I'm parked in an alley in Gastown."

"Will you be clearing there, Five-One?"

"It's hard to say."

"Is your passenger still in the car, Five-One?"

"Five-One. He's in the trunk."

There was a moment of silence. A few mike buttons clicked feebly. Lorraine was holding onto her cool with both hands.

"What is your passenger doing in the trunk, Five-One?"

"Putting on his clothes."

I hear could hear her teeth clenching. I hit the button again.

"Go ahead, say it, Lorraine."

"I'm thinking it...I'll put you On Call, Five-One."

"Five-One, right."

When the madman climbed out of the trunk he wandered off in his wet but clean clothes into the night and the steadily falling rain. I backed out of the alley, shot the bridge and was on the sedate West Van stand when Gary came on at midnight.

"Good evening, drivers. This is Gary's Graveyard Revue, helping you while away the wet wee hours of this Walpurgisnacht on wheels...It gives me great pleasure to announce that following last nights negotiated settlement between Management and the ad hoc drivers committee, light refreshments will be provided at the office for a limited time only. This full zone count this evening is cancelled due to lack of interest..."

I drove to the office and had one of Bob Sunstrom's beers. Then another. One or two trips went out, but I was well down on the board and didn't roll again until all the evening drivers booked off at two, Gary taking their pegs off the board like a convoy master taking torpedoed ships off his strategic map. When I did hit the road, it was after three, a long ramble out to Whytecliffe to pick up a guy who wanted to go to Thirteenth and St. Georges. He sat very quiet and surly in the back, ignoring my attempts at conversation as we cruised back along the Upper Levels highway. About halfway there I decided I'd had enough of that shit for one long weekend.

"Something bugging you, man?"

"Actually, yes. I'm a hemophiliac and I'm bleeding internally."

The penny dropped. Thirteenth and St. Georges was the address of Lions Gate Hospital.

"Jesus' shit! Why didn't you say so?"

I got on the radio and told Gary to call the West Van cops and the North Van RCMP and tell them I was coming in fast with an emergency. Then I punched it all the way there, busting all the red lights down Lonsdale with anarchistic glee. The rain was coming down in windblown sheets and the sidewalks were deserted. When I slowed at one intersection with a red light, a couple of drowned rat guys in mackinaws tried to flag me. They looked vaguely familiar but I gunned it through, spraying them with water from a spreading puddle created by a storm drain choked with the debris of summer. I felt so guilty I grabbed the mike and reported a flag at their location.

An RCMP cruiser, lights flashing, escorted me the last six blocks. After all that excitement, I need a break so I coasted down to the Second Street stand, figuring I could always help Rick Chang with his homework to pass the time. The stand was deserted and the Olympic looked like it expected its next customers to be the demolition crew. I parked on the stand, locked down and took a nap.

It was almost dawn when I was jerked awake by the radio. It was The Count. He was screaming into his mike and not making a lot of sense, which wasn't unusual. But I finally realized he was calling in a Code Fourteen.

"Bloot!...Zo much bloot! Helping pliss! Dere iss bloot!"

I thought he'd finally got the joke.

"Should've introduced him to my last fare..."

But it wasn't a joke. Gary came on, trying to calm him down.

"What's your location, Forty-Two?"

"Behind ze Leenvood Hotel! Hoory pliss! Eeemergency!"

I peeled rubber off the stand and blew the automatic tranny through all its phantom gears. Ted was already there when I pulled into the misty parking lot behind the Lynnwood. So were the cops. And an ambulance. And Benson, the real Captain Midnight, who'd been cruising the neighbourhood with his radio on and responded first to the Count's Code Fourteen, was sitting on the pavement, leaning against his cab, looking as vacant as the flag on his meter. The ambulance attendants were loading a bloody bundle into the meat wagon. Ted saw me and came over.

"What happened?"

"It's Rick Chang, Jack. The cops said it looked like he put up a fight and somebody shot him in the head."

I started to get out of the car. Ted put a hand on my arm.

"He's gone, man. His head was all swollen up and there's blood all over the cab. He's dead...They already got the guys. Two blocks from here...They were trying to flag a cab."

He nodded toward an RCMP cruiser parked near the hotel back door. I caught a glimpse of the profile and mackinawed shoulder of one of the occupants of the back seat. I sank back in my seat and shoved my fist in my mouth.

"Oh shit, oh shit, oh shit, oh shit..."

Ted didn't hear me. He was looking at the mountains, the rosy sky above them promising a clear day, an extension of summer's rack-rent, sunlight gilding the last overhanging rainclouds above us. He shook his head sadly.

"What kind of person would shoot somebody for a lousy fifty or sixty bucks?...What kind of person would fight and risk their life for a lousy fifty or sixty bucks?...Sometimes I don't think I understand anything."

I leaned back in the seat and lit a cigarette.

"You know the answer to the first question. You carry them around in your cab every night. Now you know the answer to the second."

I picked up my mike.

"Five-One. I'm clear at the Lynnwood."

Gary didn't answer.

"Five-One? Do you read? I'm clear at the Lynnwood."

"Ah, got you, Five-One."

"Then get me out of here."

Quietly, he gave me an address on the Reserve. I put it in gear and drove slowly away from the flashing light-show. My fare was an older native man with the stylized Mongol features of a tribal mask. He told me to drive him "out Dollarton." There was a chunk of Reserve out there on the old road to Deep Cove. We ambled along the curvy pot-holed pavement.

"Where abouts are we going?"

"I have to talk to my wife."

"Okay, man. Just tell me where to stop."

We rode for a while in silence.

"Pull over here."

I pulled over on the gravel shoulder in front of the old Indian cemetary. He got out without paying me and walked away from the cab into the graveyard, leaving the door hanging open. The city across the Inlet was only a shadow behind a gray shroud of incoming rain as the clouds took a parting shot. I watched the man as he found the grave he was looking for and stood beside it in the cold steady downpour, his lips moving silently.

I remembered driving two old men from the Reserve downtown to catch the bus for Mount Currie. As I drove onto Lions Gate Bridge, they switched from stacatto English to the soft mysterious gutturals and sibilants of the ancient Coast Salish tongue. They were discussing something they didn't want me to hear, which was fine. But the odd thing was, just then my meter suddenly stopped. The usual slap and shake wouldn't get it going again. I had to give them a flat rate. Then it worked fine again after I cleared. Must've just got stuck, I figured.

More than anything, I wished I could get out of the cab and go into that graveyard with him and talk to someone, but I didn't know anyone in there and no one in there knew me. No one in there spoke my language. I totalled my sheet, cleared the meter and paid the man's fare out of my percentage. I picked up the mike.

"Gary?"

"That you, Five-One?"

"Not any more. I'm Code Two. Forever. Tell Davidson the car is parked at the old Indian cemetary on Dollarton. The sheet's in the glove compartment. So are the keys."

"Hey, Captain Midnite? Don't tell me you're goin' AWOL..."

"I'm over the hill, man. Deserting under fire....I'll miss you."

There was silence for several moments, then Gary spoke quietly.

"*Vaya con Dios, amigo.* Go with God, Jack."

"I wish I could, man...Fifty-One is Code Two."

I switched off the radio and the top-light, locked the keys in the cab and walked away. I had a long walk ahead of me and it was raining, but there was a blue slash of sky like a doorway to the west and I needed the time and the walk to figure out where I was going and what I would say when I got there.